Dear Reader,

I can't believe that it has been thirty years since my first Long, Tall Texan book, *Calhoun*, debuted! The series was suggested by my former editor Tara Gavin, who asked if I might like to set stories in a fictional town of my own design. Would I! And the rest is history.

As the years went by, I found more and more sexy ranchers and cowboys to add to the collection. My readers (especially Amy!) found time to gift me with a notebook listing every single one of them, wives and kids and connections to other families in my own Texas town of Jacobsville. Eventually the town got a little too big for me, so I added another smaller town called Comanche Wells and began to fill it up, too.

You can't imagine how much pleasure this series has given me. I continue to add to the population of Jacobs County, Texas, and I have no plans to stop. Ever.

I hope all of you enjoy reading the Long, Tall Texans as much as I enjoy writing them. Thank you all for your kindness and loyalty and friendship. I am your biggest fan!

Love,

Diana Palmer

NEW YORK TIMES BESTSELLING AUTHOR

DIANA PALMER

LONG, TALL TEXANS:

Bentley

—

Rick

Previously published as
Tough to Tame and *True Blue*

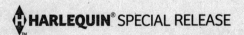

HARLEQUIN® SPECIAL RELEASE

ISBN-13: 978-1-335-00710-0

Long, Tall Texans: Bentley/Rick

Copyright © 2020 by Harlequin Books S.A.

Bentley
First published as Tough to Tame in 2010.
This edition published in 2020.
Copyright © 2010 by Diana Palmer

Rick
First published as True Blue in 2011.
This edition published in 2020.
Copyright © 2011 by Diana Palmer

Recycling programs
for this product may
not exist in your area.

This edition published by arrangement with Harlequin Books S.A.

For questions and comments about the quality of this book, please contact us at CustomerService@Harlequin.com.

® and TM are trademarks of Harlequin Enterprises Limited or its corporate affiliates. Trademarks indicated with ® are registered in the United States Patent and Trademark Office, the Canadian Intellectual Property Office and in other countries.

HARLEQUIN®
www.Harlequin.com

Printed in U.S.A.

CONTENTS

A prolific author of more than one hundred books, **Diana Palmer** got her start as a newspaper reporter. A *New York Times* bestselling author and voted one of the top ten romance writers in America, she has a gift for telling the most sensual tales with charm and humor. Diana lives with her family in Cornelia, Georgia. Visit her website at dianapalmer.com.

Books by Diana Palmer

Long, Tall Texans

Fearless

Heartless

Dangerous

Merciless

Courageous

Protector

Invincible

Untamed

Defender

Undaunted

The Wyoming Men

Wyoming Tough

Wyoming Fierce

Wyoming Bold

Wyoming Strong

Wyoming Rugged

Wyoming Brave

Morcai Battalion

The Morcai Battalion

The Morcai Battalion: The Recruit

The Morcai Battalion: Invictus

The Morcai Battalion: The Rescue

Visit the Author Profile page
at Harlequin.com for more titles.

BENTLEY

I dedicate this book to all the fine veterinarians, technicians, groomers and office workers who do so much every day to keep our furry friends healthy. Thanks!

CHAPTER ONE

CAPPIE DRAKE PEERED around a corner inside the veterinary practice where she worked, her soft gray eyes wide with apprehension. She was looking for the boss, Dr. Bentley Rydel. Just lately, he'd been on the warpath, and she'd been the target for most of the sarcasm. She was the newest employee in the practice. Her predecessor, Antonia, had resigned and run for the hills last month.

"He's gone to lunch," came an amused whisper from behind her.

Cappie jumped. Her colleague, Keely Welsh Sinclair, was grinning at her. The younger woman, nineteen to Cappie's twenty-three, was only recently married to dishy Boone Sinclair, but she'd kept her job at the veterinary clinic despite her lavish new lifestyle. She loved animals.

So did Cappie. But she'd been wondering if love of animals was enough to put up with Bentley Rydel.

"I lost the packing slip for the heartworm medicine," Cappie said with a grimace. "I know it's here somewhere, but he was yelling and I got flustered and couldn't find it. He said terrible things to me."

"It's autumn," Keely said.

Cappie frowned. "Excuse me?"

"It's autumn," she repeated.

The older woman was staring blankly at her.

Keely shrugged. "Every autumn, Dr. Rydel gets even more short-tempered than usual and he goes missing for a week. He doesn't leave a telephone number in case of emergencies, he doesn't call here and nobody knows where he is. When he comes back, he never says where he's been."

"He's been like this since I was hired," Cappie pointed out. "And I'm the fifth new vet tech this year, Dr. King said so. Dr. Rydel ran the others off."

"You have to yell back, or just smile when he gets wound up," Keely said in a kindly tone.

Cappie grimaced. "I never yell at anybody."

"This is a good time to learn. In fact…"

"Where the hell is my damned raincoat?!"

Cappie's face was a study in horror. "You said he went to lunch!"

"Obviously he came back," Keely replied, wincing, as the boss stormed into the waiting room where two shocked old ladies were sitting beside cat carriers.

Dr. Bentley Rydel was tall, over six feet, with pale blue eyes that took on the gleam of steel when he was angry. He had jet-black hair, thick and usually untidy because he ran his fingers through it in times of frustration. His feet were large, like his hands. His nose had been broken at some point, which only gave his angular face more character. He wasn't conventionally handsome, but women found him very attractive. He didn't find them attractive. If there was a more notorious woman hater than Bentley Rydel in all of Jacobs County, Texas, it would be hard to find him.

"My raincoat?" he repeated, glaring at Cappie as if it were her fault that he'd left without it.

Cappie drew herself up to her full height—the top of her head barely came to Bentley's shoulder—and took a deep breath. "Sir," she said smartly, "your raincoat is in the closet where you left it."

His dark eyebrows rose half a foot.

Cappie cleared her throat and shook her head as if to clear it. The motion dislodged her precariously placed barrette. Her long, thick blond hair shook free of it, swirling around her shoulders like a curtain of silk.

While she was debating her next, and possibly job-ending, comment, Bentley was staring at her hair. She always wore it on top of her head in that stupid pony-tail. He hadn't realized it was so long. His pale eyes narrowed as he studied it.

Keely, fascinated, managed not to stare. She turned to the old ladies watching, spellbound. "Mrs. Ross, if you'll bring—" she looked at her clipboard "—Luvvy the cat on back, we'll see about her shots."

Mrs. Ross, a tiny little woman, smiled and pulled her rolling cat carrier along with her, casting a wistful eye back at the tableau she was reluctantly foregoing.

"Dr. Rydel?" Cappie prompted, because he was really staring.

He scowled suddenly and blinked. "It's raining," he said shortly.

"Sir, that is not my fault," she returned. "I do not control the weather."

"A likely story," he huffed. He turned on his heel, went to the closet, jerked his coat out, displacing everybody else's, and stormed out the door into the pouring rain.

"And I hope you melt!" Cappie muttered under her breath.

"I heard that!" Bentley Rydel called without looking back.

Cappie flushed and moved back behind the counter, trying not to meet Gladys Hawkins's eyes, because the old lady was almost crying, she was laughing so hard.

"There, there," Dr. King, the long-married senior veterinarian, said with a gentle smile. She patted Cappie on the shoulder. "You've done well. By the time she'd been here a month, Antonia was crying in the bathroom at least twice a day, and she never talked back to Dr. Rydel."

"I've never worked in such a place," Cappie said blankly. "I mean, most veterinarians are like you—they're nice and professional, and they don't yell at the staff. And, of course, the staff doesn't yell…"

"Yes, they do," Keely piped in, chuckling. "My husband made the remark that I was a glorified groomer, and the next time he came in here, our groomer gave him an earful about just what a groomer does." She grinned. "Opened his eyes."

"They do a lot more than clip fur," Dr. King agreed. "They're our eyes and ears in between exams. Many times, our groomers have saved lives by noticing some small problem that could have turned fatal."

"Your husband is a dish," Cappie told Keely shyly.

Keely laughed. "Yes, he is, but he's opinionated, hardheaded and temperamental with it."

"He was a tough one to tame, I'll bet," Dr. King mused.

Keely leaned forward. "Not half as tough as Dr. Rydel is going to be."

"Amen. I pity the poor woman who takes him on."

"Trust me, she hasn't been born yet," Keely replied.

"He likes you," Cappie sighed.

"I don't challenge him," Keely said simply. "And I'm younger than most of the staff. He thinks of me as a child."

Cappie's eyes bulged.

Keely patted her on the shoulder. "Some people do." The smile faded. Keely was remembering her mother, who'd been killed by a friend of Keely's father. The whole town had been talking about it. Keely had landed well, though, in Boone Sinclair's strong arms.

"I'm sorry about your mother," Cappie said gently. "We all were."

"Thanks," Keely replied. "We were just getting to know one another when she was…killed. My father plea-bargained himself down to a short jail term, but I don't think he'll be back this way. He's too afraid of Sheriff Hayes."

"Now there's a real dish," Cappie said. "Handsome, brave…"

"…suicidal," Keely interjected.

"Excuse me?"

"He's been shot twice, walking into gun battles," Dr. King explained.

"No guts, no glory," Cappie said.

Her companions chuckled. The phone rang, another customer walked in and the conversation turned to business.

CAPPIE WENT HOME LATE. It was Friday and the place was packed with clients. Nobody escaped before six-thirty, not even the poor groomer who'd spent half a day on a Siberian husky. The animals had thick undercoats and it was a job to wash and brush them out. Dr. Rydel had been snippier than usual, too, glaring at Cappie as if she were responsible for the overflow of patients.

"Cappie, is that you?" her brother called from the bedroom.

"It's me, Kell," she called back. She put down her raincoat and purse and walked into the small, sparse bedroom where her older brother lay surrounded by magazines and books and a small laptop computer. He managed a smile for her.

"Bad day?" she asked gently, sitting down beside him on the bed, softly so that she didn't worsen the pain.

He only nodded. His face was taut, the only sign of the pain that ate him alive every hour of the day. A journalist, he'd been on overseas assignment for a magazine when he was caught in a firefight and wounded by shrapnel. It had lodged in his spine where it was too dangerous for even the most advanced surgery. The doctors said someday, the shrapnel might shift into a location where it would be operable. But until then, Kell was basically paralyzed from the waist down. Oddly, the magazine hadn't provided any sort of health care coverage for him, and equally oddly, he'd insisted that he wasn't going to court to force them to pay up. Cappie had wondered at her brother being in such a profession in the first place. He'd been in the army for several years. When he came out, he'd become a journalist. He made an extraordinary living from it. She'd mentioned that to a friend in the newspaper business who'd been astonished. Most magazines didn't pay that well, he'd noted, eyeing Kell's new Jaguar.

Well, at least they had Kell's savings to keep them going, even if it did so frugally now, after he paid the worst of the medical bills. Her meager salary, although good, barely kept the utilities turned on and food in the aging refrigerator.

"Taken your pain meds?" she added.

He nodded.

"Not helping?"

"Not a lot. Not today, anyway," he added with a forced grin. He was good-looking, with thick short hair even blonder than hers and those pale silvery-gray eyes. He was tall and muscular; or he had been, before he'd been wounded. He was in a wheelchair now.

"Someday they'll be able to operate," she said.

He sighed and managed a smile. "Before I die of old age, maybe."

"Stop that," she chided softly, and bent to kiss his forehead. "You have to have hope."

"I guess."

"Want something to eat?"

He shook his head. "Not hungry."

"I can make southwestern corn soup." It was his favorite.

He gave her a serious look. "I'm impacting your life. There are places for ex-military where I could stay..."

"No!" she exploded.

He winced. "Sis, it isn't right. You'll never find a man who'll take you on with all this baggage," he began.

"We've had this argument for several months already," she pointed out.

"Yes, since you gave up your job and moved back here with me, after I got…wounded. If our cousin hadn't died and left us this place, we wouldn't even have a roof over our heads, stark as it is. It's killing me, watching you try to cope."

"Don't be melodramatic," she chided. "Kell, all we have is each other," she added somberly. "Don't ask me to throw you out on the street so I can have a social life. I don't even like men much, don't you remember?"

His face hardened. "I remember why, mostly."

She flushed. "Now, Kell," she said. "We promised we wouldn't talk about that anymore."

"He could have killed you," he gritted. "I had to browbeat you just to make you press charges!"

She averted her eyes. Her one boyfriend in her adult life had turned out to be a homicidal maniac when he drank. The first time it happened, Frank Bartlett had grabbed Cappie's arm and left a black bruise. Kell advised her to get away from him, but she, infatuated and rationalizing, said that he hadn't meant it. Kell knew better, but he couldn't convince her. On their fourth date, the boy had taken her to a bar, had a few drinks, and when she gently tried to get him to stop, he'd dragged her outside and lit into her. The other patrons had come to her rescue and one of them had driven her home. The boy had come back, shamefaced and crying, begging for one more chance. Kell had put his foot down and said no, but Cappie was in love and wouldn't listen. They were watching a movie at the rented house, when she asked him about his drinking problem. He'd lost his temper and started hitting her, with hardly any provocation at all. Kell had managed to get into his wheelchair and into the living room. With nothing more than a lamp base as a weapon, he'd knocked the lunatic off Cappie and onto the floor. She was dazed and bleeding, but he'd told her how to tie the boy's thumbs together behind his back, which she'd done while Kell picked up his cell phone and called for law enforcement. Cappie had gone to the hospital and the boy had gone to jail for assault.

With her broken arm in a sling, Cappie had testified against him, with Kell beside her in court as moral support. The sentence, even so, hadn't been extreme. The boy drew six months' jail time and a year's probation. He also swore vengeance. Kell took the threat a great deal more seriously than Cappie had.

The brother and sister had a distant cousin who lived in Comanche Wells, Texas. He'd died a year ago, but the probation of the will had dragged on. Three months ago, Kell had a letter informing him that he and Cappie were inheriting a small house and a postage-stamp-size yard. But it was at least a place to live. Cappie had been uncertain about uprooting them from San Antonio, but Kell had been strangely insistent. He had a friend in nearby Jacobsville who was acquainted with a local veterinarian. Cappie could get a job there, working as a veterinary technician. So she'd given in.

She hadn't forgotten the boy. It had been a wrench, because he was her first real love. Fortunately for her, the relationship hadn't progressed past hot kisses and a little petting, although he'd wanted it to. That had been another sticking point: Cappie's impeccable morals. She was out of touch with the modern world, he'd accused, from living with her overprotective big brother for so long. She needed to loosen up. Easy to say, but Cappie didn't want a casual relationship and she said so. When he drank more than usual, he said it was her fault that he got drunk and hit her, because she kept him so frustrated.

Well, he was entitled to his opinion. Cappie didn't share it. He'd seemed like the nicest, gentlest sort of man when she'd first met him. His sister had brought her dog to the veterinary practice where Cappie worked. He'd been sitting in the truck, letting his sister wrangle a huge German shepherd dog back outside. When he'd seen Cappie, he'd jumped out and helped. His sister had seemed surprised. Cappie didn't notice.

After it was over, Cappie had found that at least two of her acquaintances had been subjected to the same sort of abuse by their own boyfriends. Some had been lucky, like Cappie, and disentangled themselves from the abusers. Others were trapped by fear into relationships they didn't even want. It was hard, she decided, telling by appearance what men would be like when they got you alone. At least Dr. Rydel was obviously violent and dangerous, she told herself. Not that she wanted anything to do with him socially.

"What was that?" Kell asked.

"Oh, I was thinking about one of my bosses," she

confided. "Dr. Rydel is a holy terror. I'm scared to death of him."

He scowled. "Surely he isn't like Frank Bartlett?"

"No," she said quickly. "I don't think he'd ever hit a woman. He really isn't the sort. He just blusters and rages and curses. He loves animals. He called the police on a man who brought in a little dog with cuts and bruises all over him. The man had beaten the dog and pretended it had fallen down stairs. Dr. Rydel knew better. He testified against the man and he went to jail."

"Good for Dr. Rydel." He smiled. "If he's that nice to animals, he isn't likely the sort of person who'd hit women," he had to agree. "I was told by my friend that Rydel was a good sort to work for." He frowned. "Your boyfriend kicked your cat on your first date."

She grimaced. "And I made excuses for him." Not long after that, her cat had vanished. She'd often wondered what had happened to him, but he returned after her boyfriend left. "Frank was so handsome, so...eligible," she added quietly. "I guess I was flattered that a man like that would look twice at me. I'm no beauty."

"You are. Inside."

"You're a nice brother. How about that soup?"

He sighed. "I'll eat it if you'll fix it. I'm sorry. About the way I am."

"Like you can help it," she muttered, and smiled. "I'll get it started."

He watched her walk away, thoughtful.

She brought in a tray and had her soup with him. There were just the two of them, all alone in the world. Their parents had died long ago, when she was ten.

Kell, who'd been amazingly athletic and healthy in those days, had simply taken over and been a substitute parent to her. He'd been in the military, and they'd traveled all over the world. A good deal of her education had been completed through correspondent courses, although she'd seen a lot of the world. Now, Kell thought he was a burden, but what had she been for all those long years when he'd sacrificed his own social life to raise a heartbroken kid? She owed him a lot. She only wished she could do more for him.

She remembered him in his uniform, an officer, so dignified and commanding. Now, he was largely confined to bed or that wheelchair. It wasn't even a motorized one, because they couldn't afford it. He did continue to work, in his own fashion, at crafting a novel. It was an adventure, based on some knowledge he'd acquired from his military background and a few friends who worked, he said, in covert ops.

"How's the book coming?" she asked.

He laughed. "Actually I think it's going very well. I spoke to a buddy of mine in Washington about some new political strategies and robotic warfare innovations."

"You know everybody."

He made a face at her. "I know almost everybody." He sighed. "I'm afraid the phone bill will be out of sight again this month. Plus I had to order some more books on Africa for the research."

She gave him a look of pride. "I don't care. You accomplish so much," she said softly. "More than a lot of people in much better shape physically."

"I don't sleep as much as most people do," he said wryly. "So I can work longer hours."

"You need to talk to Dr. Coltrain about something to make you sleep."

He sighed. "I did. He gave me a prescription."

"Which you didn't get filled," she accused. "Connie, at the pharmacy, told on you."

"We don't have the money right now," he said gently. "I'll manage."

"It's always money," she said miserably. "I wish I was talented and smart, like you. Maybe I could get a better-paying job."

"You're good at what you do," he replied firmly. "And you love your work. Believe me, that's a lot more important than making a big paycheck. I should know."

She sighed as she sipped her soup. "I guess." She gave him a quick glance. "But it would help with the bills."

"My book is going to make us millions," he told her with a grin. "It will hit the top of the *New York Times* bestseller list, I'll be in demand for talk shows and we'll be able to buy a new car."

"Optimist," she accused.

"Hey, without hope, what have we got?" He looked around with a grimace. "Unpainted walls, cracks in the paint, a car with two hundred thousand miles on it and a leaky roof."

"Oh, darn," she muttered, following his eyes to the yellow spot on the ceiling. "I'll bet another one of those stupid nails worked its way out of the tin. I wish we could have afforded a shingle roof."

"Well, tin is cheaper, and it looks nice."

She looked at him meaningfully.

"It's cheap, anyway," he persisted. "Don't you like the sound of rain on a tin roof? Just listen. It's like music."

It was like a tin drum, she pointed out, but he just laughed.

She smiled. "I guess you're right. It's better not to wish we had more than we do. We'll get by, Kell," she assured him. "We always do."

"At least we're in it together," he agreed. "But you should think about the military home."

"After I'm dead and buried, you can go into a home," she assured him. "For now, you just eat your soup and hush."

He smiled tenderly. "Okay."

She smiled back. He was the nicest big brother in the whole world, and she wasn't abandoning him while there was a breath in her body.

IT HAD STOPPED raining when she got to work the next morning. She was glad. She hadn't wanted to get out of bed at all. There was something magical about lying in the bed with rain coming down, all safe and cozy and warm. But she wanted to keep her job. She couldn't do both.

She was putting her raincoat in the closet when a long arm presented itself over her shoulder and deposited a bigger raincoat there.

"Hang that up for me, please," Dr. Rydel said gruffly.

"Yes, sir."

She fumbled it onto a hanger. When she closed the door and turned, he was still standing there.

"Is something wrong, sir?" she asked formally.

He was frowning. "No."

But he looked as if he had the weight of the world on his shoulders. She knew how that felt, because she loved her brother and she couldn't help him. Her soft gray eyes looked up into his pale blue ones. "When life gives you lemons, make lemonade?" she ventured.

A laugh escaped his tight control. "What the hell would you know about lemons, at your age?" he asked.

"It isn't the age, Dr. Rydel," she said. "It's the mile-age. If I were a car, they'd have to decorate me with solid gold accessories just to get me off the lot."

His eyes softened, just a little. "I suppose I'd be in a junkyard."

She laughed, quickly controlling it. "Sorry."

"Why?"

"You're sort of hard to talk to," she confessed.

He drew in a long breath. Just for a minute, he looked oddly vulnerable. "I'm not used to people. I deal with them in the practice, but I live alone. I have most of my life." He frowned. "Your brother lives with you, doesn't he? Why doesn't he work?"

She tightened up. "He was overseas covering a war and a bomb exploded nearby. He caught shrapnel in the spine and they can't operate. He's paralyzed from the waist down."

He grimaced. "That's a hell of a way to end up in a wheelchair."

"Tell me about it," she agreed quietly. "He was in the

military for years, but he got tired of dragging me all over the world, so he mustered out and got a job working for this magazine. He said it would mean he wouldn't be gone so much." She sighed. "I guess he wasn't, but he's in a lot of pain and they can't do much for it." She looked up at him. "It's hard to watch."

For an instant, some fellow feeling flared in his eyes. "Yes. It's easier to hurt yourself than to watch someone you love battle pain." His face softened as he looked down at her. "You take care of him."

She smiled. "Yes. Well, as much as he'll let me, anyway. He took care of me from the age of ten, when our parents died in a wreck. He wants me to let him go into some sort of military home, but I'll never do that."

He looked very thoughtful. And sad. He looked as if he badly needed someone to talk to, but he had nobody. She knew the feeling.

"Life is hard," she said gently.

"Then you die," he added, and managed a smile. "Back to work, Miss Drake." He hesitated. "Your name, Cappie. What's it short for?"

She hesitated. She bit her lower lip.

"Come on," he coaxed.

She drew in a breath. "Capella," she said.

His eyebrows shot up. "The star?"

She laughed, delighted. Most people had no idea what it meant. "Yes."

"One of your parents was an astronomy buff," he guessed.

"No. My mother was an astronomer, and my father

was an astrophysicist," she corrected, beaming. "He worked for NASA for a while."

He pursed his lips. "Brainy people."

"Don't worry, it didn't rub off on me. Kell got all that talent. In fact, he's writing a book, an adventure novel." She smiled. "I just know it's going to be a blockbuster. He'll rake in the money, and then we won't have to worry about money for medicine and health care."

"Health care." He harrumphed. "It's a joke. People going without food to buy pills, without clothes to afford gas, having to choose between essentials and no help anywhere to change things."

She was surprised at his attitude. Most people seemed to think that health care was available to everybody. Actually she could only afford basic coverage for herself. If she ever had a major medical emergency, she'd have to beg for help from the state. She hoped she could even get it. It still amazed her that Kell's employers hadn't offered him health care benefits. "We don't live in a perfect society," she agreed.

"No. Nowhere near it."

She wanted to ask him why he was so outspoken on the issue, which hit home for her, too. But before she could overcome her shyness, the phones were suddenly ringing off the hook and three new four-legged patients walked in the door with their owners. One of them, a big Boxer, made a beeline for a small poodle whose owner had let it come in without a lead.

"Grab him!" Cappie called, diving after the Boxer.

Dr. Rydel followed her, gripping the Boxer's lead firmly. He pulled up on it just enough to establish control, and held it so that the dog's head was erect. "Down, sir!" he said in a commanding tone. "Sit!"

The Boxer sat down at once. So did all the pet owners. Cappie burst out laughing. Dr. Rydel gave her a speaking glance, turned and led the Boxer back to the patient rooms without a single word.

CHAPTER TWO

WHEN SHE GOT home, Cappie told her brother about the struggle with the Boxer, and its result. He roared with laughter. It had been a long time since she'd seen him laugh.

"Well, at least he can control animals and people," he told her.

"Indeed he can." She picked up the dirty dishes and stacked them from their light supper. "You know, he's very adamant about health care. For people, I mean. I wonder if he has somebody who can't afford medicines or doctors or hospitals? He never talks about his private life."

"Neither do you," he pointed out dryly.

She made a face. "I'm not interesting. Nobody would want to know what I do at home. I just cook and clean and wash dishes. What's exciting about that? When you were in the army, you knew movie stars and sports legends."

"They're just like you and me," he told her. "Fame isn't a character reference. Neither is wealth."

"Well, I wouldn't mind being rich," she sighed. "We could fix the roof."

"One day," he promised her, "we'll get out of the hole."

"You think?"

"Miracles happen every day."

She wasn't touching that line with a pole. Just lately, she'd have given blood for a miracle that would treat her just to a new raincoat. The one she had, purchased for a dollar at a thrift shop, was worn and faded and missing buttons. She'd sewed others on, but none of them matched. It would be so nice to have one that came from a store, brand-new, with that smell that clothes had when nobody had ever worn them before.

"What are you thinking about?" Kell asked.

"New raincoats," she sighed. Then she saw his expression and grimaced. "Sorry. Just a stray thought. Don't mind me."

"Santa Claus might bring you one," he said.

She glowered at him on her way out the door. "Listen, Santa Claus couldn't find this place if he had GPS on his sleigh. And if he did, his reindeer would slide off the tin roof and fall to their doom, and we'd get sued."

He was still laughing when she got to the kitchen.

It was getting close to Christmas. Cappie dug out the old, faded artificial Christmas tree and put it up in the living room where Kell could see it from his hospital bed. She had one new string of minilights, all she could afford, and she put the old ornaments on it. Finally she plugged in the tree. It became a work of art, a magical thing, when she turned out the other lights and looked at it.

"Wow," Kell said in a soft tone.

She moved to the doorway and smiled at him. "Yeah.

Wow." She sighed. "Well, at least it's a tree. I wish we could have a real one."

"Me, too, but you spent every Christmas sick in bed until we realized you were allergic to fir trees."

"Bummer."

He burst out laughing. "Now, all we have to do is decide what we're going to put under it."

"Artificial presents, I guess," she said quietly.

"Stop that. We're not destitute."

"Yet."

"What am I going to do with you? There is a Santa Claus, 'Virginia,'" he chided. "You just don't know it yet."

She turned the lights back on and smiled at him. "Okay. Have it your way."

"And we'll put presents under it."

Only if they come prepaid and already wrapped, she thought cynically, but she didn't say it. Life was hard, when you lived on the fringes of society. Kell had a much better attitude than she did. Her optimism was losing ground by the day.

THE BEGINNING OF the week started out badly. Dr. Rydel and Dr. King had a very loud and disturbing argument over possible treatments for a beautiful black Persian male cat with advanced kidney failure.

"We can do dialysis," Dr. King argued.

Dr. Rydel's pale blue eyes threw off sparks. "Do you intend to contribute to the 'let's prolong Harry's suffering' fund?"

"Excuse me?"

"His owner is retired. All she has is her social security, because her pension plan crashed and burned during the economic downturn," he said hotly. "How the hell do you think she's going to afford dialysis for a cat who's got, at the most, a couple of weeks of acute suffering to go before he faces an end to the pain?"

Dr. King was giving him very odd looks. She didn't say anything.

"I can irrigate him and pump drugs into him and keep him alive for another month," he said through his teeth. "And he'll be in agony all that time. I can do dialysis and prolong it even more. Or do you think that animals don't really feel pain at all?"

She still hadn't spoken. She just looked at him.

"Dialysis!" he scoffed. "I love animals, too, Dr. King, and I'd never give up on one that had a ghost of a chance of a normal life. But this cat isn't having a normal life—he's going through hell on a daily basis. Or haven't you ever seen a human being in the final stages of kidney failure?" he demanded.

"No, I haven't," Dr. King said, in an unusually gentle tone.

"You can take it from me that it's the closest thing to hell on earth. And I am not, repeat not, putting the cat on dialysis and that's the advice I'm giving his owner."

"Okay."

He frowned. "Okay?"

She didn't smile. "It must have been very hard to watch," she added quietly.

His face, for an instant, betrayed the anguish of a personal loss of some magnitude. He turned away and went back into his office. He didn't even slam the door.

Cappie and Keely flanked Dr. King, all big eyes and unspoken questions.

"You don't know, do you?" she asked. She motioned them off into the chart room and closed the door. "You didn't hear me say this," she instructed, and waited until they both nodded. "His mother was sixty when they diagnosed her with kidney failure three years ago. They put her on dialysis and gave her medications to help put off the inevitable, but she lost the battle just a year later when they discovered an inoperable tumor in her bladder. She was in agony. All that time, she had only her social security and Medicaid to help. Her husband, Dr. Rydel's stepfather, wouldn't let him help at all. In fact, Dr. Rydel had to fight just to see his mother. He and his stepfather have been enemies for years, and it just got worse when his mother was so ill. His mother died and he blames his stepfather, first for not letting her go to a doctor for tests in the first place, and then for not letting him help with the costs afterward. She lived in terrible poverty. Her husband was too proud to accept a dime from any other source, and he worked as a night watchman in a manufacturing company."

No wonder Dr. Rydel was so adamant about health care, Cappie thought. She saw him through different eyes. She also understood his frustration.

"He's right, too, about Harry's owner," Dr. King added. "Mrs. Trammel doesn't have much left after she pays her own medicine bills and utilities and groceries. Certainly she doesn't have enough to afford expensive treatments for an elderly cat who doesn't have long to live no matter what we do." She grimaced. "It's wonderful that we have all these new treatments for our pets. But it's not good that we sometimes make decisions that aren't realistic. The cat is elderly and in constant pain. Are we doing it a favor to order thousands of dollars of treatments that its owner can't afford, just to prolong the suffering?"

Keely shrugged. "Bailey, Boone's German shepherd, would have died if Dr. Rydel hadn't operated on him when he got bloat," she ventured.

"Yes, and he's old, too," Dr. King agreed. "But Boone could afford it."

"Good point," Keely agreed.

"We do have medical insurance for pets now," Cappie pointed out.

"It's the same moral question, though," Dr. King pointed out. "Should we do something just because we can do it?"

The phone rang, both lines at once, and a woman with a cat in a blanket and red, tear-filled eyes rushed in the door calling for help.

"It's going to be a long day," Dr. King sighed.

CAPPIE TOLD HER brother about Dr. Rydel's mother. "I guess we're not the only people who wish we had adequate health care," she said, smiling gently.

"I guess not. Poor guy." He frowned. "How do you make a decision like that for a pet?" he added.

"We didn't. We recommended what we thought best, but let Mrs. Trammel make the final decision. She was more philosophical than all of us put together. She said Harry had lived for nineteen good years, been spoiled rotten and shame on us for thinking death was a bitter end. She thinks cats go to a better place, too, and that they have green fields to run through and no cars to run over them." She smiled. "In the end, she decided that it was kinder to just let Dr. Rydel do what was necessary. Keely's barn cat has a new litter of kittens, solid white with blue eyes. She promised Mrs. Trammel one. Life goes on."

"Yes." He was somber. "It does."

She lifted her eyebrows. "Any day now, there's going to be a breakthrough in medical research and you're going to have an operation that will put you back on your feet and give you a new lease on life."

"After which I'll win the British Open, effect détente with the eastern communists and perfect a cure for cancer," he added dryly.

"One miracle at a time," she interrupted. "And just how would you win the British Open? You don't even play tennis!"

"Don't confuse me with a bunch of irrelevant facts." He sank back into his pillows and grimaced. "Besides, the pain is going to kill me long before they find any miraculous surgical techniques." He closed his eyes with a long sigh. "One day without pain," he said quietly. "Just one day. I'd do almost anything for it."

She knew, as many other people didn't, that chronic pain brought on a kind of depression that was pervasive and dangerous. Even the drugs he took for pain only took the edge off. Nothing they'd ever given him had stopped it.

"What you need is a nice chocolate milkshake and some evil, fattening, over-salted French fries and a cholesterol-dripping hamburger," she said.

He made a tortured face. "Go ahead, torment me!"

She grinned. "I overpaid the hardware bill and got sent a ten-dollar refund," she said, reaching into her purse. "I'll go to the bank, cash it and we'll eat out to-night!"

"You beauty!" he exclaimed.

She curtsied. "I'll be back before you know it." She glanced at her watch. "Oops, better hurry or the bank will be closed!"

She grabbed her old denim jacket and her purse and ran out the door.

The ancient car was temperamental. It had over two hundred thousand miles on it, and it looked like a piece of junk. She coaxed it into life and grimaced as she read the gas gauge. She had a fourth of a tank left. Well, it was only a five-minute drive to Jacobsville from Comanche Wells. She'd have enough to get her to work and back for one more day. Then she'd worry about gas. The ten-dollar check would have come in handy for that, but Kell needed cheering up more. These spells of depression were very bad for him, and they were becoming more frequent. She'd have done anything to keep him optimistic. Even walking to work.

She cashed the check with two minutes to spare before the bank closed. Then she drove to the local fast-food joint and ordered burgers and fries and milkshakes. She paid for them—had five cents left over—and pulled out into the road. Then two things went wrong at once. The engine quit and a car flew out of a side road and right into the passenger side of her car.

She sat, shaking, amid the ruins of her car, with chocolate milkshake all over her jeans and jacket, and pieces of hamburgers on the dirty floorboard. It was quite an impact. She couldn't move for a minute. She sat, staring at the dash, wondering how she'd manage without a car, because her insurance only covered liability. She had nothing that would even pay to repair the car, if it could be repaired.

She turned her head in slow motion and looked at the car that had hit her. The driver got out, staggering. He laughed. That explained why he'd shot through a stop sign without braking. He leaned against his ruined fender and laughed some more.

Cappie wondered if he had insurance. She also wondered if she didn't have a tire iron that she could get to, before the police came to save the man.

Her car door was jerked open. She looked up into a pair of steely ice-blue eyes.

"Are you all right?" he asked.

She blinked. Dr. Rydel. She wondered where he'd come from.

"Cappie, are you all right?" he repeated. His voice was very soft, nothing like the glitter in those pale eyes.

"I think so," she said. Time seemed to have slowed to a stop. She couldn't get her sluggish brain to work. "I was taking hamburgers and shakes home to Kell," she said. "He was so depressed. I thought it would cheer him up. I was worried about spending the money on treats instead of gas." She laughed dully. "I guess I won't need to worry about gas, now," she added, looking around at the damage.

"You're lucky you weren't in one of the newer little cars. You'd be dead."

She looked toward the other driver. "Dr. Rydel, do

you have a tire tool I could borrow?" she asked conversationally.

He saw where she was looking. "You don't want to upset the police, Cappie."

"I won't tell if you won't."

Before he could reply, a Jacobsville police car roared up, lights flashing, and stopped. Obviously somebody in the fast-food place had called them.

Officer Kilraven climbed out of the police car and headed right for Cappie.

"Oh, good, it's him," Cappie said. "He'll scare the other driver to death."

Kilraven bent down on Cappie's side of the car. "You okay? Need an ambulance?"

"Heavens, no," she said quickly. As if she could afford to pay for that! "I'm fine. Just shaken up." She nodded toward the giggling driver who'd hit her. "Dr. Rydel won't loan me a tire iron, so could you shoot that man in the foot for me, please? I don't even have collision insurance and it wasn't my fault. I'll be walking to work on account of him."

"I can't shoot him," Kilraven said with a twinkle in his silver eyes. "But if he tries to hit me, I'll take him to detention in the trunk of my car. Okay?"

She brightened. "Okay!"

He straightened and said something to Dr. Rydel. A minute later, he marched over to the drunk man, smelled his breath, made a face and asked him to perform a sobriety test, which the subject refused. That would mean a blood test at the hospital, which Kilraven was fairly certain the man would fail. He told him he was under

arrest and cuffed him. Cappie vaguely heard him calling for a wrecker and backup.

"A wrecker?" She groaned. "I can't afford a wrecker."

"Just don't worry about it right now. Come on. I'll
drive you home."

Dr. Rydel helped her out of the car. She retrieved her
purse, wincing. "I hope he has a Texas-size hangover
when he wakes up tomorrow," she said coldly, watching
Kilraven putting the prisoner in the back of his squad
car. The man was still laughing.

"Oh, I hope he gets pregnant," Dr. Rydel mused,
"and it's twins."

She laughed huskily. "Even better. Thanks."

He put her into his big Land Rover. "Wait here. I'll
just be a minute."

She sat quietly, fascinated with the interior of the
vehicle. It conjured up visions of the African veldt,
of elephants and giraffes and wildebeest. She wished
she could afford even a twenty-year-old version of this
beast. She'd never have to worry about bad roads again.

He was back shortly with a bag and a cup carrier. He
put them in her lap. "Two hamburgers and fries and
two chocolate shakes."

"How...?"

"Well, it's easier to tell when you're wearing parts of
them," he pointed out, indicating chocolate milk stains
and mustard and catsup and pieces of food all over her
clothes. "Fasten your seat belt."

She did. "I'll pay you back," she said firmly.

He grinned. "Whatever."

He started the engine and drove her out of town.
"You'll have to direct me. I don't know where you live."

She named the road, and then the street. They didn't talk. He pulled up in the front yard of the dinky little house, with its peeling paint and rickety steps and sagging eaves.

He grimaced.

"Hey, don't knock it," she said. "It's got a pretty good roof and big rooms and it's paid for. A distant cousin willed it to us."

"Nice of him. Do you have any other cousins?"

"No. It's just me and Kell."

"No other siblings?"

She shook her head. "We don't have any family left."

He gave the house a speaking look.

"If we had the money to fix it up, it would look terrific," she said.

He helped her out of the car and onto the porch. He hesitated about handing her the bag with the food and the carrier of milkshakes.

"Would you like to come in and meet Kell?" she ventured. "Only if you want to," she added quickly.

"Yes, I would."

She unlocked the door and motioned him in. "Kell, I'm home!" she called. "I brought company."

"If it's wearing lipstick and has a good sense of humor, bring it in here quick!" he quipped.

Dr. Rydel burst out laughing. "Sorry, I don't wear lipstick," he called back.

"Oops."

Cappie laughed and walked toward the room a little unsteadily, motioning the vet to follow her.

Kell was propped up in bed with the old laptop. He

paused, eyebrows arched, as they walked in. "We should have ordered more food," he said with a grin.

Cappie winced. "Well, see, the food is the problem. I was pulling out of the parking lot and the engine died. A drunk man ran into the car and pretty much killed it."

"Luckily he didn't kill you," Kell said, frowning. "Are you all right?"

"Just bruised a little. Dr. Rydel was kind enough to bring me home. Dr. Rydel, this is my brother, Kell," she began.

"You're the veterinarian?" Kell asked, and his silvery-gray eyes twinkled. "I thought you had fangs and a pointed tail..."

"Kell!" she burst out, horrified.

Dr. Rydel chuckled. "Only during office hours," he returned.

"I'll kill you!" she told her brother.

"Now, now," Dr. Rydel said complacently. "We all know I'm a horror to work for. He's just saying what you aren't comfortable telling me."

"And he does have a sense of humor," Kell said. "Thanks for bringing her home," he added, and the smile faded. "My driving days are apparently over."

"There are vehicles with hand controls now," Dr. Rydel pointed out.

"We're ordering one of those as soon as we get our new yacht paid off," Kell replied with a serious expression.

Cappie burst out laughing. "And our dandy indoor swimming pool."

Dr. Rydel smiled. "At least you still have a sense of humor."

"It's the only part of me that works," Kell replied. "I've offered to check myself into a military home, but she won't hear of it."

"Over my dead body," she reiterated, and glared at him.

He sighed. "It's nice to be loved, but you can take family feeling over the cliff with you, darlin'," he reminded her.

"Sink or swim, we're a matched set," she said stubbornly. "I'm not putting you out on the street."

"Military homes can be very nice," Kell began.

Cappie grimaced. "Your milkshake is getting warm," she interrupted. She took the carrier from Dr. Rydel and handed one to Kell, along with a straw. "There's your burger and fries," she said. "Working?"

"Taking a short break to play mah-jongg," he replied. "I'm actually winning, too."

"I play Sudoku," Dr. Rydel commented.

Kell groaned. "I can't do numbers. I tried that game and thought I'd go nuts. I couldn't even get one column to line up. How do you do it?"

"I'm left-brained," the other man said simply. "Numbers and science. I'd have loved to be a writer, but I'm spelling-challenged."

Kell laughed. "I'm left-brained, too, but I can't handle Sudoku. I can spell, however," he added, tongue in cheek.

"That's why we have a bookkeeper," Dr. Rydel said. "I think people would have issues if their names and animal conditions were constantly misspelled. I had a time in college."

"So did I," Kell confessed. "College trigonometry al-

most kept me from getting my degree in the first place.
I also had a bad time with biology," he added pointedly.

Dr. Rydel grinned. "My best subject. All A's."

"I'll bet the biology-challenged loved you," Cappie
said with a chuckle. "Blew the curve every time, didn't
you?"

He nodded. "I bought pizzas for my classmates every
Saturday night to make it up to them."

"Pizza," Cappie mused. "I remember what that tastes
like. I think."

"I don't want to talk about pizza," Kell said and
sipped his milkshake. "You and your mushrooms!"

"He hates mushrooms, and I hate Italian sausage,"
Cappie commented. "I love mushrooms."

"Yuuuuck," Kell commented.

She smiled. "We'll leave you to your supper. If you
need anything, call me, okay?"

"Sure. What would you like to be called?"

She wrinkled her nose at him and went out the door.

"Nice to have met you," Kell told the vet.

"Same here," Dr. Rydel said.

He followed Cappie out into the living room. "You'd
better eat your own burger and fries before they're
cold," he said. "They don't reheat well."

She smiled shyly. "Thanks again for bringing me
home, and for the food." She wondered how she was
going to get to work the following Monday, but she
knew she'd come up with something. She could always
beg one of the other vet techs for a ride.

"You're welcome." He stared down at her quietly,
frowning. "You sure you're all right?"

She nodded. "I'm wobbly. That's because I was

scared to death. I'll be fine. It's just a little bruising. Honest."

"Would you tell me if it was more?" he asked.

She grinned.

"Well, if you think you need to go to the doctor later, you call me. Call the office," he added. "They'll take a message and page me, wherever I am."

"That's very nice of you. Thanks."

He drew in a long breath. His blue eyes narrowed on her face. "You've got a lot on your shoulders for a woman your age," he said quietly.

"Some people have a lot more," she replied. "I love my brother."

He smiled. "I noticed that."

She studied him curiously. "Do you have family?"

His face tautened. "Not anymore."

"I'm sorry."

"People get old. They die." He became distant. "We'll talk another time. Good evening."

"Good evening. Thanks."

He shrugged. "No problem."

She watched him go with a strange sense of loss. He was in many ways the saddest person she'd ever known.

She finished her supper and went to collect her brother's food containers.

"Your boss is nice," he said. "Not what I expected."

"How could you tell him what I said about him, you horrible man?" she asked with mock anger.

"He's one of those rare souls who never lie," he said simply. "He comes at you head-on, not from ambush."

"How do you know that?"

"It's in his manner," he said simply. He smiled. "I'm

that way myself. It does take one to know one. Now come here and sit down and tell me what happened."

She drew in a deep breath and sat down in the chair beside the bed. She hated having to tell him the whole truth. It wasn't going to be pretty.

CHAPTER THREE

CAPPIE HITCHED A ride to work with Keely, promising not to make a regular thing of it.

"I'll just have to get another car," she said, as if all that required was a trip to a car lot. In fact, she had no idea what she was going to do.

"My brother is best friends with Sheriff Hayes Carson," Keely reminded her, "and Hayes knows Kilraven. He told him the particulars, and Kilraven had a talk with the driver's insurance company." She chuckled. "I understand some interesting what-ifs were mentioned. The upshot is that the driver's insurance is going to pay to fix your car."

"What?"

"Well, he was drunk, Cappie. In fact, he's occupying a cell at the county detention center as we speak. You could sue his insurance company for enough to buy a new Jaguar like my brother's got."

She didn't mention that Kell had owned a Jaguar, and not too long ago. Those days seemed very far away now. "Wow. I've never sued anybody, you know."

Keely laughed. "Me, neither. But you could. Once the insurance people were reminded of that, they didn't seem to think fixing an old car was an extravagant use of funds."

"It's really nice of them," Cappie said, stunned. It was like a miracle. "I didn't know what I was going to do. My brother is an invalid, and the only money we've got is his savings and what I bring home. That's not a whole lot."

"Before I married Boone, I had to count pennies," the other girl said. "I know what it's like to have very little. I think you do very well."

"Thanks." She sighed. "You know, Kell was in the military for years and years. He went into all sorts of dangerous situations, but he never got hurt. Then he left the army and went to work for this magazine, went to Africa to cover a story and got hit with shrapnel from an exploding shell. Go figure."

Keely frowned. "Didn't he have insurance? Most magazines have it for their employees, I'm sure."

"Well, no, he didn't. Odd, isn't it?"

"They sent him to Africa to do a story," Keely added. "What sort of story? A news story?"

Cappie blinked. "You know, I never asked him. I only knew he was leaving the country. Then I got a call from him, saying he was in the hospital with some injuries and he'd be home when he could get here. He wouldn't even let me visit him. An ambulance brought him to our rented house in San Antonio."

Keely didn't say what she was thinking. But she almost had to bite her tongue.

Cappie stared at her. "That's a very strange story, even if I'm the one telling it," she said slowly.

"Maybe it's the truth," Keely said comfortingly. "After all, it's very often stranger than fiction."

"I guess so." She let it drop. But she did intend to talk it over with Kell that night.

WHEN SHE GOT HOME, there was a big SUV parked in the driveway. She frowned at it as she went up the steps and into the house. The door was unlocked.

She heard laughter coming from Kell's room.

"I'm home!" she called.

"Come on in here," Kell called back. "I've got company."

She took off her coat and moved into the bedroom. Kell's visitor was very tall and lean, with faint silvering at the temples of his black hair. He had green eyes and a somber face, and one of his hands seemed to be burned. He moved it unobtrusively into his pocket when he saw her eyes drawn to it.

"This is an old friend of mine," Kell said. "My sister, Cappie. This is Cy Parks. He owns a ranch in Jacobsville."

Cappie held out her hand, smiling, and shook the one offered. "Nice to meet you."

"Same here. You'll have to bring Kell over to the ranch to see us," he added. "I have a terrific wife and two little boys. I'd love for you to meet them."

"You, with a wife and kids," Kell said, shaking his head. "I'd never have imagined it in my wildest dreams."

"Oh, it comes to all of us, sooner or later," Cy replied lazily. He pursed his lips. "So you work for Bentley Rydel, do you?"

She nodded.

"Does he really carry a pitchfork, or is that just malicious gossip?" Cy added, tongue in cheek.

She flushed. "Kell...!" she muttered at her brother.

He held up both hands and laughed. "I didn't tell him what you said. Honest."

"He didn't," Cy agreed. "Actually Bentley makes a lot of calls at my place during calving season. He's our vet. Good man."

"Yes, he is," Cappie said. "He brought me home after a drunk ran into my car."

Cy's expression darkened. "I heard about that. Tough break."

"Well, the man's insurance company is going to fix our car," Cappie added with a laugh. "It seems they were worried that we might sue."

"We would have," Kell said, and he wasn't smiling. "You could have been killed."

"I just got bruised a little," she said, smiling. "Nice of you to worry, though."

Kell grinned. "It's a hobby of mine."

"You need to get out more," Cy told the man in the bed. "I know you've got pain issues, but staying cooped up in here is just going to make things worse. Believe me, I know."

Kell's eyes darkened. "I guess you're right. But I do have something to do. I'm working on a novel. One about Africa."

Cy Parks's face grew hard. "That place has made its mark on several of us," he said enigmatically.

"It's still making marks on other men," Kell said.

"The Latin American drug cartels are moving in there, as well," Cy replied. "Hell of a thing, as if Africa didn't have enough internal problems as it is."

"As long as power-hungry tyrants can amass fortunes

by oppressing other men, it won't lower the casualty rates for any combatants working there," Kell muttered.

"Combatants?" Cappie asked curiously.

"Two groups of people are fighting for supremacy," Kell told her.

"One good, one evil," she guessed.

"No. As far as African internal politics go, both sides have positive arguments. The outsiders are the ones causing the big problems. Their type of diplomacy is most often practiced with rapid-firing automatic weapons and various incendiary devices."

"And IEDs," Cy added.

Cappie blinked. "Excuse me?"

"Improvised explosive devices," Kell translated.

"Were you in the military, too, Mr. Parks?" Cappie asked.

Cy hesitated. "Sort of. Look at the time," he remarked, glancing at his watch. "Lisa wants me to go with her to pick out a new playpen for our youngest son," he added with a grin. "Our toddler more or less trashed the first one."

"Strong kid," Kell noted.

"Yes. Bullheaded, too."

"I wonder where he gets that from," Kell wondered aloud, with twinkling eyes.

"I am not bullheaded," Cy said complacently. "I simply have a resistance to stupid ideas."

"Same difference."

Cy made a face. "I'll come back and check on you later in the week. If you need anything…"

Kell smiled. "Thanks, Cy."

"I'd have come with Eb and Micah when they

dropped by," Cy added, "but we were out of town with the kids. It's good to see you again."

"Same here," Kell said. "I owe you."

"For what?" Cy shrugged. "Friends help friends."

"They do."

Cappie stared at her brother with a blank expression. A whole conversation seemed to be going on under her nose that she didn't comprehend.

"I'll see you," Cy said. "Nice to have met you, Miss Drake," he added, smiling.

"You, too," she replied.

Cy left without a backward glance.

After he drove away, Cappie was still staring at her brother. "You didn't say you had friends here. Why haven't I seen them?"

"They came while you were at work," he said. "Several times."

"Oh."

He averted his eyes. "I met them when I was in the service," he said. "They're fine men. A little unorthodox, but good people."

"Oh!" She relaxed. "Mr. Parks has an injury."

"Yes. He was badly burned trying to save his wife and child from a fire. He was the only one who got out. It turned him mean. But now he's remarried and has two sons, and he seems to have put the past behind him."

"Poor guy." She grimaced. "No wonder he was mean. Who were the other men he mentioned?"

"Other friends. Eb Scott and Micah Steele. Micah's a doctor in Jacobsville. Eb Scott has a sort of training center for paramilitary units."

She blinked. "You do seem to attract the oddest friends."

"Men with guns." He nodded. He grinned.

She laughed. "Okay. I'm stonewalled. What do you want for supper?"

"Nothing heavy," he said. "I had a big lunch."

"You did?" She didn't recall leaving anything out for him except sandwiches in a Baggie.

"Cy brought a whole menu full of stuff from the local Chinese restaurant," he said. "The remains are in the fridge. I wouldn't mind having some of them for supper."

"Chinese food? Real Chinese food, from a real restaurant, that I don't have to cook?" She felt her forehead. "Maybe I'm delusional."

He chuckled. "It does sound like that, doesn't it? Go dig in. Bring me some of the pork and noodles, if you will. There's sticky rice and mangoes for dessert, too."

"I have died and am now in heaven," she said in a haunted tone.

"Me, too. Get cracking. I'm on the fourth chapter of this book already!"

"You are?" She laughed. He looked so much more cheerful. More than he'd been in weeks. "Okay, then."

He pulled the laptop back into place.

"Do I get to read it?"

He nodded. "When it's done."

"That's a deal." She went into the kitchen and got out the boxes of Chinese food. It was all she could do to keep back the tears. Cy Parks was a nice man. A very nice man. Except for their splurged hamburgers and milkshakes, for which she still owed Dr. Rydel, she reminded herself, there hadn't been any convenience food for a long time. This was a feast. She put some of it in the freezer for hard times and heated up the rest. Her day was already getting better.

IT GOT EVEN better than that. A tall man with sandy hair and blue eyes came driving up in Cappie's own car two days later. The big SUV was following close behind. Cappie gaped at the sight. Her old car had been refurbished, its dents beaten out and the whole thing repainted and repaired. There were even seat covers and floor mats. She stared at it helplessly surprised.

Cy Parks got out of the SUV and followed the sandy-haired man up onto the porch. "I hope you like blue," he told Cappie. "There was a paint sale."

She could barely manage words. "Mr. Parks, I don't even know what to say…" She burst into tears. "It's so kind!"

He patted her awkwardly on the shoulder. "There, there, it's just one of those random acts of kindness we're supposed to pass around. You can do the same thing for somebody else one day."

She dabbed at her eyes. "When I strike it rich, I swear I will!"

He chuckled. "Harley Fowler, here," he introduced his companion, "is as good a mechanic as he is a ranch foreman. I had him supervise the work on your car. The insurance company paid for it all," he added when she started to protest. He grinned. "We get things done here in Jacobsville. The insurance agent locally is the sister-in-law of my top wrangler."

"Well, thank you both," she said huskily. "Thank

you so much. I was almost ashamed to ask Keely for rides. She's so nice, but it was an imposition. I live five miles out of her way."

"You're very welcome."

The front door opened and Kell wheeled himself out onto the porch. He whistled when he saw the car. "Good grief, that was quick work," he said.

Cy grinned. "You might remember that I always did know how to cut through the red tape."

"Thanks," Kell told him. "From both of us. If I can ever do anything for you…"

"You've done enough," Cy returned quietly. His green eyes twinkled. "But you could always put me in that novel you're writing. I'd like to be twenty-seven, drop-dead handsome and a linguist."

Kell rolled his eyes. "You can barely speak English," he pointed out.

Cy glared at him. "You take that back, or I'll have Harley shoot all the tires out on this car."

Kell held up both hands, his silver eyes twinkling. "Okay, you could get work as a translator at the UN any day. Honest."

Cy sighed. "Don't I wish." He frowned. "Do you still speak Farsi?"

Kell nodded, smiling.

"I've got a friend who's applying for a job with the company. Think you could tutor him? He's well-off, and he'd pay you for your time."

Kell frowned.

"It's not charity," Cy muttered, glowering at him. "This is a legitimate need. The guy wants to work overseas, but he'll never get the job unless he can perfect his accent."

Kell relaxed. "All right, then. I'll take him on. And thanks."

Cy smiled. "Thank you," he replied. "He's a nice guy. You'll like him." He glanced at Cappie, who was wondering what sort of company Cy's friend worked for. "You won't," he assured her. "I used to be a woman hater, but this guy makes me look civilized. He'll need to come over when you're at work."

Cappie was curious. "Why does he hate women?"

"I think he was married to one," Cy mused.

"Well, that certainly explains that," Kell chuckled.

"Thank you very much for fixing up my car," Cappie told Cy. "I won't forget it."

"No problem. We were glad to help. Oh, mustn't forget the keys, Harley!"

Harley handed the keys to her as Cy headed back and got into the other vehicle. "She purrs like a kitten now," Harley told her. "She drives good."

"The car is a girl?" she asked.

"Only when a guy is driving it," Kell told her with a wicked grin.

"Amen," Harley told him.

"Come on, Harley," Cy called from the SUV.

"Yes, sir." He grinned at the brother and sister and jumped into the passenger seat in Cy's SUV.

"What a nice man," Cappie said. "Just look, Kell!" She walked out to the car, opened the door and gasped. "They oiled the hinges! It doesn't squeak anymore. And look, they fixed the broken dash and replaced the radio that didn't work..." She started crying again.

"Don't do that," Kell said gently. "You'll have me wailing, too."

She made a face at him. "You have nice friends."

"I do, don't I?" He smiled. "Now you won't have to beg rides."

"It will be a relief, although Keely's been wonderful about it." She glanced at her brother. "I don't think the insurance paid for all this."

"Yes, it did," he said firmly. "Period."

She smiled at him. "Okay. You really do have nice friends."

"You don't know how nice," he told her. "But I may tell you one day. Now let's get back inside. It's cold out here today."

"It is a bit nippy." She turned and followed him inside.

THE WEEK WENT by fast. She got her paycheck on Friday and went shopping early Saturday morning in Jacobsville. Kell had said he'd love a new bathrobe for Christmas, so she went to the department store looking.

It was a surprise when she bumped into Dr. Rydel in the men's department. He gave her a curious look. She didn't realize why until she recalled that she'd left her hair long around her shoulders instead of putting it up. He seemed to find it fascinating.

"Shopping for anything particular?" he asked.

"Yes. Kell wants a bathrobe."

"Christmas shopping," he guessed, and smiled.

"Yes."

"I'm replacing a jacket," he sighed. "I made the mistake of going straight from church on a large animal call. A longhorn bull objected to being used as a pin-cushion and ripped out the sleeve."

She laughed softly. "Occupational hazard," she said.

He nodded. "Your car looks nice."

"Thanks," she said. She could imagine how her old wreck, even repainted, looked to a man who drove a new Land Rover, but she didn't say so. "Mr. Parks had his foreman supervise the work. The insurance company paid for it."

"Nice of him. He knows your brother?"

"They're friends." She frowned. "Mr. Parks doesn't look like a rancher," she blurted out.

"Excuse me?"

"There's something, I don't know, dangerous about him," she said, searching for the right word. "He's very nice, but I wouldn't want him mad at me."

He grinned. "A few drug dealers in prison could attest to the truth of that statement," he said.

"What?"

"You don't know?"

"Know what?"

"Cy Parks is a retired mercenary," he told her. "He was in some bloody firefights in Africa some years back. More recently, he and two other friends and Harley Fowler shut down a drug distribution center here. There was a gunfight."

"In Jacobsville, Texas?" she exclaimed.

"Yep. Parks is one of the most dangerous men I've ever met. Kind to people he likes. But there aren't many of those."

She felt odd. She wondered how it was that her

brother had come to know such a man, because he and Cy seemed to be old friends.

"Where do you go from here?" Dr. Rydel asked suddenly.

She blinked. "I don't know," she blurted out, flushing. "I mean, I thought I might, well, stop by the game store in the strip mall."

He stared at her blankly. "Game store?"

She cleared her throat. "There's this new video game. *Halo…*"

"…*ODST*," he said, with evident surprise. "You're a gamer?"

She cleared her throat again. "Well…yes."

He said something unprintable.

She glared at him. "Dr. Rydel!" she exclaimed. "It's not a vice, you know, playing video games. They release tension and they're fun," she argued.

He chuckled. "I have all three Halo games from Bungie, plus the campaigns," he confessed, naming the famous company whose amazing staff had engineered one of the most exciting video game series of all time. "And the new one that just came out."

Now her jaw fell open. "You do?"

"Yes. I have *Halo: ODST*," he said, pursing his lips. "Do you game online?"

She didn't want to confess that she couldn't afford the fees. "I like playing by myself," she said. "Or with Kell. He's crazy about the Halo series."

"So am I," Dr. Rydel told her. His blue eyes twinkled. "Maybe we could play split screen sometime, when we're both free."

She gave him a wicked look. "I can put down Hunters with a .45 automatic." Hunters were some of the most formidable of the alien Covenant bad guys, fearsome to engage in the Halo game because they were huge and it took a dead shot to hit them in their very few vulnerable places.

He whistled. "Not bad, Miss Drake!"

"Have you been a gamer for a long time?" she asked.

"Since college," he replied, smiling. "You?"

"Since high school. Kell was in the military and a bunch of guys in his unit would come over to the house when they were off duty and play war-game videos. We lived off base." She pursed her lips and her eyes twinkled. "I not only learned how to use tactics and weapons, I also learned a lot of very interesting and useful words to employ when I got killed in the games."

"Bad girl," he chided.

She laughed.

"I'll probably see you in the video store," he added.

She beamed. "You probably will."

He grinned and went back to the suits.

FIFTEEN MINUTES LATER, she parked in front of the video store and went inside. It was full of teenage boys mostly, but there were two men standing in front of a rack with the newest sword and sorcery and combat games. One of them was Dr. Rydel. The other, surprisingly, was Officer Kilraven.

Dr. Rydel looked up and smiled when he saw her coming. Kilraven's silver eyes cut around to follow his companion's gaze. His black eyebrows arched.

"She's Christmas shopping," Dr. Rydel announced.

"Buying video games for a relative?" Kilraven wondered aloud.

Dr. Rydel chuckled. "She's a gamer," he confided. "She can take down Hunters with a .45 auto."

Kilraven whistled through his teeth. "Impressive," he said. "I usually do that with a sniper rifle."

"I can use those, too," she said. "But the .45 works just as well, thanks to that magnified sight."

"Have you played all the Halo series?" Kilraven asked.

She nodded. "Now I'm shopping for *ODST*," she said. "Kell, my brother, likes it, too. He taught me how to play."

Kilraven frowned. "Kell Drake?"

"Yes…"

"I know him," Kilraven replied quietly. "Good man."

"Were you in the army?" she asked innocently.

Kilraven chuckled. "Once, a long time ago."

"Kell only got out a year ago," she said. "He was freelancing for a magazine in Africa and got hit by flying shrapnel. He's paralyzed from the waist down—at least until the shrapnel shifts enough so that they can operate."

Kilraven blinked. "He got hit by flying…he was working for a magazine?" He seemed incredulous. "Doing what?"

"Writing stories."

"Writing stories? Kell can write?"

"He has very good English skills," she began defensively.

"I never," Kilraven said in an odd tone. "Why did he get out of the army?" he wanted to know.

She blinked. "Well, I'm not really sure…" she began.

"Look at this one," Dr. Rydel interrupted helpfully, holding up a game. "Have you ever played this?"

Kilraven was diverted. He took the green case and stared at the description. He grinned. "Have I ever! *Elder Scrolls IV, Oblivion*," he murmured. "This is great! You don't have to do the main quest, if you don't want to. There are dozens of other quests. You can even design your own character's appearance, name him, choose from several races…ever played it?" he asked Cappie.

She chuckled. "Actually it's sort of my favorite. I love *Halo*, but I like using a two-handed sword, as well."

"Vicious girl," Kilraven mused, smiling at her.

Dr. Rydel unobtrusively moved closer to Cappie and cleared his throat. "You shopping or working today?" he asked Kilraven.

The other man looked from Cappie to Dr. Rydel and his silver eyes twinkled. "If you notice, I'm wearing a real uniform," he pointed out. "I even carry a real gun. Now would I be doing that if it was my day off?"

Dr. Rydel smiled back at him. "Would you be shopping for video games on city time?"

Kilraven glared at him. "For your information, I am here detecting crime."

"You are?"

"Absolutely. I have it on good authority that there might be an attempted shoplifting case going on here right now." He raised his voice as he said it and a young boy cleared his throat and eased a game out from under his jacket and back on the shelf. With flaming cheeks he gave Kilraven a hopeful smile and moved quickly to the door.

"If you'll excuse me," Kilraven murmured, "I'm going to have a few helpful words of advice for that young man."

"How did he know?" Cappie asked, stunned, as she watched the tall officer walk out the door and call to the departing teen.

"Beats me, but I've heard he does things like that." He smiled. "He's on his lunch hour, in case you wondered. I was just ribbing him. I like Kilraven."

She gave him a wry glance. "Sharks like other sharks, do they?" she asked wickedly.

CHAPTER FOUR

AT FIRST, BENTLEY wasn't sure he'd heard her right. Then he saw the demure grin and burst out laughing. She'd compared him to a shark. He was impressed.

"I wondered if you were ever going to learn how to talk to me without getting behind a door first," he mused.

"You're hard going," she confessed. "But so is Kell, to other people. He just walks right over people who don't talk back."

"Exactly," he returned. He shrugged his broad shoulders. "I don't know how to get along with people," he confessed. "My social skills are sparse."

"You're wonderful with animals," she replied.

His eyebrows arched and he smiled. "Thanks."

"Did you always like them?" she wondered.

His eyes had a faraway look. He averted them. "Yes. But my father didn't. It wasn't until after he died that I indulged my affection for them. It was just my mother and me until I was in high school. That's when she met my stepfather." His expression hardened.

"It must have been very difficult for you," she said quietly, "getting used to another man in your house."

He frowned as he looked down at her. "Yes."

"Oh, I'm remarkably perceptive," she said with

amusement in her eyes. "I also suffer from extreme modesty about my other equally remarkable attributes." She grinned.

He laughed again.

Kilraven came back, looking smug.

"You look like a man with a mission," Bentley mused.

"Just finished one. That young man will never want to lift a video game again."

"Good for you. Didn't arrest him?"

Kilraven arched an eyebrow. "Actually he knows some cheat codes for *Call of Duty* that even I haven't worked out. So I called our police chief."

"Cheat codes are against the law?" Cappie asked, puzzled.

Kilraven chuckled. "No. Cash has a young brother-in-law, Rory, who's nuts about *Call of Duty*, so our potential shoplifter is going to go over to Cash's house later and teach them to him. Cash may have a few words to add to the ones I gave him."

"Neat strategy," Bentley said.

Kilraven shrugged. "The boy loves gaming but he lives with a widowed mother who works two jobs just to keep food on the table. He wanted *Call of Duty*, but he didn't have any money. If he and Rory hit it off, and I think they might, he'll get to play the game and learn model citizen habits on the side."

"Good psychology," Bentley told him.

Kilraven sighed. "It's tough on kids, having an economy like this. Gaming is a way of life for the younger generation, but those game consoles and games for them are expensive."

"That's why we have a whole table of used games that are more affordable," the owner of the store, over-hearing them, commented with a grin. "Thanks, Kilraven."

The officer shrugged. "I spend so much time in here that I feel obliged to protect the merchandise," he commented.

The store owner patted him on the back. "Good man. I might give you a discount on your next sale."

Kilraven glared at him. "Attempting to bribe a police officer…"

The owner held up both hands. "I never!" he exclaimed. "I said 'might'!"

Kilraven grinned. "Thanks, though. It was a nice thought. You wouldn't have any games based on Scottish history?" he added.

The store owner, a tall, handsome young man, gave him a pitying look. "Listen, you're the only customer I've ever had who likes sixteenth-century Scottish history. And I'll tell you again that most historians think James Hepburn got what he deserved."

"He did not," Kilraven muttered. "Lord Bothwell was led astray by that French-thinking Queen. Her wiles did him in."

"Wiles?" Cappie asked, wide-eyed. "What are wiles?"

"If you have to ask, you don't have any," Bentley said helpfully.

She laughed. "Okay. Fair enough."

Kilraven shook his head. "Bothwell had admirable qualities," he insisted, staring at the shop owner. "He was utterly fearless, could read and write and speak

French, and even his worst enemies said that he was incapable of being bribed."

"Which may be, but still doesn't provide grounds for a video game," the manager replied.

Kilraven pointed a finger at him. "Just because you're a partisan of Mary, Queen of Scots, is no reason to take issue with her Lord High Admiral. And I should point out that there's no video game about her, either!"

"Hooray," the manager murmured dryly. "Oh, look, a customer!" He took the opportunity to vanish toward the counter.

Kilraven's two companions were giving him odd looks.

"Entertainment should be educational," he defended himself.

"It is," Bentley pointed out. "In this game—" he held up a Star Trek one "—you can learn how to shoot down enemy ships. And in this one—" he held up a comical one about aliens "—you can learn to use a death ray and blow up buildings."

"You have no appreciation of true history," Kilraven sighed. "I should have taught it in grammar school."

"I can see you now, standing in front of the school board, explaining why the kids were having nightmares about sixteenth-century interrogation techniques," Bentley mused.

Kilraven pursed his lips. "I myself have been accused of using those," he said. "Can you believe it? I mean, I'm such a law-abiding citizen and all."

"I can think of at least one potential kidnapper who might disagree," Bentley commented.

"Lies. Vicious lies," he said defensively. "He got

those bruises from trying to squeeze through a car window."

"While it was going sixty miles an hour, I believe?" the other man queried.

"Hey, it's not my fault he didn't want to wait for the arraignment."

"Good thing you noticed the window was cracked in time."

"Yes," Kilraven sighed. "Sad, though, that I didn't realize he had a blackjack. He gave it to me very politely, though."

Bentley glanced at Cappie. "Was it a sprained wrist or a fractured one?" he wondered.

Kilraven gave him a cold glare. "It was a figment."

"A what?"

"Of his imagination," Kilraven assured him. He chuckled. "Anyway, he's going to be in jail for a long time. The resisting-arrest charge, added to assault on a police officer, makes two felony charges in addition to the kidnapping ones."

"I hope you never get mad at me," Bentley said.

"I'd worry more about the chief," Kilraven replied. "He fed a guy a soapy sponge in front of the whole neighborhood."

"He was provoked, I hear," Bentley said.

"A felon verbally assaulted him in his own yard while he was washing his car. Of course, Cash has mellowed since his marriage."

"Not much," Bentley said. "And he's still pretty good with a sniper kit. Saved Colby Lane's little girl when she was kidnapped."

"He practices on Eb Scott's firing range," Kilraven

said. "We all do. He lets us use it free. State-of-the-art stuff, computers and everything."

"Eb Scott?" Cappie asked.

"Eb was a merc," Kilraven told her. "He and Cy Parks and Micah Steele fought in some of the bloodiest wars in Africa a few years back. They're all married and somewhat settled. But like Cash Grier, they're not really tame."

Cappie only nodded. She was recalling what her brother had said about Cy Parks.

Kilraven cleared his throat. "Oops, lunchtime is over. I've got to go. See you."

"You didn't have lunch," Bentley observed.

"I had a big breakfast," Kilraven replied. "Can't waste my lunch hour eating," he added with a grin. "See you."

"Imagine him, a gamer," Cappie commented. "I'd never have thought it."

"A lot of military men keep their hand-eye coordination skills sharp playing them," he said.

"Were you in the military?" Cappie wanted to know.

He smiled and nodded. "I have it on good authority that it's all that saved me from a life of crime. I got picked up for hanging around with a couple of bad kids who knocked over a drugstore. I was just in the car with them, but I got charged with a felony." He sighed. "My mother went to the judge and promised him her next child if he'd let me join the army instead of standing trial. He agreed." He glanced down at her with a smile. "He's in his seventies now, but I still send him a Christmas present every year. I owe him."

"That was nice."

"I thought so, too."

"Kell got into some trouble in his senior year of high school. I don't remember it, I was so young, but he told me about it. He was hanging out with one of the inner-city gangs and there was a firefight. He didn't get shot, but one of the boys in the gang was killed. Kell got arrested right along with them. He drew a female judge who had grown up in gang territory and lost a brother to the violence. She gave him a choice of facing trial or going into the service and making something of his life. He took her at her word, and made her proud." She sighed. "It was tragic, about her. She was shot and killed in her own living room during a drug deal shootout next door."

"Life is dangerous," Bentley remarked.

She nodded. "Unpredictable and dangerous." She looked up at him. "I guess maybe that's why I like playing video games. They give me something that I can control. Life is never that way."

He smiled. "No. It isn't." He watched as she took a copy of *Halo: ODST* off the shelf. "Going to make him wait until Christmas to play it?"

"Yes."

His eyes twinkled. "I could bring my copy over. Let you get a taste of it before the fact."

She looked fascinated. "You could?"

"Ask Kell." He hesitated. "I could bring a pizza with me. And some beer."

She pursed her lips. "I'm already drooling." She grimaced. "I could cook something…"

"Not fair. You shouldn't have to provide for guests.

Besides, I haven't had a decent pizza in weeks. I'll be on call tonight, but we might get lucky."

Her eyes brightened. "That would be nice. I'm sure Kell would enjoy it. We don't get much company."

"About six?"

Her heart jumped. "Yes. About six would be fine."

"It's a date."

"I'll see you then."

He nodded.

She walked, a little wobbly, to the counter and paid for her game. Her life had just changed in a heartbeat. She didn't know where it would lead, and she was a little nervous about getting involved with her boss. But he was very nice-looking and he had qualities that she admired. Besides, she thought, it was just a night of gaming. Nothing suspect about that.

SHE TOLD KELL the minute she got home.

He laughed. "Don't look so guilty," he chided. "I like your boss. Besides, it's neat to see the game I might get for Christmas." He smiled angelically.

"You might get it," she said, "and you might not."

"You might get a new raincoat," he mused.

She grinned. "Wow."

He looked at her fondly. "It's hard, living like this, I know. We were better off in San Antonio. But I didn't want us to be around when Frank got out of jail." His face hardened.

Her heart jumped. She hadn't thought about Frank for several days in a row. But now the trial and his fury came back, full force. "It was almost six months ago that he was arrested, and three months until the trial. He got credit for time served. We've been here just about three months." She bit her lower lip. "Oh, dear. They'll let him out pretty soon."

His pale eyes were cold. "It should have been a tougher sentence. But despite his past, it was the first time he was ever charged with battery, and they couldn't get more jail time for him on a first offense. The public defender in his case was pretty talented, as well."

She drew in a long breath. "I'm glad we're out of the city."

"So am I. He lived barely a block from us. We're not as easy to get to, here."

She stared at him closely. "You believe the threats he made," she murmured. "Don't you?"

"He's the sort of man who gets even," he told her. "I'm not the man I was, or we'd never have left town on the chance he might come after you. But here, I have friends. If he comes down here looking for trouble, he'll find some."

She felt a little better. "I didn't want to have him arrested again."

"It wouldn't have mattered," he told her. "The fact that you stood up to him was enough. He was used to women being afraid of him. His own sister sat in the back of the courtroom during the trial. She was afraid to get near him, because she hadn't lied for him when the police came."

"What makes a man like that?" she asked sadly. "What makes him so hard that he has to beat up a woman to make him feel strong?"

"I don't know, sis," Kell told her gently. "Honestly I don't think the man has feelings for anybody or anything. His sister told you that he threw her dog off a bridge when they were kids. He laughed about it."

Her face grew sad. "I thought he was such a gentleman. He was so sweet to me, bringing me flowers and candy at work, writing me love letters. Then he came over to our house and the first thing he did was kick my cat when it spit at him."

"The cat was a good judge of character," Kell remarked.

"When I protested, he said that animals didn't feel pain and I shouldn't get so worked up over a stupid cat. I should have realized then what sort of person he was."

"People in love are neither sane nor responsible," Kell replied flatly. "You were so crazy about him that I think you could have forgiven murder."

She nodded sadly. "I learned the hard way that looks and acts are no measure of a man. I should have run for my life the first time he phoned me at work just to talk."

"You didn't know. How could you? He was a stranger."

"You knew," she said.

He nodded. "I've known men like him in the service," he said. "They're good in combat, because they aren't bothered by the carnage. But that trait serves them poorly in civilian life."

She cocked her head at him. "Kilraven said that Eb Scott lets law enforcement use his gun range for free. Don't you know him, too?"

"Yes."

"And Micah Steele."

"Yes."

She hesitated. "They're all retired mercenaries, Kell."

"So they are."

"Were they involved with the military?" she persisted.

"The military uses contract personnel," he said evasively. "People with necessary skills for certain jobs."

"Like combat."

"Exactly," he replied. "We used certain firms to supplement our troops overseas in the Middle East. They're used in Africa for certain covert operations."

"So much secrecy," she complained.

"Well, you don't advertise something that might get you sued or cause a diplomatic upheaval," he pointed out. "Covert ops have always been a part of the military. Even what they call transparency in government is never going to threaten that. As long as we have renegade states that threaten our sovereignty, we'll have black ops." He glanced at the clock. "Shouldn't you warm up the game system?" he asked. "It's five-thirty."

"Already?" she exclaimed. "Goodness, I need to tidy up the living room! And the kitchen. He's bringing pizza and beer!"

"You don't drink," he said.

"Well, no, but you like a beer now and then. I expect somebody told him." She flushed.

"I do like a glass of beer." He smiled. "It's also nice to have friends who provide food."

"Like your friend Cy and the Chinese stuff. I'll get spoiled."

"Maybe that's the idea. Your boss likes you."

She'd gotten that idea, herself. "Don't mention horns, pitchforks or breathing fire while he's here," she said firmly.

He saluted her.

She made a face at him and went to do her chores.

"THAT'S NOT FAIR!" Cappie burst out when she'd "died" for the tenth time trying to take out one of the Hunters in the Halo game.

"Don't throw the controller," Kell said firmly.

She had it by one lobe, gripped tightly. She grimaced and slowly lowered it. "Okay," she said. "But they do bounce, and they're almost shockproof."

"She ought to know," Kell told an amused Bentley Rydel. "She's bounced it off the walls several times in recent weeks."

"Well, they keep killing me!" she burst out. "It's not my fault! These Hunters aren't like the ones in *Halo 3*… They're almost invincible, and there are so many of them…!"

"I'd worry more about the alien grunts that keep taking you out with sticky grenades," Bentley pointed out. "While you're trying to snipe the Hunters, the little guys are blowing you up right and left."

"I want a flame thrower," she wailed. "Or a rocket launcher! Why can't I find a rocket launcher?"

"We wouldn't want to make it too easy, now would we?" Bentley chided. He smiled at her fury. "Patience. You have to go slow and take them on one at a time, so they don't flank you."

She gave her boss a speaking look, turned back to the screen and tried again.

IT WAS LATE when he left. The three of them had taken turns on the controller. Bentley and Kell had wanted to try the split screen, but that would have put Cappie right out of the competition, because she was only comfortable playing by herself.

She walked Bentley outside. "Thanks for bringing the pizza and beer," she said. "Some other time, I'd like to have you over for supper, if you'd like. I can cook."

He smiled. "I'll take you up on that. I can cook, too, but I only know how to do a few things from scratch. It gets tiresome after a while."

"Thanks for bringing the game over, too," she added. "It's really good. Kell is going to love it."

"What did we all do for entertainment before video games?" he wondered aloud as they reached his car.

"I used to watch game shows," she said. "Kell liked police dramas and old movies."

"I like some of the forensic shows, but I almost never get to see a whole one," he sighed. "There's always an emergency. It's always a large animal call. And since I'm the only vet on staff who does large animal calls, it's always me."

"Yes, but you never complain, not even if it's sleeting out," she said gently.

He smiled. "I like my clients."

"They like you, too." She shook her head. "Amazing, isn't it?"

"Excuse me?"

She flushed. "Oh, no, not because of… I mean…" She grimaced. "I meant it's amazing that you never get tired of large animal calls when the weather's awful."

He chuckled. "You really have got to take an assertiveness course," he said, and not unkindly.

"It's hard to be assertive when you're shy," she argued.

"It's impossible not to be when you have a job like mine and people don't want to do what you tell them to," he returned. "Some animals would die if I couldn't outargue their owners."

"Point taken."

"If it's any consolation," he said, "when I was your age, I had the same problem."

"How did you overcome it?"

"My stepfather decided that my mother wasn't going to the doctor for a urinary tract infection. I was already in veterinary school, and I knew what happened when animals weren't treated for it. I told him. He told me he was the man of the house and he'd decide what my mother did." He smiled, remembering. "So I had a choice—either back down, or let my mother risk permanent damage to her health, even death. I told him she was going to the doctor, I put her in the car and drove her there myself."

"What did your stepfather do?" she asked, aghast.

"There wasn't much that he could do, since I paid the doctor." His face hardened. "And it wasn't the first disagreement we'd had. He was poor and proud with it. He'd have let her suffer rather than admit he couldn't afford a doctor visit or medicine." He looked down at her. "It's a hell of a world, when people have to choose between food and medicine and doctors. Or between heated houses and medicine."

"Tell me about it," she replied. She colored a little, and hoped he didn't notice. "Kell and I do all right," she said quickly. "But he'll go without medicine sometimes if I don't put my foot down. You'd think I'd be tough as nails, because I stand up to him."

"He's not a mean person."

"He could be, I think," she said. She hesitated. "There was a man I dated, briefly, in San Antonio." She hesitated again. Perhaps it was too soon for this.

He stepped closer. "A man."

His voice was very soft. Quiet. Comforting. She wrapped her arms around her chest. She had on a sweater, but it was chilly outside. The memories were just as chilling. She was recalling it, her face betraying her inner turmoil. He'd hit her. The first time, he said it was because he'd had a drink, and he cried, and she went back to him. But the second time, he'd have probably killed her if Kell hadn't heard her scream and come to save her. As it was, he'd fractured her arm when he threw her over the couch. Kell had knocked Frank out with a lamp, from his wheelchair, and made her call the police. He made her testify, too. She held her arms around herself, chilled by the memory.

"What happened?"

She looked up at him, wanting to tell him, but afraid to. Frank got a six-month sentence, but he'd already served three months and he was out. Would he come after her now? Would he be crazy enough to do that? And would Bentley believe her, if she told him? They barely knew each other. It was too soon, she thought. Much too soon, to drag out her past and show it to him. There was no reason to tell him anyway. Frank wouldn't come down here and risk being sent back to jail. Bentley might think less of her if she told him, might think it was her own fault. Besides, she didn't want to tell him yet.

"HE WAS A mean sort of person, that's all," she hedged. "He kicked my cat. I thought it was terrible. He just laughed."

His blue eyes narrowed. "A man who'll kick a cat will kick a human being."

"You're probably right," she admitted, and then she smiled. "Well, I only dated him for a little while. He wasn't the sort of person I like to be around. Kell didn't like him, either."

"I like your brother."

She smiled. "I like him, too. He was just going downhill with depression in San Antonio. We were over our ears in debt, from all the hospital bills. It's lucky our cousin died and left us this place," she added.

Bentley's eyebrows lifted. "This place belonged to Harry Farley. He got killed overseas in the military about six months ago. He didn't have any relatives at all. The county buried him, out of respect for his military service."

"But Kell said…" she blurted out.

Her expression made Bentley hesitate. "Oh. Wait a minute," Bentley said at once. "That's right, I did hear that he had a distant cousin or two."

She laughed. "That's us."

"My mistake. I wasn't thinking." He studied her quietly. "Well, I guess I'd better go. This is the first Saturday night I can remember when I didn't get called out," he added with a smile. "Pure dumb luck, I guess."

"Law of averages," she countered. "You have to get lucky sooner or later."

"I guess. I'll see you Monday."

"Thanks again for the pizza."

He opened the door of the Land Rover. "I'll take you up on the offer of supper," he said. "When we set a date, you can tell me what you want to fix and I'll bring the raw ingredients." He held up a hand when she started to protest. "It does no good to argue with me. You can't win. Just ask Keely. Better yet, ask Dr. King," he chuckled.

She laughed, too. "Okay, then."

"Good night."

"Good night."

He closed the door behind him. Cappie went back up on the porch and watched him throw up a hand as he drove away. She stood there for several seconds before she realized that the wind was chilling her. She went in, feeling happier than she had in a long time.

CHAPTER FIVE

CAPPIE FELT AWKWARD with Bentley the following Monday. She wasn't sure if she should mention that he'd been to her house over the weekend. Her coworkers were very nice, but she was nervous when she thought they might tease her about the doctor. That would never do. She didn't want to make him feel uncomfortable in his own office.

Having lived so long in San Antonio, she didn't know about life in small towns. It hadn't occurred to her that nothing that happened could be kept secret.

"How was the pizza?" Dr. King asked her.

Cappie stared at her in horror.

Dr. King grinned. "My cousin works at the pizza place. Dr. Rydel mentioned where he was taking it. And she's best friends with Art, who runs the software store, so she knew he was taking the game over to play with you and your brother."

"Oh, dear," Cappie said worriedly.

Dr. King patted her on the back. "There, there," she said in a comforting tone. "You'll get used to it. We're like a big family in Jacobs County, because most of us have lived here all our lives, and our families have lived here for generations, mostly. We know everything that's going on. We only read the newspaper to find out who got caught doing it."

"Oh, dear," Cappie said again.

"Hi," Keely said, removing her coat as she joined them. "How was the game Saturday?" she added.

Cappie looked close to tears.

Dr. King gave Keely a speaking glance. "She's not used to small towns yet," she explained.

"Not to worry," Keely told her. "Dr. Rydel certainly is." She laughed at Cappie's tormented expression. "If he was worried about gossip, you'd better believe he'd never have put a foot inside your door."

"She thinks we'll tease her," Dr. King said.

"Not a chance," Keely added. "We were all dating somebody once." She flushed. "Especially me, and very recently." She meant her husband, Boone, of course.

"And nobody teased her," Dr. King added. "Well," she qualified it, "not where Boone could hear it, anyway," she added and chuckled.

"Thanks," she said.

Dr. King just smiled. "You know, Bentley hates most women. One of our younger clients made a play for him one day. She wore suggestive clothing and a lot of makeup and when he leaned over to examine her dog, she kissed him."

Cappie's eyes widened. "What did he do?"

"He left the room, dragged me in there and told the young lady that he was indisposed and Dr. King would be handling the case."

"What did the young lady do?" Cappie asked.

"Turned red as a beet, picked up her dog and left the building. It turns out," Dr. King added with a grin, "that the dog was in excellent health. She only used it as an excuse to get Dr. Rydel in there with her."

"Did she come back?"

"Oh, yes, she was an extremely persistent young woman. The third time she showed up here, she insisted on seeing Dr. Rydel. He called Cash Grier, our police chief, and had him come in and explain the legal ramifications of sexual harassment to the young lady. He didn't smile while he was speaking. And when he finished talking, the young lady took her animal, went home and subsequently moved back to Dallas."

"Well!" Cappie exclaimed.

"So you see, Dr. Rydel is quite capable of deterring unwanted interest." She leaned closer. "I understand that you like to play video games?"

Cappie laughed. "Yes, I do."

"My husband has a score of over 16,000 on Xbox LIVE," she said, and wiggled her eyebrows.

Keely was staring at her, uncomprehending.

"My scores are around 4,000," Cappie said helpfully. "And my brother's are about 15,000." She chuckled. "The higher the score, the better the player. Also, the more often the playing."

"I guess my score would be around 200," Dr. King sighed. "You see, I get called in a lot for emergencies when Dr. Rydel is out on large animal calls. So I start a lot of games that my husband gets to finish."

"Kell had buddies in the army who could outdo even those scores. Those guys were great!" Cappie said. "They'd hang out with us when they were off duty. Kell always had nice video gaming equipment. Some of them did, too, but we always had a full fridge. Boy, could those guys eat!"

"You lived overseas a lot, didn't you?" Keely asked.

"Yes. I've seen a lot of exotic places."

"What was your favorite?"

"Japan," Cappie replied at once, smiling. "We went there when Kell was stationed in Korea. Not that Korea isn't a beautiful country. But I really loved Japan. You should see the gaming equipment they've got. And the cell phone technology." She shook her head. "They're really a long way ahead of us in technology."

"Did you get to ride the bullet train?" Keely asked.

"Yes. It's as fast as they say it is. I loved the train station. I loved everything! Kyoto was like a living painting. So many gardens and trees and temples."

"I'd love to see any city in Japan, but especially Kyoto," Keely said. "Judd Dunn's wife, Christabel, went over there with him to buy beef. She said Kyoto was just unbelievable. So much history, and so beautiful."

"It is," Cappie replied. "We got to visit a temple. The Zen garden was so stark, and so lovely. It's just sand and rocks, you know. The sand is raked into patterns like water. The rocks are situated like land. All around were Japanese black pine trees and bamboo trees as tall as the pines, with huge trunks. There was a bamboo forest, all green, and a huge pond full of Japanese Koi fish." She shook her head. "You know, I could live there. Kell said it was his favorite, too, of all the places we lived."

"Are we going to work today, or travel around the world?" came a deep, curt voice from behind them.

Everybody jumped. "Sorry, Dr. Rydel," Keely said at once.

"Me, too," Cappie seconded.

"Nihongo no daisuki desu," Dr. Rydel said, and made a polite bow.

Cappie burst out smiling. *"Nihon no tomodachi desu. Konichi wa, Rydel sama,"* she replied, and bowed back.

Keely and Dr. King stared at them, fascinated.

"I said that I liked the Japanese language," Dr. Rydel translated.

"And I said that I was a friend of Japan. I also told him hello," Cappie seconded. "You speak Japanese!" she exclaimed to Bentley.

"Just enough to get me arrested in Tokyo," Bentley told her, smiling. "I was stationed in Okinawa when I was in the service. I spent my liberties in Tokyo."

"Well, isn't it a small world?" Dr. King wondered.

"Small, and very crowded," Bentley told her. He gave her a meaningful look. "If you don't believe me, you could look at the mob in the waiting room, glaring at the empty reception counter and pointedly staring at their watches."

"Oops!" Dr. King ran for it.

So did Keely and Cappie, laughing all the way.

THERE WAS A new rapport between Dr. Rydel and Cappie. He was no longer antagonistic toward her, and she wasn't afraid of him anymore. Their working relationship became cordial, almost friendly.

Then he came to supper the following Saturday, and she found herself dropping pots and pans and getting tongue-tied at the table while the three of them ate the meal she'd painstakingly prepared.

"You're a very good cook," Bentley told her, smiling.

"Thanks," she replied, flushing even more.

Kell, watching her, was amused and indulgent. "She could cook even when she was in her early teens," he told Bentley. "Of course, that was desperation," he added with a sigh.

She laughed. "He can burn water," she pointed out. "I had so much carbon in my diet that I felt like a fire drill. I borrowed a cookbook from the wife of one of his buddies and started practicing. She felt sorry for me and gave me lessons."

"They were delicious lessons," Kell recalled with a smile. "The woman was a *cordon bleu* cook and she could make French pastries. I gained ten pounds. Then her husband was reassigned and the lessons stopped."

"Hey, a new family moved in," she argued. "It was a company commander, and she could make these terrific vegan dishes."

Kell glared at her. "I hate vegetables."

"Different strokes for different folks," she shot back. "Besides, there's nothing wrong with a good squash casserole."

Kell and Bentley exchanged horrified looks.

"What is it with men and squash?" she exclaimed, throwing up her hands. "I have never met a man who would eat squash in any form. It's a perfectly respectable vegetable. You can make all sorts of things with it."

Bentley pursed his lips. "Door props, paperweights…"

"Food things!" she returned.

"Hey, I don't eat paperweights," Bentley pointed out. She shook her head.

"Why don't you bring in that terrific dessert you made?" Kell prompted.

"I guess I could do that," she told him. She got up and started gathering plates. Bentley got up and helped, as naturally as if he'd done it all his life.

She gave him an odd look.

"I live alone." He shrugged. "I'm used to clearing the table." He frowned. "Well, throwing away plastic plates, anyway. I eat a lot of TV dinners."

She made a face.

"There is nothing wrong with a TV dinner," Kell added. "I've eaten my share of them."

"Only when I was working late and it was all you could get," Cappie laughed. "And mostly, I left you things that you could just microwave."

"Point conceded." Kell grinned.

"What sort of dessert did you make?" Bentley asked.

She laughed. "A pound cake."

He whistled. "I haven't tasted one of those in years. My mother used to make them." His pleasant expression drained away for a few seconds.

Cappie knew he was remembering his mother's death. "It's a chocolate pound cake," she said, smiling, as she tried to draw him out of the past.

"Even better," he said, smiling. "Those are rare. Barbara sells slices of one sometimes at her café, but not too often."

"A lot of people can't eat chocolate, on account of allergies," she said.

"I don't have allergies," Bentley assured her. "And I do hope it's a large pound cake. If you offered to send a slice home with me, I might let you come in an hour late one day next week."

"Why, Dr. Rydel, that sounds suspiciously like a bribe," she exclaimed.

He grinned. "It is."

"In that case, you can take home two slices," she said.

He chuckled.

Watching them head into the kitchen, Kell smiled to himself. Cappie had been afraid of men just after her bad experience with the date from hell. It was good to see her comfortable in a man's company. Bentley might be just the man to heal her emotional scars.

"Where do you want these?" Bentley asked when he'd scraped the plates.

"Just put them in the sink. I'll clean up in here later."

He looked around quietly. The kitchen was bare bones. There was an older microwave oven, an old stove and refrigerator, a table and chairs that looked as if they'd come from a yard sale. The coffeepot and Crock-Pot on the counter had seen better days.

She noticed his interest and smiled sadly. "We didn't bring a lot of stuff with us when we moved back to San Antonio. We sold a lot of things to other servicemen so we wouldn't have to pay the moving costs. Then, after Kell got wounded, we sold more stuff so we could afford to pay the rent."

"Didn't he have any medical insurance?"

She shook her head. "He said there was some sort of mix-up with the magazine's insurer, and he got left out in the cold." She removed the cover from the cake pan and got out cake plates to serve it on. Her mother's small china service had been one thing she'd managed to salvage. She loved the pretty rose pattern.

"That's too bad," Bentley murmured. But he was frowning behind her, his keen mind on some things he recalled about her mysterious brother. If Kell was friendly with the local mercs, it was unlikely he'd gotten to know them in the military. They were too old to have served anytime recently. But he did know that they'd been in Africa in recent years. So had Kell. That was more than a coincidence, he was almost sure.

His silence made her curious. She turned around, her soft eyes wide and searching.

His own pale blue eyes narrowed on her pretty face in its frame of long blond hair. She had a pert little figure, enhanced by the white sweater and blue jeans she was wearing. Her breasts were firm and small, just right for her build. He felt his whole body clench at the way she was looking at him.

He wasn't handsome, she was thinking, but he had a killer physique, from his powerful long legs in blue jeans to his broad chest outlined under the knit shirt. Beige suited his coloring, made his tan look bronzed, the turtleneck enhancing his strong throat.

"You're staring," he pointed out huskily.

She searched for the right words. Her mouth was dry. "Your ears have very nice lobes."

He blinked. "Excuse me?"

She flushed to her hairline. "Oh, good heavens!" She fumbled with the cake knife and it started to fall. He stepped forward and caught it halfway to the floor, just as she dived for it. They collided.

His arm slid around her to prevent her from going

headlong into the counter and pulled her up short, right against him. Her intake of breath was audible as she clung to him to keep her footing.

She felt his chin against her temple, heard his breath coming out raggedly. His arm contracted.

"Th…thanks," she managed to say against his throat. "I'm just so clumsy sometimes!"

"Nobody's perfect."

She laughed nervously. "Certainly not me. Thanks for saving the cake knife."

"My pleasure."

His voice was almost a purr, deep and soft and slow. He lifted his head very slowly, so that his eyes were suddenly looking right into hers. She felt his chest rise and fall against her breasts in an intimacy that grew more smoldering by the second. She looked up, but her eyes stopped at his chiseled mouth. It was very sensuous. She'd never really paid it much attention, until now. And she couldn't quite stop looking at it.

She felt his fingers curling into her long hair, as if he loved the feel of it.

"I love long hair," he said softly. "Yours is beautiful."

"Thanks," she whispered.

"Soft hair. Pretty mouth." He bent and his nose slid against hers as his mouth poised over her parted lips. "Very pretty mouth."

She stood very still, waiting, hoping that he wasn't going to draw back. She loved the way his body felt, so close to hers. She loved his strength, his height, the spicy scent of his cologne. She hung there, at his lips, her eyes half closed, waiting, waiting…

"Where's that cake?" came a plaintive cry from the living room. "I'm starving!"

They jumped apart so quickly that Cappie almost fell. "Coming right up!" Heavens, was that her voice? It sounded almost artificial!

"I'll take the coffeepot into the living room for you," Bentley said. His own voice was oddly hoarse and deep, and he didn't look at her as he went out of the room.

Cappie cut the cake, forcing her mind to ignore what had almost happened. She had so many complications in her life right now that she didn't really need another one. But she did wonder if it was possible to put this particular genie back in its bottle.

AND, IN FACT, it wasn't. When they finished the cake and a few more minutes of conversation, Bentley got a call from his answering service and hung up with a grimace.

"One of Cy Parks's purebred heifers is calving for the first time. I'll have to go. Sorry. I really enjoyed the meal, and the cake."

"So did we," Cappie said.

"We'll have to do this again," Kell added, grinning.

"Next time, I'll take the two of you out to a nice restaurant," Bentley said.

"Well…" Cappie hesitated.

"Walk me out," Bentley told her, and he didn't smile.

Cappie looked toward Kell to save her, but he only grinned. She turned and followed Bentley out the door.

He paused at the steps, looking down at her with a long, unblinking stare in the faint light that shone out from the windows.

She bit her lower lip and searched for something to say. Her mind wouldn't cooperate.

He couldn't seem to find anything to say, either. They just stared at each other.

"I hate women," he bit off.

She faltered. "I'm sorry," she said.

"Oh, what the hell. Come here."

He scooped her up against him, bent his head and kissed her with such immediate passion that she couldn't even think. Her arms went around his neck as she warmed to the hard, insistent pressure of his mouth as it parted her lips and invaded the soft, secret warmth of her mouth. It was too much, too soon, but she couldn't say that. He didn't leave her enough breath to say anything, and the pleasure throbbing through her body robbed her mind of the words, anyway.

Seconds later, he put her back on her feet and moved away. "Well!" he said huskily.

She stared up at him with her mouth open.

His eyebrows arched.

She tried to speak, but she couldn't manage a single word.

He let out a rough breath. "I really wish you wouldn't look at me in that tone of voice," he said.

"Wh…what?" she stammered.

He chuckled softly. "Well, I could say I'm flattered that I leave you speechless, but I won't embarrass you. See you Monday."

She nodded. "Monday."

"At the office."

She nodded again. "The office."

"Cappie?"

She was still staring at him. She nodded once more. "Cappie."

He burst out laughing. He bent and kissed her again. "And they say the way to a man's heart is through his stomach," he mused. "This is much quicker than food. See you."

He turned and went to his car. Cappie stood and watched him until he was all the way to the main highway. It wasn't until Kell called to her that she realized it was cold and she didn't even have on a coat.

AFTER THAT, IT was hard to work in the same office with Bentley without staring at him, starstruck, when she saw him in between patients. He noticed. He couldn't seem to stop smiling. But when Cappie started running into door facings looking at him, everybody else in the office started grinning, and that did inhibit her.

She forced herself to keep her mind on the animal patients, and not the tall man who was treating them.

Just before quitting time, a little boy came careening into the practice just ahead of a man. He was carrying a big dog, wrapped in a blanket, shivering and bleeding.

"Please, it's my dog, you have to help him!" the boy sobbed.

A worried man joined him. "He was hit by a car," the man said. "The so-and-so didn't even stop! He just kept going!"

Dr. Rydel came out of the back and took a quick look at the dog. "Bring him right back," he told the boy. He managed a smile. "We'll do everything we can. I promise."

"His name's Ben," the boy sobbed. "I've had him since I was little. He's my best friend."

Dr. Bentley helped the boy lift Ben onto the metal operating table. He didn't ask the boy to leave while he did the examination. He had Keely help him clean the wound and help restrain the dog while he assessed the damage. "We're going to need an X-ray. Get Billy to help you carry him," he told her with a smile.

"Yes, sir."

"Is he going to die?" the boy wailed.

Dr. Rydel put a kindly hand on his shoulder. "I don't see any evidence of internal damage or concussion. It looks like a fracture, but before I can reduce it, I'm going to need to do X-rays to see the extent of the damage. Then we'll do blood work to make sure it's safe to anesthetize him. I will have to operate. He has some skin and muscle damage in addition to the fracture."

The man with the boy looked worried. "Is this going to be expensive?" he asked worriedly.

The boy wailed.

"I lost my job last week," the man said heavily. "We've got a new baby."

"Don't worry about it," Dr. Rydel said in a reassuring tone. "We do some pro bono work here, and I'm overdue. We'll take care of it."

The man bit his lower lip, hard, and averted his eyes. "Thanks," he gritted.

"We all have rough patches," Dr. Rydel told him. "We get through them. It will get better."

"Thanks, Doc!" the boy burst out, reaching over to rub a worried hand over the old dog's head. "Thanks!"

"I like dogs, myself," the doctor chuckled. "Now

this is going to take a while. Why don't you leave your phone number at the desk and I'll call you as soon as your dog's through surgery?"

"You'd do that?" the man asked, surprised.

"Of course. We always do that."

"His name's Ben," the boy said, sniffing. "He's had all his shots and stuff. We take him every year to the clinic at the animal shelter."

Which meant money was always tight, but they took care of the animal. Dr. Rydel was impressed.

"We'll give her our phone number. You're a good man," the boy's father said quietly.

"I like dogs," Dr. Rydel said again with a smile. "Go on home. We'll call you."

"You be good, Ben," the boy told his dog, petting him one last time. The dog wasn't even trying to bite anybody. He whined a little. "We'll come and get you just as soon as we can. Honest."

The man tugged the boy along with him, giving the vet one last grateful smile.

"I can take care of his bill," Keely volunteered.

Dr. Rydel shook his head. "I do it in extreme cases like this. It's no hardship."

"Yes, but…"

He leaned closer. "I drive a Land Rover. Want to price one?"

Keely burst out laughing. "Okay. I give up."

Billy, the vet tech, came to help Keely get Ben in to X-ray. Cappie came back after a minute. "I promised I'd make sure you knew that Ben likes peanut butter," she said. "Who's Ben?"

"Fractured leg, HBC," he abbreviated.

She smiled. "Hit by car," she translated. "The most frequent injury suffered by dogs. They know who hit him?"

"I wish," Dr. Rydel said fervently. "I'd call Cash Grier myself."

"They didn't stop?"

"No," he said shortly.

"I'd stop, if I hit somebody's pet," Cappie said gently. "I had a cat, when we lived in San Antonio, after Kell got out of the army. I had to give him away when we moved down here." She was remembering that Frank had kicked him, so hard that Cappie took him to work with her the next day, just to have him checked out. He had bruising, but, fortunately, no broken bones. Then the cat had run away, and returned after Frank was gone. She'd given the cat away before she and Kell left town, to make sure that Frank wouldn't send somebody to get even with her by hurting her cat. He was that sort of man.

"You're very pensive," he commented.

"I was missing my cat," she lied, smiling.

"We have lots of cats around here," he told her. "I think Keely has a whole family of them out in her barn and there are new kittens. She'd give you one, if you asked."

She hesitated. "I'm not sure if I could keep a cat," she replied. "Kell wouldn't be able to look out for him, you know. He has all he can do to take care of himself."

He didn't push. He just smiled. "One day, he'll meet some nice girl who'll want to take him home with her and spoil him rotten."

She blinked. "Kell?"

"Why not? He's only paralyzed, you know, not demented."

She laughed. "I guess not. He's pretty tough."

"And he's not a bad gamer, either," he pointed out.

"I noticed."

"Cappie, have you got the charges for Miss Dill's cat in here yet?" came a call from the front counter.

She grimaced. "No, sorry, Dr. King. I'll be right there."

She rushed back out, flustered. Dr. Rydel certainly had a way of looking at her that increased her heart rate. She liked it, too.

CHAPTER SIX

CAPPIE STAYED LATE to help with the overflow of patients, held up by the emergency surgery on the dog. The practice generally did its scheduled surgeries on Thursdays, but emergencies were always accommodated. In fact, there was a twenty-four-hour-a-day emergency service up in San Antonio, but the veterinarians at Dr. Rydel's practice would always come in if they were needed. In certain instances, the long drive to the big city would have meant the death of a furry patient. They were considering the addition of a fourth veterinarian to the practice, so that they could more easily accommodate those emergencies.

The dog, Ben, came out of surgery with a mended foreleg and was placed in a recovery cage to wait until the anesthetic wore off. The next day, if he presented no complications, he would be sent home with antibiotics, painkillers and detailed instructions on postsurgical care. Cappie was glad, for the boy's sake. She felt sorriest for the children whose pets were injured. Not that grown-up people took those situations any easier. Pets were like part of the family. It was hard to see one hurt, or to lose one.

Kell was pensive when she got home. In fact, he

looked broody. She put down her coat and purse. "What's the matter with you?" she asked with a grin.

He put his laptop computer aside with deliberation. "I had a call from an assistant district attorney's office in San Antonio, from the victim support people," he said quietly. "Frank Bartlett got out of jail today."

It was the day she'd been dreading. Her heart sank. He'd vowed revenge. He would make her pay, he said, for having him tried and convicted.

"Don't worry," he added gently. "We're among friends here. Frank would have to be crazy to come down here and make trouble. In addition to the jail time, he drew a year's probation. They'll check on him. He wouldn't want to risk having to go back to jail to finish his sentence."

"You think so?" she wondered. She recalled what a hardheaded man Frank was. He got even with people. She'd heard things from one of her coworkers in San Antonio at the animal clinic, one who was friends with Frank's sister. She'd said that Frank had run a man off the road who'd reported him for making threats at one of his jobs. The man was badly injured, but he could never prove it had been Frank who'd caused the accident. Cappie was sure, now, that there had probably been other incidents, as well. Frank had admitted to her once that he'd spent time in juvenile hall as a youngster. He'd never said what for.

"He won't be able to get to you at home," Kell continued, "because I keep firearms and I know how to use them," he added grimly. "At work, I don't think he'd dare approach you. Dr. Rydel would likely propel him headfirst out the front door," he chuckled.

Cappie was reminded that Dr. Rydel had actually done that. Dr. King told her about it. A man had come in with a badly injured dog, one with multiple fractures, claiming that the animal had fallen down some steps. After examining the dog, Dr. Rydel knew better. He'd accused the man of abusing the dog, and the man had thrown a punch at him. Dr. Rydel had picked him up and literally thrown him out onto the front porch, while fascinated pet owners watched. Then he'd called the police and had the man arrested. There had been a conviction, too.

Cappie, remembering that, smiled. "Dr. Rydel gets very upset when people abuse animals," she told her brother.

"Obviously." He pursed his lips. "I wonder why he decided to become a veterinarian?"

"I'll have to ask him that."

"Yes, you will. I made macaroni and cheese for supper," he said, "when you called to say you'd be late."

She made a face before she could stop herself.

Kell just grinned. "It's frozen," he said. "I heated it up in the oven."

She sighed with relief. "Sorry. It's just that I've had my carbon for today."

He laughed. "I know I can't cook. One day, though, I'll learn how. Then watch out."

"Some men are born to be chefs. You aren't one of them. I'll make a salad to go with the macaroni."

"I did that already. It's in the fridge."

She went to kiss his cheek, bending over him in the wheelchair. "You're the nicest brother in the whole world."

"I could return the compliment." He ruffled her hair. "Listen, kid, if the surly vet proposes, you take him up on it. I can take care of myself."

"You can't cook," she wailed.

"I can buy nice frozen things to heat up," he returned.

She sighed. "As if Dr. Rydel would ever propose," she laughed. "He likes me, but that doesn't mean he'll want to marry me one day."

"You need to invite him over again and make that shrimp and pasta dish you do so well. I have it from a spy that Dr. Rydel is partial to shrimp."

"Really? Who knows that?"

"Cy Parks told me."

She gave him a suspicious look. "Did you try to pump Cy Parks for inside information?"

Kell gave her his best angelic look. "I would never do such a sneaky thing."

"Sure you would," she retorted.

"Well, Dr. Rydel knew why Cy was asking him, anyway. He just laughed and asked if there was any other inside information that Cy would like to have for us."

She flushed. "Oh, my."

"Cy said the good doctor talked more about you than he did about the heifer he was helping to deliver," Kell added. "It's well-known that Dr. Rydel can't abide women. People get curious when a notorious woman hater suddenly starts seeing a local woman."

"I wonder why he hates women?" she wondered aloud.

"Ask him. But for now, let's eat. I'm fairly empty."

"Goodness, yes, it's two hours past our usual suppertime," she agreed, moving into the kitchen. "I'm sorry I was late."

"How's the dog?" he asked, joining her at the table.

"He'll be fine, Dr. Rydel said. The poor boy was just devastated. I felt sorry for his dad. He'd just lost his job. You could see he was torn between getting the dog treated and taking care of his family. There's a new baby. Dr. Rydel didn't charge him a penny."

"Heart of gold," Kell said gently.

"We were going to take up a collection, when Dr. Rydel reminded us that he drove a Land Rover," she laughed. "He inherited money from his grandmother, Dr. King said, and he makes a good living as a vet."

"That means he'll be able to take care of you when you get married."

She made a face. "Horses before carts, not carts before horses."

"You wait and see," he replied. "That's a man who's totally hooked. He just doesn't know it yet."

She smiled from ear to ear as she started putting food on the table. She'd already pushed her fears about Frank to the back of her mind. Kell was right. He surely wouldn't risk his freedom by making trouble for Cappie again.

DR. RYDEL TOOK her to a carnival Friday night. She was shocked not only at the invitation, but at the choice of outings.

"You like carnivals?" she'd exclaimed.

"Sure! I love the rides and cotton candy." He'd smiled with reminiscence. "My grandmother used to save her egg money to take me to any carnival that came through

Jacobsville when I was a kid. She'd even go on the rides with me. I get tickled even now when I hear somebody talk about grandmothers who bake cookies and knit and sit in rocking chairs. My grandmother was a newspaper reporter. She was a real firecracker."

She was remembering the conversation as they walked down the sawdust-covered aisles between booths where carnies were enticing customers to pitch pennies or throw baseballs to win prizes.

"What are you brooding about?" he teased.

She looked up, laughing. "Sorry. I was remembering what you said about your grandmother. Did you spend a lot of time with her?"

His face closed up.

"Sorry," she said again, flushing. "I shouldn't have asked something so personal."

He stopped in the aisle and looked down at her, enjoying the glow of her skin against the pale yellow sweater she was wearing with jeans, her blond hair long and soft around her shoulders.

His big, lean hand went to her hair and toyed with it, sending sweet chills down her spine when he moved a step closer. "She raised me," he said quietly. "My mother and father never got along. They separated two or three times a year, and then fought about who got to keep me. My mother loved me, but my father only wanted me to spite her." His face hardened. "When I made him mad, he took it out on my pets. He shot one of my dogs when I talked back to him. He wouldn't let me take the dog to a veterinarian, and I couldn't save it. That's why I decided to become a vet."

"I did wonder," she confessed. "You talk about your

mother, but never about your father. Or your stepfather." Her hands went to his shirtfront. She could feel the warm muscle and hair under the soft cotton.

He sighed. His hand covered one of hers, smoothing over her fingernails. "My stepfather thought that being a vet was a sissy profession, and he said so, frequently. He didn't like animals, either."

"Some sissy profession," she scoffed. "I guess he never had to wrestle down a sick steer that weighed several hundred pounds."

He chuckled. "No, he never did. We got along somewhat. But I don't miss seeing him. I had hard feelings against him for a long time, for letting my mother get so sick that medical science couldn't save her. But sometimes we blame people when it's just fate that bad things happen. Remember the old saying, 'Man proposes and God disposes'? It's pretty much true."

"Ah, you advocate being a leaf on the river, grasshopper," she said in a heavily accented tone.

"You lunatic," he laughed, but he bent and kissed her nose. "Yes. I do advocate being a leaf on the river. Sometimes you have to trust that things will work out the way they're meant to, not the way you want them to."

"Why do you hate women?"

His eyebrows arched.

"Everybody knows that you do. You even told me so." She flushed a little as she remembered when he'd told her so; the first time he'd kissed her.

"Remember that, do you?" he teased softly. "You don't know a lot about kissing," he added.

She moved restlessly. "I don't get in much practice."

"Oh, I think I can help you with that," he said in a deep, husky tone. "And for the record, I don't hate you."

"Thank you very much," she said demurely, and peered up at him through her lashes.

He bent slowly to her mouth. "You're very welcome," he whispered. His lips teased just above hers, coaxing her to lift her chin, so that he had better access to her mouth.

Before he could kiss her, a deep voice mused from behind him, "Lewd behavior in public will get you arrested."

"Kilraven," Bentley groaned, turning to face the man. "What are you doing here?"

Kilraven, in full uniform, grinned at the discomfort in their faces as he moved closer and lowered his voice. "I'm investigating possible cotton candy fraud."

"Excuse me?" Cappie said.

"I'm going to taste the cotton candy, and the candy apples, and make sure they're not using illegal counterfeit sugar."

They both stared at him as if he'd gone mad.

He shrugged. "I'm really off duty, I just haven't gone home to change. I like carnivals," he added, laughing. "Jon, my brother, and I used to go to them when we were kids. It brings back happy memories."

"They have a sharpshooting target," Bentley told him.

"I don't waste my unbelievable talent on games," Kilraven scoffed.

"I am in awe of your modesty," Bentley said.

"Why, thank you," Kilraven replied. "I consider it one of my best traits, and I do have quite a few of them." He peered past them. Winnie Sinclair, in jeans and a pretty pink sweater and matching denim jacket, was walking around the penny-pitching booth with her brother, Boone Sinclair, and his wife, Cappie's coworker, Keely. Kilraven looked decidedly uneasy. "I'll see you around," he added.

But instead of going to the cotton candy booth, he turned on his heel and walked right out of the carnival.

"How odd," Cappie murmured, watching him leave.

"Not so odd," Bentley replied. His eyes were on Winnie Sinclair, who'd just seen Kilraven glare in her direction and then walk away. She looked devastated. "Winnie Sinclair is sweet on him," he explained, "and he's even a worse woman hater than I am."

Cappie followed his glance. Keely smiled and waved. She waved back. Winnie Sinclair smiled wanly, and turned back to the booth. "Poor thing," she murmured. "She's so rich, and so unhappy."

"Money doesn't make you happy," Bentley pointed out.

"Well, the lack of it can make you pretty miserable," she said absently.

His hand reached down and locked into hers, bringing her surprised eyes back up to meet his.

She was hesitant, because Keely was grinning in their direction.

"I don't care about public opinion," Bentley pointed out, "and she wouldn't dare tease me in my own practice," he added with a grin.

Cappie laughed. "Okay. I won't care, either."

His strong fingers linked with hers, while he held

her gaze. "I can't remember the last time I smiled so much," he said. "I like being with you, Cappie."

She smiled. "I like being with you, too."

They were still smiling at each other when two running children bumped into them and broke the spell.

BENTLEY DROVE HER HOME, but he didn't move to open the door after he cut off the lights and the engine. He unfastened her seat belt, and his own, and pulled her across the seat and into his lap. Before she could speak, his mouth was hard on hers, grinding into it, and his fingers were lazily searching under the soft hem of her sweater.

He found the hooks on her bra and loosened them with one quick motion of his hand. Then he found soft flesh and teased around it with such expertise that she squirmed backward to give him access.

"Too quick?" he whispered against her mouth.

"No," she bit off, and arched her back.

He smiled as his mouth covered hers once more, and his hand settled directly over the hard little nub that raised against his palm.

After a few minutes, kissing was no longer enough. His hand moved in at the base of her spine and half lifted her against him, so that her belly ground against his in the rapt silence of the vehicle, broken only by the force of their audible breaths, and her soft moan. She could feel him wanting her. It had been exciting with Frank, but not like this. She wanted what Bentley wanted. She was on fire for him.

He unfastened the buttons on his shirt and pulled her against him, so that her soft breasts ground against the hair-roughened muscles of his chest. His hand moved her hips against his in a slow, anguished rotation that made her moan louder.

"Oh, God," he bit off, shivering. "Cappie!"

Her nails were scoring his back as she held on for dear life and began to shudder. "Don't stop," she whimpered. "Don't stop!"

"I've...got to!"

He moved abruptly, pushing her back into her seat. He opened the door and got out of the Land Rover, standing with his back to her as he sucked in deep breaths and tried to regain the control he'd almost lost.

Embarrassed, Cappie fumbled her bra closures into place and pulled her sweater down. She was still shaky. It had been a near thing. Thank goodness they were parked in her driveway instead of on some lonely road where there might not have been as much incentive to stop. Despite her passionate response to him, Cappie didn't move with the times. Did he know that? Was he hoping for some brief fling? She couldn't. She just couldn't. Now, she reasoned with something like panic, he wouldn't want to see her again, not if she said no. And either way, how was it going to affect her job? There was only one veterinary clinic in Jacobs County, and she worked for it. If she lost her job, she couldn't get another, not in her field.

While she was torturing herself with such thoughts, the door suddenly opened.

"I know," Bentley said in a strangely calm and amused tone, "you're kicking yourself mentally for taking advantage of me in a weak moment. But it's okay. I'm used to women trying to ravish me."

She stared up at him wide-eyed and speechless. Of all the things she expected he might say, that was the last.

"Come on, come on, you're not going to get a second shot at me in the same night," he teased. "I have my reputation to think of!"

Her mind started working again, and she laughed with relief. She picked up her purse and scrambled out the door, her discarded coat over one arm.

"Listen," he said gently, "don't start brooding. We got a little too involved, too quickly, but we'll deal with it."

She hesitated. "I'm not, well, modern," she blurted out.

"Neither am I, honey," he said softly.

She could have melted into the ground at the husky endearment. She blushed.

He bent and kissed her with tender respect. "I know what sort of woman you are," he said gently. "I'm not going to push you into something you don't want."

"Thanks."

"On the other hand, you have to make me a similar promise," he pointed out. "I'm not going to keep dating you if I have to worry about being ravished every time I bring you home. I'm not that sort of man," he added haughtily.

She grinned from ear to ear. "Okay."

He walked her to the door, smiling complacently. "I'll see you at work Monday," he said. He framed her face in his hands and looked at her for a long time. "Just when you think you're safe," he mused, "you jump headfirst into the tiger trap."

"You know, I was just thinking the same thing," she said facetiously.

He chuckled as he bent to kiss her again. "We'll take it at a nice, easy pace," he whispered. "But I know already how it's going to end up. We're good together. And I'm tired of living alone."

Her heart almost burst with joy. "I… I don't think I could just live with someone," she blurted out, still a little worried.

He kissed her eyes shut. "Neither could I, Cappie," he whispered. "We can talk about licenses and rings." He lifted his head. His eyes were soft with feeling. "But not tonight. We have all the time in the world."

"Yes," she whispered. Her eyes were bright with the force of her emotions. "It's happening so fast."

He nodded. "Like lightning striking."

She felt her heart racing. But in the back of her mind, there was a sudden fear, a foreboding. She bit her lower lip. "You don't really know much about me," she began. "You see, when I lived in San Antonio, there was this man I dated…"

Before she could tell him about Frank, his phone rang. He jerked it out and answered it. "Rydel," he said. He listened, grimaced. "I'll be in the office in ten minutes. Bring the cat right in, I'll see it. Yes. Yes. You're welcome." He hung up. "I have to go."

"Be careful," she said.

He smiled. "I will. Good night."

"Good night, Dr. Rydel."

"Bentley."

She laughed. "Bentley."

He ran back to the Land Rover, started it and drove

away with a wave of his hand. Cappie watched him go, then walked into her house, feeling as if she could have floated all the way.

MONDAY MORNING, CAPPIE still felt light-headed and ecstatic. She'd half expected Bentley to phone her Saturday or Sunday, considering how involved they'd gotten when he brought her home from the carnival on Friday night. But maybe he'd had emergencies. She hoped he hadn't had second thoughts. She was so crazy about him that she couldn't bear to even think about having him reconsider what he'd said. But she knew that wasn't going to happen. They were already so close that she knew it was going to be forever.

So it came as a shock when she walked in the office and Dr. Rydel met her beaming smile with a cold glare that sent chills down her spine.

"You're late, Miss Drake," he said curtly. "Please try to be on time in the future."

She looked as if she'd been hit in the head by a brick. Keely, at the counter, gave her a sympathetic look.

"I'm... I'm sorry, sir," she stammered.

"I need you to help Keely with an X-ray," he said, and turned away abruptly.

"Right away." She put up her coat and purse and rushed to join Keely, who was going in the room where they kept the medical cages. She took a hair band out of her pocket and scrunched her thick hair into a ponytail with it. Inside, she felt numb.

"It's Mrs. Johnson's cat," Keely explained, wary of being overheard by the vet, who was just going into a treatment room. "She stepped on his paw. It's swollen, and Dr. Rydel is afraid it may be broken. Mrs. Johnson is no lightweight," she added with a grin.

"Yes, I know."

"She had to leave him with us while she went to see her heart doctor. She was very upset. She's just getting over a heart attack, and she's worried about her cat!" she said, smiling. Keely opened the cage and Cappie lifted the old cat. It just purred. It didn't even offer to bite her, although it was obvious that it was in pain.

"What a sweet old fellow," Cappie murmured as they went toward the X-ray room. "I thought he might want to bite us."

"He's a sweetheart all right. Here." Keely motioned to the X-ray table and closed the door behind them. "What in the world is wrong with Dr. Rydel?" she whispered. "He came in looking like a thundercloud."

"I don't know," Cappie said. "We went to the carnival Friday night and he was happy and laughing..."

"You didn't have a fight?" Keely persisted.

"No!" She wanted to add that they'd talked about rings, but this wasn't a good time. The tall man who met her at the door didn't look as if he'd ever said any such thing to her.

"I wonder what happened."

"So do I," Cappie said miserably.

They got the X-ray and Cappie took the old cat back to his cage while Keely developed it. Dr. King gave her a worried look, but she was too busy to say much. Cappie felt sick. She couldn't imagine what had turned Dr. Rydel into an enemy.

SHE WAITED AND worried all day through two dozen patients and one long emergency. Mrs. Johnson came to pick up her cat, his paw in a neat cast, crying buckets because she'd been so worried about him. Cappie helped her out the door, smiling even though she didn't feel like it. Earlier, she'd thought maybe Dr. Rydel would say something to her, explain, anything. But he didn't. He treated her just as he had when she first joined the practice, courteous but cold.

At the end of the day, she wanted to wait around and see if she could get him to talk to her, but a large animal call took him out the door just minutes before the staff went home. She drove to her house with her heart in her shoes.

"YOU LOOK LIKE the end of the world," Kell remarked when she walked in. "What happened?"

"I don't know," she said sadly. "Dr. Rydel looked at me as if I had some contagious disease and he didn't say one kind word all day. It was business as usual. He was just like he was when I first went to work for him."

"He seemed pleasant enough when he picked you up Friday night," he remarked.

"And when he brought me home," she added. "Maybe he got cold feet."

Kell studied her sad face. "Maybe he did. Everybody says he was the biggest woman hater around town. But if that's the case, he might warm up again when he's had time to think about it. If he's really interested, Cappie, he's not going away."

"You think so?" she asked, hopeful.

"I know so. Men who act like he did when he came to supper don't suddenly turn ice-cold for no reason. Maybe he just had a rough weekend."

Which was no reason for him to take it out on Cappie. On the other hand, she didn't really know him that well.

"Maybe I can get him to talk to me tomorrow," she said.

He smiled. "Maybe you can."

She nodded. "I'll go make supper."

"Try not to worry."

"Of course."

BUT SHE DID WORRY, and she didn't sleep. She went in to work the next morning with a feeling of foreboding.

Dr. Rydel was at the counter when she came in.

"I'm five minutes early," she said abruptly when he glared at her.

"Come into my office, please," he said.

She brightened. At last, he was going to explain. Surely it was something that didn't have anything to do with her.

He let her in and closed the door behind her. He didn't offer her a seat. He perched on the edge of his desk and stared at her coldly. "I had a visitor Saturday morning."

"You did?" An ex-girlfriend, she was thinking, and he wanted her back, was that it?

"Yes," he replied curtly. "Your boyfriend."

"My what?"

"Your boyfriend, Frank Bartlett," he said coldly.

She felt sick all the way to her toes. Frank had come down here! He'd come to Jacobsville! She held on to a chair. She should have told Bentley about him. She shouldn't have waited. "He's my ex-boyfriend," she began.

He laughed coldly. "Is he, really? Now that's not what he said."

CHAPTER SEVEN

CAPPIE COULD ALMOST imagine what sort of story Frank had told Bentley. But now she understood his anger.

"I can explain," she began.

"You told me Friday night that you had an ex-boy-friend," he said icily. "I didn't get to hear the rest of the story, but Bartlett was kind enough to fill me in. You accused him of assaulting you and had him arrested. He actually spent time in jail and now he has a felony record because of you."

Her eyes widened. "Yes, but that isn't what happened…!"

"I know all about women who like to play with men," he interrupted. "When I was in my early twenties, I worked for a veterinarian while I was in college. It supplemented my grants and scholarships. He had a vet tech who was very pretty, but never got dates. I felt sorry for her. She could only work for him part-time, because I had the full-time position. She stayed late one weekend and teased me into kissing her. Then she very calmly tore her shirt, messed up her hair and phoned the police."

Cappie felt her face go pale.

"She wanted my job," Bentley continued cynically. "I dipped into my savings to hire a private detective, who discovered that it wasn't the first time she'd pulled that stunt. She was arrested and my record was cleared. The vet hired me back in a heartbeat and spent years trying to make it up to me."

"I had no idea," she whispered.

"Of course not, or you wouldn't have tried the same stunt on me."

She blinked in disbelief. "What?"

"You were always talking about what you'd do if you had money. You knew I was well-to-do. When were you going to accuse me of assaulting you? Have you got a lawyer waiting in the wings to sue me?"

She couldn't believe her ears. He actually thought she was playing him for cash. Frank had lied to him, and with his background, Bentley had fallen for the tall tale.

"I've never accused anyone falsely," she defended herself.

"Only Frank Bartlett?"

She swallowed, hard. "He broke my arm," she said with quiet dignity. "It wasn't the first time he hit me, either."

"He told me you'd say that," he replied. "Poor guy. You ruined his life. Well, you aren't going to get the chance to ruin mine. You can work your two weeks' notice." He got to his feet.

"You're firing me?" she asked weakly.

"No, you're quitting," he returned coldly. "That way, you won't be able to let the state support you with unemployment insurance, or sue me for unlawful termination of employment."

"I see."

"Women," he muttered coldly. "You'd think I'd al-

ready learned my lesson. You all look so innocent. And
you all lie."

He opened the door. "Back to work, Miss Drake,"
he said in a formal tone. "It's going to be a long day."

She worked mechanically, even managed to smile at
old Mr. Smith's jokes and Dr. King's bland comments.
Keely was looking at her oddly, but nobody else seemed
to find her behavior out of the ordinary.

At the end of the day, she went to her car almost
gratefully. She still couldn't believe that Dr. Rydel had
fallen for Frank's lies. But she was going to do something about it. She just didn't know what. Yet.

She pulled up in the front yard, puzzled at the colorful cloth piled at the foot of the steps. Was Kell cleaning house…?

She slammed on the brakes, cut off the engine and
ran as fast as she could to the front door. That wasn't a
bundle of cloth, it was Kell. Kell! He was unconscious,
lying beside the wreck of his wheelchair and he was
bleeding from half a dozen cuts. She felt for a pulse
and, thank God, found one! At least he was still alive.

She saw the front door standing open and didn't dare
go inside, for fear someone might be waiting there.
She ran back to her car, jerked out her cell phone and
punched in 911. Then she ran back to Kell and waited.

THE NEXT HOUR was a blur of ambulance sirens, police
sirens, blue uniforms, tan uniforms and abject terror.

She waited for Dr. Micah Steele to come out and tell
her what Kell's condition was. She was sick and chilled
to the bone. If Kell died, she'd have nobody.

He came back out to the waiting room a few minutes after Kell was brought in, tall and blond and somber.

"How is he?" she asked frantically.

"Badly beaten," he told her, "which you already know. His back is one long bruise. We're still doing tests, but he has some feeling in his legs, which indicates that the shrapnel in his back may have shifted. If the tests verify that, I'm having him transported to the medical center in San Antonio. I have a friend who's an orthopedic surgeon there. He'll operate."

"You mean, Kell could walk again?" she asked, excited.

He smiled. "Yes." The smile faded. "But that's not my immediate concern. He said there were three men. One of them was a man you've had dealings with, I understand. Frank Bartlett."

"Beating up a paralyzed man, with a mob," she gritted. "What a brave little worm he is!"

"Sheriff's got an all-points bulletin out for him and his friends," Micah told her. "But you're in danger until they're found. You can't stay out there at the house by yourself."

"If you send Kell to San Antonio," she said, "I'll call a friend who works for the same veterinary practice that employed me until I moved here. She'll let me stay with her."

"You'll have to be in protective custody," Micah said firmly.

She smiled. "Her brother is a Texas Ranger. He lives with her."

"Well!"

"I'll call her as soon as I see Kell."

"That will be another twenty minutes," he said. "We have to finish the tests first. But he's going to be fine."

"Okay. Thanks, Dr. Steele."

He smiled. "Glad I can help. I like Kell."

"I do, too."

SHE PHONED BRENDA BANKS in San Antonio. Brenda's brother, Colter, was a Texas Ranger. He'd been based out of Houston until his best friend, a Houston police officer named Mike Johns, was killed trying to stop a bank robbery. Colter had asked for reassignment to Company D of the Texas Rangers, based in Bexar County, and moved in with his sister. Since Company D now had an official Cold Case sergeant, Colter applied for and obtained the job. Brenda said he loved solving old cases.

She tried the apartment, first, and sure enough, Brenda was at home and not at work. "How do you like your new job?" Brenda asked when she heard Cappie's voice.

"I like it a lot. Do you still have a spare bedroom, and is there a job opening there at the vet clinic?"

"Oh, dear."

"Yes, well, things didn't work out as well as I hoped," Cappie said quietly. "Frank and a couple of friends came down and almost beat Kell to death. He's on his way up to San Antonio for back surgery and I need a place to stay, just until after the surgery. They wanted me in protective custody, but I told them Colter lived with you…"

"You poor kid! You can come and stay as long as you like," Brenda said at once. "But Colter's out of the country on a case. He has an apartment of his own now.

What's that about Kell?" she asked worriedly. "Is he going to be all right?"

"He's just banged up, mostly," Cappie said, "but the shrapnel in his back has shifted and he has feeling in his legs. They may be able to operate."

"What a blessing in disguise," the other woman said quietly. "But what about you? Don't tell me Frank went to your house just to beat up your brother."

"He was probably looking for me," she confessed. "But he'd already done enough damage to my working relationship with my new boss. I don't have a job anymore, either."

"I'll ask Dr. Lammers about something part-time," she said immediately. "I know they'd love to have you back. The new tech doesn't have the dedication to the job that you had, and doesn't show up for work half the time, either. I'll phone her right now. Meanwhile, you come on up here. You know where the spare key's kept."

"Thanks a million, Brenda." Her voice was breaking, despite her efforts to control it.

"Honey, I'm so sorry," Brenda said gently. "If there's anything I can do, anything at all, you just tell me."

Cappie swallowed. "I've missed you."

"I've missed you, too. You just hang on. Get Kell up here and then come on yourself. We'll handle it. Okay?"

"Okay."

"I'll phone Dr. Lammers right now." She hung up.

Cappie went back to the waiting room and sat, sad and somber, while she waited for the test results and a chance to talk to Kell.

Dr. Steele was smiling when he came back. "I think it's operable," he said. "I'm going to send Kell to San

Antonio by chopper. It's quicker and it will be easier on his back. We don't want that shrapnel to shift again. You can see him, just for a minute. Want to fly up with him?"

"Yes, if I can," she said.

He nodded toward Kell's room. "Cash Grier is in there with him. He wants a word with you, too."

"Okay. Thanks, Dr. Steele."

She opened the door and walked in. Cash Grier was leaning against the windowsill, very somber. Kell looked terrible, but he smiled when she bent over to kiss him.

"Dr. Steele thinks they may be able to operate," she told him.

"So I heard." He smiled. "I don't know how I'll afford it, but maybe they take IOUs."

"You get better before you worry about money," she said firmly. "We can always sell the car."

"Sure, that will pay for my aspirin," Kell chuckled.

"Stop that. It's going to work out," she said firmly. "Hi, Chief," she greeted Cash.

"Hi, yourself. Your ex-boyfriend was after you," he said without preamble. "He won't quit. He knows he'll go back to jail for what he did to Kell. He'll get you, if he can, before we catch him."

"I'm going to fly up to San Antonio with Kell," she said slowly, "and I'll be staying with my best friend. Her brother's a Texas Ranger." She didn't add that he was out of town. After all, Cash wouldn't know. But would she be putting Brenda in danger, just by being there?

"Colter's out of the country, and Brenda doesn't own a weapon," Cash said, stone-faced. He nodded when she gasped. "I know Colter. I used to be a Texas Ranger, too. We've kept in touch. You don't want to put Brenda in the line of fire."

"I was just worrying about that." She bit her lower lip. "Then what do we do?"

"You stay in a hotel near the hospital," he said. "We're sending security up to watch you."

"Police officers from here?" she wondered.

"Not really," Cash said slowly. "Actually Eb Scott is detailing two of his men to stay with you. One is just back from the Middle East, and the other is waiting for an assignment."

"Mercenaries," she said softly.

"Exactly."

She looked worried.

"They're not the sort you see in movies," Kell assured her. "These guys have morals and they only work for good causes, not just for money."

"Do you know the men?" she asked him.

He hesitated.

"I know them," Cash said at once. "And you can trust them. They'll take care of you. Just go with Kell to the hospital and they'll meet you there."

She frowned. "I'll have to phone somebody at my office, to tell them what's happened."

"Everybody at your office already knows what happened," Cash told her. "Well, except your boss," he added, just when her heart had skipped two beats. "He had to fly to Denver on some sort of personal business. Something to do with his stepfather."

"Oh." It was just as well, she thought. Now she wouldn't have to see him again. Kell didn't know Dr.

Rydel had fired her, but this wasn't really the time to tell him. It could wait. "What about our house?"

"Kell gave me the key," he said. "I'll get it to Keely. She'll make sure the lights are off and everything's locked up and the fridge is cleaned out."

"I don't want to live there anymore," she told Kell in a subdued tone.

"We don't have to make decisions right now," he replied, wincing as he moved. "Hell, I think it was better when I couldn't feel my legs!"

"You'll enjoy walking again," Cappie said gently. "Kell, it would be like a miracle. At least some good would have come out of all this."

"Just what I was thinking." He smiled at her. "Now don't worry. It's going to work out."

"Yes, it is," Cash agreed. "Rick Marquez is going to make sure every cop in San Antonio has a personal description of Frank Bartlett, and he's talked to a reporter he knows at one of the news stations. Your nemesis Frank is going to be so famous that if he walks into a convenience store, ten people are going to tackle him and yell for the police."

"Really? But why?"

"Did I mention that there's a reward for his capture?" Cash added. "We took up a little collection."

"How kind!"

"You should stay here," Cash said seriously. "It's a good town. Good people."

Her face closed up. "I'm not living in any town that also houses Dr. Rydel."

Cash and Kell exchanged a long look.

"But Kell might like to stay," she added.

Kell wondered what was going on. Cappie had been crazy about her boss until today. "I think we need to have a talk about why you're down on your boss," he told her.

"Tomorrow," she said. "First thing."

"I'll probably be in surgery tomorrow, first thing," Kell replied.

She smiled wanly. "Then I'll tell you while you're unconscious. When do we leave?" she added.

Kell wanted to argue, but they'd given him something for pain, and he was already drooping. "As soon as the helicopter gets here. Need anything from the house? I'm sure Cash would run you over there."

She shook her head. "I've got my purse and my phone. Oh, here's the house key," she added, pulling it off her key ring and handing it to Cash. "I know you gave Kell's to Keely, but you may need mine. Thanks a lot."

"If you need anything, you can call Keely. She'll run it up to you, or her husband or her sister-in-law will."

"I'll do that."

"And try not to worry," Cash added, moving away from the window. "Things always seem darkest before the dawn. Believe me, I should know," he added with a smile. "I've seen my share of darkness."

"You're a wonderful police chief," she told him.

"Another good reason to stay in Jacobs County," he advised.

"We can agree to disagree on that point," she replied. "I might reconsider if you'd lock Dr. Rydel up and throw away the key."

"Can't do that. He's the best veterinarian around."

"I guess he is, at that."

Cash wisely didn't add to his former statement.

THE TRIP IN the helicopter was fascinating to Cappie, who'd never flown in one, despite Kell's years in the military. She'd had the opportunity, but she was afraid of the machines. Now, knowing that it was helping to save Kell's legs, she changed her opinion of them.

She sat quietly in her seat, smiling at the med techs, but not talking to them. She'd had just about all she could stand of men, she decided, for at least the next twenty years. She only hoped and prayed that Kell would be able to walk again. And that somebody would find Frank Bartlett before he came back to finish what he'd started.

BENTLEY RYDEL WALKED into his office three days later, out of sorts and even more irritable than he'd been when he left. His stepfather had suffered a stroke. It hadn't killed him, but he was temporarily paralyzed on one side and in a nursing home for the foreseeable future. Bentley had tracked down the man's younger brother and made arrangements to fly him to Denver to look after his sibling. All that had taken time. He didn't begrudge giving help, but he was still upset about Cappie. Why had he been stupid enough to get involved with her? Hadn't he learned his lesson about women by now?

The office hadn't officially opened for business; it was ten minutes until it did. He found every employee in the place standing behind the counter glaring at him as if he'd invented disease.

His eyebrows arched. "What's going on?" His face

tautened. "Cappie's suing me for asking her to quit, is she?" he asked with cold sarcasm.

Dr. King glared back. "Cappie's in San Antonio with her brother," she said. "Her ex-boyfriend and two of his friends beat Kell within an inch of his life."

He felt the blood drain out of his face. "What?"

"They've got Cappie surrounded by police and volunteers, trying to keep the same thing from happening to her," Keely added curtly. "Sheriff Carson checked into Frank Bartlett's background and found several priors for battery against women, but nobody was willing to press charges until Cappie did. She wasn't exactly willing at that—her brother forced her to, when she got out of the hospital. Bartlett beat her bloody and broke her arm. She said that she'd probably be dead if Kell hadn't managed to knock out Bartlett in time."

He felt as if his throat had been cut. He'd believed the man. How could he have done that to Cappie? How could he have suspected her of such deceit? She'd been the victim. Bentley had believed the lying ex-boyfriend and fired Cappie. Now she was in danger and it was his fault.

"Where is she?" he asked heavily.

"She told us not to tell you," Dr. King said quietly. "She doesn't want to see you again. In fact, she's got her old job back in San Antonio and she's going to live there."

He felt sick all over. No, she wouldn't want to stay in Jacobs County now. Not after the job Bentley had done on her self-esteem. It had probably been hard for her to trust a man again, having been physically assaulted.

She'd trusted Bentley. She'd been kind and sweet and trusting. And he'd kicked her in the teeth.

He didn't answer Dr. King. He looked at his watch. "Get to work, people," he said in a subdued tone.

Nobody answered him. They went to work. He went into his office, closed the door and picked up the telephone.

"Yes?" Cy Parks answered.

"Where's Cappie?" he asked quietly.

"If I tell you, I'll have to change my name and move to a foreign country," Cy replied dryly.

"Tell me anyway. I'll buy you a fake mustache."

Cy chuckled. "Okay. But you can't tell her I sold her out."

"Fair enough."

CAPPIE WAS WORN-OUT. She'd been in the waiting room around the clock until Kell was through surgery, and it had taken a long time. The chairs must have been selected for their comfort level, she decided, to make sure nobody wanted to stay in them longer than a few minutes. It was impossible to sleep in one, or even to doze. Her back was killing her. She needed sleep, but she couldn't leave the hospital until she knew Kell was out of the recovery room.

Beside her, two tall, somber men sat waiting also. One of them was dark-eyed and dark-headed, and he never seemed to smile. The other one had long blond hair in a ponytail and one pale brown eye and an eyepatch on the other. He was good-natured about his disability and referred to himself as Dead-Eye. He chuckled as he said it. She didn't know their names.

Detective Sergeant Rick Marquez had dropped by earlier in the day to talk to her about Frank Bartlett's family and friends. She did know about Frank's sister, but she hadn't met any of his friends. Detective Marquez was, she thought, really good-looking. She wondered why he didn't have a steady girlfriend.

Marquez had assured her that he was doing everything possible to track down Frank Bartlett, and that a friend of his who was a news anchor was going to broadcast a description of Bartlett and ask for help from the public to apprehend him. There was a two-thousand-dollar reward being offered for information leading to his arrest and conviction.

Brenda came with her to the hospital and stayed until she was called into her own office for an emergency surgery on a dog patient. She'd promised to return as soon as she could. She was upset that Cappie wasn't going to stay with her. She could borrow a gun, she muttered, and shoot that two-legged snake if he came near the apartment. But Cappie smiled and said she hadn't been thinking straight when she'd called and asked for a place to stay. She wasn't risking Brenda. Besides, she had security. Brenda gave the two men a long, curious glance. She did mention that she wouldn't want to mess with them, if she was a bad man. The one with the ponytail grinned at her.

After Brenda left, Cappie sat with her two somber male attachments while people came and went in the waiting room. She drank endless cups of black coffee and tried not to dwell on her fears. If Kell could just walk again, she told herself, the misery of the past few days would be worth it. If only!

Finally the surgeon on Kell's case came out to speak with her, smiling in his surgical greens.

"We removed the shrapnel," he told her. "I'm confident that we got it all. Now we wait for results, once your brother has time to heal. But I'm cautiously optimistic that he'll walk again."

"Oh, thank God," she breathed, giving way to tears. "Thank God!"

"Now, will you please go and get some sleep?" he asked. "You look like death walking."

"I'll do that. Thank you, Dr. Sims. Thank you so much!"

"You're very welcome. Leave your cell phone number at the nurses' desk and they'll phone you if they need you."

"I'll do that right now."

She went to the nurses' desk with her two companions flanking her and looking all around them covertly.

"I'm Kell Drake's sister," she told a nurse. "I want to give you my cell phone number in case you need to get in touch with me."

"Certainly," a little brunette replied, smiling. She pulled a pad over to her and held a pen poised over it. "Go ahead."

Cappie gave the number to her. "I'll always have it with me, and I won't turn it off."

The brunette looked from one man to the other curiously.

"They're with me," Cappie told her. She leaned over the counter. "You see, they're in terrible danger and I have to protect them."

The two men gave her a simultaneous glare that

could have stopped traffic. The brunette managed to smother a giggle.

"Okay, guys, I'm ready whenever you are," she told them.

The one with the eye-patch pursed his lips. "Want a head start?" he asked pointedly.

She grinned up at him. "You want one?" she countered.

He chuckled, and indicated that she could go first. He turned and winked at the little brunette, who flushed with pleasure. He was whistling as he followed Cappie out through the waiting room.

"You, protect us," the other man scoffed. "From what...bug bites?"

"Keep that up," Cappie told him, "and I'll show you a bite."

"Now, now, let's try to get along," Dead-Eye murmured as they waited for the elevator to come back up.

"I'm getting along. She's the one with the attitude problem," the other man muttered.

"Says you," Cappie told him.

He stared at Dead-Eye and pointed at Cappie.

"I never take sides in family squabbles," Dead-Eye told him.

"She is not a member of my family!" the other man said.

"A likely story," Dead-Eye said. "Anyway, how can you be sure? Have you had your DNA compared to hers?"

"I know I'm not related to you," the man told Dead-Eye.

"How do you know that?" came the dry retort.

"Because you're too ugly to be any kin to me."

"Well, I never," Dead-Eye harrumphed. "Look who's calling who *ugly*."

"Your mother dresses you funny, too."

Cappie was already light-headed with relief. These two were setting off her quirky sense of humor. "I can't take the two of you anywhere," she complained. "You embarrass me to tears."

"Can I help it if he's ugly?" the second man said. "I was only stating a fact."

"He's not ugly," Cappie defended Dead-Eye. "He's just unique."

Dead-Eye grinned at her. "We can get married first thing in the morning," he said. "I've been keeping a wedding ring in my chest of drawers for just such an emergency."

Cappie shook her head. "Sorry. I can't marry you tomorrow."

"Why not?"

"My brother won't let me date ugly men."

"You just said I wasn't ugly!" he protested.

"I lied."

"I can have my nose fixed."

She frowned. It was a very nice nose.

"I can alter it for you with my fist," the other man volunteered.

"I can alter you first," Dead-Eye informed him.

"No fighting," Cappie protested. "We'll all end up in jail."

"Some of us have probably escaped from one recently," the other man said with a pointed look at Dead-Eye.

"I didn't have to escape. They let me out on account of my extreme good looks," Dead-Eye scoffed.

"Your looks are extreme," came the reply. "Just not good."

"If you two don't stop arguing, I'm going to have my best friend come over to spend the night with us, and you two will be sharing the sofa," she assured them.

"Just shoot me now," Dead-Eye muttered, "and be done with it. I'm not sharing anything with him. Not unless he's got proof he isn't rabid."

The elevator door had opened while they were arguing. Dr. Bentley Rydel stepped off it and stared at the younger man while Cappie gaped at his sudden appearance.

"He isn't rabid," Bentley assured Dead-Eye.

"And how would you know?" Dead-Eye asked.

"I'm a veterinarian," Bentley replied curtly.

"We should go," Cappie said, avoiding Bentley's eyes.

"We?" he asked, scowling.

"These are my two new boyfriends," Cappie told him with a cold scowl. "We're sharing a room."

He knew she wasn't involved with two strangers. He had a pretty good idea of who they were and why she was with them. She probably expected him to believe the bald statement, with his track record.

"I heard about Kell," he said quietly. "How is he?"

"Out of surgery and resting comfortably, thank you," she said formally. "We have to go."

"Can we talk?" Bentley asked somberly.

"If you can get them," she indicated her companions, "to tie me up and gag me, sure. Let's go, guys."

She walked into the elevator and stood with her back to the door until she heard it close.

CHAPTER EIGHT

CAPPIE DIDN'T SLEEP, of course. She was replaying the last forty-eight hours in her mind all night, sick with worry about Kell. It was her fault that Frank Bartlett had ever gotten near them. If only she hadn't been so flattered by his attention, so crazy about him that she ignored Kell's warnings. If only she hadn't gone out with him at all.

Pity, she thought, that people couldn't set the clock backward and erase all the stupid things they did. Like getting involved with Dr. Bentley Rydel, for example, she told herself. It had surprised her to find him at the hospital. Somebody in Jacobsville must have told him what had happened, and he felt sorry for her. Maybe he was willing to overlook her smarmy past long enough to check on her brother's condition. That didn't mean he believed her innocence or wanted to get involved with her again. Which was just as well, she told herself, because she certainly wanted nothing more to do with him!

She got up and dressed…in the same clothes she'd worn the day before. She hadn't packed anything. She'd have to call Keely and ask her to go to the house and pack a few items of clothing for her and Kell. But she'd make sure Keely got an armed person to go with her, in case Frank was waiting around to see if Cappie turned back up.

When she opened her bedroom door, the two men were arguing over the coffee in the tiny little coffeepot that came, with coffee, as a perk for staying in the hotel.

"There's not enough for three people," Dead-Eye was muttering, refusing to let go of the pot.

"Then you can get yours at a café, because I'm having mine here," the other man said coldly.

"We're all having ours at the hospital, because I'm leaving right now," Cappie informed them, starting for the door.

"See what you get for starting a fight? Now neither of us is having coffee," Dead-Eye scoffed as he turned off the coffeepot and put the little carafe back in it.

"You started it first," the other man said coolly.

Cappie ignored the banter and opened the door.

"Hold it right there."

Dead-Eye was in front of her in a heartbeat, his hand under his jacket as a tall man walked into view in the hall. He stood immobile, waiting.

But it wasn't Frank. It was another man, and a woman and child suddenly appeared behind him and started talking to him.

"Nice day," Dead-Eye told them with a smile.

"Huh? Oh. Yeah." The man smiled back and herded his family ahead of him down the hall.

Dead-Eye stood aside to let Cappie out. "Wait until one of us makes sure it's safe," he told her in a kind tone. "Men who commit battery without fear of arrest are usually not planning to go back in prison, if you get my drift. He might decide a bullet is better than a fist."

"Sorry," she said. "I didn't think."

"That's what we're here for," the other man said, following her out the door and closing it. "We'll think for you."

"Were you thinking, just then?" Dead-Eye grinned.

The other man indicated his sleeve. The hilt of a large knife was in his palm. He flexed his hand and snapped it back in place. "Learned that from Cy Parks," he said. "He taught me everything I know."

"Then what are you doing with Eb?"

"Learning…diplomacy." He said it through gritted teeth. "They say my attitude needs work."

Dead-Eye opened his mouth to speak.

Cappie beat him to it. "And you think I need an attitude adjustment?" she exclaimed.

The other man shifted restlessly. "We should get to the hospital."

Cappie just smiled. So did Dead-Eye.

WHEN THEY GOT to the hospital cafeteria, it was already full. One of the tables was occupied by a somber Dr. Rydel, moving eggs around on a plate as if he couldn't decide between eating them or throwing them.

Cappie's traitorous heart jumped at the sight of him, but she didn't let her pleasure show. She was still fuming about his assumption of her guilt, without any proof except the word of a man who was a stranger.

He looked up and saw her and grimaced.

"Want me to frisk him for you?" Dead-Eye asked pleasantly. "I can do it discreetly."

"Yeah, like you discreetly frisked that guy at the airport," the dark-eyed man muttered. "Isn't he suing?"

"I apologized," Dead-Eye retorted.

"Before or after airport security showed up?"

"Well, after, but he said he understood how I might have mistaken him for an international terrorist."

"He was wearing a Hawaiian shirt and flip-flops!"

"The best disguise on earth for a spy, and I ought to know. I used to live in Fiji."

"Did you, really?" Cappie asked, fascinated. "I've always wanted to go there."

"Have you?" Dead-Eye looked past her to Bentley, who had gotten up from the table and was moving toward them. "Now might not be a bad time," he advised.

Bentley had dark circles under his eyes from lack of sleep. But he was just as arrogant as ever. He stopped in front of Cappie.

"I'd like to talk to you for a minute."

She didn't want to talk to him, and almost repeated her words of the night before. But she was tired and worried and a little afraid of Frank. It didn't matter now, anyway. Her life in Jacobsville was already over. She and Kell would start over again, here in San Antonio, once the threat was over.

"All right," she said wearily. "I'll only be a minute, guys," she told Dead-Eye and his partner. "You can get coffee."

"Finally," Dead-Eye groaned. "I'm having caffeine withdrawal."

"Is that why you look so ugly?" the other man taunted.

They moved off, still fencing verbally.

"Who are they?" Bentley asked as he seated her at his table.

"Bodyguards," she said. "Eb Scott loaned them to me."

"Want coffee?"

"Please."

He went to the counter, got coffee and a sweet roll and put them in front of her. "You have to eat," he said when she started to argue. "I know you like those. You bring them to work in the morning sometimes when you have to eat on the run."

She shrugged. "Thanks."

He pushed sugar and cream to her side of the table.

"I phoned the nurses' desk on the way here, on my cell phone," she said wearily. "They said Kell's having his bath and then breakfast, so I'd have time to eat before I went up to see him."

"I talked to him briefly last night," he said.

She lifted her eyebrows. "It's family only. They posted it on the door!"

"Oh, that. I told them I was his brother-in-law."

She glared at him over her coffee as she added cream.

"Well, they let me in," he said.

She lifted the cup and sipped the hot coffee, with an expression of absolute delight on her face.

"He was about as friendly as you are," he sighed. "I screwed up."

She nodded. "With a vengeance," she added, still glaring.

He pushed his plate of cold scrambled eggs to one side. His pale blue eyes were intent on her gray ones. "After what happened to me, I was down on women for a long time. When I finally got to the stage where I thought I might be able to trust one again, I found out that she was a lot more interested in what I could give her than what I was." His face tautened. "You get gun-shy, after a while. And I didn't know you, Cappie. We had supper a few times, and I took you to a carnival, but that didn't mean we were close."

She stared at the roll and took a bite of it. It was delicious. She chewed and swallowed and sipped coffee, all without answering. She'd thought they were getting to be close. How dumb could she be?

He drew in a long breath and sipped his own coffee. "Maybe we were getting close," he admitted. "But trust comes hard to me."

She put down the cup and met his eyes evenly. "How hard do you think it comes to me?" she asked baldly. "Frank beat me up. He broke my arm. I spent three days in the hospital. Then at the trial, his defense attorney tried his best to make it look as if I deliberately provoked poor Frank by refusing to go to bed with him! Apparently that was enough to justify the assault, in his mind."

He scowled. "You didn't sleep with him?"

The glare took on sparks. "No. I think people should get married first."

He looked stunned.

She flushed and averted her eyes. "So I live in the past," she muttered. "Kell and I had deeply religious parents. I don't think he took any of it to heart, but I did."

"You don't have to justify yourself to me," he said quietly. "My mother was like you."

"I'm not trying to justify myself. I'm saying that I have an idealistic attitude toward marriage. Frank thought I owed him sex for a nice meal and got furious when I wouldn't cooperate. And for the record, I didn't even really provoke him. He beat me up because I suggested that he needed to drink a little less beer. That was all it took. Kell barely got to me in time."

He let out a long breath. "My stepfather hit my mother once, for burning the bacon, when they were first married. I was fifteen."

"What did she do?" she asked.

"She told me. I took him out back and knocked him around the yard for five minutes, and told him if he did it again, I'd load my shotgun and we'd have another, shorter, conversation. He never touched her again. He also stopped drinking."

"I don't think that would have worked with Frank."

"I rather doubt it." He studied her wan, drawn face. "You've been through hell, and I haven't helped. For what it's worth, I'm sorry. I know that won't erase what I said. But maybe it will help a little."

"Thanks." She finished her roll and coffee. But when she got through, she put two dollar bills on the table and pushed them toward him.

"No!" he exclaimed, his high cheekbones flushing as he recalled with painful clarity his opinion of her as a gold digger.

"I pay my own way, despite what you think of me," she said with quiet pride. She stood up. "Money doesn't mean so much to me. I'm happy if I can pay bills. I'm sorry I gave you the impression that I'd do anything for it. I won't."

She turned and left him sitting there, with his own harsh words echoing in his mind.

Kell was lying on his stomach in bed. His bruises were much more obvious now, and he was pale and weak from the surgery. She sat down beside him in a chair and smiled.

"How's it going?" she asked gently.

"Badly," he said with a long sigh. "Hurts like hell. But they think I might be able to walk again. They have to wait until I start healing and the bruising abates before they'll know for sure. But I can wiggle my toes." He smiled. "I'm not going to prove it, because it hurts. You can take my word for it."

"Deal." She brushed back his unkempt hair.

"Your old boss came by last night," he said coldly. "He explained what happened. I gave him an earful."

"So did I. He's back."

"I'm not surprised. He was pretty contrite."

"It won't do any good," she said sadly. "I won't forget what he said to me. He didn't believe me."

"Apparently he's had some hard knocks of his own."

"Yes, that explains it, but it doesn't excuse it."

"Point taken." He glanced past her toward the door. "You've got bodyguards."

"Yes. Some of Eb Scott's guys. They don't like each other."

"Chet has a chip on his shoulder, and Rourke likes to take potshots at it."

"Which is which?" she asked.

"Rourke lost an eye overseas."

"Oh. Dead-Eye."

He chuckled and then winced. "That's what he calls himself. He's got quite a history. He worked for the CIA over in the South Pacific for several years. Now he's trying to get back in. His language skills are rusty, and he's not up on the latest communications protocols, so he's studying with Eb. Chet, on the other hand, is trying to land a job doing private security for overseas embassies. He has anger issues."

"Anger issues?"

"He tends to slug people who make him angry. Doesn't go over well in embassies."

"I can understand that." She frowned. "How do you know them?"

He sighed. "That's a long story. We'll have to talk about it when I get out of here."

She was adding up things and getting uncomfortable totals. "Kell, you weren't working for a magazine when you went to Africa, were you?" she asked.

He hesitated. "That's one of the things we'll talk about. But not now. Okay?"

She relented. He did look very rocky. "Okay." She laid a gentle hand on his muscular arm. "You're my brother and I love you. That won't change, even if you tell me blatant lies and think I'll never know about them."

"You're too sharp for your own good."

"I've been told that."

"Don't stray from your bodyguards," he cautioned. "I have to agree with them. I think Frank's not planning to go back to jail. He'll do whatever it takes to get even with you, and then he'll try suicide-by-cop."

"Jail would be better than dead, certainly?"

"Frank has anger issues, too."

She flexed the arm he'd broken. "I noticed."

"Don't take chances. Promise me."

"I promise. Please get well. Being an orphan is bad enough. I can't lose you, too."

He smiled. "I'm not going anywhere. After all, I've got a book to finish. I have to get well in order to do that."

She hesitated. "Kell, he wouldn't come here, and try to finish the job he did on you?" she asked worriedly.

"I have company."

"You do?"

"Move it, you military rejects," came a deep voice from the door. A tall, familiar-looking man with silver eyes and jet-black hair moved into the room, dressed in boots and jeans and a chambray shirt, carrying a foam cup of coffee.

"Kilraven?" she asked, surprised. "Aren't you working?"

He shook his head. "Not tonight," he said. "I had a couple of vacation days I was owed, so I'm babysitting your brother."

"Thanks," she said with a broad grin.

"I'm getting something out of it," he chuckled. "I'm stuck on the middle level of a video game, and Kell knows how to crack it."

"Is it *Halo: ODST*?" Dead-Eye asked. "I beat it."

"Yeah, on the 'easy' level, I'll bet," Chet chided.

"I did it on 'normal,' for your information," he huffed.

"Well, I did it on *Legendary*," Kell murmured, "so shut up and take care of my sister, or I'll wipe the floor with you when I get back on my feet."

Dead-Eye gave him a neat salute. Chet shrugged.

"See you later," Cappie said, kissing her brother's cheek again.

"Where are you going?" he asked.

"On a job interview," she said gently. "Brenda's boss might have something part-time."

"Are you sure you want to move back here?" Kell asked.

"Yes," she lied.

"Good luck, then."

"Thanks. See you, Kilraven. Thank you, too."

He grinned. "Keep your gunpowder dry."

"Tell them." She pointed to her two companions. "I hate guns."

"Bite your tongue!" Kilraven said in mock horror.

She made a face and went out the door, her two companions right behind her.

BENTLEY MET THEM at the elevator. "Where are you going now?" he asked her.

She hesitated.

"Job interview," Rourke said for her.

"You can't leave the clinic," Bentley said curtly. "I don't have anybody to replace you yet!"

"That's your problem," she shot back. "I don't want to work for you anymore!"

He looked hunted.

"Besides, Kell and I are moving back to San Antonio as soon as he heals," she said stubbornly. "It's too far to commute."

Bentley looked even more worried. He didn't say anything.

"Aren't you supposed to be at work?" she added.

"Dr. King's filling in for me," he said.

"Until when?"

His pale eyes glittered. "Until I can convince you to come home where you belong."

"Please. Hold your breath." She walked around him and into the next open elevator. She didn't even look to see which direction it was going.

IT WAS GOING UP. She was stuck between two oversize men and two perfume-soaked women. She started to cough before the women got off. The men left two floors later and the elevator slowly started down.

"Wasn't that heaven?" Rourke said with a dreamy smile, inhaling the air. "I love perfume."

"It makes me sick," Chet muttered, sniffing.

"It makes me cough," Cappie agreed.

"Well, obviously, you two don't like women as much as I do," Rourke scoffed.

They both glared at him.

He raised both hands, palms-out, in defense and grinned.

The elevator stopped at the cafeteria again and Bentley was still there, smoldering.

Cappie glared at him. It didn't help. He got on the elevator and pressed the down button.

"Where do you think you're going?" Cappie asked him.

"On a job interview," he said gruffly. "Maybe they need an extra veterinarian where you're applying."

"Does this mean that you're not marrying me?" Rourke wailed in mock misery.

Bentley gaped. "You're marrying him?" he exclaimed.

"I am not marrying anybody!" Cappie muttered.

Bentley shifted restlessly. "You could marry me," he said without looking at her. "I'm established in a profession and I don't carry a gun," he added, looking pointedly at the butt of Rourke's big .45 auto nestled under his armpit.

"So am I, established in a profession," Rourke argued. "And knowing how to use a gun isn't a bad thing."

"Diplomats don't think so," Chet muttered.

"That's only until other people start shooting at them, and you save their butts," Rourke told him.

Chet brightened. "I hadn't thought of it like that."

"Come on," Cappie groaned when the elevator stopped. "I swear, I feel like I'm leading a parade!"

"Anybody got a trombone?" Rourke asked the people waiting around the elevator.

Cappie caught his arm and dragged him along with her.

THEY TOOK A cab to the veterinarian's office. The car was full. The men were having a conversation about video games, but they left Cappie behind when they mentioned innovations they'd found on the Internet, about how to do impossible things with the equipment in the Halo series.

"Using grenades to blow a Scorpion up onto a mountain?" she exclaimed.

"Hey, whatever works," Rourke argued.

"Yeah, but you have to shoot your buddies to get enough grenades," Chet said. "That's not ethical."

"This, from a guy who lifted a policeman's riot gun right out of the trunk of his car!" Rourke said.

"I never lifted it, I borrowed it! Anyway, everybody was shooting rifles or shotguns and I only had a .45," he scoffed.

"Everybody else's was bigger than his," Rourke translated with an angelic pose.

Chet hit his arm. "Stop that!"

"See why he can't get a job with diplomats?" Rourke quipped, holding his arm in mock pain.

"I'm amazed that either of you can get a job," Cappie commented. "You really need to work on your social skills."

"I'm trying to, but you won't marry me," Rourke grumbled.

"Of course she won't, she's marrying me," Bentley said smugly.

"I am not!" Cappie exclaimed.

"No woman is going to marry a veterinarian when she can have a dashing spy," Rourke commented.

"Do you know one?" Bentley asked calmly.

Rourke glared at him. "I can be dashing when I want to, and I used to work for the CIA."

"Yes, but does sweeping floors count as a real job?" Chet wanted to know.

"You ought to know," Rourke told the other man. "Isn't that what you did in Manila?"

"I was the president's bodyguard!"

"And didn't he end up in the hospital?"

"We're here!" Cappie said loudly, indicating where the cab was stopping. "And the ride is Dutch treat," she added. "I'm not paying cab fare for bodyguards and stubborn hangers-on."

"Who's a hanger-on?" Rourke asked.

But Cappie was already out of the cab. The three men followed her when they settled their part of the fare.

She walked into the veterinarian's front office, where Kate Snow was still holding down the job of receptionist. She was twenty-four, tall, brunette and had soft green eyes and a pleasant rather than pretty face. She smiled.

"Hi, Cappie," she greeted. "Come to visit your old stomping grounds?"

"Actually I'm here to apply for something part-time," she replied.

"Brenda said that, but I didn't believe her," Kate replied, stunned. "You just moved to Jacobsville."

"Well, I'm moving back."

"I'll buzz Dr. Lammers," she said, and pressed a button on the phone. She spoke into the receiver, nodded, spoke again and hung up. "He's with a patient, but he'll be out in a minute." She looked past Cappie. "Can I help you?" she asked the three men.

"I'm with her," Rourke said.

"Me, too," Chet seconded.

"I'm applying for a job, too," Bentley said. "I thought you might need an extra vet." He smiled.

"Who are you?" Kate asked, surprised.

"He's my ex-boss," Cappie muttered.

"You're Dr. Rydel?" Kate exclaimed. "But you have your own practice in Jacobsville!"

"I do, but if Cappie moves here, I move here," he said stubbornly.

"We might move here, too," Rourke interrupted. "I can interview for a job here, too. I can type."

"Liar," Chet said. "He can't type."

"I can learn!"

"All you know how to do is shoot people," Chet scoffed.

"Sir, it's illegal to carry a concealed weapon," Kate began nervously.

Rourke gave her his most charming smile. "I'm a professional bodyguard, and I have a permit. If you'd like to see it, I'll take you to this lovely little French bistro downtown and you can look at it while we eat."

Kate stared at him as if he'd grown horns.

"There's a guy stalking her," Chet told her. "We're going to catch him if he tries anything and turn him over to local law enforcement."

"Stalking you?" Kate stammered.

Cappie glared at the two men. "Thank you so much for making me an employment liability!"

Rourke made her a bow. Chet just glowered. Bentley beamed.

"I don't mind employing you. Not one bit," Bentley said. "These two can work for the groomer and we'll protect you."

"I'm not grooming anything," Chet told him bluntly.

"Okay. Then you can deal with surly clients," Bentley compromised.

Chet gave him an appreciative look.

"Actually I know how to groom things," Rourke said. "I once shaved a monkey."

Cappie hit him.

"There you are!" Brenda exclaimed, coming out of

the back in a green-and-blue polka-dotted lab coat. "I talked to Dr. Lammers, but he said we've already got more part-timers than we can spare. I'm so sorry," she added miserably.

"What's your address?" Bentley asked. "I'll send you flowers."

"I thought you wanted to marry her," Chet pointed at Cappie.

Brenda's eyes widened. "Who are you?" she asked the dark-eyed man.

"I'm a hired…"

"…assassin," Rourke finished for him.

"I don't kill people, I just shoot them!" Chet growled.

"I only wound them," Rourke added. "Are we going back to Jacobsville, then?"

"Who are these men?" Brenda asked again.

"Well, these two are my bodyguards—" she indicated them "—and that's my ex-boss."

"Why is your ex-boss here?" she asked, all at sea.

"He was going to get a job here, too, but there are no openings for part-timers or vets, so I guess we're all going back to Jacobsville," Cappie said miserably. "That is, if Frank doesn't shoot me first."

"Nobody's shooting you," Rourke assured her.

"You can bet on that," Chet said.

Brenda smiled at them. "Thanks. She's my best friend."

Cappie hugged her. "Thanks anyway, for trying. I'll call you. See you, Kate!"

Kate waved as she picked up the ringing telephone. Her eyes were still on Rourke, who grinned at her.

"Come on, let's go," Cappie told the men.

"How's Kell?" Brenda asked, walking them out.

"He's going to make it. We won't know if he can walk for several days, though."

"If you have to go home, I'll visit him for you."

"I can't leave just yet," Cappie said. "Not until we find Frank."

Brenda stared at Bentley, who was all smiles. "Aren't you going back to your practice?"

"When we find Frank," he commented pleasantly.

"You're not part of this bodyguard unit," Chet reminded him.

"I am now," Bentley assured him. His eyes smoothed over Cappie. "I'm in it until the end."

Cappie hated the rush of pleasure that comment gave her. So she disguised it by hugging Brenda and promising to keep in touch.

CHAPTER NINE

BENTLEY WENT WITH them back to the hotel where Cappie was staying. He left them at the desk to get a room for himself. He managed one on the same floor, two doors down, and then went back to the other hotel where he'd been staying to pack his bags and check out.

"Great," Cappie muttered when they were back in her suite. "Now we're really going to be a parade."

"He likes you," Rourke pointed out. "And at this point, the more eyes, the better. He might see something we'd miss. After all, he knows what Frank looks like. We only have a mug shot. And you said it didn't really look much like him," he added, because he'd shown it to her earlier.

"All right," she sighed. She moved to the window and looked down at the busy street. "At least Kell's in good hands. I wouldn't want to walk in on Kilraven, even if he was in a good mood, with evil intent."

"There's an odd bird," Rourke commented. "We can't even find out which branch of the government he really works for, and we've tried. His brother works for the FBI, but Kilraven's true affiliations are less obvious."

She turned to him. "Is he CIA?"

"If he was, he wouldn't say so. And just for the record," he added with a grin, "no CIA office address is ever listed, in any city where we have offices. We don't even mention which cities those are."

"What a shadowy bunch you are," she commented.

He just grinned. "That's why we're so good at what we do."

"What we *do?*" she asked, hitting on the obvious assumption.

"I didn't say I was still with them," he pointed out.

"You didn't say you weren't, either," she replied.

He made a face at her.

"At least my job is up-front and everybody knows what it is," Chet said.

They both looked at him with wide eyes.

He glared at them. "I'm a bodyguard!"

"Well, so am I, right now," Rourke said. "But it's not what I do full-time." He gave the other man a narrow-eyed appraisal. "And it isn't what you do full-time, either."

Chet looked uncomfortable.

"What does he do full-time?" Cappie asked, curious.

"It involves long-range rifles and black ops."

"It does not," Chet muttered.

"It used to."

"Well, after I broke my leg, I was less enthusiastic about jumping out of Blackhawks," he muttered.

"You broke both legs, I heard."

Chet sighed. "And an arm. Breaks never heal properly, even with good medical care." He sighed again. "You try getting good medical care in…" He caught himself and closed his mouth.

"I wasn't going to say a word," Rourke told him.

"Well, don't. I'm out of cigarettes. I'm going down

the street and see if I can find anybody in the mob to sell me a pack under the table, if the police aren't looking."

"Smoking's not illegal, is it?" Cappie asked.

"Any day now, it probably will be," Chet said despondently. "Can't spit without a federal permit these days," he said, and kept muttering all the way out the door.

"Quick, tell me," Cappie said to Rourke, "was he a sniper?"

"I've never been sure," he told her with a grin. "But he and Cash Grier are pretty chummy."

"Should that mean something?"

"Grier was a high-level government assassin in his younger days, but I didn't tell you that," he said firmly. "Some secrets have to be kept to save one's skin."

"Well!" she exclaimed. "I'd never have guessed."

"Neither would most other people. I'm going down the hall to loiter and see if I see anybody I recognize. Keep the door locked and don't answer it unless you recognize my voice, or Chet's. Got that?"

She nodded. "Thanks."

"When I do a job, I do a job," he told her. He closed the door behind him when he left.

SHE WAS JUMPY. With her protection, she shouldn't have been, but she kept remembering her last sight of Frank Bartlett, cursing her for all he was worth when the judge announced his sentence. He'd been yelling vengeance at the top of his lungs, and he'd almost managed to get away from the sheriff's deputy who had him in handcuffs. It had been a scary moment. Almost as scary as the memory of the night he'd beaten her.

She wrapped her arms around her rib cage and closed

her eyes. She did hope they'd catch him before he got to her. Surely the job he'd done on Kell would guarantee him some quality prison time. But what if he got out again, after that? Would she have to live her entire life being afraid of Frank? After all, he could get out on good behavior, no matter how long his sentence was. Or he could hang a jury at his next trial. Or he could break out of prison. There were plenty of horrible possibilities, all of which would leave Cappie hiding behind locked doors as long as she lived. It wasn't a possibility she looked forward to.

The sudden knock on the door brought a cry of panic to her lips. She moved toward the door, but she didn't touch the knob. "Who…is it?" she called.

"Room service. We're checking to see if your veterinarian has been delivered yet."

She burst out laughing. She knew that curt voice, as well as she knew her own. "Bentley!" She moved closer to the door. "I don't recall ordering a veterinarian."

"Well, we're delivering one to you anyway, just in case you regret not ordering him later," he drawled.

She unlocked the door and gave him a droll look. "Nice tactics."

He shrugged. "I'm desperate. You wouldn't let me in if I just asked." He looked behind her and the smile faded. "Where are your bodyguards?"

"Chet went looking for cigarettes and Rourke is down the hall checking for intruders."

"And you're in here alone."

"Well, the door was locked until you asked to come in," she pointed out.

"Fair enough. Want to come downstairs and have coffee and pie with me? Then we can go to see Kell."

"I guess that would be okay. But I have to tell Rourke where I'm going…"

"He already knows," came an amused voice from the general direction of her purse.

"How did you get in here?" she asked, lifting the purse.

"I hid a microphone in there earlier, in case you escaped."

"I'm going downstairs to have coffee and pie, then Bentley and I are going to see Kell."

"Okay. I'll be around. Have fun. And don't hit him with the pie. You will be going to a hospital."

"On your way to a hospital is the best time to hit people with things," she retorted. "There are doctors there."

"Yes, I know," Bentley spoke into her purse. "I am one."

"You're a veterinarian," Rourke shot back.

"I can treat injuries if I want to."

"Try not to let her give you any."

"You stop that," Cappie told her purse. Nobody answered. "Hello?" she said, looking inside it.

"Don't do that in public, okay?" Bentley asked as they walked to the door. "There are probably psychiatrists around the hospital, too."

She rolled her eyes and went out into the hall just ahead of him.

THE HOSPITAL CAFETERIA was crowded. They found a table, but they had to share it with an elderly couple who'd come all the way from the Mexican border to visit their daughter, who'd just had a baby. They had photographs, and showed every single one to Bentley and Cappie, who made the correct responses between sips of coffee and bites of apple pie.

Finally the elderly couple finished their soft drinks and went off toward the elevator.

"Alone at last," Bentley teased.

"One more photograph would have done me in," she confessed. "I swear, if I ever have a grandchild…"

"…you'll have even more photos than they did, and show them to total strangers, too," he chuckled.

She shrugged and smiled. "Yes. I guess I would."

"Babies are nice. I used to think I'd like one or two, myself."

"You don't anymore?" she asked.

He moved his coffee mug around on the table. "I sort of gave up hope. Until you came along." He didn't look at her as he said it.

She felt her toes tingle. She hated the rush of pleasure she felt. "Really?"

He looked up. His pale blue eyes made sparks as they met hers. "Really."

She hesitated.

"I never should have believed a man I just met, who sat in my office and told lies about you with perfect innocence. But, then, I was afraid you were too good to be true."

"Nobody's perfect."

"I realize that. You don't have to be perfect. I just don't want to get in over my head and get kicked in the teeth again."

"I'm not that sort of person," she told him.

His eyes narrowed on her face. "He really hurt you, didn't he?"

"I thought I loved him," she said quietly. "He seemed to be kind and considerate…but the first date we had, he kicked my cat. I should have known then. Kind people aren't cruel to animals, ever. I found out later that he'd been abusive to at least two other women he dated, but they were too afraid of him to press charges." She smiled wanly. "Well, so was I. But Kell insisted. He said that Frank might end up killing someone if I didn't have him prosecuted. Then I'd have it on my conscience. I just didn't realize that it might be me that Frank killed." She put her face in her hands. "It won't ever end. Even if he goes back to trial, he could get off, or they could release him for good behavior, or he could break out… I'll never be free of him as long as I live."

"Don't talk like that," he said softly. "I won't let him hurt you."

She took her hands away. She looked older. "What if he hurt you? What if he killed you? Anybody around me will be a target. I almost put Brenda in danger without even realizing it."

"I'm not afraid of the little weasel," he told her. "And you're not going to be afraid of him, either. That's how he controls women. With fear. Don't give him a foothold in your mind."

She bit her lip. "I'm just scared, Bentley."

"Yes, but you did the right thing. And you'll do it again, anytime you have to. You aren't the type of person who runs from trouble, any more than I am."

"You think so?"

"I know so."

She searched his eyes. "I was scared to death of you, at first. Then I was in a wreck and you drove me home." She smiled. "You aren't as horrible as you seem."

"Thanks. I think." He smiled back.

"Okay. I'll stick it out. If Frank escapes another jail sentence, maybe I can get Rourke to hide him in a jungle overseas, so deep that he'd never find his way out."

"Ahem," her purse replied, "I do not kidnap American citizens and carry them out of the country for nefarious purposes. Not even for pretty women."

"Spoilsport," she told him.

"However, I know people who would," he added, with a smile in his voice.

"Good man," Bentley said.

"Why don't you marry him?" Rourke asked. "At least he'd make sure you were never in harm's way."

"If you'll give me your boss's telephone number," Bentley told the purse, "I'll call him and give you a glowing recommendation."

"What a pal!"

"I always…"

Bentley stopped talking because three people were standing at their table with open mouths, watching him speak into Cappie's purse. He cleared his throat. "There, the radio's turned off now," he said in a deep, deliberate tone. He handed her back the purse.

The three people looked sheepish, smiled and left the cafeteria in a bit of a rush.

Cappie burst out laughing. Bentley's cheeks were the color of bubble gum.

"Quick thinking, there, Dr. Rydel," Rourke called over the radio. "Want to come work for us?"

"Go away," Cappie told him. "I am not going to consider marrying anybody in your line of work."

"Spoilsport," Rourke said. "Shutting up now."

Cappie met Bentley's eyes, and they both laughed.

KELL WAS GROGGY and quiet. The pain must have been pretty bad, Cappie thought, once the anesthetic wore off. He was much less talkative than he'd been when he was just out of the recovery room. He was pale and he looked as if it was an effort to say anything at all. They only stayed a couple of minutes. Kell was asleep before they got out the door.

"Do you think it would be safe to step outside just for a minute and get a breath of air?" Cappie asked. "There are people everywhere."

"I don't know," Bentley said, his eyes roving.

"Rourke, what do you think?" she asked her purse.

But there was no reply. She looked around. She didn't see Rourke or Chet. That was odd. They'd been visible every minute since she came to San Antonio.

"Maybe it would be all right," she said. "I just want to stretch my legs for a minute."

"All right," Bentley said. "But you stay close to me." He slid his big hand into her small one and closed it warmly. "I'll take care of you."

She smiled wearily and laid her head against his shoulder for a minute. "Okay."

They walked out into the cold night air. The sidewalk was crowded. Traffic passed by. There was a policeman on the corner, leaning back against a storefront, talking into a cell phone. Nearby, two men in suits were talking, oblivious to passersby.

All around them, neon signs and holiday lights brightened the darkness. "It's almost Christmas," she exclaimed. "With all that's happened, I forgot." She grimaced. "We won't get to open presents under the tree this year. Kell will never be able to go home by Christmas Eve."

"Then we'll put up a small tree in his room and transfer the presents up here from Jacobsville," he promised her. "We'll have Christmas here."

She looked up at him with soft, quiet eyes. "We?"

His jaw tautened. "I'm not leaving you again. Not even for a day," he said huskily.

The words made tears brim in her eyes. The way he said it was so poignant, so passionate. He didn't even need to say what he was feeling. She read it in his face.

He pulled her into his arms and held her close, hugged her tight, buried his face in her long, soft hair. "Marry me."

She closed her eyes. "Yes. Yes!" she whispered.

His chest rose and fell heavily. "Of all the places to get engaged," he groaned. "With a thousand eyes watching."

"It doesn't matter," she whispered.

No, he thought. It didn't.

"Hold him! I'll get her!"

The voices came suddenly into what was the sweetest dream of Cappie's life. She was so relaxed, so happy, that it took precious seconds for her to realize what was about to happen. She felt Bentley torn from her arms. Two men were pulling his arms behind him. A violent jerk brought her around as two bruising hands caught her shoulders and twisted them. Above her,

Frank Bartlett's angry, contorted features came into view, his narrow dark eyes promising retribution.

"Got you at last, didn't I?" he growled. "Now, you're going to pay for what you did to me!"

She cried out and tried to pull away from him, but his hands were too strong. He drew one back and slapped her as hard as he could, so hard that she staggered and would have fallen if he hadn't jerked her back up brutally with the other hand.

Her face stung like fire. There would be a bruise. But it only made her mad. She drew back her high-heeled foot and kicked him in the calf muscle as hard as she could. He yelled in pain and slapped her again. But before he could draw back another time, he suddenly went down under a vicious tackle.

"That's the way, brother!" came a cheering cry from the sidelines.

"Go get him!" came another hearty voice.

Bentley was knocking the stuffing out of Frank Bartlett, his big fists making the other man, a match for him pound for pound, cry out in pain.

"Now isn't he talented?" Rourke murmured as he drew a shaky Cappie back from the crowd. He looked at her bruised face and winced. "Sorry we didn't rush right in, but we wanted to make sure we had plenty of witnesses and an excellent case for the prosecution." He jerked his head toward Chet and the two men in suits. They had the two men with Frank subdued and handcuffed. The uniformed officer who'd been on the corner was standing with them.

"We had you staked out," Rourke told her. "I

wouldn't have done it this way, if there had been any other choice."

She reached up and patted his cheek. "You did good, Dead-Eye," she said with a smile, and winced when it hurt. "I'm going to look like an accident victim for a few days, I'm afraid."

"No doubt about that. Your poor face!"

She glanced back toward Frank. Bentley was still pounding him. "Shouldn't you save Bentley?"

"Bentley?" he exclaimed.

"From a homicide charge, I mean," she clarified.

"Oh. Right. Probably should."

He moved forward and pulled Bentley off the other man. It took some doing. The veterinarian was obviously reluctant to give up his pastime.

"Now, now," Rourke calmed him, "we have to have enough left to prosecute. Besides, Cappie needs some TLC. She's pretty bruised."

Bentley was catching his breath as he walked quickly back to Cappie. He winced at the sight of her face. "My poor baby," he exclaimed, bending to kiss her bruised cheek with exquisite tenderness. "Let me just go back over there and hit him one more time…!"

"No," she protested, grabbing his suit coat. "Rourke's right, we have to have enough of him left to prosecute. Bentley, you were magnificent!"

"So were you, kicking him in the leg," he chuckled.

"I guess we make a pretty good team," she mused.

"You can say that again."

She put a hand to her cheek. "Boy, that stings."

"It looks like hell. You'll have to see a doctor."

"Fortunately there are plenty of those right inside,"

Rourke came back in time to reply. "See the letters? They spell out *hospital*."

She drew back a fist.

Rourke held up both hands. "Now, now, I'm on your side." He nodded toward one of the men in suits who had a long black ponytail. "Recognize him?"

She frowned. "No…"

"That's Detective Sergeant Rick Marquez," he told her. "He was just on his way to the opera when we phoned and said an assault with intent was going down in front of the hospital. He broke speed records getting here."

"How kind of him," Cappie said.

"Not really. He always goes to the opera alone. He can't get women."

"But, why not?" she wondered. "He's a dish."

"He carries a gun," Rourke pointed out.

"You carry a gun."

"I can't get women, either."

"What a shame."

He moved closer. "I'm available."

She laughed as Bentley stepped in front of her, glowering.

"Wait, scratch that, I just remembered, I'm not available," Rourke said quickly.

"Even if you were, she's not," Bentley said.

"There you are, again, starting trouble," Rick Marquez chuckled, joining them. He looked at Cappie's face and grimaced. "Damn, I'm sorry we didn't get here sooner," he apologized. "I couldn't get a cab and I had to run all the way."

"Fortunately you're in great shape," Rourke said.

"Fortunately I am," Marquez agreed. "What are you and Billings doing here?"

"Trading favors with Eb Scott." Rourke grinned. "We're bodyguards. Well, not anymore. Not now that you have those three jackals in custody."

Marquez moved a step closer to him. "How about telling Chet that he's not allowed to smoke here?"

"Why don't you tell him?" Rourke asked, surprised.

"Too many windows overlook my apartment," came the amused reply. "He might not be able to resist the temptation to get even."

"Good point. I'll just pass that along. About the smoking!" Rourke added quickly. "Anyway, he wouldn't shoot you. He's not sanctioned."

"Yet," Marquez enunciated.

Rourke shrugged, grinned and went to find his partner.

"They really were great," Cappie told the detective. "I've never felt safer. Well, until tonight."

"We let you walk into the trap," Marquez replied quietly. "It was the only way we could guarantee a case against Bartlett that he couldn't escape. His sort doesn't give up."

"Yes, but he could get out again…"

"He won't," Marquez said curtly. "I promise you that. See that guy I was standing with? He's the assistant D.A. who put Frank away in the first place."

"I thought he looked familiar," Cappie returned.

"He cursed a blue streak because the judge gave him such an easy sentence. He's been working behind the scenes to get depositions in case Frank slipped." He grinned. "And did Frank ever slip! In front of all these witnesses, too." He indicated the uniformed officer, and two others who'd joined him, who were questioning bystanders. "Frank is going back in jail for a long time."

"What about his friends?" Cappie asked.

"I know what they helped him do to your brother. We couldn't have proved it, before, but I'm betting one of them will be happy to turn state's evidence in return for a reduced sentence."

"Meanwhile," Bentley said, sliding an affectionate arm around Cappie, "we're going to have a nice Christmas celebration with Kell in the hospital and then plan a wedding."

"A wedding?" Marquez sighed. "I used to think I'd find a nice woman someday who liked cops and opera, who'd love to marry me. But, I'm really happy to be single. I mean, I have all sorts of free time, and I get to watch whatever television programs I like, and TV dinners are just wonderful. In fact, I think I might like to do commercials for them." He smiled.

"They have psychiatrists in there, don't they?" Bentley asked, nodding toward the hospital.

Marquez glared at him. "I'm happy, I said! I love living alone! I never want my private life messed up by some sweet, loving woman who can cook!"

"Anybody got a straitjacket?" Bentley asked.

Marquez threw up his hands and walked away.

Cappie felt her face begin to throb. Tears stung her eyes. "Could we go back inside and find the emergency room, you think?" she asked Bentley.

"Right this minute," he said with obvious concern.

Marquez followed them inside. "I've got my digital camera with me," he said, suddenly all business. "We want to get photos, to make sure a jury sees what Frank did to you."

"Be my guest," Cappie replied. "But then I want aspirin and an ice pack!"

"You can come down to my office in the morning to give me a statement. For now, we'll get the photos and have a doctor look at your face. After that, you can even have a beer if you like, and I'll buy," Marquez promised.

She made a face. "Sorry, but I'd rather have the ice pack."

Bentley's arm contracted. "Then we have to find some way to keep Kell from seeing your poor face, until he's through the worst of his own ordeal."

"Yes, we do," she said. "That isn't going to be easy."

Marquez, seeing the bruising increase by the second, had to agree. And she didn't know yet how it was going to look a day later. But he did.

THEY DID TAKE X-rays of Cappie's face. Marquez got his photos and left. The doctor treating her came back into the cubicle where she and Bentley were waiting in the busy emergency room.

"There are two small broken bones," he said. "I want you to take these X-rays to your primary physician and let him refer you to a good plastic surgeon. Meanwhile, I'm going to write you something for pain. Keep ice on the swelling. Nothing is going to disguise the bruises, I'm afraid." He glanced curiously at Bentley.

"I didn't do it," Bentley said easily. "The man who did was taken away in a squad car, with his accomplices, and he's going to be prosecuted to the full extent of the law. Those X-rays we asked for a copy of are going to help put him away."

The young resident nodded somberly. "I see far too many injuries like this. A boyfriend?" he queried.

"No," Cappie said heavily. "An ex-boyfriend who spent six months in jail for breaking my arm," she added. "He got out and came looking for me. This time, I hope he'll stay as a guest of the state for much longer."

"I'll be happy to testify," the resident said. He pulled a card out of his wallet and handed it to her. "That happens too often, you know, a brutal man seeking revenge. We had a young woman killed a few weeks ago for the same thing."

Cappie felt sick to her stomach.

Bentley put his arm around her. "Nobody's killing you," he said.

She leaned her head against him. "Thanks."

They took the extra X-ray in its envelope, paid the bill and left the emergency room, hand-in-hand.

"Do you want to go and see Kell tonight?" Bentley asked.

She shook her head, wincing, because it hurt. "I'm too sick. I just want to lie down." She looked up. "Will you go with me to Marquez's office in the morning?"

"You'd better believe I will."

"Thanks."

His arm contracted around her. "Not necessary. Let's get you back to your room. It's been a long day."

"Tell me about it," she mused. At least, she thought, her ordeal was over for the moment. Tomorrow she could worry about the details, including telling poor Kell what had happened.

CHAPTER TEN

CAPPIE GROANED AT her own reflection in the hotel mirror when she climbed out of bed the next morning. One whole side of her face was a brilliant purple, and swollen to boot.

"You okay in there?"

She smiled. Bentley had insisted on sleeping on the sofa in the suite, just in case. Rourke and Chet were already up and packing their things for the trip back to Jacobsville. Cappie and Bentley were staying for another day or two, while she gave statements to the police and looked after Kell.

"I think so," she said. "I just can't bear to look at myself."

"I'll bet Chet knows exactly how that feels!" Rourke called from the doorway of the room he and Chet had shared.

"Will you shut up?" Chet muttered.

"Now, that's a good example of how much work your diplomatic skills need," Rourke admonished.

"I'm through trying to be diplomatic," Chet said curtly. "I'm going back to the company and let them send me off on lone assignments, all by myself. Anywhere I don't have to try to be nice to people!"

"Yes, and you can take those smokes with you,"

Rourke added. "Having to share a room with you is punishment enough for any lawbreaker! Man, you reek!"

"Cigarette smoke is beneficial," Chet told him.

"It is not!"

"If your quarry smokes, you can smell him from five hundred meters," Chet returned, and he actually smiled.

Rourke's jaw dropped. He'd never seen the other man smile.

Chet gave him a haughty, arrogant stare, picked up his bag and walked out. "Hope things go well for you, Miss Drake," he said as she came out of her room wrapped in a thick robe. He winced. "It will look much better in a week or so," he assured her.

She tried to smile, but it hurt too much. "Thanks for helping keep me alive, Chet."

"My pleasure. See you back at Scott's place, Rourke."

"You wait for me—I'm not paying cab fare back to Jacobsville all alone," Rourke said. He picked up his own bag, shook hands with Bentley and bent to kiss Cappie's undamaged cheek. "If he ever walks out on you, just get word to me, and I'll bring him back to you in a net," he said in a stage whisper.

"Thanks, Rourke. But I don't think that will ever happen."

Bentley smiled. "I can guarantee it won't."

"Cheers, then. See you."

They waved the two men off. Bentley studied her poor, damaged face warily. "I wish there had been some way to prevent that."

"Me, too. But it's insurance. Let's get breakfast. Then we can go down to Detective Marquez's office and start giving statements. Later," she added reluctantly, "we can go see Kell and try not to upset him too much when we tell him what happened."

"Suits me."

DETECTIVE MARQUEZ HAD a small office in a big department. It was noisy and people seemed to come and go constantly. The phones rang off the hook.

"This looks like those crime shows on television," Cappie remarked.

Marquez chuckled. "It's much worse. You can't get five minutes' peace to type up a report." He got up to retrieve the report he'd typed at the computer as he questioned her. He took it out of the printer tray and handed it to her. "Check over that, if you will, and see if I've got it right." He pulled out another one. "This one's for you, Dr. Rydel." He handed the vet another sheet of paper.

They went over their statements, made a couple of corrections. Marquez inserted the corrections and printed the statements out again. They signed them.

"I'll bet Frank's foaming at the mouth," Cappie mused.

"He really is, but this time he's not going to fool any jury into thinking he's the injured party," Marquez assured her.

"I'll bet that judge is feeling bad about now," Bentley muttered.

"The judge did feel bad," Marquez agreed. "So did the district attorney, especially after Frank and his cohorts beat up your brother. The whole justice system here in San Antonio went into overdrive to catch the perp."

"Really?" Cappie asked, surprised.

"Really. The assistant district attorney who prose-cuted your case was in the vanguard."

"Somebody needs to take him out for a big steak dinner," Cappie commented.

"I'm taking him out for one, at my mother's café in Jacobsville," he chuckled. "Of course, he's eligible and so is my mother."

"I see wheels turning in your head," Cappie said.

He grinned. "Always," Marquez said easily. "He and I have worked several cases together. I like him."

"Me, too," Cappie said. She hesitated. "Frank won't get out until the trial, will he?"

Marquez shook his head. "The assistant D.A. is hav-ing the bond set in the six-figure range. I don't think Frank knows a bail bondsman who'll take a chance on him for that amount of money."

"Let's hope not," Bentley said.

Marquez gave him a keen glance. "He'll probably stay in jail voluntarily, to keep from having you come at him again. That was some tackle."

Bentley shrugged. "I used to play football in college."

"I played soccer. Don't get to do much tackling, but I can knock a ball half a block with my head."

"Is that why it looks that way?" a familiar voice drawled from the cubicle doorway.

"Kilraven," Marquez grumbled, "will you stop stalk-ing me?"

"I'm not stalking you," the tall man said easily. "I'm just waiting for you to answer my ten phone calls, six voice mails and twenty e-mails." He glowered at the younger man.

Marquez held up his hands. "Okay. Just let me finish up with Miss Drake and Dr. Rydel and I'll be right with you. Honest."

"No hurry," Kilraven said, smiling. "I'll be standing right out here, intimidating lawbreakers."

"Thanks for looking out for Kell," Cappie told him.

"What are friends for?" he asked.

"How would you know, Kilraven, you don't have any friends," a passing detective drawled.

"I have lots of friends!"

"Oh, yeah? Name one."

"Marquez!"

"He's your friend?" the detective asked Marquez, sticking his head into the cubicle.

"He is not," Marquez said without looking up as he glanced over the statements one last time.

"I am so," Kilraven said in a surly tone.

Marquez gave him a speaking glance.

Kilraven moved back out of the cubicle, muttering to himself in some foreign language.

"I know what that means in Arabic," Marquez called after him. "Your brother speaks Farsi fluently and he taught me what those words mean!"

A rolling barrage in yet another language came lilting into the cubicle.

"What's that?" Marquez asked.

Kilraven poked his head in and grinned. "Lakota. And Jon can't teach you that—he doesn't speak it. Ha!"

He left.

Marquez grimaced.

"He's really very nice," Cappie said.

Marquez leaned toward her. "He is, but I'm not saying it out loud." His expression became somber. "I'm working on a cold case with him and another detective," he said quietly. "It involves him. He's impatient, because we got a new lead."

Bentley nodded quietly. "I know about that one. One of my vet techs is married to the best friend of our local sheriff. I hear most of what's going on."

"Tragic case," Marquez agreed. "But hopefully we're going to crack it."

Bentley got to his feet, tugging Cappie up with him. He winced as she turned toward him.

"I appreciate the copies of those X-rays," Marquez added, walking out with them. "Everything we can throw against Bartlett will help put him away."

"He'd better hope he never gets out," Cappie said. "My brother will be waiting for him if he does."

Marquez chuckled. "If it hadn't been three to one against, and your brother hadn't been in a wheelchair, I'd probably be helping defend him on homicide charges."

"No doubt," Bentley replied somberly.

Cappie frowned. "Is there a conversation going on that I don't know anything about?" she asked.

Bentley and Marquez exchanged covert glances. "Just commenting on your brother's justifiable anger," Bentley told her easily. He caught her fingers in his. "Let's go see your brother and tell him he's about to have a new brother-in-law."

KELL WAS A little better, until he saw Cappie's face. He swore brilliantly.

"I know how you feel," Bentley said. "But for what

it's worth, Bartlett probably looks much worse. It took two detectives to pull me off him."

Kell brightened. "Good man." He winced at his sister's face, though. "I'm so sorry."

"I'll heal." She didn't mention the potential surgery she might have to undergo. There was no need to worry him even more. "Detective Marquez said that Frank won't get out for a long time. He expects one of Frank's accomplices to turn state's evidence. If they charge him with battery on both of us, he'll do some serious time."

"I expected Hayes Carson to show up here and ask me for a statement for what Frank did to me in Comanche Wells," he murmured.

"I imagine he's giving you time to get over the surgery," Cappie said.

"Probably so."

"Have you spoken to the surgeon yet?" Cappie asked.

He smiled. "Yes. He's optimistic, especially since I have feeling in my legs now."

"At least something good may come out of all this misery," she said gently.

Kell was looking at Bentley. "Just before we came up here to the hospital, she said she didn't want to live in a town that also contained you. You told me part of the story, but not any more than you had to. She was going to explain, then they knocked me out with a shot. Care to comment?"

"I made a stupid decision," Bentley said with a sigh. "I expect to be apologizing for it for the rest of my life. But she's going to marry me anyway." He gave her a tender smile, which she returned. "I can eat crow at every meal, for however long it takes."

"I stopped being mad at you while you were beating the stuffing out of Frank Bartlett," she pointed out.

He glanced at his bruised, swollen knuckles. "I'll have permanent mementoes of the occasion, I expect."

"You're getting married?" Kell asked.

"Yes," Cappie said. She touched her face gingerly. "Not until the swelling goes down, though."

"And not until I'm able to walk down the aisle and give you away," Kell interjected.

Bentley pursed his lips. "I could get Chet and Rourke to carry you down the aisle to give her away," he offered.

"The last wedding Chet went to, he spent the night in jail for inciting a riot," Kell pointed out.

Cappie frowned. "Exactly how well do you know Chet and Rourke?" she asked pointedly.

He groaned. "Oh. The pain. I need to rest. I really can't talk anymore right now."

Cappie's eyes narrowed on the drip catheter. "Doesn't that thing automatically inject painkiller into the drip while you're post-surgical?" she asked.

Kell kept his eyes closed. "I don't know. I feel terrible. You have to leave now." He opened one eye. "You can come back later, when I'll be much better as long as you don't ask potentially embarrassing questions. If you do, I may have a relapse."

"All right," Cappie sighed.

He brightened. "Be good and I'll tell you how to get past the Hunters in *ODST*."

"Cash told you?" she asked.

He chuckled and winced, because moving hurt. "Not without a bribe."

"What sort of bribe?"

"Remember that old Bette Davis movie, where she murders her lover and then has to blackmail the man's widow over a letter that could convict her?" he asked.

"Yes. It's called *The Letter*…it's one of my favorite…" She stopped. "You didn't!"

"Hey, it's not as if you watch it that much," Kell protested.

"Kell!"

"Do you want to get past the Hunters, or don't you?" he asked.

She sighed. "I guess I can always find another copy of it somewhere."

"That's a nice sister," Kell said.

"If I buy you another one," Bentley interrupted, "will you tell *me* how to get past the Hunters?" he asked her.

They all laughed.

Two weeks later, Kell was walking down the hall, wobbling a little, in his pajamas and robe while Cappie held him up. The swelling in her cheek had gone down, but it still had a yellowish tinge to it. Kell was much better. He was learning how to walk all over again, courtesy of the rehab department in the Jacobsville hospital.

"This is slow," he muttered.

"It is not," Bentley retorted, and the sound of gunfire came from the television in the living room. "Ha! That's one Hunter down!"

"Rub it in," she called. "It wasn't even your favorite movie you had to sacrifice to learn how to do that!"

"I bought you a new one. It's in the DVD player," he called back.

"Fat lot of good it's doing me, since that game console hasn't been off for five minutes all day," she muttered.

"Stop picking on my future brother-in-law," Kell chided. "It isn't every man who can make tortillas from scratch."

"He only did it to butter you up," she told him.

"It worked. When's the wedding, again?"

"Three weeks from now. Micah Steele says you'll be able to manage the church aisle with just a cane by then. And we can hope there won't be a large animal emergency anywhere in the county during the ceremony!" she raised her voice.

"I'm borrowing a vet from San Antonio to cover the practice for me until we're back from our honeymoon in Cancún," he said. They'd picked the exotic spot because it had been the dream of Cappie's life to see Chichen Itza, the Mayan ruin.

"I hope the vet knows he's covering for you," she said.

He chuckled. "He does."

"The guest list just keeps growing," Cappie sighed. "I've already sent out fifty invitations."

"Did you put Marquez and the assistant D.A. on the list?"

"Yes," she said. "And Rourke and Chet, too."

Kell groaned.

"Chet won't start any riots. I'll have a talk with him," she promised. "They took good care of me in San Antonio," she added.

"Yes, but I was the one who took down Frank," Bentley called. "Can you believe that little weasel tried to sue me for assault?" he added huffily.

"He didn't get as far as first base," Kell assured him. "Blake Kemp had a long talk with his attorney."

"Why would our D.A. be talking to a defense attorney in San Antonio?" Cappie wanted to know.

"Because the defense attorney wasn't aware of the familial connections of the defendant's assailant," Bentley murmured. "Ha! There went another Hunter!" he exclaimed.

Cappie blinked. "Familial connections…?"

Kell leaned down to her ear. "Don't ask. The upshot is that the lawsuit is going nowhere. Fast."

Cappie was still staring at Bentley. "What familial connections?" she persisted.

"The governor is my first cousin. Ha! Another one!"

"Our governor?" she exclaimed.

"We only have one. This game is great!"

Cappie sighed. She looked up at her handsome big brother. "The game is not going with us on our honeymoon," she said firmly.

Bentley gave her a roguish glance. "Not even if I tell you how to get past the Hunters?"

"Well, in that case, maybe I could reconsider," she chuckled.

KELL DID MAKE it down the aisle with a cane. The little country church in Comanche Wells was filled to capacity. Only people they knew got an invitation, but there was still standing room only. A good many of the guests were in uniform, either military or law enforcement, on one side of the church, while a number of Eb

Scott's guys were seated across the aisle from them. Covert glares were exchanged. Down the center aisle marched Cappie in her lovely white gown with what seemed acres of lace and a pretty fingertip veil. She was carrying a bouquet of yellow roses and wearing a smile that went from ear to ear.

She held on to Kell's arm tightly, so proud of his progress that she beamed with happiness. He was already talking about a new job working for Eb Scott at his anti-terrorism school. She was really curious about how well her brother seemed to know any number of Eb's employees, but she hadn't made any comments. She was still indebted to Eb for lending her Chet and Rourke, who were seated together in the front of the church. Around them were her former and present co-workers, including Keely and Boone Sinclair. Boone's sister, Winnie, was being watched with real intensity by Kilraven, dressed in an expensive suit in the row behind her.

She and Kell stopped at the altar, where he gave her hand to Bentley. He was beaming, too, so handsome that Cappie just sighed, looking up at him with gray eyes that adored him.

The wedding service was brief, but poignant. Bentley lifted the veil and bent to kiss her with such tenderness that she had to fight tears.

Then he led her down the aisle to the back of the church. The people who hadn't been able to squeeze into the church were waiting outside with what seemed like buckets of rice and confetti. They were totally drenched in both as they ran to the white limousine that was to take them to the town civic center, for the reception.

THEY FED EACH other cake, posed for wedding pictures and generally had a wonderful time. There was a live band and they danced together to a slow, romantic tune, which lasted for all of two minutes before Cash Grier, with his beautiful wife, Tippy, signaled to the band leader.

There were grins, a fanfare and then a furious and delicious rendition of the classic tune "Brazil." But Cash didn't start dancing, as everyone expected him to. He glanced toward Bentley with a chuckle and a flourish.

Bentley gave Cappie a wicked look. "Shall we?"

"But, Bentley, you can't dance…can you?" she exclaimed.

"I couldn't," he confessed, taking her onto the dance floor. "But Cash gave me lessons. Okay. One, two… three!"

He twirled her around in the most professional sort of way, in a mixture of samba, cha-cha and mambo that she followed with consummate ease while people on the sidelines began to clap.

"You're terrific!" Cappie panted.

"So are you, gorgeous," he chuckled. "Are we good, or what?"

ABOUT A DAY and a half later, they repeated the same exact dialog to each other, but for a totally different reason.

Lying exhausted and bathed in sweat in a huge double bed in a beachfront hotel in Cancún, they could barely move.

"And I thought you danced well!" she laughed. "You're just amazing!"

"Why, thank you," he drawled, grinning. "May I return the compliment?"

"Yes, well, I think I'm a quick study," she sighed.

"Not so nervous anymore, I notice," he murmured.

She laughed. She was almost a basket case of nerves when they checked into the hotel that afternoon. She loved Bentley, but she had no real idea of what it was going to be like when they were alone together. But he was understanding, patient and gentle as he cradled her in his arms in a big easy chair and fed her shrimp from a big platter of seafood that room service had brought up. Of course, he'd also fed her champagne in increasing amounts, until she was so relaxed that nothing he suggested seemed to disturb her.

Slow, tender kisses grew slower and more insistent. He coaxed her out of her clothing with such ease that she barely noticed until she felt the cool air on her skin. Even then, the way he was touching her was so electrifying that her only conscious thought was to see how much closer to him she could get. There was one little flash of pain, easily forgotten as he kissed her with delicate sensuality and lifted her back into the fiery hunger the hesitation had briefly interrupted. Her mind had gone into eclipse while her body demanded and pleaded for an end to the tension which he built in her so effortlessly. Finally, finally, she fell over the edge of it into a blazing heat of fulfillment that exceeded her wildest expectations.

"And I used to think you were reserved!" she laughed.

"Only when I'm wearing a white lab coat," he murmured drowsily. He opened his eyes, rolled over and studied her pretty pink nudity with lazy appreciation. "Would you like me to get up and put on a lab coat, and be reserved?"

"I would not," she retorted, pulling him back down. She kissed him intensely. "I'd like you to be unreserved all over again, starting right now."

He slid over her, his hair-roughened chest grazing the hard tips of her pretty breasts. "I can't think of anything I'd enjoy more, Mrs. Rydel."

She would have answered him back, but she was much too involved for speech.

THEY WANDERED THROUGH the ruins at Chichen Itza hand in hand, fascinated as they strolled around the wide plain that contained the pyramidal Castillo and the other buildings that made up the Mayan complex.

"It must have looked much different when it was occupied, all those hundreds of years ago," Cappie mused, her eyes everywhere.

"There were probably even more people," he chuckled, glancing at the crowds of tourists that abounded, even this time of year. He handed her his huge water bottle and waited for her to take a sip before he followed suit. The bus trip here was hours long, and it would be after dark before they got back to their hotel. It was something they'd both wanted to see.

"It's a lot different, being here, than seeing it on television," she remarked.

"Most things are," he replied. "Until they can discover a way to let you touch and smell distant ruins, it won't be as much fun to watch it on a small screen."

She stopped and looked up at him with her heart in

her gray eyes. "I never thought being married would be so much fun."

He hugged her close. "And we're only at the beginning of our marriage," he agreed, his blue eyes soft as they scanned her face. "I hope we have a hundred years ahead of us."

"Me, too." She pressed into his arms and closed her eyes. "Me, too, Bentley."

SHE WENT BACK to work for him in the practice. She'd argued that if Keely, who was happily married and well-off, could keep working, she could, too. He hadn't protested too much. It delighted him to be able to see her all day long.

"Don't you want a cat?" Keely coaxed the week after they came back from their honeymoon. "I've got six little white kittens that Grace Grier asked me to find homes for, and I've only placed four of them."

Cappie laughed. "I'd love one."

"Me, too," Bentley agreed, poking his head around the corner. "Did Cy Parks call back about that new bull of his that got cut on the barbed wire?"

"He did. He said if you'd drop by on your way home, he and Lisa would feed you both," Keely chuckled. "They're having homemade chili and corn bread."

"My favorite," Bentley said.

"Mine, too," Cappie replied almost at the same time as Bentley.

"He said you could bring Kell along," the other girl added.

"Kell's gone off somewhere with Rourke and Chet," Cappie sighed. "No telling where. They vanish for days

at a time, and nobody knows where. He's my own
brother. You'd think he could trust me."

"And me," Bentley added.

"I'm sure he has his reasons," Cappie said. "Whatever they are."

"It's bound to be something covert and dangerous
and exciting," Keely said out loud.

"More than likely, they're helping Detective Marquez
stake out a nightclub or something," Bentley chuckled.
"He did mention that he needed a couple of willing volunteers for a special project he and that assistant district
attorney are working on."

"We owe that district attorney," Cappie agreed. "He
talked Frank's accomplices into testifying against him
for reduced sentences. He says Frank won't get out until
his hair turns gray. Made my day," she added.

"Mine, too," Bentley assured her. "Okay, people,
back to work."

"Yes, sir, Dr. Rydel, sir," Cappie said, saluting him.

He made a face at her. Then he grinned.

She grinned back, turning back to her coworker behind the counter. "Who's next, Keely?"

"Mrs. Anderson and her Chihuahua. Got the chart
right here."

Cappie took it from her and went out into the waiting
room, which was full. Her eyes were bright with happiness as she exchanged a glance with her handsome
husband, just before he went into the back to examine
a surgical patient. She felt as if she could walk on air.

"Okay, Mrs. Anderson," she told an elderly little
woman with a smile. "If you'll bring Tweedle on back,
we'll get Dr. Rydel to take a look at his bruised paw."

"He's a very nice doctor," the little woman told Cappie. "You're a lucky young woman!"

"Yes, you are!" Bentley called from the back. "Not every woman gets a husband who's as accomplished and modest as I am! You should be proud of yourself!"

"I am, dear, and how do you like your potatoes… burned or charbroiled?"

There was a pause. "Not every husband gets a wife as accomplished and modest as you are, dear!" he called back.

She chuckled. "Now that will get you a nice scalloped potato dish and a beautifully cooked pot roast!"

An amused Mrs. Anderson wiggled her eyebrows at Cappie as she followed her to a treatment room. Cappie just grinned.

* * * * *

RICK

CHAPTER ONE

"WE COULD LOSE the case," San Antonio Detective Sergeant Rick Marquez muttered as he glared at one of the newest detectives on his squad.

"I'm really sorry," Gwendolyn Cassaway said, wincing. "I tripped. It was an accident."

He stared at her through narrowed dark eyes, his sensual lips compressed. "You tripped because you're nearsighted and you won't wear glasses." Personally, he didn't think the lack of them did anything for her, if vanity was the issue. She had a pleasant face, and an exquisite complexion, but she was no raving beauty. Her finest feature was her wealth of thick platinum-blond hair that she wore in a high bun on top of her head. She never wore it down.

"Glasses get in my way and I can't ever get them clean enough," she muttered. "That coating just causes smears unless you use the proper cleaning materials. And I can't ever find them," she said defensively.

He drew in a long, exasperated breath and perched on the edge of the desk in his office. In the posture, his .45 Colt ACP in its distinctive leather holster was displayed next to his badge on his belt. So were his powerful legs, and to their best advantage. He was tall and muscular, without it being obvious. He had a light olive complexion and thick long black hair that he wore in a ponytail. He was very attractive, but he couldn't ever seem to wind up with a serious girlfriend. Women found him useful as a sympathetic shoulder to cry on over their true loves. One woman refused to date him when she realized that he wore his pistol even off duty. He'd tried to explain that it was a necessary thing, but it hadn't given him any points with her. He went to the opera, which he loved, all alone. He went everywhere alone. He was almost thirty-one, and lonelier than ever. It made him irritable.

And here was Gwen making it all worse, messing up his crime scene, threatening the delicate chain of evidence that could lead to a conviction in a complex murder.

A college freshman, pretty and blonde, had been brutally assaulted and killed. They had no suspects and trace evidence was very sketchy already. Gwen had almost contaminated the scene by stepping too close to a blood smear.

He was not in a good mood. He was hungry. He was going to be late for lunch, because he had to chew her out. If he didn't, the lieutenant surely would, and Cal Hollister was even meaner than Marquez.

"You could also lose your job," Marquez pointed out. "You're new in the department."

She grimaced. "I know." She shrugged. "I guess I could go back to the Atlanta P.D. if I had to," she said with grim resignation. She looked at him with pale green eyes that were almost translucent. He'd never seen eyes that color.

"You just have to be more careful, Cassaway," he cautioned.

"Yes, sir. I'll do my best."

He tried not to look at the T-shirt she was wearing under a lightweight denim jacket with her jeans. It was unseasonably warm for November but a jacket felt good against the morning chill.

On her T-shirt was a picture of a little green alien, the sort sold in novelty shops, with a legend that read, Have You Seen My Spaceship? He averted his eyes and tried not to grin.

She tugged her jacket closer. "Sorry. But they don't have any regulations against T-shirts here, do they?"

"If the lieutenant sees that one, you'll find out," he said.

She sighed. "I'll try to conform. It's just that I come from a very weird family. My mother worked for the FBI. My father was, uh, in the military. My brother is…" She hesitated and swallowed. "My brother *was* in military intelligence."

He frowned. "Deceased?"

She nodded. She still couldn't talk about it. The pain was too fresh.

"Sorry," he said stiffly.

She shifted. "Larry died very bravely during a covert ops mission in the Middle East. But he was my only sibling. It's hard to talk about."

"I can understand that." He stood up, glancing at the military watch he wore on his left wrist. "Time for lunch."

"Oh, I have other plans…" she began quickly.

He glared at her. "It was a remark, not an invitation. I don't date colleagues," he said very curtly.

She blushed all the way down to her throat. She swallowed and stood taller. "Sorry. I was... I meant...that is..."

He waved the excuses away. "We'll talk about this some more later. Meanwhile, please do something about your vision. You can't investigate a crime scene you can't see!"

She nodded. "Yes, sir. Absolutely."

He opened the door and let her go out first, noticing absently that her head only came up to his shoulder and that she smelled like spring roses, the pink ones that grew in his mother's garden down in Jacobsville. It was an elusive, very faint fragrance. He approved. Some women who worked in the office seemed to bathe in perfume and always had headaches and allergies and never seemed to think about the connection. Once, a fellow detective had had an almost-fatal asthma attack after a clerical worker stood near him wearing what smelled like an entire bottle of perfume.

Gwendolyn stopped suddenly and he plowed into her, his hands sweeping out to grasp her shoulders and steady her before she fell from his momentum.

"Oh, sorry!" she exclaimed, and felt a thrill of pleasure at the warm strength of the big hands holding her so gently.

He removed them at once. "What is it?"

She had to force her mind to work. Detective Sergeant Marquez was very sexy and she'd been drawn to him since her first sight of him several weeks before. "I meant to ask if you wanted me to check with Alice

Fowler over at the crime lab about the digital camera we found in the murdered woman's apartment. By now, she might have something on the trace evidence."

"Good idea. You do that."

"I'll swing past there on my way back to the office after lunch," she promised, and beamed, because it was a big case and he was letting her contribute to solving it. "Thanks."

He nodded, his mind already on the wonderful beef Stroganoff he was going to order at the nearby café where he usually had lunch. He'd been looking forward to it all week. It was Friday and he could splurge.

Tomorrow was his day off. He was going to spend it helping his mother, Barbara, process and can a bushel of hothouse tomatoes she'd been given by an organic gardener with a greenhouse. She owned Barbara's Café in Jacobsville, and she liked to use her organic vegetables and herbs in the meals she prepared for her clients. They would add to the store of canned summer tomatoes that she'd already processed earlier in the year.

He owed her a lot. He'd been orphaned in junior high school and Barbara Ferguson, who'd just lost her husband in an accident, and suffered a miscarriage, had taken him in. His mother had once worked for Barbara at the café just briefly. Then his parents—well, his mother and stepfather—had died in a wreck, leaving a single, lonely child all on his own. Rick had been a terrible teen, always in trouble, bad-tempered and moody. He'd been afraid when he lost his mother. He had no other living relatives of whom he was aware, and no place to go. Barbara had stepped in and given him a home. He loved her no less than he'd loved his real mother, and he was quite protective of her. He never spoke of his stepfather. He tried not to remember him at all.

Barbara wanted him to marry and settle down and have a family. She harped on it all the time. She even introduced him to single women. Nothing helped. He seemed to be an eternally on-sale item in the matrimonial market that everybody bypassed for the fancier merchandise. He laughed shortly to himself at the thought.

Gwen watched him leave and wondered why he'd laughed. She was embarrassed that she'd thought he was asking her to lunch. He didn't seem to have a girlfriend and everybody joked about his nonexistent love life. But he wasn't attracted to Gwen in that way. It didn't matter. No man had ever liked her, really. She was everybody's confidante, the good girl who could give advice about how to please other women with small gifts and entertainments. But she was never asked out for herself.

She knew she wasn't pretty. She was always passed over for the flashy women, the assertive women, the powerful women. The women who didn't think sex before marriage was a sin. She'd had a man double over laughing when she'd told him that, after he expected a night in bed in return for a nice meal and the theater. Then he'd become angry, having spent so much money on her with nothing to show for it. The experience had soured her.

"Don Quixote," she murmured to herself. "I'm Don Quixote."

"Wrong sex," Detective Sergeant Gail Rogers said as she paused beside the newcomer. Rogers was the mother of some very wealthy ranchers in Comanche Wells, but she kept her job and her own income. She was an amazing peace officer. Gwen admired her tremendously. "And what's that all about?" she asked.

Gwen sighed, glancing around to make sure they weren't being overheard. "I won't give out on dates," she whispered. "So men think I'm insane." She shrugged. "I'm Don Quixote, trying to restore morality and idealism to a decadent world."

Rogers didn't laugh. She smiled, very kindly. "He was noble, in his way. An idealist with a dream."

"He was nutty as a fruitcake." Gwen sighed.

"Yes, but he made everyone around him feel of worth, like the prostitute whom he idealized as a great lady for whom he quested," came the surprising reply. "He gave dreams to people who had given them up for harsh reality. He was adored by them."

Gwen laughed. "Yes, I suppose he wasn't so bad at that."

"People should have ideals, even if they get laughed at," Rogers added. "You stick to your guns. Every society has its outcasts." She leaned down. "Nobody who conformed to the rigid culture of any society ever made history."

Gwen brightened. "That's true." Then she added, "You've lived through a lot. You got shot," Gwen recalled hearing.

"I did. It was worthwhile, though. We broke a cold case wide-open and caught the murderer."

"I heard. That was some story."

Rogers smiled. "Indeed it was. Rick Marquez got blindsided and left for dead by the same scoundrels who shot me. But we both survived." She frowned. "What's wrong? Marquez giving you a hard time?"

"It's my own fault," Gwen confided. "I can't wear contacts and I hate glasses. I tripped in a crime scene and came close to contaminating some evidence." She grimaced. "It's a murder case, too, that college freshman they found dead in her apartment last night. The defense will have a field day with that when the perp is caught and brought to trial. And it will be my fault. I just got chewed out for it. I should have, too," she said quickly, because she didn't want Rogers to think Marquez was being unfair.

Rogers's dark eyes searched hers. "You like your sergeant, don't you?"

"I respect him," Gwen said, and then flushed helplessly.

Rogers studied her warmly. "He's a nice man," she said. "He does have a temper and he does take too many chances. But you'll get used to his moods."

"I'm working on that." Gwen chuckled.

"How did you like Atlanta?" Rogers asked conversationally as they headed for the exit.

"Excuse me?" Gwen said absently.

"Atlanta P.D. Where you were working."

"Oh. Oh!" Gwen had to think quickly. "It was nice. I liked the department. But I wanted a change, and I've always wanted to see Texas."

"I see."

No, she didn't, Gwen thought, and thank goodness for that. Gwen was keeping secrets that she didn't dare divulge. She changed the subject as they walked together to the parking lot to their respective vehicles.

Lunch was a salad with dressing on the side, and half a grilled cheese sandwich. Dessert, and her drink, was a cappuccino. She loved the expensive coffee and could only afford it one day a week, on Fridays. She ate an inexpensive lunch so that she could have her coffee.

She sipped it with her eyes closed, smiling. It had an aroma that evoked Italy, a little sidewalk café in Rome with the ruins visible in the distance...

She opened her eyes at once and looked around, as if someone could see the thoughts in her head. She must be very careful not to mention that memory, or other similar ones, in regular conversation. She was a budding junior detective. She had to remember that. It wouldn't do to let anything slip at this crucial moment.

That thought led to thoughts of Detective Marquez and what would be a traumatic revelation for him when the time came for disclosure. Meanwhile, her orders were to observe him, keep her head down and try to discover how much he, or his adoptive mother, knew about his true background. She couldn't say anything. Not yet.

She finished her coffee, paid for her meal and walked out onto the chilly streets. So funny, she thought, the way the weather ran in cycles. It had been unseasonably cold throughout the South during the spring then came summer and blazing, unrelenting heat with drought and wildfires and cattle dying in droves. Now it was November and still unseasonably warm, but some weather experts said snow might come soon.

The weather was nuts. There had been epic drought throughout the whole southern tier of America, from Arizona to Florida, and there had been horrible wildfires in the southwestern states. Triple-digit temperatures had gone all summer in south Texas. There had been horrible flooding on the Mississippi River due to the large snowmelt, from last winter's unusually deep snows up north.

Now it was November and Gwen was actually sweating long before she reached her car, although it had been chilly this morning. She took off her jacket. At least the car had air-conditioning, and she was turning it on, even if it was technically almost winter. Idly, she wondered how people had lived in this heat before air-conditioning was invented. It couldn't have been an easy life, especially since most Texans of the early twentieth century had worked on the land. Imagine, having to herd and brand cattle in this sort of heat, much less plow and plant!

Gwen got into her car and drove by the crime lab to see if Alice had found anything on that digital camera. In fact, she had. There were a lot of photos of people who were probably friends—Gwen could use face recognition software to identify them, hopefully—and there was one odd-looking man standing a little distance behind a couple who was smiling into the camera against the background of the apartment complex where the victim had lived. That was interesting and suspicious. She'd have to check that man out. He didn't look as if he belonged in such a setting. It was a mid-range apartment complex, and the man was dingy and ill kempt and staring a little too intently. She drove back to her precinct.

Her mind was still on Marquez, on what she knew, and he didn't. She hoped he wasn't going to have too hard a time with his true history, when the truth came out.

BARBARA GLARED AT her son. "Can't you just peel the tomato, sweetie, without taking out most of it except the core?"

He grimaced. "Sorry," he said, wielding the paring knife with more care as he went to work on what looked like a bushel of tomatoes, a gift from an organic gardener with a hothouse, that his mother was canning in her kitchen at home. Canning jars simmered in a huge tub of water, getting ready to be filled with fragrant tomato slices and then processed in the big pressure cooker. He glared at it.

"I hate those things," he muttered. "Even the safest ones are dangerous."

"Baloney," she said inelegantly. "Give me those."

She took the bowl of tomatoes and dunked them into a pot of boiling water. She left them there for a couple of minutes and fished them out in a colander. She put them in the sink in front of Rick. "There. Now they'll skin. I keep telling you this is a more efficient way than trying to cut the skins off. But you don't listen, my dear."

"I like skinning them," he said with a dark-eyed smile in her direction. "It's an outlet for my frustrations."

"Oh?" She didn't look at him, deliberately. "What sort of frustrations?"

"There's this new woman at work," he said grimly.

"Gwen." She nodded.

He dropped the knife, picked it back up and stared at her.

"You talk about her all the time."

"I do?" It was news to him. He didn't realize that.

She nodded as she skinned tomatoes. "She trips over

things that she doesn't see, she messes up crime scenes, she spills coffee, she can't find her cell phone…" She glanced at him. He was still standing there, with the knife poised over a tomato. "Get busy, there, those tomatoes won't peel themselves."

He groaned.

"Just think how nice they'll taste in one of my beef stew recipes," she coaxed. "Go on, peel."

"Why can't we just get one of those things that sucks the air out of bags and freeze them instead?"

"What if we have a major power outage that lasts for days and days?" she returned.

He thought for a minute. "I'll go buy twenty bags of ice and several of those foam coolers."

She laughed. "Yes, but we can't tell how the power grid is going to cope if we have one of those massive CMEs like the Carrington Event in 1859."

He blinked. "Excuse me?"

"There was a massive coronal mass ejection in 1859 called the Carrington Event," she explained. "When it hit earth, all the electrics on the planet went crazy. Telegraph lines burned up and telegraph units caught fire." She glanced at him. "There wasn't much electricity back in those days—it was in its infancy. But imagine if such a thing happened today, with our dependence on electricity. Everything is connected to the grid these days, banks, communications corporations, pharmacies, government, military and the list goes on and on. Even our water and power are controlled by computers. Just imagine if we had no way to access our computers."

He whistled. "I was in the grocery store one day when the computers went offline. They couldn't process credit cards. Most people had to leave. I had enough cash for bread and milk. Then another time the computers in the pharmacy went down, when you had to have those antibiotics for the sinus infection last winter. I had to come home and get the checkbook and go back. People with credit cards had real problems."

"See?" She went back to her tomatoes.

"I suppose it would be a pretty bad thing. Is it going to happen, you think?"

"Someday, certainly. The sun has eleven year cycles, you know, with a solar minimum and a solar maximum. The next solar maximum, some scientists say, is in 2012. If we're going to get hit, that would have my vote for the timeline."

"Twenty-twelve," he groaned, rolling his eyes. "We had this guy come in the office and tell us we needed to put out a flyer."

"What about?"

"The fact that the world is ending in 2012 and we have to have tin-foil hats to protect us from electromagnetic pulses."

"Ah. EMPs," she said knowledgeably. "Actually, I think you'd have to be in a modified and greatly enlarged version of a Leiden jar to be fully protected. So would any computer equipment you wanted to save." She glanced at him. "They're developing weapons like that, you know," she added. "All it would take is one nicely placed EMP and our military computers would go down like tenpins."

He put down the knife. "Where do you learn all this stuff?" he asked, exasperated.

"On the internet." She pulled an iPod out of her

pocket and showed it to him. "I have Wi-Fi in the house, you know. I just connect to all the appropriate websites." She checked her bookmarks. "I have one for space weather, three radars for terrestrial weather and about ten covert sites that tell you all the stuff the government won't tell you…"

"My mother, the conspiracy theorist," he moaned.

"You won't hear this stuff on the national news," she said smartly. "The mainstream media is controlled by three major corporations. They decide what you'll get to hear. And mostly it's what entertainer got drunk, what television show is getting the ratings and what politician is patting himself on the back or running for reelection. In my day—" she warmed to her theme "—we had real news on television. It was local and we had real reporters out gathering it. Like the Jacobsville paper still does," she added.

"I know about the Jacobsville paper," he said with a sigh. "We hear that Cash Grier spends most of his time trying to protect the owner from getting assassinated. She knows all the drug distribution points and the drug lords by name, and she's printing them." He shook his head. "She's going to be another statistic one day. They've killed plenty of newspaper publishers and reporters over the border for less. She's rocking the boat."

"Somebody needs to rock it," Barbara muttered as she peeled another tomato skin off and tossed it into a green bag to be used for mulch in her garden. She never wasted any organic refuse. "People are dying so that another generation can become addicted to drugs."

"I can't argue that point," he said. "The problem is that nothing law enforcement is doing is making much of a dent in drug trafficking. If there's a market, there's going to be a supply. That's just the way things are."

"They say Hayes Carson actually talked to Minette Raynor about it."

That was real news. Minette owned the *Jacobsville Times*. She had two stepsiblings, Shane, who was twelve, and Julie, who was six. She'd loved her stepmother very much. Her stepmother and her father had died within weeks of each other, leaving a grieving Minette with two little children to raise, a newspaper to run and a ranch to manage. She had a manager to handle the ranch, and her great-aunt Sarah lived with her and took care of the kids after school so that Minette could keep working. Minette was twenty-five now and unmarried. She and Hayes Carson didn't get along. Hayes blamed her, God knew why, for his younger brother's drug-related death, even after Rachel Conley left a confession stating that she'd given Bobby Carson, Hayes's brother, the drugs that killed him.

Rick chuckled. "If there's ever a border war, Minette will stand in the street pointing a finger at Hayes so the invaders can get him first."

"I wonder," Barbara mused. "Sometimes I think where there's antagonism, there's also something deeper. I've seen people who hate each other end up married."

"Cash Grier and his Tippy," Rick mused.

"Yes, and Stuart York and Ivy Conley."

"Not to mention half a dozen others. Jacobsville is growing by leaps and bounds."

"So is Comanche Wells. We've got new people there, too." She was peeling faster. "Did you notice that Grange bought a ranch in Comanche Wells, next to the property that his boss owns?"

Rick pursed his sensual lips. "Which boss?"

She blinked at him. "What do you mean, which boss?"

"He works as ranch manager for Jason Pendleton. But he also works on the side for Eb Scott," he said. "You didn't hear this from me, but he was involved in the Pendleton kidnapping," he added. "He went to get Gracie Pendleton back when she was kidnapped by that exiled South American dictator, Emilio Machado."

"Machado."

"Yes." He peeled the tomato slowly. "He's a conundrum."

"What do you mean?"

"He started out, we learned, as a farm laborer down in Mexico, from the time he was about ten years old. He was involved in protests against foreign interests even as a teenager. But he got tired of scratching dirt for a living. He could play the guitar and sing, so he worked bars for a while and then through a contact, he got a job as an entertainer on a cruise ship. That got boring. He signed on with a bunch of mercs and became known internationally as a crusader against oppression. Afterward, he went to South America and hired on with another paramilitary group that was fighting to preserve the way of life of the native people in Barrera, a little nation in the Amazon bordering Peru. He helped the paramilitary unit free a tribe of natives from a foreign corporation that was trying to kill them to get the oil-rich land on which they were living. He developed a taste for defending the underdog, moved up in the ranks of the military until he became a general." He smiled. "It seems that he was a natural leader, because when the small country's president died four years ago, Machado was elected by acclamation." He glanced at her. "Do you realize how rare that is, even for a small nation?"

"If people loved him so much, how is it that he's in Mexico kidnapping people to get money to retake his country?"

"He wasn't ousted by the people, but by a vicious and bloodthirsty military subordinate who knew when and how to strike, while Machado was on a trip to a neighboring country to sign a trade agreement and offer an alliance against foreign corporate takeovers."

"I didn't know that."

"It's sort of privileged info, so you can't share it," he told her. "Anyway, the subordinate killed Machado's entire staff, and sent his secret police to shut down newspapers and television and radio stations. Overnight, influential people ended up in prison. Educators, politicians, writers—anyone who might threaten the new regime. There have been hundreds of murders, and now the subordinate, Pedro Mendez by name, is allying himself with drug lords in a neighboring country. It seems that cocaine grows quite nicely in Barrera and poor farmers are being 'encouraged' to grow it instead of food crops on their land. Mendez is also nationalizing every single business so that he has absolute control."

"No wonder the general is trying to retake his country," she said curtly. "I hope he makes it."

"So do I," Rick replied. "But I can't say that in public," he added. "He's wanted in this country for kidnapping. It's a capital offense. If he's caught and convicted he could wind up with a death penalty."

She winced. "I don't condone how he's getting the money," she replied. "But he's going to use it for a noble reason."

"Noble." He chuckled.

"That's not funny," she said shortly.

"I'm not laughing at the word. It's Gwen. She goes around mumbling that she's Don Quixote."

She laughed out loud. "What?"

He shook his head. "Rogers told me. It seems that our newest detective won't give out on dates and she groups herself with Don Quixote, who tried to restore honor and morality to a decadent world."

"My, my!" She pursed her lips and smiled secretively.

"I don't want to marry Gwen Cassaway," he said at once. "I just thought I'd mention that, because I can read minds, and I don't like what you're thinking."

"She's a nice girl."

"She's a woman."

"She's a nice girl. She has a very idealistic and romantic attitude for someone who lives in the city. And I ought to know. I have women from cities coming through here all the time, talking about unspeakable things right in public with the whole world listening." Her lips made a thin line. "Do you know, Grange was having lunch next to a table of them where they were discussing men's, well, intimate men parts," she amended, clearing her throat, "and Grange got up from his chair, told them what he thought of them for discussing a bedroom topic in public in front of decent people and he walked out."

"What did they do?"

"One of them laughed. One of the others cried. Another said he needed to start living in the real world instead of small town 'stupidville.'" She grinned. "Of course, she said it after he'd already left. While he was talking, they didn't say a word. But they left soon after. I was glad. I can't choose my clientele and I've only ever ordered one person to leave my restaurant since I've owned it," she added.

She dragged herself back to the present. "But the topic of conversation was getting to me, too. People need to talk about intimate things in private, not in a public place with their voices raised. We don't all think alike."

"Only in some ways," he pointed out, and hugged her impulsively. "You're a nice mother. I'm so lucky to have you for an adoptive parent."

She hugged him back. "You've enriched my life, my sweet." She sighed, closing her eyes in his warm embrace. "When I lost Bart, I wanted to die, too. And then your mother and stepfather died, and there you were, as alone as I was. We needed each other."

"We did." He moved away and smiled affectionately. "You took on a big burden with me. I was a bad boy."

She groaned and rolled her eyes. "Were you ever! Always in fights, in school and out. I spent half my life in the principal's office and once at a school board meeting where they were going to vote to throw you right out of school altogether and put you in alternative school." Her face hardened. "In their dreams!"

"Yes, you took a lawyer to the meeting and buffaloed them. First time it ever happened, I heard later."

"I was very mad."

"I felt really bad about that," he said. "But I put my nose to the grindstone after, and tried hard to make it up to you."

"Joined the police force, went to night school and got your associate degree, went to the San Antonio Police Department and worked your way up in the ranks to sergeant," she agreed, smiling. "Made me *so* proud!"

He hugged her again. "I owe it all to you."

"No. You owe it to your hard work. I may have helped, but you pulled yourself up."

He kissed her forehead. "Thank you. For everything."

"You're my son. I love you very much."

He cleared his throat. Emotions were difficult for him, especially considering his job. "Yeah. Me, too."

She grinned. The smile faded as she searched his large, dark eyes. "Do you ever wonder about your mother's past?"

His eyebrows shot up. "What a question!" He frowned. "What do you mean?"

"Do you know anything about her friends? About any male friends she had before she married your stepfather?"

He shrugged. "Not really. She didn't talk about her relationships. Well, I wasn't old enough for her to confide in me, either, you know. She never was one to talk about intimate things," he said quietly. "Not even about my real father. She said that he died, but she never talked about him. She was very young when I was born. She did say she'd done things she wanted forgiveness for, and she went to confession a lot." He studied her closely. "You must have had some reason for asking me that."

She put her lips tightly together. "Something I overheard. I wasn't supposed to be listening."

"Come on, tell me," he said when she hesitated.

"Cash Grier was having lunch with some fed. They were discussing Machado. The fed mentioned a woman named Dolores Ortíz who had some connection to General Machado when he lived in Mexico."

CHAPTER TWO

"Dolores Ortíz?" he asked, the paring knife poised in midair. "That was my mother's maiden name."

"I know."

Rick frowned. "You mean my mother might have been romantically involved with Emilio Machado?"

"I got that impression," Barbara said, nodding. "But I wasn't close enough to hear the entire conversation. I just got bits and pieces of it."

He pursed his lips. "Well, my father died around the time I was born, so it's not impossible that she did meet Machado in Mexico. Although, it's a big country."

"You lived in the state of Sonora," she pointed out. "That's where Machado had his truck farm, they said."

He finished skinning the tomato and reached for another one. "Wouldn't that be a coincidence, if my mother actually knew him?"

"Yes, it would."

"Well, it was a long time ago," he said easily. "And she's dead, and I never knew him. So what good would it do for them to dig up an old romance now?"

"I have no idea. It bothered me, a little. I mean, you're my son."

"Yes, I am." He glanced at her. "I love it when people get all flustered and start babbling when you introduce me. You're blonde and fair and I'm dark and obviously Hispanic."

"You're gorgeous, my baby," she teased. "I just wish women would stop crying on your shoulder about other men and start trying to marry you."

He sighed. "Chance would be a fine thing. I carry a gun!" he said with mock horror.

She glowered at him. "All off-duty policemen carry guns."

"Yes, but I might shoot somebody accidentally, and it would get in the way if I tried to hug somebody."

"I gather that somebody female mentioned that?"

He sighed and nodded. "A public defender," he said. "She thought I was cute, but she doesn't date men who carry. It's a principle, she said. She hates guns."

"I hate guns, too, but I keep a shotgun in the closet in case I ever need to defend myself," Barbara pointed out.

"I'll defend you."

"You work in San Antonio," she said. "If you're not here, I have to defend myself. By the time Hayes Carson could get to my place, I'd be...well, not in any good condition if somebody tried to harm me."

That had happened once, Rick recalled with anger. A man he'd arrested, after he'd been released, had gone after Rick's adoptive mother for revenge. It was just chance that Hayes Carson had stopped by when he was off duty, in his unmarked truck, to ask her about catering an event. The ex-convict had piled out of his car and come right up on the porch with a drawn gun—in violation of parole—and banged on the door demanding that Barbara come outside. Hayes had come outside, disarmed him, cuffed him and taken him right to jail. The man was now serving another term in prison, for assault on a police officer, trespassing, attempted assault, possessing a firearm in violation of parole and resisting arrest. Barbara had testified at his trial. So had Hayes.

Rick shook his head. "I hate having you in danger because of my job."

"It was only the one time," she said, comforting him. "It could have been somebody who carried a grudge because their apple pie wasn't served with ice cream or something."

He smiled. "Dream on. You even make the ice cream you serve with it. Your pies are out of this world."

"Don't you have an in-house seminar coming up at work?" she asked.

He nodded.

"Why don't you take a couple of pies back with you?"

"That would be nice. Thank you."

"My pleasure." She pursed her lips. "Does Gwen like apple pie?"

He turned and stared at her. "Gwen is a colleague. I never, never date colleagues."

She sighed. "Okay."

He went back to work on the tomatoes. This could turn into a problem. His mother, well-meaning and loving, nevertheless was determined to get him married. That was one area in which he wanted to do his own prospecting. And never in this lifetime did he want to end up with someone like Gwen, who had two left feet and the dress sense of a Neanderthal woman. He laughed at the idea of her in bearskins carrying a spear. But he didn't share the joke with his mother.

WHEN HE WENT to work the next day, it was qualifying time on the firing range. Rick was a good shot, and he kept excellent care of his service weapon. But the testing was one of the things he really hated about police work.

His lieutenant, Cal Hollister, could outshoot any man in the precinct. He scored a hundred percent regularly. Rick could usually manage in the nineties but never a perfect score. He always seemed to do the qualifying when the lieutenant was doing his, and his ego suffered.

Today, Gwen Cassaway also showed up. Rick tried not to groan out loud. Gwen would drop her pistol, accidentally kill the lieutenant and Rick would be prosecuted for manslaughter…

"Why are you groaning like that?" Hollister asked curtly as he checked the clip for his .45 in preparation for target shooting.

"Just a stray thought, sir, nothing important." His eyes went involuntarily to Gwen, who was also loading her own pistol.

On the firing range, shooters wore eye protection and ear protection. They customarily loaded only six bullets into the clip of the automatic, and this was done at the time they got into position to fire. The pistol would be held at low or medium ready position, after being carefully drawn from its snapped holster for firing, with the safety on. The pistol, even unloaded, would never be pointed in any direction except that of the target and the trigger finger would never rest on the trigger. When in firing position, the safety would be released, and the shooter would fire at the target using either the Weaver, modified Weaver or Isosceles shooting stance.

One of the most difficult parts of shooting, and one of the most important to master, was trigger pull. The pressure exerted on the trigger had to be perfect in order to place a shot correctly. There were graphs on the firing range that helped participants check the efficiency of their trigger pull and help to improve it. Rick's was improving. But his lieutenant consistently showed him up on the gun range, and it made him uncomfortable. He tried not to practice or qualify when the other man was around. Unfortunately, he always seemed to be on the range when Rick was.

Hollister followed Rick's gaze to Gwen. He knew, as Rick did, that she had some difficulty with coordination. He pursed his lips. His black eyes danced as he glanced covertly at Gwen. "It's okay, Marquez. We're insured," he said under his breath.

Rick cleared his throat and tried not to laugh.

Hollister moved onto the firing line. His thick blond hair gleamed like pale honey in the sunlight. He glanced at Gwen. "Ready, Detective?" he drawled, pulling the heavy ear protectors on over his hair.

Gwen gave him a nice smile. "Ready when you are, sir."

The Range Master moved into position, indicated that everything was ready and gave the signal to fire.

Hollister, confident and relaxed, chuckled, aimed at the target and proceeded to blow the living hell out of it.

Rick, watching Gwen worriedly, saw something incredible happen next. Gwen snapped into a modified Weaver position, barely even aimed and threw six shots into the center of the target with pinpoint accuracy.

His mouth flew open.

She took the clip out of her automatic, checked the cylinder and waited for the Range Master to check her score.

"Cassaway," he said eventually, and hesitated. "One hundred percent."

Rick and the lieutenant stared at each other.

"Lieutenant Hollister," the officer continued, and was obviously trying not to smile, "ninety-nine percent."

"What the hell…!" Hollister burst out. "I hit dead center!"

"Missed one, sir, by a hair," the officer replied with a twinkle in his eyes. "Sorry."

Hollister let out a furious bad word. Gwen marched right up to him and glared at him from pale green eyes.

"Sir, I find that word offensive and I'd appreciate it if you would refrain from using it in my presence," she said curtly.

Hollister's high cheekbones actually flushed. Rick tensed, waiting for the explosion.

But Hollister didn't erupt. His black eyes smiled down at the rookie detective. "Point taken, Detective," he said, and his deep voice was even pleasant. "I apologize."

Gwen swallowed. She was almost shaking. "Thank you, sir."

She turned and walked off.

"Not bad shooting, by the way," he commented as he removed the clip from his own pistol.

She grinned. "Thanks." She glanced at Rick, who was still gaping, and almost made a smart remark. But she thought better of it in time.

Rick let out the breath he'd been holding. "She trips

over her own feet," he remarked. "But that was some damned fine shooting."

"It was," the lieutenant agreed. He shook his head. "You can never figure people, can you, Marquez?"

"True, sir. Very true."

LATER THAT DAY, Rick noted two dignified men in suits walking past his office. They glanced at him, spoke to one another and hesitated. One gestured down the hall quickly, and they kept walking.

He wondered what in the world was going on.

Rogers came into his office a few minutes later, frowning. "Odd thing."

"What?" he asked, his eyes on his computer screen where he was running a case through VICAP.

"Did you see those two suits?"

"Yes, they hesitated outside my office. Who are they, feds?"

"Yes. State Department."

He burst out laughing as he looked at her with large, dancing brown eyes. "They think I'm illegal and they're here to bust me?"

"Stop that," she muttered.

"Sorry. Couldn't resist it." He turned to her. "We have high level immigration cases all the time where the State Department gets involved."

"Yes, but mostly we deal with the enforcement branch of the Department of Immigration and Naturalization, with ICE. Or we deal with the DEA in drug cases, I know that. But these guys aren't from Austin. They're from D.C."

"The capitol?"

"That's right. They've been talking to the lieutenant all morning. They're taking him to lunch, too."

"What's going on? Any idea?"

She shook her head. "Only that gossip says they're on the Machado case."

"Yes. He's wanted for kidnapping." He didn't add what Barbara had told him, that his own birth mother might have once known Machado in the past.

"He's not in the country."

"And how would you know that?" Rick asked her with pursed lips. "Another psychic insight?" he added, because she had a really unusual sixth sense about cases.

"No. I ran into Cash Grier over at the courthouse. He was up here on a case."

"Our police chief from Jacobsville," he acknowledged.

"The very same. He mentioned that Jason Pendleton's foreman is on temporary leave because of Machado."

"Grange," Rick recalled, naming the foreman. "He went into Mexico to retrieve Gracie Pendleton when she was kidnapped by Machado's men for ransom."

"Yes. It seems the general took a liking to him, had him investigated and offered him a job."

Rick blinked. "Excuse me?"

"That's what I said when Grier told me." She laughed. "The general really does have style. He said somebody had to organize his mercs when he goes in to retake his country. Grange, being a former major in the army, seemed the logical choice."

"His country is Barrera," Rick mused. "Nice name,

since it sits on the Amazon River bordering Colombia, Peru and Bolivia. Barrera is Spanish for barrier."

"I didn't know that, only having completed two years of college Spanish," she replied blithely.

He made a face at her.

"Anyway, it seems Grange likes the idea of being a crusader for democracy and freedom and human rights, so he took the job. He's in Mexico at the moment helping the general come up with a plan of attack."

"With Eb Scott offering candidates, I don't doubt," Rick added. "He's got the cream of the crop at his counterterrorism training center in Jacobsville, as far as mercs go."

"The general is gathering them from everywhere. He has a couple of former SAS from Great Britain, a one-eyed terror from South Africa named Rourke whose nickname is Dead-Eye…"

"I know him," Rick said.

"Me, too," Rogers replied. "He's a pill, isn't he? Rumored to be the natural son of K. C. Kantor, who was one of the more successful ex-mercs."

"Yes, Kantor became a billionaire after he gave up the lifestyle. He has a daughter who married Dr. Micah Steele in Jacobsville, and a godchild who married into the ranching Callister family up in Montana." His eyes narrowed. "Where is the general getting the money to finance his revolution?"

"Remember that he gave Gracie back without any payment. But then he nabbed Jason Pendleton for ransom, and Gracie paid it with the money from her trust fund?"

"Forgot about that," Rick said.

"It ran to six figures. So he's bankrolled. We hear he also charged what's left of the Fuentes cartel for protection while he was sharing space with them over the border."

"Charging drug lords rent in their own turf?" Rick asked.

"And getting it. The general has a pretty fearsome reputation," she added. She laughed. "He's also incredibly handsome," she mused. "I've seen a photograph of him. They say he has a charming personality, reveres women and plays the guitar and sings like an angel."

"A man of many talents."

"Not the least of which is inspiring troops." Rogers sighed. "But it has to be unsettling for the State Department, especially since the Mexican government is up in arms about having Machado recruit mercs to invade a sovereign nation in South America while living in their country."

"Why are they protesting to us? We aren't helping him," Rick pointed out.

"He's on our border."

"If they want us to do something about Machado, they could do something about the militant drug cartels running over our borders with automatic weapons to protect their drug runners."

"Chance would be a fine thing."

"I guess so. None of that explains why the State Department is gumming up our office," he added. "This is San Antonio. The border is that way." He pointed out the window. "A long, long drive that way."

"I know. That's what puzzled me. So I pumped Grier for information."

"What did he tell you?"

"He didn't. Tell me anything," she added grimly. "So I had my oldest son pump his best friend, Sheriff Hayes Carson, for information."

"Did you get anything from him?"

She bit her lower lip. "Bits and pieces." She gave him a worried look. She couldn't tell him what she found out. She'd been sworn to secrecy. "But nothing really concrete, I'm sorry to say."

"I suppose they'll tell us eventually."

"I suppose so."

"When is this huge invasion of Barrera going to take place? Any timeline on that?"

"None that presented itself." She sighed. "But it's going to be a gala occasion, from what we hear. The State Department would have good reason to be concerned. They can't back a revolution..."

"One of the letter agencies could help with that, of course, without public acknowledgment."

Letter agencies referred to government bureaus like the CIA, which Rick assumed would have been in the forefront of any assistance they could legally give to help install a democratic government friendly to the United States in South America.

"Kilraven used to belong to the CIA," Rick murmured. "Maybe I could ask him if he knows anything."

"I'd keep my nose out of it for the time being," Rogers cautioned, foreseeing trouble ahead if Rick tried to interfere at this stage of the game. "We'll know soon enough."

"I guess so." He glanced at her and asked, "Hear about what happened on the firing range this morning?"

Her eyes brightened. "Did I ever! The whole department's talking about it. Our rookie detective outshot the lieutenant."

"By a whole point." Rick grinned. "Imagine that. She falls into potted plants and trips over crime evidence, but she can shoot like an Old West gunslinger." He shook his head. "I thought I'd pass out when she started firing that automatic. It was beautiful. She never even seemed to aim. Just snapped off the shots and hit in the center every single time."

"The lieutenant's a good loser, though," Rogers commented. "He bought a single pink rose and laid it on her desk after lunch."

Rick's eyes narrowed and his expression grew cold. "Did he, now?"

The lieutenant was a widower. Nobody knew how he lost his wife, he never spoke of her. He didn't even date, as far as anyone knew. And here he was giving flowers to Gwen, who was young and innocent and impressionable...

"I said, do you think that could be construed as sexual harassment?" Rogers repeated.

"He gave her a flower!"

"Well, yes, but he wouldn't have given a man a flower, would he?"

"I'd have given Kilraven a flower after he nabbed the perp who blindsided me in the alley and left me for dead," he said, tongue-in-cheek.

She sighed. She felt in her pocket for the unopened pack of cigarettes she kept there, pulled it out and looked at it with sad eyes. "I miss smoking. The kids made me quit."

"You're still carrying around cigarettes?" he exclaimed.

"Well, it's comforting. Having them in my pocket, I mean. I wouldn't actually smoke one, of course. Unless we have a nuclear attack, or something. Then it would be okay."

He burst out laughing. "You're incorrigible, Rogers."

"Only on Mondays," she said after a minute. She glanced at her watch. "I have to get back to work."

"Let me know if you find out anything else, okay?"

"Of course I will." She smiled.

She felt a twinge of guilt as she walked out of his office. She wished she could tell him the truth, or at least prepare him for what she knew was coming. He had a surprise in store. Probably not a very nice one.

"But I MADE corned beef and cabbage," Barbara groaned when Rick phoned her Friday afternoon to say he wasn't coming home that night.

"I know, it's my favorite, and I'm sorry," he said. "But we've got a stakeout. I have to go. It's my squad." He sighed. "Gwen's on it, and she'll probably knock over a trash can and we'll get burned."

"You have to think positively." She hesitated. "You could bring her home with you tomorrow. The corned beef will still be good and I'll cook more cabbage."

"She's a colleague," he repeated. "I don't date colleagues."

"Does your lieutenant date colleagues?" she asked with glee. "Because I heard he left her a single rose on her desk. What a lovely, romantic man!"

He gnashed his teeth and hoped the sound didn't

carry. He was tired of hearing that story. It had gone the rounds at work all week.

"You could put a rose on her desk…"

"If I did, it would be attached to a pink slip!" he snapped.

She gasped, hesitated and turned off the phone. It was the first time he'd ever snapped at her.

Rick groaned and dialed her number back. It rang and rang. "Come on. Please?" he spoke into the busy signal. "I'm sorry. Come on, let me apologize…"

"Yes?" Barbara answered stiffly.

"I'm sorry. I didn't mean to snap at you. I really didn't. I'll come home for lunch tomorrow and eat corned beef and cabbage. I'll even eat crow. Raw." There was silence on the end of the line. "I'll bring a rose?"

She laughed. "Okay, you're forgiven."

"I'm really sorry. Things have been hectic at work. But that's no excuse for being rude to you."

"No, it's not. But I'm not mad."

"You're a nice mother."

She laughed. "You're a nice son. I love you. I'll see you at lunch tomorrow."

"Have a good night."

"You have a careful one," she said solemnly. "Even rude sons are hard to come by these days," she added.

"I'll change my ways. Honest. See you."

"See you."

He hung up and sighed heavily. He couldn't imagine why he'd been so short with his own mother. Perhaps he needed a vacation. He only took time off when he was threatened. He loved his job. Being sergeant of an eight-detective squad in the Homicide Unit, in the Murder/Attempted Murder detail, was heady and satisfying. He assigned lead detectives to cases, reviewed cases to make sure everything necessary was done and kept up with what seemed like tons of paperwork, as well as reporting to the lieutenant on caseloads. But maybe a little time off would improve his temper. He'd talk to the lieutenant about it next week, he resolved. For now, he had work to do.

GWEN HAD BEEN assigned as lead detective on the college student's murder case downtown. It was an odd sort of case. The woman had been stabbed by person or persons unknown, in her own apartment, with all the doors locked and the windows shut. There were no signs of a struggle. She was a pretty young woman with no current boyfriend, no apparent enemies, who led a quiet life and didn't party.

Gwen wanted very much to solve the case. She'd told Rick that Alice Fowler had found prints on a digital camera that featured an out-of-place man in the background. Gwen was checking that out. She was really working hard on the mystery.

But in the meantime, she'd been pressed into service to help Rick with a stakeout of a man wanted for shooting a police officer in a traffic stop. The officer lived, but he'd be in rehab for months. They had intel that the shooter was hiding out in a low class apartment building downtown with some help from an associate. But they couldn't find him there. So Rick decided to stake out the place and try to catch him. The fact that it was a Friday night meant that the younger, single detectives were trying to find ways not to get involved. Even the night detectives had excuses, pending cases that they simply couldn't spare time away from. So Rick ended up with Gwen and one young and eager patrol officer, Ted Sims, from the Patrol South Division who'd volunteered, hoping to find favor with Rick and maybe get a chance at climbing the ladder, and working as a detective one day.

They were set up in a ratty apartment downtown, observing a suspect across the alley in another run-down apartment building. They had all the lights off, a telescope, a video camera, listening devices, warrants to allow the listening devices and as much black coffee as three detectives could drink in an evening. Which was quite a lot.

"I wish we had a pizza." Officer Sims sighed.

Rick sighed, too. "So do I, but the smell would carry and the perp would know we were watching him."

"Maybe we could put the pizza outside his door and he'd go nuts smelling it and rush out to grab it and we could grab him," Sims mused.

"What do you have in that bottle besides water?" Gwen asked, with twinkling green eyes.

Sims made a face. "Just water, sadly. I could really use a cold beer."

"Shut up," Marquez groaned. "I'm dying for one."

"We could ask Detective Cassaway to investigate the beer rack at the local convenience store and confiscate a six-pack for the crime scene investigation unit," Sims joked. "Nobody would have to know. We could threaten the owner with health violations or something."

Gwen gave him a cold look. "We don't steal."

Marquez gave him an even more vicious look. "Ever."

He flushed. "Hey," he said, holding up both hands, "I was just kidding!"

"I'm not laughing," she returned, unblinking.

"Neither am I," Marquez seconded. His face was hard with suppressed anger. "I don't want to hear talk like that from a sworn police officer."

"Sorry," he said, swallowing hard. "Really. Bad joke. I didn't mean I'd actually do it."

Gwen shrugged. Sims was very young. "I'm missing that new science fiction show I got hooked on," she groaned. "It's making me twitchy."

"I watch that one, too," Rick replied. "It's not bad."

"You could record it," Sims suggested. "Don't you have a DVR?"

She shook her head. "I'm poor. I can't afford one."

Rick glared at her. "We work for one of the best-paying departments in the southwest," he rattled off. "We have a benefits package, expense accounts, access to excellent vehicles…"

"I have a monthly rent bill, a monthly insurance bill, a car payment, utilities payments and I have to buy bullets for my gun," she muttered. "Who can afford luxuries?" She glared at him. "I haven't had a new suit in six months. This one looks like moths have nested in it already."

Rick's eyebrows arched up. "Surely, you've got more than one suit, Cassaway."

"Two suits, twelve blouses, six pair of shoes and assorted…other things," she said. "Mix and match and I'm sick of all of it. I want haute couture!"

"Good luck with that," Rick remarked.

"Luck won't do it."

"Hey, is this the guy we're looking for?" Sims asked suddenly, looking through the telescope.

CHAPTER THREE

RICK AND GWEN joined him at the window. Rick snapped a photo of the man across the street, using the telephoto feature, plugged it into his small computer and, using a new face recognition software component, compared it to the man he'd photographed.

"Positive ID. That's him," Rick said. "Let's go get him."

They ran down the steps, deploying quickly to the designations planned earlier by Rick.

The man, yawning and oblivious, stepped out onto the sidewalk next to a bus stop sign.

"Now," Rick yelled.

Three people came running toward the stunned man, who started to run, but it was far too late. Rick tackled him and took him down. He cuffed his hands behind his back and chuckled as the man started cursing.

"I ain't done nothin'!" he wailed.

"Then you don't have a thing to worry about."

The man only groaned.

"THAT WAS A nice takedown," Gwen said as they cleared their equipment out of the rented apartment, after the man had been taken away by the patrol officer.

"Thanks. I try to keep in shape."

She didn't dare look at him. She was having a hard enough time not noticing how very attractive he was.

"You know," he mused, "that was some fine shooting down at HQ."

She beamed. "Thanks." She glanced up. "At least I do have one saving grace."

"Probably more than one, Cassaway."

She shouldered her purse. "Are we done for the night?"

"Yes. I'll input the report and you can sign it tomorrow. I snapped at my mother. I have to go home and try to make it up to her."

"She's very nice."

He turned, frowning. "How do you know?"

"I came through Jacobsville when I had to interview a witness in that last murder trial," she reminded him. "I had lunch at the café. It's the only one in town, except for the Chinese restaurant, and I like her apple pie." She added that last bit to make sure he knew she wasn't frequenting his mother's café just because she was his mother.

"Oh."

"Has she owned the restaurant a long time?"

He nodded. "She opened it a couple of years before I was orphaned. My mother worked for her as a cook just briefly."

Gwen nodded, trying to be low-key. "Is your mother still alive? Your biological mother?" she asked while looking through her purse for her car keys.

"She and my stepfather died in a wreck when I was almost in my teens. Barbara had just lost her husband and had a miscarriage the month before it happened.

She was grieving and so was I. Since I had no other family, and she knew me, she adopted me."

She flushed. "Oh. Sorry, I didn't mean to pry. I was just curious."

He shrugged. "Most everybody knows," he said easily. "I was born in Mexico, in Sonora, but my mother and stepfather came to this country when I was a toddler and lived in Jacobsville. My stepfather worked at one of the local ranches."

"What did he do?"

"Broke horses." The way he said it was cold and short, as if he didn't like being reminded of the man.

"I had an uncle who worked ranches in Wyoming," she confided. "He's dead now."

He studied her through narrowed eyes. "Wyoming. But you're from Atlanta?"

"Not originally."

He waited.

She cleared her throat. "My people are from Montana, originally."

"You're a long way from home."

"Yes, well, my parents moved to Maryland when I was small."

"I guess you miss the ocean."

She nodded. "A lot. It wasn't a long drive from our house. But I go where they send me. I've worked a lot of places—" She stopped dead, and could have bitten her tongue.

His eyebrows were arching already. "The Atlanta P.D. moves you around the country?"

"I mean, I've worked a lot of places around Atlanta."

"Mmm-hmm."

"I didn't always work for Atlanta P.D.," she muttered, trying to backpedal. "I worked for a risk organization for a year or two, in the insurance business, and they sent me around the country on jobs."

"A risk organization? What sort of work did you do?"

"I was a sort of security consultant." It wasn't quite the truth, but it wasn't quite a lie, either. She glanced at her watch as a diversion. "Oh, goodness, I'll miss my television show!"

"God forbid," he said dryly. "Okay. We're done here."

"It didn't take as long as I expected," she commented on the way out. "Usually stakeouts last for hours if not days."

"Tell me about it," he said drolly. "Is your car close by?"

She turned at the foot of the steps. "It's across the street, thanks," she said, because she knew he was offering to walk her to it. He was a gentleman, in the nicest sort of way.

He nodded. "I'll see you Monday, then."

She smiled. "Yes, sir."

She turned and walked away. Her heart was pounding and she was cursing herself mentally. She'd almost blown the whole thing sky-high!

BARBARA WAS HER USUAL, smiling self, but her eyes were sad when Rick showed up at the door the night before he was due home.

"You said tomorrow?" she murmured.

He stepped into the house and hugged her, hard, rocking her in his arms. He heard a muffled sob. "I felt bad," he said at her ear. "I upset you."

"Hey," she murmured, drawing away to dab at her eyes, "that's what kids are supposed to do."

He smiled. "No, it's not."

"Want some coffee?"

"Yes!" he said at once, pulling off his suit coat and loosening his tie as he followed her to the kitchen. He swung the coat around one of the high-back kitchen chairs at the table and sat down. "I've been on stake-out, with convenience-store coffee." He made a face. "I think they keep it in the pot all day to make sure it doesn't pass for hot brown water."

She laughed as she made a fresh pot. "There's that profit margin to consider," she mused.

"I guess."

"Did you catch a crook?"

"We did, actually. That new face recognition software we use is awesome. Pegged the guy almost immediately."

"New technology." She shook her head. "Cameras everywhere, face recognition software, pat downs at the airport…" She turned and looked at him. "Isn't all that supposed to make us feel safer?"

"No, it's supposed to actually make you safer," he corrected. "It makes it harder for the bad guys to hide from the law."

"I guess so." She got out cups and saucers. "I made apple pie."

"You don't even need to ask. I had a hamburger earlier."

"You live on fast food."

"I work at a fast job," he replied. "No time for proper meals, now that I'm in a position of responsibility."

She turned and smiled at him. "I was so proud of you for that promotion. You studied hard."

"I might have studied less if I'd realized how much paperwork would be involved," he quipped. "I have eight detectives under me, and I'm responsible for all the major decisions that involve them. Plus I have to co-ordinate them with other services, work around court dates and emergency assignments… Life was a lot easier when I was just a plain detective."

"You love your job, though. That's a bonus."

"It is," he had to agree.

She cut the pie, topped it with a scoop of homemade ice cream and served it to him with his black coffee. She sat down across from him and watched him eat it with real enjoyment, her hands propping up her chin, elbows on the tablecloth.

"You love to cook," he responded.

She nodded. "It isn't an independent woman thing, I know," she said. "I should be designing buildings or running a corporation and yelling at subordinates."

"You should be doing what you want to do," he replied.

"In that case, I am."

"Good cooks are thin on the ground." He finished the pie and leaned back with his coffee cup in his hand, smiling. "Wonderful food!"

"Thanks."

He sipped coffee. "And the best coffee anywhere."

"Flattery will get you another slice of pie."

He chuckled. "No more tonight. I'm fine."

"Are you ever going to take a vacation?" she asked.

"Sure," he replied. "I've already arranged to have Christmas Eve off."

She glared at him. "A vacation is longer than one night long."

He frowned. "It is? Are you sure?"

"There's more to life than just work."

"I'll think about that, when I have time."

"Have you watched the news today?" she asked.

"No. Why?"

"They had a special report about violence on the border. It seems that the remaining Fuentes brother sent an armed party over the border to escort a drug shipment and there was a shootout with some border agents."

He grimaced. "An ongoing problem. Nobody knows how to solve it. Bottom line, if people want drugs, somebody's going to supply them. You stop the demand, you stop the supply."

"Good luck with that" She laughed hollowly. "Never going to happen."

"I totally agree."

"Anyway, they mentioned in passing that one of the captured drug runners said that General Emilio Machado was recruiting men for an armed invasion of his former country."

"The Mexican Government, we hear, is not pleased with that development and they're angry at our government because they think we aren't doing enough to stop it."

"Really?" she exclaimed. "What else do you know?"

"Not much, but you can't repeat anything I tell you," he added.

She grinned. "You know I'm as silent as a clam. Come on. Talk."

"Apparently, the State Department sent people into our office," he replied. "We know they talked to our lieutenant, but we don't know what about."

"State Department!"

"They do have their fingers on the pulse of foreign governments," Rick reminded her. "If anybody knows what's really going on, they do."

"I would have thought one of those other government agencies would have been more involved, especially if the general's trying to recruit Americans for a foreign military action," she pondered.

His eyebrows arched.

"Well, it seems logical, doesn't it?" she asked.

"Actually, it does," he agreed. "I know the FBI and the CIA have counterterrorism units that infiltrate groups like that."

"Yes, and some of them die doing it," Barbara recalled. She grimaced. "They say undercover officers in any organization face the highest risks."

"The military also has counterterrorism units," he replied. He sipped his cooling coffee. "That must be an interesting sort of job."

"Dangerous."

He smiled. "Of course. But patriotic in the extreme, especially when it comes to foreign operatives trying to undermine democratic interests."

"Doesn't the general's former country have great deposits of oil and natural gas?" she wondered aloud.

"So we hear. It's also in a very strategic location, and the general leans toward capitalism rather than socialism or communism. He's friendly toward the United States."

"A point in his favor. Gracie Pendleton says he sings like an angel," she added with a smile.

"I heard."

"Yes, we had that discussion earlier." She was also remembering another discussion over the phone and her face saddened.

He reached across the table and caught her hand in his. "I really am sorry, Mom," he said gently. "I don't know what came over me. I'm not usually like that."

"No, you're not." She hesitated. She wanted to remark that it wasn't until she asked about the lieutenant giving Gwen a rose that he'd gone ballistic. But in the interests of diplomacy, it was probably wiser to say nothing. She smiled. "How about I warm up that coffee?" she asked instead.

GWEN ANSWERED THE phone absently, her mind still on the previews of next week's episode of her favorite science fiction show.

"Yes?" she murmured, the hated glasses perched on her nose so that she could actually see the screen of her television.

"Cassaway, anything to report?"

She sat up straighter. "Sir!"

"No need to get uptight. I'm just checking in. The wife and I are on our way to a party, but I wanted to make sure things are progressing well."

"They're going very slowly, sir," she said, curling up in her bare feet and jeans and long-sleeved T-shirt on her sofa. "I'm sorry, I haven't found a diplomatic way to get him talking about the subject and find out what he knows. He doesn't like me...."

"I find that hard to believe, Cassaway. You're a good kid."

She winced at the description.

He cleared his throat. "Sorry. Good woman. I try to be PC, you know, but I come from a different generation. Hard for us old-timers to work well in the new world."

She laughed. "You do fine, sir."

"I know this is a tough assignment," he replied. "But I still think you're the best person for the job. You have a way with people."

"Maybe another type of woman would have been a better choice," she began delicately, "maybe someone more open to flirting, and other things..."

"With Marquez? Are you kidding? The guy wrote the book on staunch outlooks! He'd be turned off immediately."

She relaxed a little. "He does seem to be like that."

"Tough, patriotic, a stickler for doing the right thing even when the brass disapproves, and he's got more guts than most men in his position ever develop. Even went right up in the face of a visiting politician to tell him he was putting his foot in his mouth by interfering with a homicide investigation and would regret it when the news media got hold of the story."

She laughed. "I read about that."

"Takes a moral man to be that fearless," her boss continued. "So yes, you're the right choice. You just have to win his confidence. But you're going to have to move a little faster. Things are heating up down in

Mexico. We can't be caught lagging when the general makes his move, you know? We have to have intel, we have to be in position to take advantage of any opportunities that present themselves. The general likes us. We want him to continue liking us."

"But we can't help."

He sighed. "No. We can't help. Not obviously. We're in a precarious position these days, and we can't be seen to interfere. But behind the scenes, we can hope to influence people who are in a position to interfere. Marquez is the obvious person to liaison with Machado."

"It's going to be traumatic for him," Gwen said worriedly. "From the little intel I've been able to acquire, he has no idea about his connection to Machado. None at all."

"Pity," he replied. "That's going to make it harder." He put his hand over the receiver and spoke to someone. "Sorry, my wife's ready to leave. I have to go. Keep me in the loop, and watch your back," he added firmly. "We're trying to get the inside track. There are other people, other operatives, around who would love nothing better than to see us fall on our faces. Other countries would do anything to get a foothold in Barrera. I don't need to tell you who they are, or from what motives they work."

"No, sir, you don't," she agreed. "I'll do the best I can."

"You always do," he said, and there was faint affection in his tone. "Have a good evening. I'll be in touch."

"Yes, sir."

She hung up the cell phone and sat staring at it in her hand. She felt a chill. So much was riding on her ability to be diplomatic and quick and discreet. It wasn't her first difficult assignment; she was not a novice. But until now, she'd had no personal involvement. Her growing feelings for Rick Marquez were complicating things. She shouldn't care so much about how it would hurt him, but she did. If only there was a way, any way, that she could give him a heads-up before the fire hit the fan. Perhaps, she thought, she might be able to work something out if she spoke to Cash Grier. They shared a similar background in covert ops and he knew Marquez. It was worth a try.

So FRIDAY MORNING, her day off, Gwen got in her small, used foreign car and drove down to Jacobsville, Texas.

Cash Grier met her at the door of his office, smiling, and led her inside, motioning to a chair as he closed the door behind him, locked it and pulled down the shade.

She pursed her lips with a grin. "Unusual precautions," she mused.

He smiled. "I'd put a pillow over the telephone if I thought there might be a wire near it. An ambassador's family habitually did that in Nazi Germany in the 1930s. Even did it in front of the head of the Gestapo once."

Her eyebrows arched as she sat down. "I missed that one."

"New book, about the rise of Hitler, and firsthand American views on the radical changes in society there in the 1930s," he said as he sat down and propped his big booted feet on his desk. "I love World War II history. I could paper my walls with books on the European Theatre and biographies of Patton and Rommel and Montgomery," he added, alluding to three famous World War II generals. "I like to read battle strategies."

"Isn't that a rather strange interest for a guy who worked alone for years, except with an occasional spotter?" she asked, tongue-in-cheek. It was pretty much an open secret that Grier had been a sniper in his younger days.

He chuckled. "Probably."

"I like history, too," she replied. "But I lean more toward political history."

"Which brings us to the question of why you're here," he replied and smiled.

She drew in a long breath and leaned forward. "I have a very unpleasant assignment. It involves Rick Marquez."

He nodded and his face sobered. "I know. I still have high-level contacts in your agency."

"He has no idea what's about to go down," she said. "I've argued with my boss until I'm blue in the face, but they won't let me give Marquez even a hint."

"I think his mother knows," he said. "She asked me about it. She overheard some visitors from D.C. talking about connections."

"Do you think she's told him anything?"

"She might know that his mother was romantically involved with Machado at some point. But she wouldn't know the rest. His mother was very close about her private life. Only one or two people even knew what happened." He grimaced. "The problem is that one of the people involved had a cousin who married a high-level agent in D.C., and he spilled his guts. That started this whole chain of events."

"Hard to keep a secret like that, especially one that would have been so obvious." She frowned. "Rick's stepfather must have known. From what little information I've been able to gather about his past, he and his stepfather didn't get along at all."

"The man beat him," Grier said harshly. "A real jewel of a human being. It's one reason Rick had so many problems as a kid. He was in trouble constantly right up until the wreck that killed his mother and stepfather. It was a tragedy that produced golden results. Barbara took him in, straightened him out and put him on a path that turned him into an exemplary citizen. Without her influence…" He spread his hands expressively.

Gwen stared at her scuffed black loafers. Idly, she noticed that they needed some polish. She dressed casually, but she liked to be as neat as possible. One day her real identity would come out, and she didn't want to give the agency a black eye by being slack in her grooming habits.

"You want me to tell him, don't you?" Grier asked.

She looked up. "You know him a lot better than I do. He's my boss, figuratively speaking. He doesn't like me very much, either."

"He might like you more if you'd wear your damned glasses and stop tripping over evidence in crime scenes," he said, pursing his lips. "Alice Mayfield Jones Fowler, who works in the Crime Scene Unit in San Antonio, was eloquent about the close call."

Gwen flushed. "Yes, I know." She pushed the hated glasses up on her nose, where they'd slipped. "I'm wearing my glasses now."

"I didn't mean to be critical," he said, noting her

discomfort. "You're a long way from the homicide detective you started out to be," he added. "I know it's a pain, trying to relearn procedure on the fly."

"It really is," she said. "My credentials did stand up to a background check, thank goodness, but I feel like I'm walking on eggshells. I let slip that my job involved a lot of traveling and Marquez wondered why, since I was apparently working for Atlanta Homicide."

"Ouch," he said.

"I have to remember that I've never been out of the country. It's pretty hard, living two lives."

"I haven't forgotten that aspect of government work," he agreed. "It's why I never had much of a personal life, until Tippy came along."

Everybody local knew that Tippy had been a famous model, and then actress. She and Cash had a rocky trip to the altar, but they had a little girl almost two years old and it was rumored that they wanted another child.

"You got lucky," she said.

He shrugged. "I guess I did. I never could see myself settling down in a small town and becoming a family man. But now, it's second nature. Tris is growing by leaps and bounds. She has red hair, and green eyes, like her mama's."

Gwen noted the color photo on his desk, with himself and Tippy, with Tris and a boy who looked to be in his early teens. "Is that Tippy's brother?" she asked, indicating the photo.

"Rory," he agreed. "He's fourteen." He shook his head. "Time flies."

"It seems to." She leaned back again. "I miss my dad. He's been overseas for a long time, although he's coming back soon for a talk with some very high-level people in D.C. and rumors are flying. Rick Marquez has no idea what sort of background I come from."

"Another shock in store for him," he added. "You should tell him."

"I can't. That would lead to other questions." She sighed. "I'd love to meet my dad at the airport when he flies in. We've had a rough six months since my brother, Larry, died overseas. Dad still mourns my mother, and she's been gone for years. I miss her, too."

"I heard about your brother from a friend in the agency. I'm truly sorry." His dark eyes narrowed. "No other siblings?"

She shook her head.

"My mother's gone, too. But my dad's still alive, and I have three brothers," he replied with a smile. "My older brother, Garon, is SAC at the San Antonio FBI office."

"I've met him. He's very nice." She studied his face. He was a striking man, even with hair that was going silver at the temples. His dark eyes were piercing and steady. He looked intimidating sitting behind a desk. She could only imagine how intimidating he'd look on the job.

"What are you thinking so hard about?" he queried.

"That I never want to break the law in your town." She chuckled.

He grinned. "Thanks. I try to perfect a suitably intimidating demeanor on the job."

"It's quite good."

He sighed. "I'll talk to Marquez's mother and plant

clues. I'll do it discreetly. Nobody will ever know that you mentioned it to me, I promise."

"Least of all my boss, who'd have me on security details for the rest of my professional life," she said with a laugh. "I don't doubt he'd have me transferred as liaison to a police department for real, where he'd make sure I was assigned to duty at school crossings."

"Hey, now, that's a nice job," he protested. "My patrolmen fight over that one." He said it tongue-in-cheek. "In fact, the last one enjoyed it so much that he transferred to the fire department. It seems that a first-grader kicked him in the leg, repeatedly."

Her fine eyebrows arched. "Why?"

"He told the kid to stay in the crosswalk. Seems the kid had a real attitude problem. The teachers couldn't deal with him, so they finally called us, after the kicking incident. I took the kid home, in the patrol car, and had a long talk with his mother."

"Oh, dear."

His face was grim. "She's a single parent, living alone, no family anywhere, and this kid is one step away from juvy," he added, referencing the juvenile justice system. "He's six years old," he said heavily, "and he already has a record for disobedience and detention at his school."

"They put little kids in detention in grammar school?" she exclaimed.

"Figure of speech. They call it time-out and he sits in the library. Last time he had to go there, he stood on one of the library tables and recited the Bill of Rights to the head librarian."

Her eyes widened in amusement. "Not only a troublemaker, but brilliant to boot."

He nodded. "Everybody's hoping his poor mother will marry a really tough hombre who can control him before he does something unforgivable and gets an arrest record."

She laughed. "The things I miss because I never married," she mused, shaking her head. "It's not an incentive to become a parent."

"On the other end of the spectrum, there's Tippy and me," he replied with a smile. "I love being a dad."

"It suits you," she said.

She got to her feet. "Well, I have to get back to San Antonio. If Sergeant Marquez asks, I had to talk to you about a case, okay?"

"In fact, we really do have a case that might connect," he said surprisingly. "Sit back down and I'll tell you about it."

CHAPTER FOUR

SERGEANT MARQUEZ CAME into the office two days later, looking grim. He motioned to Gwen, indicated a chair and closed the door.

She remembered her trip to Cash Grier's office, and wondered if Grier had had time to talk to her superior officer's mother and the information had trickled down.

"The cold case squad has a job for us," he said as he sat down, too.

"What sort of job?"

"They dug up an old murder. It was committed back in 2002 and a man went to prison on evidence largely given by one person. Now it seems the person who gave evidence has been arrested and convicted for a similar crime. They want to know if we can find a connection."

"Well, by chance, that was the case I just spoke to Chief Grier about down in Jacobsville," she told him, happy that she could make a legitimate connection to her impromptu trip out of town. "He has an officer who knew the prisoner's family and could place the man at a party during the murder."

"Did he give evidence?" he asked.

She shook her head. "He was never called to testify," she said. "Nobody knows why."

"Isn't that interesting."

"Very. So the cold case squad wants us to wear out some shoe leather on their behalf?"

He grimaced. "They have plenty of manpower, but they've got two people out sick, one just transferred to the white collar crime unit and their sergeant said they don't want to let this case get buried. Especially not when a similar crime was just committed here. Your case. The college woman who was murdered. It needs investigation, and they don't have enough people." He smiled. "Besides, there's the issue of not stepping on the toes of another unit's investigation."

"I can understand that."

"So, we'll see if we can make a connection, based on available evidence. I'm assigning you as lead detective on this case, as well as on the college freshman murder. Find a connection. Catch the perp. Make me proud."

She grinned at him. "Actually, that might be possible. I just got some new information from running a check on the photo of that odd man in the murder victim's camera. The one I mentioned to you?"

"Yes, I recall that."

She pulled up a file on her phone. "This is him. I used face recognition software to pick him out." She showed him the mug shot on her phone. "The perp. His name is Mickey Dunagan. He has a rap sheet. It's a long one. He's been prosecuted in two aggravated assault cases, never convicted. Here's the clincher. He has a thing for young college girls. He was arrested for attempted assault a few months ago, on a girl who went to the same college as our victim. I have a detective from our unit en route to question her today, and we're interviewing people at the apartment complex about the man in the photograph. If his DNA is on file, and I'm betting it is since he's served time during his trials, and there's enough DNA from the crime scene to type and match…"

"Good work!" he said fervently.

She grinned. "Thanks, sir."

"I wish we could get ironclad evidence that he killed the victim." He grimaced. "Not that ironclad evidence ever got a conviction when some silver-tongued gung-ho public defender got the bit between his teeth."

"Impressive mixing of metaphors, sir," she murmured dryly.

He actually made a face at her. "Correct my grammar, get stakeout duty for the next two months."

"I would never do that!" she protested with wicked, twinkling eyes.

He smiled back. She was very pretty when she smiled. Her mouth was full and lush and sensuous…

He sat back in his chair and forced himself not to notice that. "Get busy."

"I'll get on it right now."

"Just out of curiosity, who was the officer who could place the convicted murderer at a party when the other murder was committed?"

"Officer Dan Travis," she said. "He's at the Jacobsville Police Department. I'm going to drive down and talk to him tomorrow." She checked the notes on her phone. "Dunagan was arrested for assault by a patrolman in South Division named Dave Harris. I'm going to talk to him afterward. He might remember something that would be helpful."

"Good. Keep me in the loop."

"I will." She got up and started for the door.

"Cassaway."

She turned at the door. "Sir?"

His dark eyes narrowed. He seemed deep in thought. He was. He had a strange sense that she knew something important that she was hiding from him. He read body language very well after his long years in law enforcement. He'd once tripped a bank robber up when he noticed the man's behavior and deliberately engaged him in conversation. During the conversation, he'd gotten close enough to see the gun the man was holding under his long coat. Rick had quickly subdued him, cuffed him and taken him in for questioning. The impromptu encounter had solved a whole string of unsolved bank robberies for the cold case unit, and their sergeant, Dave Murphy, had taken Rick out to lunch in appreciation for the help.

"Sir?" Gwen prompted when he didn't reply.

He sat up straight. His eyes narrowed further as he stared at her. She was almost twitching. "What do you know," he said softly, "that you aren't telling me?"

Her face flushed. "No…nothing. I mean, there's… nothing," she faltered, and could have bitten her tongue for making things worse.

"You need to think about your priorities," he said curtly.

She drew in a long breath. "Believe me, I am."

He grimaced and waved his hand in her direction. "Get to work."

"Yes, sir."

She almost ran out of the office. She was flushed

and unsettled. Lieutenant Hollister met her in the hall, and frowned.

"What's up?" he asked gently.

She bit her lip. "Nothing, sir," she said. She drew in a long breath. She wanted, so badly, to tell somebody what was going on.

Hollister's black eyes narrowed. "Come into my office for a minute."

He led her back the way she'd come, past a startled Marquez, who watched the couple go into the lieutenant's office with an expression that was hard to classify.

"Sit down," Hollister said. He went behind his desk and swung up his long, powerful legs, propping immaculate black boots on the desk. He crossed his arms and leaned back precariously in his chair. "Talk."

She shifted restlessly. "I know something about Sergeant Marquez that I'm not supposed to discuss with anybody."

He lifted a thick blond eyebrow. He even smiled. "I know what it is."

Her green eyes widened.

"The suits who came to see me earlier in the week were feds," he said. "I know who you really are, and what's going on." He sighed. "I want to tell Marquez, too, but my hands are tied."

"I went to see Cash Grier," she said. "He's out of the loop. He can't do anything directly, but he might be able to let something slip at Barbara's Café in Jacobsville. That would at least prepare Sergeant Marquez for what's about to go down."

"Nothing can prepare a man for that sort of revelation, believe me." His eyes narrowed even more. "They want Marquez as a liaison, don't they?"

She nodded. "He'd be the best man for the job. But he's going to be very upset at first and he may refuse to do anything."

"That's a risk they're willing to take. They don't dare interfere directly, not in the current political climate," he added. "Frankly, I'd just go tell him."

"Would you?" she asked, and smiled.

He laughed deeply and then he shook his head. "Actually, no, I wouldn't. I'm too handsome to spend time in prison. There would be riots. I'd be so much in demand as somebody's significant other."

She laughed, too. She hadn't realized he had a sense of humor. Her face flushed. She looked very pretty.

He cocked his head. "You could just ask Marquez to the ballet and tell him yourself."

"My boss would have me hung in Hogan's Alley up at the FBI Academy with a placard around my neck as a warning to other loose-lipped agents," she told him.

He grinned. "I'd come cut you down, Cassaway. I get along well with the feds. But I'm not prejudiced. I also get along with mercenaries."

"There's a rumor that you used to be one," she fished.

His face closed up, although he was still smiling. "How about that?"

She didn't comment.

He swung his long legs off the desk and stood up. "Let me know how it goes," he said. He walked her to the door. "It's not a bad idea, about asking him to the ballet. He loves ballet. He usually goes alone. He can't get girlfriends."

"Why not?" she asked. She cleared her throat. "I mean, he's rather attractive."

"He wears a gun."

"So do you," she pointed out, indicating the holster. "In fact, we all wear them."

"True, but he likes women who don't," he replied. "And they don't like men who wear guns. He doesn't date colleagues, he says. But you might be able to change his mind."

"Fat chance." She sighed. "He doesn't like me."

"Go solve that murder for the cold case unit, and they'll lobby him for you," he teased.

"How do you know about that?" she asked, surprised.

"I'm the lieutenant," he pointed out. "I know everything," he added smugly.

She laughed. She was still laughing when she walked down the corridor.

Rick heard her from inside his office. He threw a scratch pad across the room and knocked the trash can across the floor with it. Then he grimaced, in case anybody heard and asked what was going on. He couldn't have told them. He didn't know himself why he was behaving so out of character.

THE MAN GWEN was tracking in her semiofficial disguise was an unpleasant, slinky individual who had a rap sheet that read like a short story. She'd gone down to Jacobsville and interviewed Officer Dan Travis. He seemed a decent sort of person, and he could swear that the man who was arrested for the murder was at a holiday party with him, and had never even stepped outside. He had told the assistant DA, but the attorney refused to

entertain evidence he considered hearsay. Travis gave
her the names of two other people she could contact,
who would verify the information. She took notes and
arranged for a deposition to be taken from him.

Her next stop was Patrol South Division, in San Antonio, to talk to the arresting officer who'd taken Dunagan in for the attempted assault on a college woman
a few months ago, Dave Harris. He was working that
day, but was working a wreck when she phoned him.
So she arranged to meet him for lunch at a nearby fast
food joint.

They sat together over hamburgers and fries and soft
drinks, attracting attention with his uniform and her
pistol and badge, conspicuously displayed.

"We're being watched," she said in a dramatic tone,
indicating two young women at a nearby booth.

"Oh, that's just Joan and Shirley," he said. He looked
toward the women, waved and grinned. One of them
flushed and almost knocked over her drink. He was
blond and blue-eyed, nicely built and quite handsome.
He was also single. "Joan's sweet on me," he added in
a whisper. "They know I always eat here, so they come
by for lunch. They work at the print shop downtown.
Joan's a graphic artist. Very talented."

"Nice," she murmured, biting into the burger.

"Why are you doing a cold case?" he asked as he
finished his salad and sipped black coffee.

"It ties in with a current one we're working on," she
said, and related what Cash Grier had told her.

His dark eyebrows arched. "They never called a
prime witness in the case?"

"Strange, isn't it?" she agreed. "That would be

grounds for a mistrial, I'd think, but I'll need to talk to the city attorney's office first. The man who was convicted has been in prison for almost a year."

"Shame, if he's innocent," the patrolman replied.

"I know. Fortunately, such things don't happen often."

"What about the suspect in your current case?"

"A nasty bit of work," she replied. "I can place him at the scene of the crime, and if there's enough trace evidence to do a DNA profile, I think I can connect him with it. Her neighbors reported seeing him around her apartment the morning before the murder. If he's guilty, I don't want him to slip through the cracks on my watch, especially since Sergeant Marquez assigned me to the case as chief investigator."

"Really? How many other people are helping you with the case?"

"Let's see, right now, there's me and one other detective that I borrowed to help question witnesses."

He sighed. "Budget issues again?"

"Afraid so. I can manage. If I need help, the cold case unit will lend me somebody."

"Nice group, that cold case unit."

She smiled. "I think so, too."

"Now about the perp," he added, leaning forward. "This is how it went down."

He described the scene of the assault where he'd arrested Dunagan, the persons involved, the witnesses and his own part in the arrest. Gwen made notes on her phone and saved the file.

"That's a big help," she told him. "Thanks."

He smiled. "You're very welcome." He checked his

watch. "I have to get back on patrol. Was there any other information you needed?"

"Nothing I can't find in the file. I appreciate the summary of the case, and your thoughts on it. That really helps."

"You're welcome. Anytime."

"Shame about the latest victim," she added as they got up and headed to the trash bin with their trays. "She was very pretty. Her neighbors said she went out of her way to help people in need." She glanced at him. "We had one of your fellow officers on stakeout with us the other night. Sims."

He paused as he dumped the paper waste and placed the tray in its stack on the refuse container top. "He's not our usual sort of patrol officer."

"What do you mean?" she asked, frowning.

"I really can't say anything. It's just that he has an interesting background. There are people in high positions with influence," he added. He smiled. "But he's not my problem. I think you'll do well in the homicide unit. You've got a knack for sorting things out, and you're thorough. Good luck on the case."

"Thanks. Thanks a lot."

He smiled. "You're welcome."

She drove back to the office with her brain spinning. What she'd learned was very helpful. She might crack the case, which would certainly give her points with Rick Marquez. But there was still the problem of what she knew and couldn't tell him. She only hoped that Cash Grier would be able to break some ground with her sergeant.

CASH GRIER HAD a thick ham sandwich with homemade fries and black coffee and then asked for a slice of Barbara's famous apple pie and homemade ice cream.

She served it with a grin. "Don't eat too much of this," she cautioned. "It's very fattening." She was teasing, because he was still as trim as men ten years his junior, and nicely muscled.

He pursed his lips and his black eyes twinkled. "As you can see, I'm running to fat."

She laughed. "That'll be the day."

He studied her quietly. "Can you sit down for a minute?"

She looked around. The lunchtime rush was over and there were only a couple of cowboys and an elderly couple in the café. "Sure." She sat down across from him. "What can I do for you?"

He sipped coffee. "I've been enlisted to get some information to your son without telling him anything."

She blinked. "That's a conundrum."

"Isn't it?" He put down the coffee cup and smiled. "You're a very intelligent woman. You must have some suspicions about his family history."

"Thanks for the compliment. And yes, I have a lot." She studied his hard face. "I overheard some feds who ate here talking about Dolores Ortíz and her connection to General Machado. Dolores worked for me just briefly. She was Rick's birth mother."

"Rick's stepfather was a piece of work," he said coldly. "I've heard plenty about him. He mistreated livestock and was fired for it on the Ballenger feedlot. Gossip is that he did the same to his stepson."

Her face tautened. "When I first adopted him, I lifted

my hand to smooth back his hair—you know, that thing mothers do when they feel affectionate. He stiffened and cringed." Her eyes were sad. "That's when I first knew that there was a reason for his bad behavior. I've never hit him. But someone did."

"His stepfather," Grier asserted. "With assorted objects, including, once, a leather whip."

"So that's where he got those scars on his back," she faltered. "I asked, but he would never talk about it."

"It's a blow to a man's pride to have something like that done to him," he said coldly. "Jackson should have been sent to prison on a charge of child abuse."

"I do agree." She hesitated. "Rick's last name is Marquez. But Dolores said that was a name she had legally drawn up when Rick was seven. I never understood."

"She didn't dare put his real father's name on a birth certificate," he replied. "Even at the time, his dad was in trouble with the law in Mexico. She didn't want him to know about Rick. And, later, she had good reason to keep the secret. She married Craig Jackson to give Rick a settled home. She didn't know what sort of man he was until it was too late," he added coldly. "He knew who Rick's real father was and threatened to make it public if Dolores left him. So she stayed and Rick paid for her silence."

Barbara was feeling uncomfortable. "Would his real father happen to be an exiled South American dictator, by any chance?"

Grier nodded.

"Oh, boy."

"And nobody can tell him, because a certain federal agency is hoping to talk him into being a go-between for them, to help coax Machado into a comfortable trade agreement with our country when he gets back into power. Which he certainly will," he added quietly. "The thug who took over his government has human rights advocates bristling all over the world. He's tortured people, murdered dissenters, closed down public media outlets… In general, he's done everything possible to outrage anyone who believes in democracy. At the same time, he's pocketing money from sources of revenue and buying himself every rich man's perk that he can dream up. He's got several Rolls-Royce cars, assorted beautiful women, houses in most affluent European cities and his own private jet to take him to them. He doesn't govern so much as he flaunts his position. Workers are starving and farmers are being forced to grow drug crops to support his extravagant lifestyle." He shook his head. "I've seen dictators come and go, but that man needs a little lead in his diet."

She knew what he was alluding to. "Any plans going to take care of that?" she mused.

"Don't look at me," he warned. "I'm retired. I have a family to think about."

"Eb Scott might have a few people who would be interested in the work."

"Yes, he might, but the general isn't lacking for good help." He glanced up as one of Barbara's workers came, smiling, to refill his coffee cup. "Thanks."

She grinned. "You're welcome. Boss lady, you want some?"

Barbara shook her head. "Thanks, Bess, I'm already flying on a caffeine high."

"Okay."

"So who has to do the dirty work and tell Rick the truth?" Barbara asked.

Grier didn't speak. He just smiled at her.

"Oh, darn it, I won't do it!"

"There's nobody else. The feds have forbidden their agents to tip him off. His lieutenant knows, but he's been gagged, too."

"Then how in the world do they expect him to find out? Why won't they just tell him?"

"Because he might get mad at them for being the source of the revelation and refuse to cooperate. And there isn't anybody else they can find to do the job of contacting Machado."

"They could ask Grange," Barbara said stubbornly. "He's already working for the general, isn't he?"

"Grange doesn't know."

"Why me?" she groaned. "He'll be furious!"

"Yes, but you're his mother and he loves you," he replied. "If you tell him, he'll get over it. He might even be receptive to helping the feds. If they tell him, he'll hold a grudge and they'll never find anyone halfway suitable to do the job."

She was silent. She stared at the festive tablecloth worriedly.

"It will be all right," he assured her gently.

She looked up. "We've already had a disagreement recently."

"You have? Why?" he asked, surprised, because Rick's devotion to his adopted mother was quite well-known locally.

She grimaced. "His lieutenant gave the new detective, Gwen Cassaway, a rose, and I mentioned it in a teasing way. He went ballistic and I hung up on him. He won't admit it, but I think he's got a case on Gwen."

"Well!" he mused.

That was a new and interesting proposition. "Couldn't she tell him?" she asked hopefully.

"She's been cautioned not to."

She sighed. "Darn. Does everybody know?"

"Rick doesn't."

"I noticed."

"So you have to tell him. And soon."

"Or what?"

He leaned forward. "Or six government agencies will send operatives down here to disparage your apple pie and accuse you of subverting government policy by using organic products in your kitchen."

She burst out laughing. "Yes, I did hear that a SWAT team of federal agents raided a farm that was selling unpasteurized milk. Can you believe that? In our country, in this day and time, with all the real problems going on, we have to send armed operatives against people living in a natural harmony with the earth?"

"You're kidding!" he exclaimed.

"I wish I was," she replied. "I guess we're all going to be force-fed Genetically Modified Organisms from now on."

He burst out laughing. "You need to stop hanging out on those covert websites."

"I can't. I'd never know what was really going on in the world, like us having bases on the moon."

He rolled his eyes. "I have to get back to work." He stood up. "You'll tell him, then."

She stood up, too. "Do I have a choice?"

"You could move to Greenland and change your name."

She made a face at him. "That's no choice. Although I would love to visit Greenland. They have snow."

"So do we, occasionally."

"They have lots of snow. Enough to make many snowmen. South Texas isn't famous for that."

"The pie was great, by the way."

She smiled. "Thanks. I do my best."

"I'd have to leave town if you ever closed up," he told her. "I can't live in a town that doesn't have the best food in Texas."

"That will get you extra ice cream on your next slice of apple pie!" she promised him with a grin.

But she wasn't grinning when she went home. It disturbed her that she was going to have to tell her son something that would devastate him. He wasn't going to be pleased. Other than that, she didn't know what the outcome would be. But Grier was right about one thing; it was better that the information came from his mother rather than from some bureaucrat or federal agent who had no personal involvement with Rick and didn't care how the news affected him. It did make her feel good that so far, they hadn't blurted it out. By hesitating, they did show some compassion.

RICK WENT TO his mother's home tired. It had been a long day of meetings and more meetings, with a workshop on gun safety occasioned by the accidental discharge of a pistol by one of the patrol officers. The bullet went into the asphalt but fortunately didn't ricochet and hit anything, or anyone. The officer was disciplined but the chain of command saw an opportunity to emphasize gun safety and they took it. The moral of the story was that even experienced officers could mishandle a gun.

Privately, Marquez wondered how Officer Sims ever got through the police academy, because he was the officer involved. The same guy who'd gone on stakeout with him and Cassaway. He didn't think a lot of the young man's ethics and he'd heard that Sims had an uncle high up in the chain of command who made sure he kept his job. It was disturbing.

"You look worn-out," Barbara said gently. "Come sit down and I'll put supper on the table."

"It's late," he commented, noting his watch.

"We can have supper at midnight," she teased. "Nobody's watching. I'll even pull down the shades if it makes you happy."

He laughed and hugged her. "You're a treasure, Mom. I'll never marry unless I can find a girl like you."

"That's sweet. Thanks."

She started heating up roast beef and buttered rolls, topping off his plate with homemade potato salad. She put the plate in front of him. "Thank goodness for microwave ovens." She laughed. "The cook's best friend."

"This is delicious." He closed his eyes, savoring every bite. "I had a sandwich for lunch and I only had time to eat half of it between meetings."

"I didn't even eat lunch," she said, dipping into her own roast beef.

"Why not?"

"I had a talk with Cash Grier and afterward I lost my appetite."

He stopped eating and stared at her with narrowed eyes. "What did he tell you?"

"Something everybody knows and nobody has the guts to tell you, my darling," she said, stiffening herself mentally. "I have some very unpleasant news."

He put down his fork. "You've got cancer." His face paled. "That's it, isn't it? You should have told me...!"

He got up and hugged her. "We'll get through it together. I'll never leave your side..."

She pulled back, flattered. "I'm fine," she said. "I don't have anything fatal. That isn't what I meant. It's about you. And your real father."

He blinked. "My real father died not long after I was born..."

She took a deep breath. "Rick, your real father is across the border in Mexico amassing a private army in preparation for invading a South American country."

He sat down, hard. His light olive complexion was suddenly very pale. All the gossip and secrecy suddenly made sense. The feds were all over his office, not because they were working on shared cases, but because of Rick.

"My father is General Emilio Machado," he said with sudden realization.

CHAPTER FIVE

"My father is a South American dictator," Rick repeated, almost in shock.

"I'm afraid so." Barbara pulled up a chair facing him and held his hand that was resting on the table. "They made me tell you. Nobody else wanted to. I'm so sorry."

"But my mother said my father was dead," he repeated blankly.

"She only wanted to protect you. Machado was in trouble with the Mexican authorities when he lived in the country because he was opposed to foreign interests trying to take over key industries where he lived. He organized protests even when he was in his teens. He was a natural leader. Later, Dolores didn't dare tell you because Machado was the head of a fairly well-known international paramilitary group and that would have made you a target for any extremist with a grudge. He was in the news a lot when you were a child."

"Does he know?" Rick persisted. "Does he know about me?"

Barbara bit her lower lip. "No. She never told him." She sighed. "After Cash told me who your father was, I remembered something that Dolores told me. She said your father was only fourteen when he fathered you. She was older, seventeen, and there was no chance that her family would have let her marry him. She wanted you very much. So she had you, and never even told her parents who the father was. She kept her secret. At least, until she married your stepfather. Cash said that your stepfather got the truth out of her and used it to keep her with him. She didn't dare protest or he'd have made your real identity known. A true charmer," she added sarcastically.

"My stepfather was a sadist," he said quietly. "I've never spoken of him to you. But he made my life hell, and my mother's as well. I got in trouble with the law on purpose. I thought maybe somebody would check out my home life and see the truth and help us. But nobody ever did. Not until you came along and offered my mother work."

"I tried to help," she agreed. "Dolores liked cooking for me, but your stepfather didn't like her having friends or any interest outside of him. He was insanely jealous."

"He also couldn't keep a job. Money was tight. You used to sneak me food," he recalled with a warm smile. "You even came to visit me in the detention center. My mother appreciated that. My stepfather wouldn't let her come."

"I knew that. I did what I could. I tried to get our police chief at the time to investigate, but he was the sort of man who didn't want to rock the boat." She laughed. "Can you imagine Cash Grier turning a blind eye to something like that?"

"He'd have had my stepfather pilloried in the square." Rick smiled, then sobered. "My father is a dictator," he repeated again. It was hard to believe. He'd spent his whole life certain that his biological father was long dead.

"A deposed dictator," Barbara corrected. "His country is going to the dogs under its new administration. People are dying. He wants to accomplish a military coup, but he needs all the help he can get. Which brings us to our present situation," she added. "A paramilitary group is going down to Barrera with him, including some of Eb Scott's guys, some Europeans, one African merc and with ex-army Major Winslow Grange, Jason Pendleton's foreman on his Comanche Wells ranch, to lead them."

"All that firepower and the government hasn't noticed?"

"It wouldn't do them a lot of good. Machado's in Mexico, just over the border," Barbara said. "They can't mount an invasion to stop him. But they can try to find a way to be friendly without overt aid."

"Ah. I see. I'm the goat."

She blinked. "Excuse me?"

"They're going to tether me out to attract the puma."

"Puma." She laughed. "Funny, but one of my customers said that's what the local population calls 'El General.' They say he's cunning and dangerous like a cat, but that he can purr when he wants to." Her face softened. "For a dictator, he's held in high esteem by most democracies. He's intelligent, kind, he reveres women and he isn't afraid to fight for justice."

"Does he wear a red cape?" Rick murmured.

She shook her head. "Sorry."

"Who's in on this?" he asked narrowly. "Does my lieutenant know?"

"Yes," she said. "And there's a covert operative somewhere in your organization," she added. "I got that tidbit from a patrol officer who has a friend on the force in San Antonio. A guy named Sims."

"Sims." His face closed up. "He's got connections. And he's a total ethical wipeout. I hate having a guy like that on the force. He got careless with a pistol and almost shot himself in the foot. He's the reason we just had a gun safety workshop."

"Learning gun safety is not a bad thing."

He sighed. "I know." He was trying to adjust to the shock of his parentage. "Why didn't my mother tell me?" he burst out.

"She was trying to protect you. I'm certain that she would have told you eventually," she added. "She just didn't have time before she died."

He grimaced. "What am I supposed to do now, walk over the border, find the general and say, hey, guess what, I'm your kid?"

"I don't really think that would be wise," she replied. "I'm not sure he'd believe it in the first place. Would you?"

"Now there's a question." He leaned back in the chair, his dark eyes focused on the tablecloth. "I suppose I could have a DNA profile done. There's a private company that can at least rule out paternity by blood type. If mine is compatible with the general's, it might help convince him... Wait a minute," he added coldly. "Why the hell should I care?"

"Because he's your father, Rick," she said gently. "Even though he doesn't know."

"And the government's only purpose in telling me is to help reunite us," he returned angrily.

"Well, no, they want someone to convince the general to make a trade agreement with us once he's back in power. They're certain that he will be, which is why they want you to make friends with him."

"I'm sure he'll be overjoyed to know he has a grown son who's a cop," he said coldly. "Especially since he's wanted by our government for kidnapping."

She leaned forward with her chin resting in her hands, propped by her elbows. "You could arrest him," she pointed out. "And then befriend him in jail. Like the mouse that took the thorn out of the lion's paw and became its friend."

He made a face at her. "I can't walk across the border and arrest anyone. I might have been born in Mexico, but I'm an American citizen. And I did it the hard way," he added firmly. "Legally."

She grimaced.

"Sorry," he said after a minute. "I know you sympathize with all the people hiding out here who couldn't afford to wait for permission. In some of their countries, they could be killed just for paying too much attention to the wrong people."

"It's very bad in some Central American states," she pointed out.

"It's very bad anywhere on our border."

"And getting worse."

He got up and poured himself another cup of coffee. His big hand rested on the coffeemaker as he switched it off. "Who's the mole in my office?"

"I honestly don't know," she replied. "I only know

that Sims told his friend, Cash Grier's patrolman, about it. He said it was someone from a federal agency, working undercover."

"I wonder how Sims knew."

"Maybe he's the mole," she teased.

"Unlikely. Most feds have too much respect for the law to abuse it. Sims actually suggested that we confiscate a six-pack of beer from a convenience store as evidence in some pretended case and threaten the clerk with jail if he told on us."

"Good grief! And he works for the police?" she exclaimed, horrified.

"Apparently," he replied. "I didn't like what he said, and I told him so. He seemed repentant, but I'm not sure he really was. Cocky kid. Real attitude problem."

"Doesn't that sound familiar?" she asked the room at large.

"I never suggested breaking the law after I went through the academy and swore under oath to uphold it," he replied.

"Are you sure you didn't overreact, my darling?" she asked gently.

"If I did, so did Cassaway. She was hotter under the collar than I was." He laughed shortly. "And then she beat the lieutenant on the firing range and he let out a bad word. She marched right up to him and said she was offended and he shouldn't talk that way around her." He glanced at her ruefully. "Hence, the rose."

"Oh. An apology." She looked disappointed. "Your lieutenant is very attractive," she mused. "And eligible. I thought he might find Miss Cassaway interesting. Or something."

"Maybe he does," he said vaguely. "God knows why. She's good with a gun, I'll give her that, but she's a walking disaster in other ways. How she ever got a job with the police, I'll never know." He didn't like talking about Cassaway and the lieutenant. It got under his skin, for reasons he couldn't understand.

"She sounds very nice to me."

"Everybody sounds nice to you," he replied. He smiled at her. "You could find one good thing to say about the devil, Mom. You look for the best in people."

"You look for the worst," she pointed out.

He shrugged. "That's my job."

He was thoughtful, and morose. She felt even more guilty when she saw how disturbed he really was.

"I wish there had been some other way to handle this," she muttered angrily. "I hate being made the fall guy."

"Hey, I'm not mad at you," he said, and bent to kiss her hair. "I just...don't know what to do." He sighed.

"'When in doubt, don't,'" she quoted. She frowned. "Who said that?"

"Beats me, but it's probably good advice." He put down his cooling coffee and stretched, yawning. "I'm beat. Too many late nights finishing paperwork and going on stakeouts. I'm going to bed. I'll decide what to do in the morning. Maybe it will come to me in a dream or something," he added.

"Maybe it will. I'm just sorry I had to be the one to tell you."

"I'll get used to the idea," he assured her. "I just need a little time."

She nodded.

BUT TIME WAS in short supply. Two days later, a tall, elegant man with dark hair and eyes, wearing a visitor's tag but no indication of his identity, walked into Rick's office and closed the door.

"I need to talk to you," he said.

Rick stared at him. "Do I know you?" he asked after a minute, because the man seemed vaguely familiar.

"You should," he replied with a grin. "But it's been a while since we caught Fuentes and his boys in the drug sting in Jacobsville. I'm Rodrigo Ramirez. DEA."

"I knew you looked familiar!" Rick got up and shook the other man's hand. "Yes, it has been a while. You and your wife bought a house here last year."

He nodded. "I work out of San Antonio DEA now instead of Houston, and she works for the local prosecutor, Blake Kemp, in Jacobsville. With her high blood pressure, I'd rather she stayed at home, but she said she'd do it when I did it." He shrugged. "Neither of us was willing to try to change professions at this late date. So we deal with the occasional problem."

"Are you mixed up in the Barrera thing as well?" Rick asked curiously.

"In a way. I'm related, distantly, to a high official in Mexico," he said. "It gives me access to some privileged information." He hesitated. "I don't know how much they've told you."

Rick motioned Ramirez into a chair and sat down behind his desk. "I know that El General has a son who's a sergeant with San Antonio P.D.," he said sarcastically.

"So you know."

"My mother told me. They wanted me to know, but nobody had the guts to just say it," he bit off.

"Yes, well, that could have been a big problem. Depending on how you were told, and by whom. They were afraid of alienating you."

"I don't see what help I'm going to be," Rick said irritably. "I didn't know my biological father was still alive, much less who he was. The general, I'm told, has no clue that I even exist. I doubt he'd take my word for it."

"So do I. Sometimes government agencies are a little thin on common sense," he added. He crossed his elegant long legs. "I've been elected, you might say, to do the introductions, by my cousin."

"Your cousin…?"

"He's the president of Mexico."

"Well, damn!"

Ramirez smiled. "That's what I said when he told me to do it."

"Sorry."

"No problem. It seems we're both stuck with doing something that goes against the grain. I think the general is going to react very badly. I wish there was someone who could talk to him for us."

"Like my mother talked to me for the feds?" he mused.

"Exactly."

Rick frowned. "You know, Gracie Pendleton got along quite well with him. She refused to even think of pressing charges. She was asked, in case we could talk about extradition of Machado with the Mexican government. She said no."

"I heard. She's my sister-in-law, although she's not related to my wife. Don't even ask," he added, waving his hand. "It's far too complicated to explain."

"I won't. But I remember Glory very well," he reminded Ramirez. "Cash Grier and I taught her how to shoot a pistol without destroying cars in the parking lot," he added with a grin.

Ramirez laughed. "So you did." He sobered. "Gracie might be willing to speak to the general, if we could get word to him," Ramirez said.

"We had a guy in jail here who was one of the higher-ups in the Fuentes organization. He's going on probation tomorrow."

"An opportunity." Ramirez chuckled.

"Apparently, a timely one. I'll ask him if he'd have the general call Gracie. Now, how do you get Gracie to do that dirty work for you?"

"I'll have my wife bribe her with flowers and chocolate and Christmas decorations."

"Excuse me?" Rick asked.

"Gracie loves to decorate for Christmas. My wife has access to a catalog of rare antique decorations. Gracie can be bribed, if you know how," he added.

Rick smiled. "An assistant district attorney working a bribe. What if somebody tells her boss?"

"He'll laugh," Ramirez assured him. "It's for a just cause, after all."

RICK STARTED DOWN to the jail in time to waylay the departing felon. He spoke to the probation officer on the way and arranged the conversation.

The man was willing to take a message to the general, for a price. That put them on the hot seat, because neither man could be seen offering illegal payment to a felon.

Then Rick had a brainstorm. "Wait a second." He'd spotted the janitor emptying trash baskets nearby. He took the man to one side, handed him two fifties and told him what to do.

The janitor, confused but willing to help, walked over to the prisoner and handed him the money. It was from him, he added, since the prisoner had been pleasant to him during his occupation in the jail. He wanted to help him get started again on the outside.

The prisoner, smiling, understood immediately what was going on. He took the money graciously, with a bow, and proceeded to sing the janitor's praises for his act of generosity. So the message was sent.

GWEN CASSAWAY WAS sitting at Rick's desk when he went back to his office, in the chair reserved for visitors. He hated the way his heart jumped at the sight of her. He fought down that unwanted feeling.

"Do they have to issue us these chairs?" she complained when he came in, closing the door behind him. "Honestly, only hospital waiting rooms have chairs that are more uncomfortable."

"The idea is to make you want to leave," he assured her. "What's up?" he added absently as he removed his holstered pistol from his belt and slid it into a desk drawer, then locked the drawer before he sat down. "Something about the case I assigned you to?"

She hesitated. This was going to be difficult. "Something else. Something personal."

He stared at her coolly. "I don't discuss personal issues with colleagues. We have a staff psychologist if you need counseling."

She let out an exasperated sigh. "Honestly, do you have a steel rod glued to your spine?" she burst out. Then she realized what she'd said, clapped her hand over her mouth and looked horrified at the slip.

He didn't react. He just stared.

"I'm sorry!" she said, flustered. "I'm so sorry! I didn't mean to say that…!"

"Cassaway," he began.

"It's about the general," she blurted out.

His dark eyes narrowed. "Lately, everything is. Don't tell me. You're having an affair with him and you have to confess for the sake of your job."

She drew in a long breath. "Actually, the general *is* my job." She got up, opened her wallet and handed it to Rick.

He did an almost comical double take. He looked at her as if she'd grown leaves. "You're a fed?"

She nodded and grimaced. She took back the wallet after he'd looked at it again, just to make sure it didn't come from the toy department in some big store.

She put it back in her fanny pack. "Sorry I couldn't say something before, but they wouldn't let me," she said heavily as she sat down again, with her hands folded on her jeans.

"What the hell are you doing pretending to be a detective?" he asked with some exasperation.

"It was my boss's idea. I did start out with Atlanta P.D., but I've worked in counterterrorism for the agency for about four years now," she confessed. "I'm sorry," she repeated. "This wasn't my idea. They wanted me to find out how much you knew about your family his-

tory before they accidentally said or did something that
would upset you."

He raised an eyebrow. "I've just been presented
with a father who's an exiled South American dictator,
whose existence I was unaware of. They didn't think
that would upset me?"

"I asked Cash Grier to talk to your mother," she said.
"You can't tell anybody. I was ordered not to talk to you
about it. But they didn't say I couldn't ask somebody
else to do it."

He was touched by her concern. Not that he liked her
any better. "I wondered about your shooting skills," he
said after a minute. "Not exactly something I expect in
a run-of-the-mill detective."

She smiled. "I spend a lot of time on the gun range,"
she replied. "I've been champion of my unit for two
years running."

"Our lieutenant was certainly surprised when he
found himself outdone," he remarked.

"He's very nice."

He glared at her.

She wondered what he had against his superior officer, but she didn't comment. "I was told that a DEA
officer is going to try to get someone to speak to General Machado about you."

"Yes. Gracie Pendleton will talk with him. Machado
likes her."

"He kidnapped her!" she exclaimed. "And the man
she's now married to!"

He nodded. "I know. He also saved her from being
assaulted by one of Fuentes's men," he added.

"Oh. I didn't know that."

"She's fond of him, too," he replied. "Apparently, he makes friends even of his enemies. A couple of feds I know think he's one of the better insurgents," he added dryly.

"He did install democratic government in Barrera," she pointed out. "He instituted reforms that did away with unlawful detention and surveillance, he invited the foreign media in to oversee elections and he ousted half a dozen petty politicians who were robbing the poor and making themselves into feudal lords. From what we understand, one of those petty politicians helped Machado's second-in-command plan the coup that ousted him."

"While he was out of the country negotiating trade agreements," Rick agreed. "Stabbed in the back."

"Exactly. We'd love to have him back in power, but we can't actually do anything about it," she said quietly. "That's where you come in."

"The general doesn't even know me, let alone that I'm his biological son," he repeated. "Even if he did, I don't think he's going to jump up and invite me to baseball games."

"Soccer," she corrected. "He hates baseball."

His eyebrows lifted. "How do you know that?"

"I have a file on him," she said. "He likes strawberry ice cream, his favorite musical star is Marco Antonio Solís, he wears size 12 shoes and he plays classical guitar. Oh, he was an entertainer on a cruise ship in his youth."

"I did know about that. Not his shoe size," he added with twinkling dark eyes.

"He's never been romantically linked with any particular woman," she continued. "Although he was good friends with an American anthropologist who went to live in his country. She'd found an ancient site that was revolutionary and she was involved in a dig there. Apparently, there are some interesting ruins in Barrera."

"What happened to her?"

"Nobody knows. We couldn't even ascertain her name. What I was able to ferret out was only gossip."

He folded his hands on his desk. "So, you're a fed, I'm one detective short and you're supposed to be heading a murder investigation for me," he said curtly. "What do I do about that?"

"I've been working on it," she protested. "I'm making progress, too. As soon as we get the DNA profile back, I may be able to make an arrest in the college freshman's murder, and solve a cold case involving another dead coed. I have lots of information to go on, now, including eyewitness testimony that can place the suspect at the murdered woman's apartment just before she was killed."

He sat up. "Nice!"

"Thank you. I have an appointment to talk to her best friend, also, the one who took the photo that the suspect showed up in. She gave a statement to the crime scene detective that the victim had complained about visits from a man who made her uneasy."

"They'll let you continue to work on my case, even though you're a fed?"

"Until something happens in the general's case," she said. "I'm keeping up appearances."

"You slipped through the cracks," he translated.

She laughed. "Thanksgiving is just over the horizon

and my boss gets a lot of business done in D.C. going from one party to another with his wife."

"I see."

"When is Mrs. Pendleton going to talk to the general, did the DEA agent say?"

He shook his head. "It's only a work in progress right now." He leaned back in his chair. "I thought my father was dead. My mother told me he was killed when I was just a baby. I didn't realize I had a father who never even knew I was on the way."

"He loves children," she pointed out.

"Yes, but I'm not a child."

"I noticed."

He glared at her.

She flushed and averted her eyes.

He felt guilty. "Sorry. I'm not dealing with this well."

"I can understand that," she replied. "I know it must be hard for you."

She had a nice voice, he thought. Soft and medium in pitch, and she colored it in pastels with emotion. He liked her voice. Her choice of T-shirts, however, left a lot to be desired. She had on one today that read Save a Turkey, Eat a Horse for Thanksgiving. He burst out laughing.

"Do you have an open line to a T-shirt manufacturer?" he asked.

"What? Oh!" She glanced down at her shirt. "Well, sort of. There's this online place that lets you make your own T-shirts. I do a lot of business with them, designing my own."

Now he understood her quirky wardrobe.

"Drives my boss nuts," she added with a grin. "He thinks I'm not dignified enough on the job."

"I'm sure you have casual days, even in D.C."

"I don't work in D.C.," she said. "I get sent wherever I'm needed. I live out of a suitcase mostly." She smiled wanly. "It's not much of a life. I loved it when I was younger, but I'd really love to have someplace permanent."

"You could get a job in a local office."

"I guess." She shrugged. "Meanwhile, I've got one right here. I'm sorry I didn't tell you who I was at first," she added. "I would have liked to be honest."

He sensed that. He grimaced. "It's hard for me, too, trying to understand the past. My mother, my adopted mother," he said, just to clarify the point, "said that the general was only fourteen when he fathered me. I'll be thirty-one this year, in late December. That would make him—" he stopped and thought "—forty-five." His eyebrows arched. "That's not a great age for a dictator."

She laughed. "He was forty-one when he became president of Barrera," she said. "In those four years, he did a world of good for his country. His adopted country."

"Yes, well, he's wanted in this country for kidnapping," he reminded her.

"Good luck trying to get him extradited," she cautioned. "First the Mexican authorities would have to actually apprehend him, and he's got a huge complex in northern Sonora. One report is that he even has a howitzer."

"True story," he said, leaning back in his chair. "Pancho Villa, who fought in the Mexican Revolution, was a folk hero in Mexico at the turn of the twentieth century. John Reed, a Harvard graduate and journalist, actually lived with him for several months."

"And wrote articles about his adventures there. They made them into a book," she said, shocking him. "I had to buy it from a rare book shop. It's one of my treasures."

CHAPTER SIX

"I'VE READ THAT BOOK," Rick said with a slow smile. "*Insurgent Mexico*. I couldn't afford to buy it, unfortunately, so I got it on loan from the library. It was published in 1914. A rare book, indeed."

She shifted uncomfortably. She hadn't meant to let that bit slip. She was still keeping secrets from him. She shouldn't have been able to afford the book on her government salary. Her father had given it to her last Christmas. That was another secret she was keeping, too; her father's identity.

"And would you know Pancho Villa's real name?" he asked suddenly.

She grinned. "He was born Doroteo Arango," she said. The smile faded a little. "He changed his name to Pancho Villa, according to one source, because he was hunted by the authorities for killing a man who raped his younger sister. It put him on a path of lawlessness, but he fought all his life for a Mexico that was free of foreign oppression and a government that worked for the poor."

He smiled with pure delight. "You read Mexican history," he mused, still surprised.

"Well, yes, but the best of it is in Spanish, so I studied very hard to learn to read it," she confessed. She flushed. "I like the colonial histories, written by priests in the sixteenth century who sailed with the *conquistadores*."

"Spanish colonial history," he said.

She smiled. "I also like to read about Juan Belmonte and Manolete."

His eyebrows arched. "Bullfighters?" he exclaimed.

"Well, yes," she said. "Not the modern ones. I don't know anything about those. I found this book on Juan Belmonte, his biography. I was so fascinated by it that I started reading about Joselito and the others who fought bulls in Spain at the beginning of the twentieth century. They were so brave. Nothing but a cape and courage, facing a bull that was twice their size, all muscle and with horns so sharp…" She cleared her throat. "It's not PC to talk about it, I know."

"Yes, we mustn't mention blood sports," he joked. "The old bullfighters were like soldiers who fought in the world wars—tough and courageous. I like World War II history, particularly the North African theater of war."

Her eyes opened wide behind the lenses of her glasses. "Rommel. Patton. Montgomery. Alexander…"

His lips fell open. "Yes."

She laughed with some embarrassment. "I'm a history major," she said. "I took my degree in it." She didn't add that she came by her interest in military history quite naturally, nor that her grandfather had known General George S. Patton, Jr., personally.

"Well!"

"You have an associate's degree in criminal justice

and you're going to night school working on your B.A.," she blurted out.

He laughed. "What's my shoe size?"

"Eleven." She cleared her throat. "Sorry. I have a file on you, too."

He leaned forward, his large dark eyes narrow. "I'll have to compile one on you. Just to be fair."

She didn't want him to do that, but she just nodded. Maybe he couldn't dig up too much, even if he tried. She kept her private life very private.

She stood up. "I need to get back to work. I just wanted to be honest with you, about my job," she said. "I didn't want you to think I was being deliberately deceitful."

He stood up, too. "I never thought that."

He walked with her to the door. "Uh, is the lieutenant still bringing you roses?" he asked, and could have slapped himself for even asking the question.

"Oh, certainly not," she said primly. "That was just an apology, for using bad language in front of me."

"He's a widower," he said as they reached the door.

She paused and looked up at him. He was very close all of a sudden and she felt the heat from his body as her nostrils caught the faint, exotic scent of the cologne he used. He smelled very masculine and her heart went wild at the proximity. Her head barely topped his shoulder. He was tall and powerfully built, and she had an almost overwhelming hunger to lay her head on that shoulder and press close and bury her lips in that smooth, tanned throat.

She caught her breath and stepped back quickly. She looked up into his searching eyes and stood very still, like a cat in the sights of a hunter. She couldn't even think of anything to say.

Rick was feeling something similar. She smelled of wildflowers today. Her skin was almost translucent and he noticed that she wore little makeup. Her hair was caught up in a high ponytail, but he was certain that if she let it down, it would make a thick platinum curtain all the way to her waist. He wanted, badly, to loosen it and bury his mouth in it.

He stepped back, too. The feelings were uncomfortable. "Better get back to work," he said curtly. He was breathing heavily. His voice didn't sound natural.

"Yes. Uh, m-me, too," she stammered, and flushed, making her skin look even prettier.

He started to open the door for her. But he paused. "Someone told me that you like *The Firebird*."

She laughed nervously. "Yes. Very much."

"The orchestra is doing a tribute to Stravinsky Friday night." He moved one shoulder. He shouldn't do this. But he couldn't help himself. "I have two tickets. I was going to take Mom, but she's going to have to cater some cattlemen's meeting in Jacobsville and she can't go." He took a breath. "So I was wondering…"

"Yes." She cleared her throat. "I mean, if you were going to ask me…?" she blurted, embarrassed.

Her nervousness lessened his. He smiled at her in a way he never had, his chiseled mouth sensuous, his eyes very dark and soft. "Yes. I was going to ask you."

"Oh." She laughed, self-consciously.

He tipped her chin up with his bent forefinger and looked into her soft, pale green eyes. "Six o'clock? We'll have dinner first."

Her breath caught. Her heartbeat shook her T-shirt. "Yes," she whispered breathlessly.

His dark eyes were on her pretty bow of a mouth. It was slightly parted, showing her white teeth. He actually started bending toward it when his phone suddenly rang.

He jerked back, laughing deeply at his own helpless response to her. "Go to work," he said, but he grinned.

"Yes, sir." She started out the door. She looked back at him. "I live in the Oak Street apartments," she said. "Number 92."

He smiled back. "I'll remember."

She left, with obvious reluctance.

It took him a minute to realize that his phone was still ringing. He was going to date a colleague and the whole department would know. Well, what the hell, he muttered to himself. He was really tired of going to concerts and the ballet alone. She was a fed and she wouldn't be here long. Why shouldn't he have companionship?

GWEN GOT BACK to her own office and leaned back against the door with a long sigh. She was trembling from the encounter with Rick and so shocked at his invitation that she could barely get her breath back. He was going to date her. He wanted to take her out. She could barely believe it!

While she was savoring the invitation, her cell phone rang. She noted the number and opened it.

"Hi, Dad," she said, smiling. "How's it going?"

"Rough, or don't you watch the news, pudding?"

he asked with a laugh in his deep voice as he used his nickname for her.

"I do," she said. "I'm really sorry. Politicians should let the military handle military matters."

"Come up to D.C. and tell the POTUS that," he murmured.

"Why can't you just say President of the United States?" she teased.

"I'm in the military. We use abbreviations."

"I noticed."

"How's it going with you?"

"I'm working on a sensitive matter."

"I've been talking to your boss about it," he replied. "And I told him that I don't like having you put on the firing line like this."

She winced. She could imagine that encounter. Her boss, while very nice, was also as bullheaded as her father. It would have been interesting to see how it ended.

"And he told you...?"

He sighed. "That I could mind my own damned business, basically," he explained. "We're a lot alike."

"I noticed."

"Anyway, I hope you're packing, and that the detective you're working with is, also."

"We both are, but the general isn't a bad man."

"He's wanted for kidnapping!"

"Yes, well, he's desperate for money, but he didn't really hurt anybody."

"A man was killed in his camp," he returned curtly.

"Yes, the general shot him for trying to assault Gracie Pendleton," she replied. "He caught him in the act.

Gracie was bruised and shaken, but he got to her just in time. The guy was one of the Fuentes organization."

There was a long silence. "I didn't hear that part."

"Not many people have."

He sighed. "Well, maybe he's not as bad a man as I thought he was."

"We want him on our side. He has a son that he didn't know about. We're trying to get an entrée into his camp, to make contact with him. It isn't easy."

"I know about that, too." He paused. "How's your love life?" he teased.

She cleared her throat. "Actually, Sergeant Marquez just invited me to a symphony concert."

There was a longer pause. "He likes classical music?"

"Yes, and the ballet." Her eyes narrowed. "And no smart remarks, if you please."

"I like classical music."

"But you hate ballet," she pointed out. "And you think anybody who does is nuts."

"So I have a few interesting flaws," he conceded.

"He's also a military history buff," she added quickly. "World War II and North Africa."

"How ironic," he chuckled.

She smiled to herself. "Yes, isn't it?"

He drew in a long sigh. "You coming home for Christmas?"

"Of course," she agreed. She smiled sadly. "Especially this year."

"I'm glad." He bit off the words. "It hasn't been easy. Larry's wife calls me every other night, crying."

"Lindy will adjust," she said softly. "It's just going to take time. She and Larry were married for ten years and they didn't have children. That will make it harder for her. But she's strong. She'll manage."

"I hope so." There was a scraping sound, as if he was getting up out of a chair. "His commanding officer got drunk and wrecked a bar up in Maryland, while he was on R&R," he said.

"Larry's death wasn't his fault," she replied tersely. "Any officer who goes into a covert situation knows the risks and has to be willing to take them."

"I told him that," her father replied. "Damn it, he cried…!" He cleared his throat, choking back the emotion. "I called up Brigadier Langston and told him to get that man some help before he becomes a statistic. He promised he would."

"General Langston was fond of Larry, too," she said quietly. "I remember him at the funeral…"

There was a pause. "Let's talk about something else."

"Okay. How do you feel about giving chickens the vote?"

He burst out laughing.

"Or we could decide where we're going to eat on Christmas Eve, because I'm not spending my days off in the kitchen," she said.

"Good thing. We'd starve or die of carbon monoxide poisoning," he replied.

"I can cook! I just don't like to."

"If you'd use timers, we'd have food that didn't turn black before we got to eat it," he said. "I can cook anything," he added smugly.

"I remember." She sighed. "Rick's mom is a great cook," she replied. "She owns a restaurant."

"She does? You should marry him. You'd never have to worry about cooking again." He chuckled.

She blushed. "It's just a date, Dad."

"Your first one in how many years…?"

"Stop that," she muttered. "I date."

"You went to the Laundromat with a guy who lived in your apartment building," he burst out. "That's not a date!"

"It was fun. We ate potato chips and discussed movies while our clothes got done," she replied.

He shook his head. "Pudding, you're hopeless."

"Thanks!"

"I give up. I have to go. I've got a meeting with the Joint Chiefs in ten minutes."

"More war talk?"

"More withdrawal talk," he said. "There's a rumor that the POTUS is going to offer me Hart's job."

"You're kidding!"

"That's what they're saying."

"Will you take it?" she asked, excited.

"Watch the news and we'll find out."

"That would be great!"

"I might be in a position to do something more useful," he said. "But, we'll see. I guess I'd do it, if they ask me."

"Good for you!"

"Say, do you ever see Grange?"

"Grange? You mean, the Pendletons' foreman?" she asked, disconcerted.

"Yes. Winslow Grange. He was in my last overseas command." He smiled. "Had a real pig of an officer, who sent him into harm's way understrength and with a battle plan that some kindergarten kid could have come up with. Grange tied him up, put him in the trunk of his own car and led the assault himself. He was invited to leave the army with an honorable discharge or be court-martialed. He left. But he came back to testify against his commanding officer, who was dishonorably discharged after a nasty trial."

"Good enough for him," she said curtly.

"I do agree. Anyway, Winslow is a friend of mine. I'd love to see him sometime. You might pass that along. We could always use someone like him in D.C. if he gets tired of horse poop."

She wondered if she should tell her father what his buddy Grange was rumored to be doing right now, but that was probably a secret she should keep. "If I see him, I'll tell him," she promised.

"Take care of yourself, okay? You're the only family I've got left." His deep voice was thick with emotion.

"Same here," she replied. "Love you, Dad."

"Mmm-hmm." He wasn't going to say it out loud. He never did. But he loved her, so she didn't make a smart remark.

"I'll call you in a few days, just to check in. Okay?"

"That's a deal." His hand went over the receiver. "Yes, I'm on my way," he told someone else. "Gotta go. See you, kid."

"Bye, Dad."

He hung up. She put the phone back in her pocket. It seemed to be a day for revelations.

SHE HAD A beautiful little couture black dress, with expensive black slingbacks and a frilly black shawl that she'd gotten in Madrid. She wore those for her date with Rick, and she let her hair down, brushing it until it was shiny, like a pale satin curtain down her back. She left her glasses off for once. If she wasn't driving, she didn't need them, and a symphony concert didn't really require perfect vision.

Rick wore a dinner jacket and a black tie. His own hair was still in its elegant ponytail, but tied with a neat black ribbon. He looked very sharp.

He stared at her with disconcerting interest when she opened the door, taking in the nice fit of her dress with its modest rounded neckline and lacy hem that hit just at mid-calf. Her pretty little feet were in strappy high heels that left just a hint of the space between her toes visible. It was oddly sexy.

"You look…very nice," he said, his eyes taking in her flushed, lovely complexion and her perfect mouth, just dabbed with pale lipstick.

"Thanks! So do you," she replied, laughing nervously.

He produced a box from behind his back and handed it to her. It was a beautiful cymbidium orchid, much like the ones she had back at her father's home that the housekeeper faithfully misted each day.

"It's lovely!" she exclaimed.

He raised one shoulder and smiled self-consciously. "They wanted to give me one you wore around the wrist, but I explained that we weren't going to a dance and I wanted one that pinned."

"I like this kind best." She took it out of the box and pinned it to the dress, smiling at the way it complemented the dark background. "Thanks."

"My pleasure. Shall we go?"

"Yes!"

She grabbed her evening bag, closed the door and locked it and let him help her into his pickup truck.

"I should have something more elegant to drive than this," he muttered as he climbed in beside her.

"But I love trucks!" she exclaimed. "My dad has one that he drives around our place when he's home."

He grinned. "Well, maybe I'll get a nice car one day."

"It doesn't matter what you go in, as long as it gets you to your destination," she pointed out. "I even like Humvees."

His eyebrows arched. "And where do you get to ride in those?"

She bit her tongue. "Uh…"

"I forgot. Your brother was in the military, you said," he interrupted. "Sorry. I didn't mean to bring back sad memories for you."

She drew in a long breath. "He died doing what he felt was important for his country," she replied. "He was very patriotic and spec ops was his life."

His eyebrows arched.

"He died in a classified operation," she added. "His commanding officer just went on a huge bender. He feels responsible. He ordered the incursion."

His eyes softened. "That's the sort of man I wouldn't mind serving under," he said quietly. "A man with a conscience, who cares about his men."

She smiled. "My dad's like that, too. I mean, he's a man with a conscience," she said quickly.

He didn't notice the slip. He reached out and touched

her soft cheek. "I'm sorry for your loss," he said. "I don't have siblings. But I wish I did."

She managed a smile. "Larry was a wonderful brother and a terrific husband. His wife is taking it hard. They didn't have any kids."

"Tough."

She nodded. "It's going to be hard to get through Christmas," she said. "Larry was a nut about it. He came home to Lindy every year and he brought all sorts of foreign decorations with him. We've got plenty that he sent us…"

He moved closer. His big hands framed her face and lifted it. Her pale green eyes were swimming in tears. He bent, helpless, and softly kissed away the tears.

"Life is often painful," he whispered. "But there are compensations."

While he spoke, his chiseled lips were moving against her eyelids, her nose, her cheeks. Finally, as she held her breath in wild anticipation, his lips hovered just over her perfect bow of a mouth. She could feel his breath, taste its minty freshness, see the hard curve of his lips that filled her vision to the exclusion of anything else.

She hung there, at his mouth, her eyes half-closed, her skin tingling from the warm strength of his hands framing her face, waiting, waiting, waiting…!

He drew in an unsteady breath and bent closer, logic flying out the window as the wildflower scent of her made him weak. Her mouth was perfect. He wanted to feel its softness under his lips, taste her. He was sure that she was going to be delicious…

The sudden sound of a horn blowing raucously on

the street behind them shocked them apart. He blinked, as if he was under the influence of alcohol. She didn't seem much calmer. She fumbled with her purse.

"I guess we should go," he said with a forced laugh. "We want to have enough time to eat before the concert."

"Y...yes," she agreed.

"Seat belt," he added, nodding toward it.

"Oh. Yes! I usually put it on at once," she added as she fumbled it into place.

He laughed, securing his own.

Her shy smile made him feel taller. Involuntarily, his fingers linked with hers as he started the truck and pulled out into traffic. He wouldn't even let himself think about how he'd gone in headfirst with a colleague, against all his best instincts. He was too happy.

They ate at a nice restaurant in San Antonio, one with a flamenco theme and a live guitarist with a Spanish dancer in a beautiful red dress with puffy sleeves and the ruffled, long-trained dress that was familiar to followers of the dance style. The performance was short, but the applause went on for a long time. The duet was impressive.

"What a treat," she said enthusiastically. "They're so good!"

"Yes, they are." He grinned. "I love flamenco."

"So do I. I bought this old movie, *Around the World in 80 Days,* and it had a guy named Jose Greco and his flamenco dance troupe in it. That's when I fell in love with flamenco. He was so talented," she said.

"I've seen tapes of Jose Greco dancing," he replied. "He truly was phenomenal."

"My mother used to love Latin dances," she said dreamily, smiling. "She could do them all."

"Is she still alive?" he asked carefully.

She hesitated. She shook her head. "We lost her when I was in my final year of high school. Dad was overseas and couldn't even come back for the funeral, so Larry and I had to do everything. Dad never got over it. He was just starting to, when Larry died."

"Why couldn't your father come home?" he asked, curious.

She swallowed. "He was involved in a classified mission," she said. She held up a hand when he started to follow up with another question, smiling to lessen the sting. "Sorry, but he couldn't even tell me what he was doing. National security stuff."

His eyebrows arched. "Your dad's in the military?"

She hesitated. But it wouldn't hurt to agree. He was. But Rick would be thinking of a regular soldier, and her dad was far from regular. "Yes," she replied.

"I see."

"You don't, but I can't say any more," she told him.

"I guess not. Wouldn't want to tick off the brass by saying something out of turn, right?" he teased.

"Right." She had to fight a laugh. Her father was the brass; one of the highest ranking officers in the U.S. Army, in fact.

The waiter who took their order was back quickly with cups of hot coffee and the appetizers, buffalo wings and French fries with cheese and chili dip.

Rick tasted the wings and laughed as he put it quickly back down. "Hot!" he exclaimed.

"I'm glad I'm wearing black," she sighed. "If I had

on a white dress, it would be red-and-white polka dotted when I finished eating. I wear most of my food."

His dark eyebrows arched and he grinned. "Me, too."

She laughed. "I'm glad it's not just me."

He tried again with the French fries. "These are really good. Here. Taste."

She let him place it at her lips. She bit off the end and sighed. "Delicious!"

"They have wonderful food, including a really special barbecue sauce for the wings. Want to know where they got it?" he asked mischievously.

"From your mother?" she guessed.

He shook his head. "It seems that FBI senior agent Jon Blackhawk came here to eat with his brother, Kilraven, one night. Jon tasted their barbecue sauce, made a face, got up, walked into the kitchen and proceeded to have words with the chef."

"You're kidding!"

"I'm not. It didn't come to blows, but only because Jon put on an apron and showed the chef how to make a proper barbecue sauce. When the chef tasted it, so the story goes, he asked which cordon bleu academy in Paris Mr. Blackhawk had attended. He got the shock of his life when Jon named it." He grinned. "You see, he actually went to Paris and took courses. His new wife is one lucky woman. She'll never have to go in the kitchen unless she really wants to."

"I heard about them," she replied. "That's one interesting family."

He munched a French fry thoughtfully. "I'd love to have kids," he said solemnly. "A big family to make up for what I never had." His expression was bitter. "Barbara is the best mother on the planet, but I wish I'd had brothers and sisters."

"You do at least still have a father living," she pointed out.

"A father who's going to get the shock of his life when he's introduced to his grown-up son," he said. "And I wonder if Ramirez has had any luck getting his sister-in-law to approach the general."

As if in answer to the question, his cell phone began vibrating. He checked the number, gave her a stunned glance and got to his feet. "I'll be right back. I have to take this."

She nodded. She liked his consideration for the other diners. He took the call outside on the street, so that he wouldn't disturb other people with his conversation.

He was back in less than five minutes. He sat back down. "Imagine that," he said on a hollow laugh. "Gracie talked to the general. He wants us to come to the border Monday morning for a little chat, as he put it."

Her eyebrows arched. "Progress," she said, approving.

He sighed. "Yes. Progress." He didn't add that he had misgivings and he was nervous as hell. He just finished eating.

CHAPTER SEVEN

RICK WAS PREOCCUPIED through the rest of the meal. Gwen didn't talk much, either. She knew he had to be unsettled about the trip to the border, for a lot of reasons.

He held her hand on the way to the car, his strong fingers tangling in hers.

"It will be all right," she blurted out.

They reached the passenger door and he paused, looking down at her. "Will it?"

"You're a good man," she said. "He'll be very proud of you."

He was uncertain. "You think?"

She loved the smell of his body, the warm strength of it near her. She loved everything about him. "Yes."

He smiled tenderly. She made him feel tall, powerful, important. Women had made him feel undervalued for years, mostly by thinking of him as nothing more than a friend. Gwen was different. She was a working girl, from his own middle-class strata. She was pretty, in her way, and smart. And she knew her way around a handgun, he thought amusedly. But she also stirred his senses in a new and exciting way.

"You're nice," he said suddenly.

She grimaced. "Rub it in."

"No. Nice, in a very positive way," he replied. His expression was somber. "I don't like sophisticated women. I like brains in a woman, and even athletic outlooks. But I do mind women who think of themselves as party favors. You get me?"

She smiled. "I feel the same way about men like that."

He smiled. "You and I, we don't belong in a modern setting."

"We'd look very nice in a Victorian village," she agreed. "Like Edward in the Twilight vampire series of books and movies. I love those. I guess I've seen the movies ten times each and read the books on my iPod every night."

"I don't watch vampire movies. I like werewolves."

"Oh, but there are werewolves in them, too. Nice werewolves."

"You're kidding."

She hesitated. "I've got all the DVDs. I was wondering…"

He moved a step closer, so that she was backed into the car door. "You were wondering?"

"Uh, yes, if you'd like to maybe watch the movies with me?" she asked him. "I could make a pizza. Or we could…order…one…?"

She was whispering now, and her voice was breaking because his mouth had moved closer with every whispered word until it was right against her soft lips.

"Gwen?"

"Hmm?"

"Shut up," he whispered against her lips, and his

crushed down on them with warm, sensual, insistent hunger.

A muffled sob broke from her throat as she lifted her arms and pressed her body as close as she could get it to his tall, powerful form. He groaned, too, as the insane delight pulsed through him like fire.

He moved, shifting her, so that one long leg was between her skirt, and his mouth was suddenly invasive, starving.

"Detective!"

He heard a voice. It sounded close. And shocked. And angry. He lifted his head, still reeling from Gwen's soft mouth.

"Hmm?" he murmured, turning his head.

"Detective Sergeant Marquez," a deep, angry voice repeated.

"Sir!" He jumped back, almost saluted, and tried to look normal. He hoped his jacket was covering a blatant reminder of his body's interest in Gwen's.

"What the hell are you doing?" Lieutenant Hollister asked gruffly.

"It's okay, sir," Gwen faltered. "He was, uh, helping me get my earring unstuck from my dress."

He blinked and scowled. "What?"

"My earring, sir." She dangled it in her hand. "It caught on my dress. Detective Marquez was helping me get it loose. I guess it did look odd, the position we were in." She laughed with remarkable acting ability.

"Oh. I see." Hollister cleared his throat. He shoved his hands in his pockets. "I'm very sorry. It looked, well, I mean…" He cleared his throat again. He scowled. "I thought you didn't date colleagues," he shot at Marquez, who had by reciting multiplication tables made a remarkably quick recovery.

"I don't, sir," Marquez agreed. "We both like flamenco, and there's a dancer here…"

Hollister held up his hand and declared, "Say no more. That's why I came. Alone, sadly," he added with a speculative and rather sad look at Gwen.

"She's a great dancer," Gwen said. "And that guitarist!"

He nodded. "Her husband."

"Really!" Gwen exclaimed.

"Oh, yes. They've appeared all over Europe. I understand they're being considered for a bit part in a movie that's filming near here next year."

"That would be so lovely for them," Gwen enthused.

Rick checked his watch. "We'd better go. I've got an appointment early Monday morning. I thought I'd brush up on my Spanish over the weekend," he added dryly.

"Yes, I heard about that," Hollister said quietly. "It will go all right," he told Rick. "You'll see."

Rick was touched. "Thanks."

Hollister shrugged. "You're a credit to my department. Don't let him talk you into going to South America, okay?"

Rick smiled. "I'm not much good with rocket launchers."

"Me, neither," the lieutenant agreed. He glanced at Gwen and smiled. "Well, sorry about the mistake. Have a good evening."

"You, too, sir," Gwen said, and Rick nodded assent.

Hollister nodded back and walked, distracted, toward the restaurant.

Rick helped Gwen into the truck and burst out laughing. So did she.

"Did I ever tell you that I minored in theater in college?" she asked. "They said I had promise."

"You could make movies," he said flatly. He shook his head as he started the truck. "Quick thinking."

"Thanks." She flushed a little.

Neither of them mentioned that they'd been so far gone that anything could have happened, right there in the parking lot, if the lieutenant hadn't shown up. But it was true. Also true was the look the lieutenant had been giving them. He seemed to have more than the usual interest in Gwen. He wasn't really the sort of man to put a rose on a woman's desk unless he meant it. Rick was thinking that he had some major competition there, if he didn't watch his step. Hollister's tone hadn't been one of outraged decorum so much as jealous anger.

RICK LEFT GWEN at her door. He was more cautious this time, but he did pull her close and kiss her good-night with barely restrained passion.

She held him, kissing him back, loving the warm, soft press of his mouth on hers.

"I'm out of practice," he murmured as he stepped back.

"Me, too," she said breathlessly, her eyes full of stars as they met his in the light from the security lamps.

"I guess we could practice with each other," he murmured dryly.

She flushed and laughed nervously. "I'd like that."

"Yes. So would I." He bent again, brushing his mouth

lightly over hers and forcing himself not to go in head-first. "Are you coming along, in the morning?"

She nodded. "I have to."

He smiled. "Good. I could use the moral support."

She smiled back. "Thanks."

"Well. I'll see you at the office Monday."

"Yes."

He turned and took a step. He stopped. He turned. She was still standing there, her expression confused, waiting, still...

He walked back to her. "Unlock the door," he said quietly.

She fumbled the key into the lock and opened it. He closed it behind him, his arms enveloping her in the dark hallway, illuminated by a single small lamp in the living room. His mouth searched for hers, found it, claimed it, possessed it hungrily.

His arms were insistent, locking her against the length of his powerful body. She moaned, a sound almost like a sob of pleasure.

He was feeling something very similar.

"What the hell," he whispered into her lips as he bent and lifted her, still kissing her, and carried her to the long, soft sofa.

They slid down onto it together, his body covering hers, one long leg insinuating itself between her skirt, between her soft thighs. His lean hands went to the back of the dress, finding the hook and the zipper.

She was drowning in pleasure. She'd never felt anything remotely similar to the sensations that were washing over her like ripples of unbelievable delight.

He slid the dress off her arms, along with the tiny

straps of the black slip she wore under it, exposing a small, black-lace bra that revealed more than it covered. She had pretty little breasts, firm and very soft.

His hand slid under the bra, savoring the warm softness of the flesh, exciting the hard little tip, making her shiver with new sensations.

She hadn't done this before. He knew it without being told. He smiled against her mouth. It was exciting, and new, to be the first man. He never had been. Not that there had even been that many women that he'd been almost intimate with. And, in recent years, nobody. Like Gwen, he'd never indulged in casual sex. He was as innocent, in his way, as she was. Well, he knew a little more than she did. When he touched his mouth to her breast, she lifted toward his lips with a shocked little gasp. He smiled as his mouth opened, taking the hard tip inside and pulling at it gently with his tongue.

Her nails bit into the muscles of his arms as he removed his jacket and tie and shirt, wanting so badly to be closer, closer...

She felt air on her skin and then the hard, warm press of hair and muscle as they locked together, both bare from the waist up.

His mouth was insistent now, hungry, demanding. She felt his hand sliding up her bare thigh and she knew that very soon they would reach a point from which there was no return.

"N...no," she whispered, pushing at his chest. "Rick? Rick!"

He heard her voice through a bloodred haze of desire that locked his muscles so tightly that he could barely move for the tension. She was saying something. What? It sounded like…no?

He lifted his head. He looked into wide, uneasy green eyes. He felt her body tensed, shivering.

"I'm sorry…" she began.

He blinked once, twice. He drew in a breath that sounded as ragged as he felt. "Good Lord," he exhaled.

She swallowed. They were very intimate. Neither of them had anything on above the waist. His hand was still on her thigh. He removed it quickly and lifted up just a little, his high cheekbones flushing when he got a sudden, stark, uninterrupted view of her pretty pink breasts with tight little dusky pink tips very urgently stating the desire of the owner for much more than looking.

Embarrassed, she drew her hands up over them as he levered himself away and sat up.

"I'm sorry," he said, averting his eyes while she fumbled her dress back on. "I didn't mean to…"

"Of c-course not," she stammered. "Neither did I. It's all right."

He laughed. His body felt as if it had been hit with a bat several times in strategic places and he ached from head to toe. "Sure it is."

"Oh, I'm sorry!" she groaned. She wasn't experienced, but she had friends who were, and she knew what was wrong with him. "Here, just a sec."

She went to the kitchen and came back with a cold beer from the fridge. "Detective Rogers comes over from time to time and she likes this brand of light beer," she explained. "I don't drink, but I think people need to sometimes. You need to, a little…?"

He gave her an exasperated sigh. "Gwen, I'm a police detective sergeant!"

"Yes, I know…"

"I can't take a drink and drive!"

She stared at him, looked at the beer. "Oh."

He burst out laughing. It broke the ice and slowly he began to feel normal again.

She looked around them. His jacket and shirt and tie, and her shoes and his holster and pistol were lying in a heap beside the sofa.

His gaze followed hers. He laughed again. "Well."

"Yes. Uh. Well." She looked at the can of beer, laughed and set it down. Her glasses were where she'd tossed them on the end table but she didn't put them on. She didn't want to see his expression. She was already embarrassed.

He put his shirt and tie back on and slipped into his jacket before he replaced the holstered pistol on his belt. "At least you don't object to the gun," he mused.

She shrugged. "I usually have a concealed carry in my purse," she confessed.

His eyebrows arched. "No ankle holster?" he asked.

She made a face. "Weighs down my leg too much."

He nodded. He looked at her in a different way now. Possessively. Hungrily. He moved forward, but he only took her oval face in his hands and searched her eyes, very close up. He was somber.

"From now on," he said gently, "we say good-night at the door. Right?"

He was hinting at a relationship. "From now on?" she said hesitantly.

He nodded. He searched her eyes. "There aren't that

many women running around loose who belong to the
Victorian era, don't mind firearms and like to watch
flamenco dancing."

She smiled with pure delight. "I was going to say the
same about you—well, you're not a woman, of course."

"Of course."

He bent and kissed her very softly. He lifted his head
and his large brown eyes narrowed. "If Hollister puts
another rose on your desk, I'm going to deck him, and
I don't care if he fires me."

Her face became radiant. "Really?"

"Really." His jaw tautened. "You're mine."

She flushed. She lowered her eyes to his strong neck,
where a pulse beat very strongly. She nodded.

He hugged her close, rocked her in his arms. He drew
in a long breath, finally, and let her go. He smiled ruefully. "After we get through talking with the general,
Monday, I'm going to take you to meet my mother."

"You are?"

"You'll love her. She'll love you, too," he promised.
He glanced at his watch and grimaced. "I have to get
going. I'll pick you up here at 6:00 a.m. sharp, okay?"

"I could drive to the office…"

"I'll pick you up here."

She smiled. Her eyes were bright with pleasure.
"Okay."

He chuckled. "Lock the door after me."

"I will. I really enjoyed the flamenco."

"So did I. I know another Latin dance club over on
the west side of town. We'll go there next time. Do you
like Mexican food?"

"Love it."

He smiled. "Theirs is pretty hot."

"No worries, I don't have any taste buds left. I eat jalapenos raw," she added with a grin.

"Whew! My kind of girl."

She grinned. "I noticed."

He laughed, kissed her hair and walked out the door.

After he climbed back into the pickup truck, he paused and waited until she was safely in her apartment before he drove off.

She didn't sleep that night. Not a wink. She was too excited, exhilarated and hungrily, passionately really in love for the first time in her life.

RICK WAS SOMBER and nervous Monday morning when he picked Gwen up for the drive to the border. It had turned cold again and she was wearing a sweater and thick jeans with a jacket and boots.

"Summer yesterday, winter today," she remarked, readjusting her seat belt.

"That's Texas," he said fondly.

"Is Ramirez going to meet us at the border station?"

"Yes," he said. "He and Gracie."

Her eyebrows arched. "Mrs. Pendleton is coming, too? Isn't that dangerous?"

"We're not going over the border," he reminded her. "Just up to it."

"Oh. Okay."

He glanced at her, warm memories of the night before still in his dark eyes. She was lovely, he thought. Pretty and smart and good with a gun.

She felt his eyes but she didn't meet them. She was nervous, too. She worried about how he might feel when he learned the truth about her own background. She was still keeping secrets. She hoped he wouldn't feel differently when he learned them.

But right now, the biggest secret of all was about to be revealed to a man who had no apparent family and seemed to be content with his situation. Gwen wondered how the general would feel when he was introduced to a son he didn't even know existed.

They pulled up to the small border station, which wasn't much more than an adobe building beside the road, next to a cross arm that was denoted as the Mexican-American border, with appropriate warning signs.

A tall, sandy-haired man came out to meet them. He introduced himself as the border patrol agent in charge, Don Billings, and indicated a Lincoln town car sitting just a little distance way. He motioned.

The car pulled up, stopped and Rodrigo Ramirez got out, going around to open the door for his sister-in-law, Gracie Pendleton. They came forward and introductions were made.

Gracie was blonde and pretty and very pregnant. She laughed. "The general is going to be surprised when he sees me," she said with a grin. "I didn't mention my interesting condition. Jason and I are just over the moon!"

"Is it a boy or a girl?" Gwen wanted to know.

"We didn't let them tell us," she said. "We want it to be a surprise, so I bought everything yellow instead of pink or blue."

Gwen laughed. "I'd like it to be a surprise, too, if I ever had a baby." Her eyes were dreamy. "I'd love to have a big family."

Rick was watching her and his heart was pounding.

He'd like a big family, too. Her family. He cleared his throat. Memories of last night were causing him some difficulty in intimate places. He thought of sports until he calmed down a little.

"He should be here very soon," Ramirez said.

Even as he spoke, a pickup truck came along the dusty road from across the border, stopped and was waved through by the border agent.

The truck stopped. Two doors opened. Winslow Grange, wearing one of the very new high-tech camouflage patterned suits with an automatic pistol strapped to his hip, came forward. Right beside him was a tall, elegant-looking Hispanic man with thick, wavy black hair and large black eyes in a square face with chiseled lips and a big grin for Gracie.

"A baby?" he enthused. "How wonderful!"

She laughed, taking his outstretched hands. "Jason and I think so, too. How have you been?"

"Very busy," he said, indicating Grange. "We're planning a surprise party." He wiggled his eyebrows at the border agent. "I'm sorry that I can't say more."

"So am I." The border patrolman chuckled.

Gwen came forward, her eyes curious and welcoming at the same time. "You and I haven't met, but I think you've heard of me," she said gently. She held out her hand. "I'm Gwendolyn Cassaway. CIA."

He shook her hand warmly, and then raised it to his lips. He glanced at the man with her, a tall young man with long black hair in a ponytail and an oddly familiar face. "Your boyfriend?" he asked, lifting an eyebrow at the reaction the young man gave when he kissed Gwen's hand.

"Uh, well, uh, I mean…" She cleared her throat. "This is Detective Sergeant Ricardo Marquez, San Antonio Police Department."

General Emilio Machado looked at the younger man with narrowed, intent eyes. "Marquez."

"Yes."

Machado was curious. "You look familiar, somehow. Do I know you?"

He studied the general quietly. "No. But my birth mother was Dolores Ortíz. She was from Sonora. I look like her."

Machado stared at him intently. "She lived in Sonora, in a little village called Dolito. I knew her once," he said. "She married a man named Jackson," he added coldly.

"My stepfather," Rick said curtly.

"I have heard about your late stepfather. He was a brutal man."

Rick liked Machado already. "Yes. I have the scars to prove it," he added quietly.

Machado drew in a long breath. He looked around him. "This is a very unusual place to meet with federal agents, and I feel that I am being set up."

"Not at all," Gwen replied. "But we do have something to tell you. Something that might be upsetting."

Nobody spoke. There were somber, grim faces all around.

"You brought a firing squad?" Machado mused, looking from one to the other. "Or you lured me here to arrest me for kidnapping Gracie?"

"None of the above," Gwen said quietly. She took a deep breath. This was a very unpleasant chore she'd been given. "We were doing a routine background check on you for our files and we came across your relationship with Dolores Ortíz. She gave birth to a child out of wedlock down in Sonora. Thirty-one years ago."

Machado was doing quick math in his head. He looked at Rick pointedly, with slowly growing comprehension. The man had looked familiar. Was it possible…? He moved a step closer and cocked his head as he studied the somber-faced young man.

Then he laughed coldly. "Ah. Now I see. You know that I have spies in my country who are even now planting the seeds of revolution. You know that I have an army and that I am almost certain to retake the government of Barrera. So you are searching for ways to ingratiate yourself with me…excuse me, with my oil and natural gas reserves as well as my very strategic location in South America." He gave Rick a hard glance. "You produce a candidate for my son, and think that I will accept your word that he is who he says he is."

"I haven't said a damned thing," Rick snapped back icily.

Machado's eyebrows shot up. "You deny their conclusion?"

Rick glared at him. "You think I'm thrilled to be lined up as the illegitimate son of some exiled South American dictator?"

Machado just stared at him for a minute. Then he burst out laughing.

"Rick," Gwen groaned from beside him.

"I was perfectly content to think my real father was in a grave somewhere in Mexico," Rick continued.

"And then she showed up with this story..." He pointed at Gwen.

She raised her hand. "Cash Grier told your mother," she reminded him quickly. "I had nothing to do with telling you."

"All right, my mother told me," he continued.

"Your mother is dead," Machado said, frowning.

"Barbara Ferguson, in Jacobsville, adopted me when my mother and stepfather were killed in an auto accident," Rick continued. "She runs the café there."

Machado didn't speak. He'd never considered the possibility that Dolores would become pregnant. They'd been very close until her parents discovered them one night in an outbuilding and her father threatened to kill Machado if he ever saw him again. He'd gone to work for a big landowner soon afterward and moved to another village. He hadn't seen Dolores again.

Could she have been pregnant? They'd done nothing to prevent a child. But he'd only been fourteen. He couldn't have fathered a son at that age, surely? In fact, he'd never fathered another child in the years since, and he had been coaxed into trying, at least once. The attempt had ended in total failure. It had hurt his pride, hurt his ego, made him uncertain about his manhood. He had thought, since then, that he must be sterile.

But here was, if he could believe the statement, proof of his virility. Could this really be his son?

He moved forward a step. Yes, the man had his eyes. He had Dolores's perfect teeth, as well. He was tall and powerfully built, as Machado was. His hair was long and black and straight, without the natural waves that were in Machado's. But, then, Dolores had long black hair that was smooth as silk and thick and straight.

"You think I would take your word for something this important, even with Gracie's help?" he asked Rick.

"Hey, I didn't come here to convince you of anything," Rick said defensively. "She—" he indicated Gwen "—got him—" he nodded at Ramirez "—to call her—" he pointed toward Gracie "—to have you meet us here. I got pulled into it because some feds think you'll listen to me even if you won't listen to them." He shrugged. "Of course, they haven't decided what to have me tell you just yet. I presume that's in the works and they'll let me know when they can agree on what day it is."

Machado listened to him, pursed his lips and laughed. "Sounds exactly like government policy to me. And I should know. I was head of a government once." His eyes narrowed and glittered. "And I will be, once again."

"I believe you," Gwen agreed.

"But for now," Machado continued, studying Rick. "What evidence exists that you really are my son? And it had better be good."

CHAPTER EIGHT

"DON'T LOOK AT ME," Rick said quietly. "I didn't come here to prove anything."

Gwen moved forward, removing a paper from her purse. "We were sure that you wouldn't accept anyone's word, General," she said gently. "So we took the liberty of having a DNA profile made from Sergeant Marquez's last physical when blood was drawn." She gave Rick an apologetic glance. "Sorry."

Rick sighed. "Accepted."

The general read the papers, frowned, read some more and finally handed them back. "That's pretty convincing."

Gwen nodded.

He glanced at Rick, who was standing apart from the others, hard-faced, with his hands deep in the pockets of his slacks.

The general studied him from under thick black eyelashes, with some consternation. His whole life had just been turned upside-down. He had a son. The man was a law enforcement officer. He was not bad-looking, seemed intelligent, too. Of course, there was that severe attitude problem...

"I don't like baseball," Rick said curtly when he noticed how the general was eyeing him.

Machado's thick eyebrows levered up. "You don't like baseball…?"

"In case you were thinking of father-son activities," Rick remarked drolly. "I don't like baseball. I like soccer."

Machado's dark eyes twinkled. "So do I."

"See?" Gwen said, grasping at straws, because this was becoming awkward. "Already, something in common…"

"Get down!"

While she was trying to understand the quick command from the general, Rick responded by tackling her. Rodrigo had Gracie in the limo, which had bulletproof glass, and Machado hit the ground with his pistol drawn at the same time Grange opened up with an army-issue repeating rifle.

"What the hell…!" Rick exclaimed as he leveled his own automatic, along with Gwen, at an unseen adversary, tracking his direction from the bullets hitting the dust a few yards away.

"Carver, IED, now!" Grange called into a walkie-talkie.

Seconds later, there was a huge explosion, a muffled cry, and a minute later, the sound of an engine starting and roaring, a dust cloud becoming visible as a person or persons unknown took off in the distance.

Grange grinned. "I always have a backup plan," he remarked.

"Good thing," Gwen exclaimed. "I didn't even consider an ambush!"

"Your father would have," Grange began.

She held up her hand and gave a curt shake of her head.

"You know her father?" Rick asked curiously.

"We were poker buddies, a few years back," Grange said. "Good man."

"Thanks," Gwen said, and she wasn't referring totally to the compliment. Grange would keep her secret; she saw it in his eyes.

Rick was brushing thick dust off his jacket and slacks. "Damn. They just came back from the dry cleaner."

"You should wear cotton. It cleans better," Machado suggested, indicating his own jeans and cotton shirt.

"Who was that, do you think?" Gwen asked somberly.

"Fuentes." Machado spat. "He and I have parted company. He amuses himself by sniping at me and my men."

"The drug lord? I thought his family was dead!" Gwen exclaimed.

"Most of it is. This is the last one of the Fuentes brothers, the stupid one, and he's clinging to power by his fingernails," the general told her. "He spies on me for a federal agency. Not yours," he told Gwen with a smile.

Ramirez left Gracie in the car and came back. "I don't think she should risk coming out here in the open," he said.

"I agree. She is all right?" Machado asked with some concern.

"Yes. Gracie really has guts," he replied. He frowned. "Which agency is Fuentes spying for?"

"Yours, I think, my friend," Machado told the DEA agent.

Ramirez let out a sigh. "We know there's a mole in our agency, someone very high level. We've never found out who it is."

"You should set Kilraven on him," Gwen mused dryly.

"I probably should," Ramirez agreed. "But we have our hands full right now with Mexican military coming over the border to protect drug shipments." He glanced toward the border patrol agent, who was talking to Gracie through a cracked window. "Our men on the border are in peril, always. We almost lost one some months ago, an agent named Kirk. He was very nearly killed. He left the agency and went back to his brothers on their Wyoming ranch. A great loss. He was good at his job, and he had contacts that we now lack."

"I can get you all the contacts you need," Machado promised. He glanced toward the distant hill where the sniper had been emplaced. "First I must deal with Fuentes."

"I didn't hear you say that," Gwen said firmly.

"Nor I," Ramirez echoed.

"Well, I did," Rick replied coldly. "And you're still wanted on kidnapping charges in my country, even though Mrs. Pendleton refuses to press them."

Machado's large eyes widened. "You would turn your own father in to the authorities?"

Rick's eyes narrowed. "The law is the law."

"You keep a book of statutes on your person?" the general asked.

Rick glared at him. "I've been a cop for a long time."

"Amazing. I have spent my life breaking most of the laws that exist, and here I find a son, a stranger, who goes by the book." His eyes narrowed. "I think perhaps they rigged the DNA evidence." He gave the detective a disparaging look. "I would never wear a suit like that, or grow my hair long. You look like a—what is the expression?—a hippie!"

Rick glared at him.

The general glared back.

"Uh, the sniper?" Ramirez reminded them. "He may have gone for reinforcements."

"True." Machado turned to Grange. "Perhaps you should order a sweep on the surrounding hills."

Grange smiled. "I already have."

"Good man. We will soon have a proper government in my country and you will be the commander of the forces in my country."

Ramirez choked. Gwen colored. Rick looked at them, trying to figure out why the hell they were so disturbed.

"We should go," Ramirez said, indicating the car. "I promised her husband that I would have her home very quickly. He might send a search party for us. Not a man to make an enemy of."

"Absolutely," Grange agreed.

"Thank you for making this meeting possible," Machado said, extending his hand to Ramirez.

Ramirez shook it, and then grinned. "It wasn't my idea. I'm related to the president of Mexico. He thought it would be a good idea."

Machado was impressed. "When I retake my country, perhaps you can speak to him for me about a trade agreement."

Ramirez admired the confidence in the other man's voice. "Yes, perhaps I can. Keep well."

"And you."

Gwen and Marquez waved them off before turning back to Machado.

"We should be going, too," Marquez said stiffly. "I have to get back to work."

Machado nodded. He studied his son with curious, strange eyes. "Perhaps, later, we can meet again."

"Perhaps," Rick replied.

"In a place where we do not have to fear an attack from my enemies," Machado said, shaking his head.

"I don't think we can get to Mars yet," Rick quipped.

Machado laughed. "Grange, we should go."

"Yes, sir."

Machado took Gwen's hand and kissed the back of it tenderly. "It has been a pleasure to meet you, *señorita*," he said with pure velvet in his deep voice.

Rick stepped in, took Gwen's hand and pulled her back. He glared at Machado, which made Gwen almost giddy with delight.

Machado's dark eyes twinkled. "So it is like that, huh?"

"Like what?" Rick asked innocently. He dropped Gwen's hand and looked uncomfortable.

"Never mind. I will be in touch."

"Thank you for coming," Gwen told the general.

"It was truly a pleasure." He winked at her, gave Rick a droll look and climbed back into the truck with Grange. They disappeared over the border. Rick stood staring after the truck with mixed feelings. Then he turned, said goodbye to the border agent and walked back to his truck with Gwen.

RICK KEPT TO himself for the next couple of days. Gwen didn't intrude. She knew that he was dealing with some emotional issues that he had to resolve in his own mind.

Meanwhile, she went on interviews with neighbors of the murdered college freshman, the case she'd been assigned to as lead detective.

"Did she have any close friends that you know of?" she asked the third neighbor, an elderly woman who seemed to have a whole roomful of cats. They were clean, brushed, well fed and there was no odor, so she must be taking excellent care of them.

"Oh, you've noticed the cats?" the woman asked her with a grin that made her seem years younger. "I'm babysitting."

Gwen blinked. "Excuse me?"

"Babysitting. I have four neighbors with cats, and we've had a problem with animals disappearing around here. So they leave their cats with me while they're at work, and I feed them. It's a nice little windfall for me, since I'm disabled, and the owners have emotional security since they don't have to worry about their furry 'families' going missing."

Gwen laughed. "Impressive."

"Thanks. I love animals. I wish I could afford to keep a cat, but I can't. This is the next best thing."

Gwen noted several pill bottles on the end table by the elderly lady's recliner.

"By the time I pay for all those out of my social security check," she told Gwen, "there's not much left over for bills and food."

Gwen winced. "That's not right."

The woman sighed. "The economy is terrible. I expect something awful will have to happen to finally set things right." She looked at Gwen over her glasses. "I don't expect to still be around then. But if aliens exist, and they want somebody to experiment on…" She raised her hand. "I'm ready to go. To some nice, green planet with lots of meadows and trees and no greedy humans destroying it all for a quick profit."

"You and I would get along," Gwen said with a smile.

The woman nodded. "Now, back to my neighbor. I do keep a watch on the apartment complex, mostly to try to protect myself. I can't fight off an intruder and I don't own a gun. So I make sure I know who belongs here and who doesn't." Her eyes narrowed. "There was a grimy young man with greasy hair who kept coming to see the college girl. She was trying to be nice, you could tell from her expression, but she never let him inside. Once, the last time he came, the police went to her apartment and stayed for several minutes."

Gwen's heart jumped. If there had been police presence, there would be a report, with details of the conversation. She jotted that down on her phone app, making virtual notes.

"That thing is neat," the elderly lady said. "One of my cat-owning friends has one. He can surf the net on it, buy groceries, books, all sorts of things. I never realized we had such things in the modern world. I suppose I live in the past."

Gwen made a mental note to make sure this nice lady

got a phone and several phone cards for Christmas, from an anonymous source. It would revolutionize her life.

"Yes, they are quite nice," Gwen said. She smiled. "Thanks for talking to me. You've been a very big help."

"It was my pleasure. I know you young folks don't have much free time, but if you're ever at a loose end, you can come and see me and I'll tell you about the FBI in the seventies."

Gwen stared at her.

"I was a federal agent," the woman told her. "One of the first women in the bureau."

"I would love to hear some stories about those days," Gwen told her. "And I'll make time."

The wrinkled face lit up. "Thank you!"

"No, thank you. I'm fond of pioneers," she replied.

She told Rick about the elderly woman.

"Yes, Evelyn Dorsey." He nodded, smiling. "She's something of a legend over at the FBI field office. Garon Grier goes to see her from time to time." He was the SAC, the special agent in charge, at the San Antonio Field Office now. "She shot it out with a gang of would-be kidnappers right over on the 410 Loop. Hit two of them before they shot her, almost fatally, and escaped. But she had a description of the car, right down to the license plate number, and she managed to get it out on the radio before she passed out. They nabbed the perps ten miles away. Back in those days, the radio was in the car, not on a belt. It was harder to be in law enforcement."

"I expect so. Ms. Dorsey was very helpful on our college freshman case, by the way. We did have a patrol unit respond to the freshman's call. I'm tracking down the officer who filed the report now."

"I hope we can catch the guy," he replied.

"The cold case unit wants him very badly. They think he's connected to the old case they're working on," she said. "One of those detectives was related to the victim in it."

"Sad."

"Yes." She moved closer to the desk. "You doing okay?"

He grimaced. "No," he said, with a faint smile.

"Why don't you come over and watch the Twilight movies with me tonight? We can order a pizza."

He cocked his head and the smile grew. "You know, that sounds like a very good idea."

She grinned. "Glad you think so. I like mushrooms and cheese and pepperoni."

His eyebrows lifted. "Have you been checking out my profile?"

"No. Why?"

"That's my favorite."

She beamed. "Another thing in common."

"We'll find more, I think."

"Yes."

RICK WASN'T COMFORTABLE with so-called chick flicks, but he was drawn into the movie almost at once. He barely noticed when the pizza delivery girl showed up, and only lifted his hand for the plate and coffee cup without taking his eyes off the screen.

Gwen was delighted. It was her favorite film. She kicked off her shoes and curled up beside him on the sofa to watch it again, sipping coffee and munching pizza in a contented silence. It was amazing, she thought, how comfortable they were with each other, even at this early stage of their relationship.

He glanced at her while the vampire was showing off his skills to the heroine on the screen. "You're right. This is very good."

"So are the books. I love all of them."

"I guess I'll have to buy them. It isn't often you find so many likable people in a story chain."

She sipped coffee. "You know, I hadn't thought of it that way, but you're right. Even the vampires are likable."

"Odd, isn't it? Likable monsters."

"But they aren't really monsters. They're just misunderstood living-challenged people."

He burst out laughing.

"More pizza?" she asked.

"I think I could hold one more slice."

"Me, too." She jumped up and went to get it.

After they finished eating, she curled up against him through the heroine's introduction to her boyfriend's family, the baseball game in the rain, the arrival of the more dangerous vampires, the heroine's brush with death and, finally, her appearance at the prom in a cast with her boyfriend.

"That was a roller coaster ride," he remarked. "Are there more?"

"Two more. Want to watch the next one?"

He turned toward her, his dark eyes on her radiant face. He pursed his lips. "Yes, I would. But not right now." He pulled her across his lap. "I'm suffering from affection deprivation. Do you think you could assist me?"

"Could I!" she whispered as his mouth came down on hers.

Each kiss became harder, more urgent. As they grew accustomed to the feel and taste of each other, the pleasure grew and it became more difficult to pull back.

He actually groaned when he found himself lying over her with half their clothes out of the way, just like before. He buried his face in her warm, frantically pulsing throat.

"I'm dying," he ground out.

"Me, too," she whispered back, shivering.

He lifted his head. His eyes were tormented. "How do you feel about marriage?"

She blinked.

He realized that he, the most non-impulsive man on earth, was doing something totally out of character. But he was already crazy about Gwen and the lieutenant was lurking. Even Machado had been giving her long looks. He didn't want her to end up with some other man while he was waiting for the right moment to do something. And besides, he was traditional, so was she, and there was this incredible, almost unbelievable physical compatibility.

He sighed. "Look, we get along very well. We're incredibly suited physically. We have similar jobs, outlooks on life, philosophies, and we're on the same social level. Why don't we drive over the border and get married? Right now. Afterward," he added with a speaking glance, "we can do what we're both dying to do without lingering feelings of guilt."

Her lips parted. She should have challenged that social level comparison immediately, but her body was on fire and all she could think of was relief. She loved him. He was at least fond of her. They both wanted kids. It would work. She would make it work.

"Yes," she blurted out.

He forced himself to get up and he pulled out his cell phone, scrolled down a list of names and punched in a button. "Yes. Ramirez? Sorry to call so late. Can you get me a direct line to the general? I need his help on a—" he glanced at Gwen "—personal matter."

Ramirez sighed. "All right. But you owe me one."

"Yes, I do."

There was a pause, another pause. Rick motioned Gwen for a pencil and paper. He wrote down a number. "Thanks!" he told Ramirez, and hung up. He dialed the number.

"Yes, it's your—" he hesitated "—your son. How do you feel about giving away the bride at a Mexican wedding? Oh, in about thirty minutes."

There was a burst of Spanish from the other end of the line. Rick replied in the same language, protesting that he wasn't up to anything immoral, he was trying to make sure everything was done properly and that meant a proper wedding. The general seemed to calm down. Another hesitation. Rick grinned.

"Thanks," he said, and hung up. He turned to Gwen and pursed his lips. "Do you have a white dress?"

"Do I have a white dress!" she exclaimed, and ran into the next room to put it on.

She left her hair long. The dress was close-fitting, with puffy sleeves and a draped beaded shawl. She looked young and very innocent. And most incredibly sexy.

Rick's body reacted to her visibly. He cleared his throat. "Don't notice that," he said curtly.

"Oh. Okay." She giggled as she joined him and looked up into his dark eyes. "Are you sure?" she asked hesitantly.

He framed her face in his hands and kissed her with breathless tenderness. "I don't know why, but I've never been so sure of anything. No cold feet?"

She shook her head. Her eyes were full of dreams. "Oh, no. Not at all."

He smiled. "Same here. We can share ammunition, too, so it will be cost effective to get married."

She burst out laughing. "I'll be sure to tell my father that when I explain why I didn't invite him to the ceremony."

He grimaced. "I'll have to do the same for my mother. But we don't have time to get them all together. We're eloping."

"Your father will have to be the audience," she said.

"My father." He smiled. "Let's go."

THE GENERAL WAS waiting for them at the border. They followed him down a long dusty road to a small village and stopped in front of a mission church with a shiny new bell.

"I donated the bell," the general informed them proudly. "They are good people here, and the priest is a nice young man, from the United States." He hesitated, glancing from one to the other. "I did not think to ask which religious denomination...?"

"Catholic." They both spoke at once, stared at each other and then burst out laughing.

"We hadn't discussed it before," Rick said.

"Well, it will be good," the general said with a big smile. "Come, the priest is waiting. You two, you're sure about this?"

Gwen looked at Rick with her heart in her eyes. "Very."

"Very, very," Rick added, his dark eyes shining.

"Then we shall proceed."

The general took Gwen down the aisle of the church on his arm. The whole village came to watch, including a number of small children who seemed to find the blonde lady's hair fascinating.

The priest smiled benevolently, read the marriage service. Then they came to the part about a ring.

Rick turned white. "Oh, no."

The general punched him. "Here. I remember everything." He handed him a small circle of gold that looked just right for Gwen's hand. "Something old. It belonged to my *abuela*," he added, "my grandmother." He smiled. "She would want it to stay in the family."

"It's beautiful," Gwen whispered. "Thank you."

The general nodded. Rick took the small circle of gold and slid it gently onto Gwen's finger, where it was a perfect fit. The priest pronounced them man and wife, and Rick bent to kiss her. And they were married.

NEITHER OF THEM remembered much about the rest of the evening. Back at Gwen's apartment, there was a feverish removal of cotton and lace, followed by an incredibly long session in bed that left them both covered in sweat, boneless with pleasure and totally exhausted.

Not that exhaustion stopped them. As soon as they

were breathing normally again, they reached for each other, and started all over.

"You know, it never occurred to me that marriage would be so much fun," Rick commented when they were finally sleepy.

Gwen, curled up against him, warm and satisfied, laughed softly. "Me, either. I always thought of it as something a little more dignified. You know, for children and..." She stopped.

He turned and looked down at her guilty face. "Hey. You want kids. I want kids. What's the problem?"

She relaxed. "You make it seem so simple."

"It is simple. Two people fall in love, get married and have a family." His eyes were on fire with his feelings. "We'll grow old together. But not right away. Maybe not at all," he added worriedly, "when my mother realizes that I got married without even telling her."

"My dad is going to go ballistic, too," she replied. "But he couldn't have come even if I'd had time to ask him. He's tied up with military stuff right now."

"Is he on active duty?"

"Oh, yes," she said, and there was another worry. She still had to tell Rick who her dad was, and all about the family he'd married into. That might be a source of discord. So she wasn't about to face it tonight.

She curled up close and wound her arms around him. "For a guy who never indulged, you're very good."

He laughed. "Compliment returned." He hugged her close. "They said it comes naturally. I guess it does. Of course, there were all these books I read. For educational purposes only."

She grinned. "I read a few of those, too."

He bent and brushed his mouth gently over hers. "I'm glad we waited," he said seriously, searching her eyes. "I know we're out of step with the world. But I don't care. This was right for us."

"Yes, it was. Thank you for having enough restraint," she added. "We couldn't have counted on me for it. I was on fire!"

"So was I. But I was thinking about later, generations later, when we tell our grandchildren and great-grand-children about how it was when we fell in love and got married." He closed his eyes. "It's a golden memory. Not a legalization of something that had gone on before."

She pressed her mouth into his warm, muscular shoulder with a smile. "And the nicest thing is that you're already my best friend."

"You're mine, too." He kissed her hair. "Go to sleep. We'll get up tomorrow and face the music."

"What?"

"I was just thinking," he mused, "that the lieutenant is going to foam at the mouth when we tell him."

"What?" she exclaimed.

"Just a hunch." He thought the lieutenant had a case on Gwen. Maybe, maybe not. But he was expecting fireworks the next day.

CHAPTER NINE

"FIREWORKS" WAS, IF ANYTHING, an understatement.

"You're married?" Lieutenant Hollister exclaimed.

Gwen moved a little closer to Rick. "Yes. Sorry, we would have invited you, but we didn't want the expense of a big wedding, so we eloped," she told him, stretching the truth.

"Eloped." Hollister leaned back in his chair with a grumpy sigh. He glared at Marquez. "Well, it was certainly quick."

"We knew how we felt at once," Rick replied with a smile at his wife. "No sense having a long engagement."

She smiled back. "Absolutely."

"Well, congratulations," Hollister said after a minute. He got up, smiled and shook hands with both of them. "How did your mother take it?" he asked Rick.

Rick grimaced. "Haven't told her."

"Why don't you two take the day off and call it a honeymoon," Hollister suggested. "Gail Rogers can sub for you," he told Rick. "I don't want Barbara coming after me with a bazooka because she heard the news from somebody else."

"Good idea," Rick said. "Thanks!"

"My pleasure. A wedding present. A short one," he

added. "You have to be back on the job tomorrow. And when are we losing you?" he asked Gwen.

She wasn't sure what he meant, and then she realized that she belonged to a federal agency. "I'm not sure. I'll have to talk to my boss and he'll have to discuss it with the captain here."

Hollister nodded. "You've done very well. I'll be sorry to lose you."

She smiled. "I'll be sorry to go. I may have to make some minor adjustments in my career path, as well," she added with a worried glance at Rick. "I don't really want to keep a job that sends me around the world every other week. Not now."

Hollister pursed his lips. "We can always use another detective," he pointed out. "You'd pick it back up in no time, and we have all sorts of workshops and training courses."

She beamed. "You mean it?"

"Of course," he assured her.

"Wait a minute, you'd give up working for the feds, for me?" Rick asked, as if he couldn't quite believe it.

"I would," she said solemnly. "I'm tired of living out of a suitcase. And I really like San Antonio." She didn't add that she was also very tired of the D.C. social scene and being required to hostess parties for her dad. It was never enjoyable. She didn't like crowds or parties. To give him his due, neither did her father. But he was certainly going to be in the center of the Washington social whirl very soon. She dreaded having to tell Rick about it.

"Well," Rick said, and couldn't resist a charming smile.

She laughed. "And now for the really hard part. We have to break the news to your mother."

"She'll kill me," he groaned.

"No. We'll take her a pot of flowers," Gwen said firmly. "She's a gardener. I know she wouldn't mind a bribe that she could plant."

They all laughed.

And actually, Barbara wasn't mad. She burst into tears, hugged them both and rambled on for several minutes about how depressed she'd been that women never seemed to see Rick as a potential mate as much as a shoulder to cry on.

"I'm just so happy!"

"I'm so glad," Gwen enthused. "But we still brought you a bribe."

"A bribe?" Barbara asked, wiping away tears.

Gwen went onto the porch and came back inside carrying a huge potted plant.

"It's an umbrella plant!" Barbara exclaimed. "I've wanted one for years, but I could never find one the right size. It's perfect!"

"I thought you could plant it," Gwen said.

"Oh, no, I'll let it live inside. I'll put grow lights around it and fertilize it and…" She hesitated. "You two didn't have to get married?"

They howled.

"She's as Victorian as we are," Rick told his mother with a warm smile.

"That's wonderful! Welcome to the stone age, my dear!" she told Gwen and hugged her, hard.

"Where are you going to live? In San Antonio?" Barbara asked, resigned.

Gwen and Rick had discussed this. "The old Andrews place is up for sale, right in downtown Jacobsville," Rick said, "next door to the Griers. In fact, I put in an offer for it this morning."

"Oh!" Barbara started crying again. "I thought you'd want to live where your jobs are."

Explanation about Gwen's job could come later, Rick decided. "We want to live near you," Rick replied.

"Because when the kids come along," Gwen added with a grin, "you'll want to be able to see them."

Barbara felt her forehead. "Maybe I'm feverish. You want to have kids?"

"Oh, yes," Gwen replied, smiling.

"Lots of kids," Rick added.

"I can buy a toy store," Barbara murmured to herself. "But first I need to stock up on organic seeds, so that I can make healthy stuff for the baby."

"We just got married yesterday," Rick pointed out.

"That's right, and this is November." She went looking for a calendar. "And nine months from now is harvest season!" she called back.

Rick and Gwen shook their heads.

They stayed for supper, a delicious affair, and then settled down to watch the news. Gwen, sitting contentedly beside her husband, had no warning of what was about to happen.

A newscaster smiled as a picture of a four-star general, very well-known to the public, was splashed across the screen. "And this just in. Amid rumors that he was retiring or resigning from the service, we have just learned that General David Cassaway, former U.S. Commander in Iraq, has been named director of the

Central Intelligence Agency. General Cassaway, a former covert ops commander, has commanded American troops in Iraq for the past two years. He was rumored to be retiring from the military, but it seems that he was only considering a new job."

Barbara glanced at Gwen. "Why, what a coincidence. That's your last name."

The newscaster was adding, "General Cassaway's only son, Larry, died in a classified operation in the Middle East just a few months ago. We wish General Cassaway the best of luck in his new position. Now for other news…"

Rick was staring at Gwen as if she'd grown horns. "Your brother's name was Larry, wasn't it?" he asked. "The one who was killed in action?"

Barbara was staring. So was Rick.

Gwen took a deep breath. "He's my father," she confessed.

Rick wasn't handling this well. "Your father is the new head of the CIA?"

"Well, sort of," she said, nodding worriedly.

Rick knew about Washington society from people in his department who had to deal with the socialites in D.C. He was certain that there were no poor generals in the military, and the head of the CIA would certainly not be in line for food stamps.

"What sort of place do you live in, when you go home?" Rick asked very quietly.

Gwen sighed. "We have a big house in Maryland, on several acres of land. My dad likes horses. He raises, well, thoroughbreds." She was almost cringing by now.

"And drives a…?"

She swallowed. "Jaguar."

Rick got up and turned away with an exasperated sigh. "Why didn't you tell me?"

"Because I was afraid you'd do just what you're doing now," Gwen moaned. "Judging me by the company I keep. I hate parties. I hate receptions. I hate hostessing! I'm perfectly happy working a federal job, or a police job, any sort of job that doesn't require me to put on an evening gown and look rich!"

"Rich." Rick ran his fingers through his hair.

"I'm not rich," she pointed out.

"But your father is."

She grimaced. "He was born into one of the founding families. He went to Harvard, and then to West Point," she said. "But he's just a regular person. He doesn't put on airs."

"Sure."

"Rick—" she got up and went to him "—I'm not my family. I don't have money. I work for my living. For heaven's sake, this suit is a year old!"

He turned around. His face was hard. "My suit is three years old," he said stiffly. "I drive a pickup truck. I can barely afford tickets to the theater."

She gave him a strained look. "You'll get used to this," she promised him. "It will just take a little time. You've had one too many upsets in the past few weeks."

He sighed heavily. "We should have waited to get married," he ground out.

"No," she returned. "If we'd waited and you'd found out, you'd never have married me at all."

Before Rick could open his mouth and destroy his future, Barbara got up and stood between them. "She's right," she told her son. "You need to stop before you say something you'll regret. Let Gwen go home for tonight, and you sleep on it. Things will look better in the morning." She went to get her cell phone and dialed a number. She waited until the call was answered. "Cash? Gwen Cassaway's going back to San Antonio for the night and I don't want her driving up there alone, do you have someone who can take her?"

"No…!" Gwen protested.

Barbara held up a hand. She grinned. "I thought you might. Thanks! I owe you a nice apple pie." She hung up. "One of Cash's men lives in San Antonio and he's on his way home. He'll swing by and give you a lift. He won't mind, and he's very nice. His name is Carlton Ames. He'll take good care of you."

Rick was cursing himself for not letting Gwen drive her car down instead of insisting that she come with him. He didn't like the idea of her riding with another man. They were married. At least, temporarily.

"Go home and don't worry," Barbara said, hugging her. "It will be all right."

Gwen managed a smile. She looked at Rick, but he wouldn't meet her eyes. She drew in a long breath and put on her coat and picked up her purse. She walked out to the front porch with Barbara, who closed the door behind them.

"He's still upset about meeting his father," Barbara said gently. "He'll get over this. You just get a good night's sleep and don't worry. It will work out. I'm so happy he married you!" She hugged the younger woman again. "You're going to be very happy together once he gets over the shock."

"I hope you're right. I should have told him. I was afraid to."

"Have you talked to your father?"

She shook her head. "I have to do that tonight." She grimaced. "He's not going to be happy, either."

"Does he have prejudices…?" Barbara worried at once.

Gwen laughed. "Heavens, no! Dad doesn't see color or race or religion. He's very liberal. No, he'll be hurt that I didn't tell him first."

"That's all right then. You'll make it up with him. And with Rick. Oh, there's Carlton!"

She waved as an off-duty police car pulled up at the porch. A nice young man got out and smiled. "I'm going to have company for the ride, I hear?" he asked.

"Yes, this is my new daughter-in-law, Gwen." Barbara introduced them. "That's Carlton," she added with a grin. "She didn't drive her own car and she has to get back to San Antonio to pick it up. Thanks for giving her a ride."

"Should I follow you back down here, then?" he offered.

Gwen shook her head. "I have things to get together in my apartment. But thanks."

"No problem. Shall we go?"

Gwen looked toward the porch, but the door was still closed. She saw Barbara wince. She managed a smile. "I'll see you later, then," she said. "Have a good night."

"You, too, dear," Barbara said. She forced a smile. "Good night."

She watched them leave. Then she went back in the house and closed the door. "Rick?"

He was on the phone. She wondered who he could be calling at this hour of the night. Perhaps it was work.

He hung up and came into the living room, looking more unapproachable than she'd ever seen him. "I'm going for a drive. I won't be long."

"She was very upset," she said gently. "She can't help who her father is, any more than you can."

He looked torn. "I know that. But she should have told me."

"I think she was afraid to. She's very much in love, you know."

He flushed and looked away. "I won't be long."

She watched him go, feeling a new and bitter distance between them, something she'd never felt before. She hoped they could work things out. She liked Gwen a lot.

RICK PULLED UP to the country bar, locked the truck and walked inside. It was late and there were only a couple of cowboys sitting in booths. A man in the back motioned to Rick, who walked down the aisle to sit across from him.

The older man gave him an amused smile. "Should I be flattered that you called me when you needed sympathy? Why not talk to your mother?"

Rick sighed. "It's not really something a woman would understand," he muttered.

General Machado pursed his lips. "No? Perhaps not." He motioned to the waiter, who came over at once, grinning. "Coffee for my young friend, please."

"At once!"

Rick's eyebrows arched at the man's quick manner.

"He wants to go and help liberate my country," Machado told Rick with a grin. "I have the ability to inspire revolutions."

"I noticed," Rick said dryly.

General Emilio Machado leaned back against the booth, studying the young man who looked so much like himself. "You know, we do favor each other."

"A bit."

The waiter came back with the coffee, placing a mug in front of Rick, along with small containers of cream and sugar, and a spoon. "Anything else for you, sir?" he asked the general with respect.

"No, that will do for now, thank you."

"A pleasure! If you need anything, just call."

"I will."

The waiter scampered away. Machado watched Rick sip hot coffee. "Just married, and already you quarrel?"

"She lied to me. Well, she lied by omission," he corrected coolly.

"About what?"

"It turns out that her father is the new head of the CIA."

"Ah, yes, General Cassaway. He and Grange are friends."

Rick recalled an odd conversation that Gwen and Grange had shared at the first meeting with Machado at the border. It had puzzled him at the time. Now he knew that she had been cautioning Grange not to give away her identity. It made him even sadder.

"He's rich," Rick said curtly.

"And you are not." Machado understood the problem. "Does it matter so much, if you care for the woman?

What if it was your mother who was wealthy, and her father who was poor?"

He shifted restlessly. "I don't know."

"But of course you do. You would not care."

Rick sipped more coffee. He was losing the argument.

Machado toyed with his own cup. "I was a millionaire, in my country," he confided. "I had everything a man could possibly want, right down to a Rolls-Royce and a private helicopter. Perhaps I had too much, and God resented the fact that I spent more money on me than I did on the poor villagers who were being displaced and murdered by my underling's minions as he worked to bring in foreign oil corporations. The oil and natural gas are quite valuable, and the villagers considered them a nuisance that interfered with the fishing." He smiled. "They have no interest in great wealth. They live from day to day, quietly, with no clocks, no supermarkets, no strip malls. Perhaps they have the right idea, and the rest of the world has gone insane from this disease called civilization."

Rick smiled back. "It would be a less hectic life."

"Yes, indeed." His dark eyes were thoughtful. "I was careless. I will never be careless again. And the man who usurped my place and made my people suffer will pay a very high price for his arrogance and greed, I promise you." The look on his face gave Rick cold chills.

"We've heard what he did to private citizens," Rick agreed.

"That is my fault. I should have listened. A…friend of mine, an archaeologist, tried to warn me about what his people were doing to the native tribes. I thought she was overstating, trying to get me to clamp down on foreign interests in the name of preserving archaeological treasures."

"A female archaeologist?"

He chuckled. "There are many these days. Yes, she taught at a small college in the United States. She was visiting my country when she stumbled onto a find so amazing that she hesitated to even announce it before she had time to substantiate her claim with evidence." His face hardened. "There was gossip that they put her in prison. I shudder to think what might have been done to her. That will be on my soul forever, if she was harmed."

"Maybe she escaped," Rick said, trying to find something comforting to say. "Rumors and gossip are usually pretty far off the mark."

"You think so?" Machado's dark eyes were sad but hopeful.

"Anything is possible."

Machado sighed. "I suppose."

The waiter came scurrying up looking worried. "El General, there is a police car coming this way," he said excitedly.

Machado looked at Rick.

"I'm not involved in any attempts to kidnap or arrest you," he said dryly.

"Is the car local?" Machado asked.

"Yes. It is a Jacobsville police car."

Machado weighed his options. While he was trying to decide whether to make a break out the back door, a tall, imposing man in a police uniform with large dark eyes and his long hair in a ponytail came in the door, looked around and spotted Rick with the general.

Rick relaxed. "It's all right," he said. "That's Cash Grier."

"You know him?"

"Yes. He's our police chief. He's a good man. Used to be a government assassin, or that's the rumor," Rick mused.

Machado laughed under his breath.

Cash walked over to their table. He wasn't smiling. "I'm afraid I have some bad news."

"You're here to arrest me?" Machado asked dryly.

Cash glanced at him. "Have you broken the law?" he asked curiously. It was obvious that he didn't recognize the bar's famous patron.

"Not lately," Machado lied.

Cash looked back at Rick, who was going tense.

"Gwen," he burst out.

Cash grimaced. "I'm afraid so. There's been a wreck…"

Rick was out of the booth in a flash. "How badly is she hurt?" he asked at once, white-faced. "Is she all right?"

"They've transported her and Ames to Jacobsville General," he said quietly. "Ames is pretty bad. Ms. Cassaway has at the very least a broken rib…!" Rick was already out of the bar, running for his truck.

"Wait! I'm coming with you!" Machado called after him, and stopped just long enough to pay the waiter, who bowed respectfully.

Cash, confused by the two men, got back in his patrol car and followed the pickup truck down the long road to the hospital. To his credit, he didn't pull out his ticket book when he pulled in behind Rick at the emergency entrance.

"My wife, Gwen Cassaway," Rick told the clerk at the desk. "They just brought her in."

The clerk studied him. "Oh, that's you, Detective Marquez," she said, smiling. "Yes, and she's your wife? Congratulations! Yes, she's in X-ray right now. Dr. Coltrain is treating her..."

"Copper or Lou?" Rick asked, because the married Coltrains were both doctors.

"Lou," came the reply.

"Thanks."

"You can have a seat right over there," the clerk said gently, "and I'll have someone ask Dr. Coltrain to come see you, okay?"

Rick wanted to rush behind the counter, but he knew better. He ground his teeth together. "Okay."

"Be just a sec." The clerk picked up the phone.

"She will be all right," Machado told his son with a warm smile. "She has great courage for one so young."

Rick felt rocked to the soles of his feet. He never should have reacted as he had. He'd upset her. But... she hadn't been driving, and Ames was one of Cash's better drivers...

He turned to the police chief. "Ames wrecked the car? How?"

"That's what I'd like to know," Cash said curtly. "There was another set of tracks in the dirt nearby, as if a car had sideswiped them. I've got men tracking right now."

"If you need help, I can provide a tracker who might even excel your own," Machado offered quietly.

Cash had been sizing the other man up. He pursed his lips. "You look familiar."

"There are very few photographs of me," Machado replied.

"Yes, but we've met. I can't remember where. Maybe it will come back to me."

Machado raised an eyebrow. "It would be just as well if your memory lapses for the next few hours. My son can use the company."

"Your son?" Cash's dark eyes narrowed on the older man. "Machado."

The older man nodded and smiled.

"Gwen had a photo of you. I had to break the news to Rick's mother, about your connection to him."

"Ah, yes, that was how he was told. Ingenious." The general's expression sombered. "I hope she and the officer will be all right."

"So do I," Cash said. "I can't help being concerned about that other car."

Machado came a step closer. "The Fuentes bunch have much reason to interfere with my plans. They are being paid by my successor to spy on me. There is also a very high level mole in the DEA. I do not know who it is," he added. "But even I am aware of him."

"Damn," Cash muttered.

"Yes, things are quite complicated. I did not mean to involve the children in my war," he added, with a rueful glance at Rick, who was pacing the floor.

"No parent would. Sometimes fate intervenes. Her father should be told."

"Yes," Machado replied. "He should." He excused himself and spoke to Rick.

"Her father." Rick groaned. "How am I going to find him?"

Machado grinned. "I think I can solve that problem." He pulled out his disposable cell phone, one of many, and dialed a number. "Grange? Yes. Gwen has been injured in an automobile accident. I need you to call her father and tell him. We don't know details yet. She has at least a broken rib. The rest we don't know... but he should come."

There was a pause. "Yes. Thank you. She is at the Jacobsville hospital. Yes. All right." He hung up. "Grange and her father are friends. He will make the call."

Rick averted his eyes. "Hell of a way to meet in-laws," he muttered.

"I do agree," Machado said. He put an affectionate arm around his son's neck. "But you will get through it. Come. Sit down and stop pacing, before you wear a hole in the floor."

Rick allowed himself to be led to a chair. It was kind of nice, having a father.

DR. LOUISE COLTRAIN came into the room in her white lab coat, smiling. She was introduced to Gwen's husband and father-in-law with some surprise, because no one locally knew about the wedding.

"Congratulations," she told Rick. "She'll be all right," she added quickly. "She does have a broken rib, but the other injuries are mostly bruises. Patrolman Ames has a head injury," she told Cash. "His prognosis is going to be trickier. I'm having him airlifted to San Antonio, to the Marshall Center. He's holding his own so far, though. Do you have a way to notify his family?"

Cash shook his head. "He doesn't have any family that I'm aware of. Just me," he added with a grim smile. "So I'm the one to notify."

She nodded. "I'll keep you in the loop. Detective Marquez, you can see your wife now. I'll take you back…"

"Where the hell is my daughter?"

Rick felt a shiver go down his spine. That voice, deep and cold with authority, froze everyone in the waiting room. Rick turned to find the face that went with it, and understood at once how this man had risen to become a four-star general. He was in full uniform, every button polished, his hat at the perfect angle, his hard face almost bristling with antagonism, his black eyes glittering with it.

"And who's responsible for putting her in the hospital?" he added in a tone that was only a little less intimidating.

While Rick was working on an answer, Barbara came in the door, worried and unsettled by his call. She paused beside the military man who was raising Cain in the waiting room.

"My goodness, someone had his razor blade soup this morning, I see!" she exclaimed with pure hostility. "Now you calm down and stop shouting at people. This is a hospital, not a military installation!"

CHAPTER TEN

GENERAL CASSAWAY TURNED and looked down at the willowy blonde woman who was glaring up at him.

"Who the hell are you?" he demanded.

"The woman who's going to have you arrested if you don't calm down," she replied. "Rick, how is she?" she asked, holding out her arms.

Rick came and held her close. "Broken rib," he said. "And some bruising. She'll be all right."

"Who are you?" General Cassaway demanded.

Rick turned. "I'm Gwen's husband. Detective Sergeant Rick Marquez," he said coldly, not backing down an inch.

"Her husband?"

"Yes. And he's my son," Barbara added.

"And also my son," General Machado said, joining them. He smiled at Barbara, who smiled back.

"You two are married?" Cassaway asked.

Barbara laughed. "No. He's much too young for me," she said.

Machado gave her an amused look. "I do like older women," he admitted.

She just shook her head.

"I want to see my daughter," Cassaway told Lou Coltrain.

"Of course. Come this way. You, too, Rick."

Cassaway was surprised at the first name basis.

"We all know each other here," Lou told him. "I'm a newcomer, so to speak, but my husband is from here. He's known Rick since Barbara adopted him."

"I see."

Gwen was heavily sedated, but her eyes opened and she brightened when she saw her husband and her father walk into the recovery room.

"Dad! Rick!"

Rick went on one side to take a hand, her father on the other.

"I'm so sorry," she began.

"Don't be absurd." Rick kissed her forehead. "I was an idiot. I'm sorry! I never should have let you go with Ames."

"Ames! How is he?" she asked. "The other car came out of nowhere! We didn't even see it until it hit us. There were three men in it…"

"Did you recognize any of them?"

"No," she replied. "But it could have been Fuentes. The last of the living brothers, the drug lords."

"By God, I'll have them hunted down like rats," Cassaway said icily.

"My father will beat you to it," Rick replied coolly.

"Just who is your father?" Cassaway asked suddenly. "He looks very familiar."

"General Emilio Machado," Rick said, and with a hint of pride that reflected in the tilt of his chin.

Cassaway pursed his lips. "Grange's boss. Yes, we know about that upcoming operation. We can't be involved, of course."

"Of course," Rick replied with twinkling eyes.

"But we are rooting for the good guys," came the amused comment.

Rick chuckled.

"So you're married," Cassaway said. He shook his head. "Your mother would have loved seeing you married." He winced. "I would have, too."

"I'm so sorry," she said. "But I hadn't told Rick who you were." She bit her lip.

"What did that have to do with anything?" the older man asked, puzzled.

"I'm a city detective," Rick said sardonically. "I wear three-year-old suits and I drive a pickup truck."

"Hell, I drive a pickup truck, too," the general said, shrugging. "So what?"

Rick liked the man already. He grinned.

"See?" Gwen asked her husband. "I told you he wasn't what you thought."

"Snob," the general said, glaring at Rick. "I don't pick my friends for their bank accounts."

"Sorry," Rick said. "I didn't know you."

"You'll get there, son."

"Congratulations on the appointment," Rick said.

The general shrugged. "I don't know how long I'll last. I don't kiss butt, if you know what I mean, and I say what I think. Not very popular to speak your mind sometimes."

"I think honesty never goes out of style, and has value," Rick replied.

The general's eyes twinkled. "You did good," he told his daughter.

She just smiled.

OUT IN THE waiting room, Cash Grier was talking on the phone to someone in San Antonio while the general thumbed through a magazine. Barbara paced, worried. Gwen's father was a hard case. She hoped he and Rick would learn to get along.

Cash closed his flip phone grimly. "They found a car, abandoned, a few miles outside of Comanche Wells," he said. "We can't say for sure that it's the one that hit Ames, but it has black paint on the fender, and Ames's car is black. We ran wants and warrants on it—it was stolen."

"Fuentes," Machado said quietly. His dark eyes narrowed. "I have had just about enough of him. I think he will have to meet with a similar accident soon."

"I didn't hear you say that," Cash told him.

"Did I say something?" Machado asked. "Why, I was simply voicing a prediction."

"Terroristic threats and acts," he said, waving a finger at Machado. "And I'm conveniently forgetting your connection with the Pendleton kidnapping for the next hour or so. After that," he added with pursed lips, "things could get interesting here."

Machado grinned. "I will be long gone by then. My son needed me."

Cash smiled. "I have a daughter," he said. "She's going on three years old. Red hair and green eyes and a temper worse than mine."

"I would like to have known my son when he was small," Machado said sadly. "I did not know about him. Dolores kept her secret all the way to the grave. A pity."

"It was nice for me, that you didn't know," Barbara said gently. "When I adopted him, he gave me a reason to live." She stood up. "Do you think things happen for a reason?" she asked philosophically.

"Yes, I do," Machado replied with a smile. "Perhaps fate had a hand in all this."

"Well, I suppose…" she began.

"I have to get back home," General Cassaway was saying as he walked out with Rick. "But it's been a pleasure meeting you, son." He shook hands with Rick.

"Same here," Rick told him. "I'll take better care of your daughter from now on. And I won't be so inflexible next time she springs a surprise on me," he added with a laugh.

"See that you aren't. Remember what I do for a living now," he told the younger man with a grin. "I can find you anywhere, anytime."

"Yes, sir," Rick replied.

The general turned to Machado. "And you'd better hightail it out of Mexico pretty soon," he said in a confidential tone. "Things are going to heat up in Sonora. A storm's coming. You don't want to be in its way."

Machado nodded. "Thank you."

"Oh, I have ulterior motives," Cassaway assured him. "I want that rat out of Barrera before he turns your country into the world's largest cocaine distribution center."

"So do I," Machado replied quietly. "I promise you, his days of power will soon come to an end."

"Wish I could help," Cassaway told him. "But I think you have enough intel and mercs to do the job."

"Including a friend of yours," Machado replied, smiling.

"A very good one. He'll get the job done." He shook

hands with Machado. Then he turned to Barbara. "You've got a smart mouth on you."

She glared at him. "And you've got a sharp tongue on you."

He smiled. "I like pepper."

She shifted. "Me, too."

"She's a great cook," Rick said, sliding his arm around her shoulders. "She owns the local café here, and does most of the cooking for it."

"Really! I'm something of a chef myself," Cassaway replied. "I grow my own vegetables and I get a local grandmother to come over and help me can every summer."

Barbara moved closer. "I can, too. I like to dry herbs as well."

"Now I've got a herb garden of my own," the general said. "But it isn't doing as well as I'd like."

"Do you have a composter?" Barbara asked.

His eyebrows lifted. "A what?"

"A composter, for organic waste from the kitchen." She went on to explain to him how it worked and what you did with it.

"A fellow gardener," Cassaway said with a beaming smile. "What a surprise! So few women garden these days."

"Oh, we have plenty around Jacobsville who plant gardens," Barbara said. "You'll have to come and visit us next summer. I can show you how to grow corn ten feet high, even in a drought," she added.

Cassaway moved a step closer. He was huge, Barbara thought, tall and good-looking and built like a tank. He had thick black hair and black eyes and a tan complexion. Nice mouth.

Cassaway was thinking the same thing about Barbara. She was tall and willowy and very pretty.

"I might visit sooner than that," he said in a low, deep tone. "Is there a hotel?"

"Yes, but I have a big Victorian house. Rick and Gwen can stay there, too. We'll have a family reunion." She flushed a little, and laughed, and then looked at Machado. "That invitation includes you, also," she added. "If you're through with your revolution by then," she said ruefully.

"I think that is a good possibility, and I will accept the invitation," Machado said. He kissed her hand and bowed. "Thank you for taking such good care of my son."

She smiled. "He's been the joy of my life. I had nobody until Rick needed a home."

"I only have a daughter," General Cassaway said sadly. "I lost my son earlier this year to an IED, and my wife died some years ago."

"I'm so sorry," Barbara said with genuine sympathy. "I miscarried the only child I ever had. It must be terrible to lose one who's grown."

"Worse than death," Cassaway agreed. He cleared his throat and looked away. He drew in a long breath. "Well, my adjutant is doing the ants' dance, so I guess we'd better go," he said, nodding toward a young officer standing in the doorway.

"The ants' dance?" Barbara asked.

"He moves around like that when he's in a hurry to do something, like he's got ants climbing his legs.

Good man, but a little testy." He shrugged. "Like me. He suits me." He shook hands with Rick. "I've heard good things about you from Grange. Your police chief over there—" he nodded toward Cash, who was talking on the phone again "—speaks highly of you."

Rick smiled. "Nice to know. I love my job. I like to think I'm good at it."

"Take care of my little girl."

"You know I will."

He paused at Barbara and looked down at her with quiet admiration. "And I'll see you later."

She grinned. "Okay!"

He nodded at the others, and walked toward the young man, who was now motioning frantically.

Cash joined them a minute later. "Sorry, I wasn't trying to be rude. I've got a man working on the hit-and-run, and I've been checking in. There was an incident at the border crossing over near Del Rio," he added. "Three men jumped a border agent, knocked him out and took off over the crossing into Mexico. We think it was the same men who ran Ames off the road."

"Great," Rick muttered. "Just great. Now we work on trying to get them extradited back to the States. That will be good for a year, even if we can get a positive identification of who they are."

Machado pursed his lips. "I would not worry about that. Such men are easy to find, for a good tracker, and equally easy to deal with."

"I didn't hear that," Cash said.

Machado chuckled. "Of course not. I was, again, making a prediction."

"Thanks for coming with me," Rick told Machado. "And for the shoulder earlier."

Machado embraced his son in a bear hug. "I will always be around, whenever you need me." He searched the younger man's face. "I am very proud to have such a man for my son."

Rick swallowed hard. "I'm proud to have such a man for my father."

Machado's eyes were suspiciously bright. He laughed suddenly. "We will both be wailing in another minute. I must go. Grange is waiting for me in the parking lot."

"I can't say anything officially," Cash told the general. "But privately, I wish you good luck."

Machado shook his hand. "Thank you, my friend. I hope your patrolman will be all right."

"So do I," Cash said.

Rick walked Machado to the door. Outside, Winslow Grange was sitting behind the wheel of Machado's pickup truck, waiting.

Machado turned to his son. "When the time comes, I will be happy to let you become my liaison with the American authorities. And it will come," he added solemnly. "My country has many resources that will appeal to outside interests. I would prefer to deal with republics or democracies rather than totalitarian states."

"A wise decision," Rick said. "And when the time comes, I'll be here."

Machado smiled. *"Que vayas con Dios, mi hijo,"* he said, using the familiar tense that was only applied to family and close friends.

It made Rick feel warm inside, that his father already felt affection for him. He waved as the two men in the truck departed. He hoped his father wouldn't get killed in the attempt to retake Barrera. But, then, Machado was a general, and he'd won the title fairly, in many battles. He would be all right. Rick was certain of it.

GWEN CAME HOME two days later. She wore a rib belt and winced every time she moved. The lieutenant had granted her sick leave, but she was impatient to get back on the job. Rick had to make threats to keep her in bed at all, at Barbara's house.

"And I'm a burden on your poor mother," Gwen protested. "She has a business to run, and here she is bringing me food on trays…!"

"She doesn't mind," Rick assured her.

"Of course she doesn't mind," Barbara said as she brought in soup and crackers. "She's working on planning a fantastic Thanksgiving dinner in a couple of weeks. I'm going to invite your father," she told Gwen and then flushed a little. "I guess that would be all right. I don't know," she hesitated, looking around her. "He's head of the CIA and used to crystal and fine china…"

"He doesn't use the good place settings at home," Gwen said dryly. "He likes plain white ceramic plates and thick Starbucks coffee mugs and just plain fare to eat. He isn't a fancy mannered person, although he can blend into high society when he has to. He'll think of it as a welcome relief from the D.C. whirl. Which I'm happy to be out of," she added heavily. "I never liked having to hostess parties. I like working in law enforcement."

"Me, too," Rick said, smiling warmly at his wife. "I'm just sorry about what happened to you and Ames."

"Yes. Have we heard anything about Ames?"

"Cash Grier said that he regained consciousness this morning," Barbara said with a smile. "It's all coming back to him. He remembered what the men looked like. He got a better view of them than you did," she told the younger woman. "He recognized Fuentes."

"Fuentes himself?" Gwen was shocked. "Why would he do his own dirty work?"

"Fuentes knows that you're married to me, and that I'm General Machado's son," Rick said somberly. "I think he was trying to get back at the general, in a roundabout way. He may have thought it was me driving. He wouldn't have known that you were with Ames."

"Yes," Barbara said worriedly. "And he may try again. You can't go anywhere alone from now on, at least until Fuentes is arrested."

"He won't be," Rick said coldly. "Dozens of policemen have tried to pin him down, nobody has succeeded. He has a hideout in the mountains and guards at every checkpoint. An undercover agent died trying to infiltrate his camp a few weeks ago. I'd love to see him behind bars. It's trying to get him there that's the problem."

"Well, your father's not too happy with him right now," Barbara remarked.

"And the general has ways and means that we don't have access to," Gwen agreed.

"True," Rick said.

"I think we may hear some good news soon about Fuentes and his bunch," Barbara said. "But for now, my main focus is getting your wife back on her feet," she told her son. "Good food and a little spoiling always does the trick."

"You're a nice mother," Rick said.

"A very nice mother and I'm so happy that you're going to be mine, too," Gwen told her with a warm smile. She shifted in the bed and groaned.

"Time for meds," Barbara said, and went out to get them.

Rick bent and kissed Gwen gently between her eyes. "You get better," he whispered. "I have erotic plans for you at some future time very soon."

She laughed, wincing, and lifted her mouth to touch his. "You aren't the only one with plans. Darn this rib!"

"Bad timing, and Fuentes's fault," Rick murmured as he brushed her mouth tenderly with his. "But we have forever."

"Yes," she whispered, beaming. "Forever."

THANKSGIVING CAME SUDDENLY and with, of all things, snow! Rick and Gwen walked out into the yard at Barbara's house and laughed as it piled down on the bare limbs of the trees around the fence line.

"Snow!" she exclaimed. "I didn't know it snowed in Texas!"

"Hey, it snowed in South Africa twice in August," he pointed out. "The weather is loopy."

She smiled and hugged him, still wincing a little, because her rib was tender. She was healing quickly, though. Soon, she would be whole again and ready for more amorous adventures with her new husband.

"Is your father coming down?" he asked Gwen.

"Oh, yes. He said he wouldn't miss a homemade

Thanksgiving dinner for the world. He can cook, but he hates doing it on holidays, and he mostly eats out. He's very excited. And not only about the meal," she added with an impish grin. "I think he likes your mother."

"Wouldn't that be a match?" he mused.

"Yes, it would. They're both alone and about the same age. Dad's quite a guy."

"But he's head of a federal agency. He lives in D.C. and she owns a restaurant here," Rick pointed out.

"If they really want to, they'll find a way."

"I guess so." He turned to her, in the white flaky curtain, and drew her gently to his chest. "The best thing I ever did in life was marry you," he said somberly. "I may not say it a lot but I love you very much."

She caught her breath at the tenderness in his deep voice. "I love you, too," she whispered back.

He bent and drew her mouth under his, teasing the upper lip with his tongue, parting her lips so that his could cover them hungrily. He forgot everything in the flashpoint heat of desire. His arms closed around her, enveloping her so tightly that she moaned.

He heard that, and drew back at once. "Sorry," he said quickly. "I forgot!"

She laughed breathily. "It's okay. I forgot, too. Just another week or two, and I'll be in fine shape."

He lifted an eyebrow and looked down at her trim, curvy body in jeans and a tight sweater. "I'll say you're in fine shape," he murmured dryly.

"Oh, you!" She punched him lightly in the chest.

"Shapely, sexy and sweet. I'm a lucky man."

She reached up and kissed him back. "We're both lucky."

He sighed. "I suppose we should go back inside and offer to peel potatoes."

"I suppose so."

He kissed her again, smiling. "In a minute."

She sighed. "Yes. In a minute…or two…or three…"

Ten minutes later, they went back inside. Barbara gave them an amused look and handed Rick a huge pan full of potatoes and a paring knife. He sighed and got to work.

The general came with an entourage, but they were housed in the local hotel in Jacobsville. General Cassaway did allow his adjutant and a clerk to move into Barbara's house with him, with her permission of course, and he had a case full of electronic equipment that had to find living space as well.

"I have to keep in touch with everyone in my department, monitor the web, answer queries, inform the proper people at Homeland Security about my activities," the general said, rattling off his duties. "It's a great job, but it takes most of my time. That's why I've been remiss in the email department," he added with a smile at Gwen.

"I think you do very well, considering how little free time you have, Dad," she told him.

"Thanks." He dug into the dressing, closing his eyes as he savored it and the giblet gravy. "This is wonderful, Barbara."

"Thank you," she replied, with a big smile. "I love to cook."

"Me, too," Gwen added. "Barbara's teaching me how to do things properly."

"She's a quick study, too," Barbara replied, smiling at her daughter-in-law. "Her corn bread is wonderful, and I didn't teach her that…it's her own recipe. She's very talented."

"Thanks."

"What about this Fuentes character who sideswiped that car you were in?" he asked Gwen suddenly.

"Strange thing," she replied, tongue-in-cheek. "Fuentes seems to have gone missing. Nobody's seen him since the wreck."

"How very odd," the general remarked.

"Isn't it?"

"How about the young man who was driving you?" he added as he dipped his fork into potato salad.

"He's out of the hospital and back at work," Gwen said warmly. "He's going to be fine, thank goodness."

"I'm glad about that." He glanced across the table at Rick. "I understand that your father has left Mexico."

Rick smiled. "Yes, I did hear about that."

"So things are going to heat up in Barrera very soon, I would expect," the general added.

Rick nodded. "Very soon."

"No more talk of revolution," Barbara said firmly. She got to her feet with a big grin. "I have a surprise."

She went into the kitchen and came back in with a huge coconut cream pie. She put it on the table.

"Is that…?"

"Coconut cream." Barbara nodded. "I heard that it's someone's favorite."

"Mine!" General Cassaway said. "Thanks!"

"My pleasure." She cut it into slices and put one on a saucer for him. "If you still have room after all that turkey and dressing…"

"I'll make room," he said with such fervor that everyone laughed.

THE GENERAL STAYED for two days. Rick and Gwen and Barbara drove him around Jacobsville and introduced him to people. He fit in as if he'd been born there. He was coming back for Christmas, he assured them. He had to do a vanishing act to get out of all those holiday parties in Washington, D.C.

Rick heard from his father, too. The mercenaries had landed in a country friendly to Machado, near the border of Barrera, and they were massing for an attack. Machado told Rick not to worry, he was certain of victory. But just in case, he wanted Rick to know that the high point of his life so far had been meeting his own son. Rick had been overwhelmed with that statement. He told Gwen later that it had meant more to him than anything. Well, anything except marrying her, of course.

They moved back into her apartment, because it was closer to their jobs, leaving Rick's vacant for the moment.

She went home early one Friday night and when Rick walked in the door, he found her standing by the sofa wearing a negligee set that sent his heart racing like a bass drum.

"Here I was trying on my new outfit and there you

are, home early. What perfect timing!" she purred, and moved toward him with her hair long and soft around her shoulders, her arms lifting to envelope him hungrily.

He barely got the door closed in time, before they wound up in a feverish tangle on the carpet....

CHAPTER ELEVEN

"YOUR RIBS," RICK GASPED.

"Are fine," Gwen whispered, lifting to the slow, hard rhythm. Her eyes rolled back in her head at the overwhelming wave of pleasure that accompanied the movements. "Oh, my gosh!" she groaned, shivering.

"It just gets better…and better," he bit off.

"Yes…!" A high-pitched little cry escaped her tight throat. She opened her eyes wide as he began to shudder and she watched him. His body rippled in the throes of ecstasy. He closed his eyes and groaned helplessly as he arched up and gave himself to the pleasure.

Watching him set her own body on fire. She moved involuntarily, lifting, lifting, tightening as she felt the pleasure grow and grow and grow, like a volcano throwing out rocks and flame before it suddenly exploded and sent fiery rain into the sky. She was like the volcano, echoing its explosions, feeling her body burn and flame and consume itself in the endless fires of passion.

She couldn't stop moving, even when the pinnacle was reached and she was falling from the hot peak, down into the warm ashes.

"No," she choked. "No…it's too soon…!"

"Shhhhh," he whispered at her ear. "I won't stop until you ask me to." He brushed her mouth with his and

moved back into a slow, deep rhythm that very quickly brought her from one peak to an even higher one.

He lifted his head and looked down at her pretty pink breasts, hard-tipped and thrusting as she lifted to him, her flat belly reaching up to tempt his to lie on it, press it into the soft carpet as the rhythm grew suddenly quick and hard and urgent.

"Now, now, now," she moaned helplessly, shivering as the pleasure began to grow beyond anything she'd experienced before in his arms. "Oh, please, now!"

He pushed down, hard, and felt her ripple around him, a flutter of motion that sent him careening off the edge into space. He cried out, his body contracting as he tried to get even closer.

They shuddered and shuddered together, until the pleasure finally began to seep into manageable levels. He collapsed on her, his body heavy and hard and hot, and she held him while they started to breathe normally again.

"That was incredible," she whispered into his throat.

"I thought we'd already found the limit," he whispered back. "But apparently, we hadn't." He laughed weakly. He lifted his head. "Your rib," he said suddenly.

"It's fine," she assured him. "I wouldn't have felt it if it wasn't fine," she added with a becoming flush. She searched his dark eyes. "You're just awesome."

He grinned. "So are you." He lifted an eyebrow. "I hope you plan to make a habit of meeting me at the door in a see-through pink negligee. Because I have to tell you, I really like it."

She laughed softly. "It was impromptu. I was trying it on and I heard your key in the door. The rest is history."

He kissed her softly. "History indeed."

He started to lift away and she grimaced.

"Sorry," he said, and moved more gently. "We went at it a little too hard."

"No, we didn't," she denied, smiling even through the discomfort.

He led her into the bedroom and tucked them both into bed, leaving the clothes where they'd been strewn.

"We haven't had supper," she protested.

"We had dessert. Supper can wait." He pulled her into his arms and turned out the light. And they slept until morning.

CHRISTMAS DAY BROUGHT a huge meal, the whole family except for General Machado, and holiday music around the Christmas tree in the living room of Barbara's house. Rick and Gwen had bid on the nearby house and the family selling it accepted. They were signing the papers the following month. It was an exciting time.

Barbara and General Gene Cassaway were getting along from time to time, but with minor and unexpected explosions every few hours. The general was very opinionated, it seemed, and he had very definite ideas on certain methods of cooking. Considering that he'd only started being a chef five years before, and Barbara had been doing it for years, they were bound to clash. And they did. The more they discussed recipes, the louder the arguments became.

Gwen had resigned her federal job, with her father's

blessing, and was now working full-time as a detective on Rick's squad at San Antonio P.D.

Her fledgling efforts had resulted in murder charges against Mickey Dunagan, the man arrested but not convicted on assault charges concerning a college coed. He was also the subject of another investigation on a similar cold case, in which charges were pending. He'd been seen at the most recent victim's apartment before her death in San Antonio.

Faced with ironclad evidence of his guilt, a partial fingerprint and conclusive DNA matching fluids found on the victim's body, he'd confessed. A public defender had tried to argue that the Miranda rights hadn't been read, but the prisoner himself had assured his legal counsel that he'd been read them, and that he stood on his confession. He'd started crying. He hadn't meant to hurt any of them, but they were so pretty and he could never even get a girl to go out with him. He'd killed that other girl, too, because she'd made fun of him and laughed.

This girl he'd just killed, she'd been kind. He didn't care if he went to prison, he told Gwen. He didn't want to hurt anybody else.

She'd handed him over to the prosecutor's office with a sad smile. A murderer with a conscience. How unusual. But it didn't bring the dead women back. On the other hand, the cold case squad was feeling a sense of satisfaction. They owed Gwen a nice dinner, they told her, and would deliver any time she asked. She also spoke with the parents of the dead women, and gave them some consolation, in the fact that the killer would be brought to justice and, most likely, without a long and painful trial that would only bring back horrible memories of the tragedies.

The San Antonio patrolman, Sims, who'd gone on stakeout with Rick and Gwen had been resigned from the force suddenly, with no reason given. Nobody in the department knew what had happened.

Patrolman Ames in Jacobsville was happily back on the job and with no apparent ill effects.

Down in Barrera, there were rumors of an invasion. It was all over the news. General Cassaway, when asked about the truth of those rumors, just smiled.

Gwen handed Rick a wrapped gift and waited patiently for him to open it.

He looked inside and then back at her with wonder. "How did you know...?"

She grinned and nodded toward Barbara, who laughed.

"Thanks!" he said, pulling out a DVD of an important United States vs. Mexico soccer match that he'd had to miss because of work. "I'll really enjoy it."

"I know you saw the results, but it was a great game," Gwen said.

"Here. Open yours," he said, and handed her a small present.

She pulled it open. It was a jeweler's box. She pulled the lid up and there was a small, beautiful diamond ring.

He pulled it out and slid it onto her finger. "I thought you should have one. It isn't the biggest around, but it's given with my whole heart."

He kissed it. She burst into tears and hugged him close. "I wouldn't care if it was a cigar band," she said.

"I know. That's why I wanted you to have it."

"Sweet man," she murmured.

He sighed. "Happy man," he added, kissing her hair.

She looked up at him with eyes full of love. "You know," she said, glancing toward his mother and General Cassaway, who were looking at recipe books they'd given each other, "I think this is the best Christmas of my life."

"I know it's the best of mine," he replied. "And only the first of many."

"Yes," she said, smiling from ear to ear as she touched his cheek with her fingertips. "The first of many. Merry Christmas."

He kissed her. "Merry Christmas."

The sudden buzz of his cell phone interrupted them. He reached into his pocket with a grimace. It was probably a case and he'd have to go to San Antonio on Christmas Day....

He looked at the number. It was an odd sort of number....

"Hello?" he said.

"Feliz Navidad," a deep voice sang, "Feliz Navidad, Feliz Navidad, something-somethingy felicidad!"

"You forgot the words?" Rick laughed, delighted. "Shame! It's '*Feliz Navidad, próspero año y felicidad,*'" he added smugly.

"Yes, shame, but I am very busy and my mind is on other things. Happy Christmas, my son."

"Happy Christmas to you, Dad," he said, glowing because his father had taken time out of a revolution to wish him well.

"Things are going fine here. Perhaps soon you and

your lovely wife will come to visit me, and I will send a plane for you."

"That would be nice," Rick said. He mouthed "Dad" to Gwen, who grinned.

"Meanwhile, be a good boy and Santa Claus will send you something very nice in the near future."

"I didn't get you anything," Rick said with sadness.

There was a deep chuckle. "You did. The hope of grandchildren. That is a gift beyond measure."

"I'll do my best," Rick replied, tongue in cheek.

There was an interruption. "Yes, I will be right there. Sorry. I have to go. Wish me luck."

"You know I do."

"And Happy Christmas, my son."

"Happy Christmas."

He hung up.

"That was a very nice surprise," Rick said.

She smiled. "Yes."

"It's not a simple recipe," the general was growling. "Nobody can make that right! It's a stupid recipe, it curdles every time!"

"It's not stupid, and yes, you can," Barbara growled back.

"I'm telling you, it's impossible! I know, I've tried!"

"Oh, for heaven's sake! Come on in here and I'll show you. It's not hard!"

"That's what you think!"

"Stop growling. It's Christmas."

The general made a face. "All right, damn it."

"Gene!"

He sighed. "Darn it."

"Much better," she said with a grin.

"I won't be reformed by a cook," he informed her. "And just in case you didn't notice, I'm head of the CIA!"

"In this house, you're an apprentice chef. Now stop muttering and come on. This is one of the easiest sauces in the world, and you won't curdle it if you'll just pay attention."

The general was still muttering as he followed Barbara into the kitchen. There was a loud rattle of pots and pans and the opening of the fridge. Voices murmured.

Rick pulled Gwen into his arms and kissed her hungrily. "I love you."

"I love you, too."

"See? I told you! That's curdling!"

"It's not curdling, it's reducing!"

"Damn it, you put the butter in too soon!" the general was raging.

"I did not!"

Rick rolled his eyes. "Do you think you could do something about your father?"

"If you'll do something about your mother," she returned with a grin.

"I'm not raising the heat. That book is wrong!" the general snapped.

Rick looked at Gwen. Gwen looked at Rick. In the kitchen, the voices were growing louder. Without a word, they went to the front door, opened it and ran for their car.

Rick was laughing. "They won't even miss us," he

said as he started the vehicle. "And maybe if they're left alone, they'll make peace."

"You think?" she teased.

He drove off to the house they were buying, cut off the engine and stared at it.

"We're going to be very happy here," Gwen said, sighing. "I'll make a garden and your mother can teach me how to can."

"Yes." He pulled her close. "If she and your father don't kill each other," he added.

"They'll have to learn to get along."

"Ha!"

The phone rang. Rick opened it. "Hello?"

"Could you come home for a minute?" Barbara asked.

"Sure. If it's safe," he teased. "What do you need?"

"Well, we could use a little help in the kitchen."

"Making the sauce?"

"Getting hollandaise sauce out of hair. And curtains. And cabinets. And on walls…"

"Mom!" he exclaimed. "What happened?"

"He thought I was making it wrong and I thought he was making it wrong, and, well, we sort of, uh, tossed the pan up."

"Are you okay?"

"Actually, you know, I think he was right. It tastes pretty good with less salt."

"I see."

"He's looking for another frying pan, so could you hurry?" she whispered, and then hung up.

"What's going on?" Gwen asked.

He grinned as he started the car. "War of the Worlds Part I. We get to help clean up the carnage in the kitchen."

"Excuse me?"

"They trashed the hollandaise sauce all over the kitchen."

"At least they're speaking," she pointed out.

He just shook his head. The general and his mother might eventually agree to a truce, but Rick had a feeling that it was going to be a long winter.

He pulled Gwen close and kissed the top of her head. He could manage anything, he thought, as long as he had her.

She sighed and closed her eyes. "Too many cooks spoil the broth?" she wondered aloud.

"I was thinking the same thing," he agreed. "Let's go referee."

"Done!"

They drove home through the colorful streets, with strings of red and blue and yellow and green lights and garlands of holly and fir. In the middle of the town square was a huge Christmas tree full of decorations, under which were wooden painted presents.

"One day," Rick said, "we'll bring our kids here when they light the tree."

She beamed. "Yes," she said, and it was a promise. "One day."

The tree grew smaller and smaller in the rearview mirror as they turned down the long road that led to Barbara's house. It was, Rick thought, truly the best Christmas of his life. He looked down at Gwen, and he saw in her eyes that she was thinking the very same thing.

Two lonely people, who found in each other the answer to a dream.

* * * * *

SPECIAL EXCERPT FROM

*As teenagers, they couldn't get enough of each other.
So when Sunny Dalton returns to her hometown of Lone
Star Ridge, Texas, and is reunited with Shaw Jameson,
the sparks they both assumed had long fizzled out are
quickly reignited. But too many old secrets lay hidden
below the surface, threatening the happily-ever-after
they've never given up on...*

Read on for a sneak peek at
Tangled Up in Texas,
the first book in Lone Star Ridge from
USA TODAY *bestselling author Delores Fossen.*

Shaw looked up when he heard the sound of the
approaching vehicle. Not coming from behind but rather
ahead—from the direction of the ranch. It was a dark
blue SUV barreling toward him, and it screeched to a
stop on the other side of the intimate apparel he'd found
lying on the road.

Because of the angle of the morning sunlight and the
SUV's tinted windshield, Shaw couldn't see the driver,
but he sure as heck saw the woman who stepped from the
passenger's side.

Talk about a gut punch of surprise. The biggest
surprise of the morning, and that was saying something
considering the weird underwear on the road.

Sunny Dalton.

She was a blast from the past and a tangle of memories. And here she was walking toward him like a siren in her snug jeans and loose gray shirt.

And here he was on the verge of drooling.

Shaw did something about that and made sure he closed his mouth, but he knew it wouldn't stay that way. Even though Sunny and he were no longer teenagers, his body just steamed up whenever he saw her.

Sunny smiled at him. However, he didn't think it was so much from steam but rather a sense of polite frustration.

"Shaw," she said on a rise of breath.

Her voice was smooth and silky. Maybe a little tired, too. Even if Shaw hadn't seen her in a couple of years, he was pretty sure that was fatigue in her steel blue eyes.

She'd changed her hair. It was still a dark chocolate brown, but it no longer hung well past her shoulders. It was shorter in a nonfussy sort of way, which would have maybe looked plain on most women. On Sunny, it just framed that amazing face.

And Shaw knew his life was about to get a whole lot more complicated.

Don't miss
Tangled Up in Texas *by Delores Fossen,*
available March 2020 wherever
HQN Books and ebooks are sold!

HQNBooks.com

"Don't look at me like that, April."

She raised her gaze to his. "Like what?"

His fingers tightened in her hair and her mouth ran dry. She swallowed. Moistened her lips.

She wasn't sure if she moved first. Or if it was him.

But then his mouth was on hers and like everything else about him, she felt engulfed by an inferno. Or maybe the burning was coming from inside her.

There was no way to know.

No reason to care.

Her hands slid up the granite chest, behind his neck, where his skin felt even hotter beneath her fingertips, and slipped through his thick hair, which was not hot, but instead felt cool and unexpectedly silky.

His arm around her tightened, his hand pressing her closer while his kiss deepened. Consuming. Exhilarating.

Her head was whirling, sounds roaring.

It was only a kiss.

But she was melting.

She was flying.

And then she realized the sounds weren't just inside her head.

Someone was laying on a horn.

She jerked back, her gaze skittering over Jed's as they both turned to peer through the curtain of white light shining over them.

"Mind getting at least one of these vehicles out of the way?" The shout was male and obviously amused.

"Oh for cryin'—" She exhaled. "That's my uncle Matthew," she told Jed, pushing him away. "And I'm sorry to say, but we are probably never going to live this down."

Don't miss
A Promise to Keep *by Allison Leigh,*
available March 2020 wherever
Harlequin Special Edition books and ebooks are sold.

Harlequin.com

Love Harlequin romance?

DISCOVER.

Be the first to find out about promotions,
news and exclusive content!

Facebook.com/HarlequinBooks

Twitter.com/HarlequinBooks

Instagram.com/HarlequinBooks

Pinterest.com/HarlequinBooks

ReaderService.com

EXPLORE.

Sign up for the Harlequin e-newsletter and
download a free book from any series at
TryHarlequin.com

CONNECT.

Join our Harlequin community to
share your thoughts and connect
with other romance readers!
Facebook.com/groups/HarlequinConnection

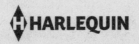